NEW THREATS LURK IN THE SHADOWS...

Its long, boney limbs poked out from a tattered black robe like the spindly legs of a giant spider. The skin was thick and crusted like a protective scab. Its hands and feet ended in three-inch long, yellowed claws that glistened with fresh blood from where it had pinned the woman's shoulders down. The creature slowly lifted its head revealing the most horrifying sight Laila had ever seen. The creature's face had been ripped away, revealing the bones of the skull beneath. Where eyes should have been was nothing but pits of endless darkness.

"Odin's eye," whispered Laila stepping back, but she bumped into the wall behind her.

Faster than Laila could have imagined, the creature rose and rushed her, only stopping when it collided with the shield that Laila had conjured. Standing face to face with her, the creature opened its mouth and unleashed a piercing shriek. Laila felt her own face contort in a silent scream of terror.

BOOKS BY
KATHRYN BLANCHE

Laila of Midgard series

Caught by Demons
Summoned by Demons
Infiltrated by Demons
Hunted by Demons

INFILTRATED
BY
DEMONS

LAILA OF MIDGARD
❖ BOOK 3 ❖

KATHRYN BLANCHE

First published in the United States of America in May 2019 by Kathryn Blanche
Library of Congress Control Number:

ISBN: 978-1-7326651-6-3 (Paperback)

Also available:
ISBN: 978-1-7326651-7-0 (Hardcover Edition)
ISBN: 978-1-7326651-8-7 (Electronic Edition)

The characters and events in this book are fictitious. Any similarity to real persons, living or dead, is coincidental and not intended by the author.

Editing by The Crimson Quill
Cover Art by: Damonza.com

Printed and bound in the United States of America
First printing May 2019

Distributed by Ingram
www.ingramcontent.com

Printed by Lightning Source

Visit www.kathrynblanche.com

DEDICATION

To the brave men and women in law enforcement who risk their lives to keep us safe.

INFILTRATED
BY
DEMONS

CHAPTER 1

"Darien, this is ridiculous," muttered Laila sinking back into the passenger seat of the SUV. "I've been looking for this creature all day."

"Sure, but all the reports state it comes out at night," pointed out the Vampire. He was dressed in his typical ripped up jeans, black muscle-T, biker boots, and a leather jacket. His black hair was spiked and contrasted with his deathly pale skin. Thanks to his blood-red Vampire eyes, that were gifted with excellent night vision, he navigated the Old City's streets with unnatural ease despite the obstacles that littered their path.

No one bothered to clean up the streets back here. Most people wouldn't even venture into this remote part of the Old City. They were somewhere out in Hollywood, or at least what used to be known as Hollywood. Now it was just lumped together with the other sections east of the 405 Freeway in Los Angeles.

Ordinarily, their team didn't respond to calls out in this area, even those desperate souls who dwelled in the Old City avoided this part, but her team had received ten calls this week regarding a giant skeleton. One or two Laila could chalk up to drugs, or a prank. But ten was a lot, and it was their job as agents with the Inter-Realm Security Agency, or IRSA, to investigate.

Laila wasn't sure how a creature like that would have gotten into the city. She suspected it was released during one of the many summoning rituals that had taken place in the city last month. Her team managed to track down those responsible for the illegal rituals, but they were still discovering more sites as well as the Supernatural creatures that had been summoned. The majority of the past month had involved tracking down these creatures before they harmed anyone.

"Where in the worlds would a giant skeleton be hiding during the day?" asked Jerrik from the back seat. "That's not exactly inconspicuous."

Jerrik Torhild was a Svartálfr or Dark Elf. He had the same tall, lean build that Laila had, but the main difference was their skin. While Laila's skin had a warm glow like a human, Jerrik's skin had a silvery hue to it. He looked as if he'd just stepped out of an old black and white film. Their kingdoms had once been one, but long ago the Dark Elves separated from the Light Elves and built their capital city in the world of Svartalfheim.

Jerrik was the newest member of their team. He wasn't truly an agent, and his status was more provisional than anything. But their supervisor, Colin, had recommended him for an expedited training program in order to increase the size of their team. She wouldn't have minded, except for the fact no one had told her. Given their romantic history together, it made things awkward at best.

He joined her on the day-long search for the creature, and the two of them were running short on patience. They'd been snapping at each other all evening, although Darien didn't seem to notice. Or maybe he didn't care. In any case, Laila had the feeling he was happy to be driving around instead of sitting in the office.

"Thor's hammer," whispered Laila as they rounded the corner, "it looks like we found it."

Before them towered, what was unmistakably, a giant skeleton. Laila's jaw dropped. She had never seen anything quite like this. It was nearly twice the size of the surrounding buildings and seemed to glow in the pale light of the moon. Its bones chattered and creaked as it took a step towards them. She bristled at the sound and fought the shiver creeping down her spine.

"How the hell did we miss *that*!?!" Jerrik stared, mouth agape.

"Beats me," Darien stopped the car, "But let's figure that out later."

He stepped out of the SUV to face the skeleton. The men reached for the heavy artillery in the back of the vehicle, but Laila shook her head. Why did they always assume guns were the answer?

"Let's see if we can reason with it first." She took a step towards the creature and shouted, "Freeze where you are!"

The creature gave no sign of understanding. She tried a variety of other languages to no avail. It was getting closer and looking more threatening by the second. Its massive feet were large enough to flatten a sedan like a pancake.

"Step aside." Darien hefted a rocket launcher onto his shoulder.

"Where in Odin's name did you get that!?!" she spluttered.

"Found it." He gave her a nonchalant grin.

Laila shot him an incredulous look and shook her head. "Put it back! You'll destroy everything around us."

"It's the Old City, it's already been destroyed," scoffed the Vampire as he ignored her command.

"Look out!" shouted Jerrik, bringing Laila's attention back to the skeleton, who had just picked up a dumpster and thrown it at them. Laila dove out of the way and rolled across the sidewalk as the dumpster landed in the middle of the street.

Ducking behind an overturned car, Laila focused on her magic and a spell that would trap the skeleton's feet. She heated the asphalt in front of the creature. With its next step, its giant feet sunk into the soft black goop, making a squelching sound as the asphalt worked its way through its bones. It glanced down confused, buying Jerrik the time to cast a spell of ice, cooling the asphalt and trapping the skeleton where it stood.

Laila would have expected the creature to cry out in rage, but the only sound was the gnashing of its teeth. She found it deeply unsettling, like the sound of a hundred breaking bones, but she didn't stop to think about it. This trap bought her limited time to reach out and examine the energy of the creature, searching for some sort of weakness.

"Okay," she said as the others joined her, "it's held together with Ghostly energy."

"It doesn't look like a Ghost to me. Are you sure it's not Necromancy?" asked Darien.

Laila shuddered. "Luckily no, but that makes it even more bizarre."

"I see what you mean." Jerrik concentrated as he examined the magic. "The spell that's animating it feels like hundreds of Ghosts are moving in unison, sort of like a school of fish."

"So how do we kill it?" Darien ducked further behind the car sheltering them as the skeleton threw a minivan. It hit the ground and rolled past them but collided with the building behind. Cracks spread across the walls like black spider webs, as stucco rained down.

Ghost were creatures of pure energy trapped in between the planes of the worlds after death. They only had so much energy at their disposal. Every time they chose to manifest and make themselves seen, or to affect objects—as in this case— they expended more of their energy. They were like batteries, once they ran out of energy they ceased to function and were forced on to the next life. They could recharge by stealing energy from the living, but at the moment there weren't many living things around they could siphon energy from.

Laila threw up a shield, protecting them from the debris. "If

it's like a Ghost, then when we use up its energy, it should collapse. The more it moves and the harder it works to keep itself
assembled and standing, the faster the energy will be used up."

"Now *that* I can do." Darien grinned.

In a flash, the Vampire was across the street.

"Hey numbskull!" he shouted enthusiastically. "Over here!"

He lifted the rocket launcher and deployed one of the rock-
ets. It collided with the giant skeleton's ribcage in a fiery explosion that shook the ground. Bone fragments rained down, and
Laila and Jerrik ducked to avoid the falling debris.

"Damn!" Jerrik peered around the overturned car at Darien's
rocket launcher, his eyes wide. "I'm getting one of those!"

Laila rolled her eyes. Picking up a piece of bone, she realized it was, in fact, an ordinary human femur.

"What the—" she began, but an invisible force jerked the
bone out of her grasp as the skeletal giant reassembled itself.

"Just like the Zombies." Jerrik frowned.

Chills ran down her spine. The Zombies from The Event
had the same ability. She truly hoped this was not the work of
a Necromancer. The last time a group of them launched an
attack, they nearly destroyed the humans with hordes of reas-
sembling Zombies. That horrific period of time—now known
as The Event—was the reason that Supernatural creatures now
roamed Earth freely. An age-old treaty was broken, and Supernaturals were now allowed to travel to Earth and openly interact
with humans.

Laila searched the street for anything that could help. On
the far side of the skeleton was a fire hydrant.

"Cover me!" she shouted as she sprinted across the cracked
asphalt.

Jerrik hurtled a volley of magical fireballs at the creature as
she sprinted through its legs. The skeleton spotted her, swatting
at her like a bug. She jumped over the hand and kept running.

"Take cover!" shouted Darien as he deployed another rocket.

The explosion rang out above her. She called up a magical shield as bones fell from the sky.

She reached the hydrant and used a spell to remove the rusty screw, but there was no water.

"Come on!" she groaned, magically coaxing the water out at a painfully slow rate. It had been years since the water had been shut off, but there was still some remaining in the pipes. After a minute, water began to flood the street.

She directed the stream to climb up along the skeleton's legs and along its entire body. Then she froze it into a thick layer of glittering ice. *That should hold*, she thought smugly.

A loud crack echoed through the night as the ice fractured, one long fissure running up the creature's right leg. The ice quivered as the giant skeleton fought to free itself. Chunks of ice fell to the ground and shattered as the giant broke free. Laila backed up, swearing, and quickly reassessed the situation.

Darien launched another rocket, which took out the skeleton's knee. It teetered back and forth for a moment before falling backwards in her direction.

"Laila!" shouted Jerrik.

Laila ran full tilt away from the falling stack of bones. She was starting to weave a shield spell when the ground lurched out from underneath her.

Looking up, she saw familiar claws grabbing her forearms. It was Frej, her Air Dragon boyfriend.

The Dragon unleashed a roar as he turned and dropped her close to the ground next to the SUV. She rolled to cushion the impact and turned to watch Frej climb higher into the dark sky.

"A bit dramatic if you ask me," scoffed Jerrik with an irritated look.

"Nobody was," muttered Laila, dusting herself off.

As the giant skeleton tried to pick itself up, Frej appeared out of the night sky, colliding with the skeleton and clawing at it. As he climbed in altitude for another pass, Darien let loose his last rocket, obliterating the skull, but still it continued to fight back. When Laila reached out to feel the Ghostly energy of the creature, she could tell it was quickly diminishing—they were almost there.

Laila resumed her cover with Jerrik behind the overturned car as they took turns casting spells at the creature, scattering the bones across the block. A massive hand grabbed for them and lifted the car. Laila scrambled back but froze when she saw Jerrik pinned against the car by a large, bone finger.

"Hold on!" she cried.

She ran and jumped, clinging onto the rusty car bumper as it rose higher and higher in the air. Climbing as fast as she dared, she reached Jerrik.

"Take my hand," she shouted.

He clasped her hand as she blasted through the bone finger with a spell. The sudden lurch of Jerrik's weight strained her arms as she struggled to hold onto the bumper, but she didn't let go. The Dark Elf quickly found his footing.

"Thanks!" He winked at her before leaping onto the giant's ribcage.

Laila followed suit and together they climbed down the giant skeleton, quickly reaching the asphalt.

With one last pass, Frej slammed into the giant's spine. The skeleton fell apart, disintegrating into a massive pile of human bones as the last of the Ghostly energy was used up. Laila and the others scattered to avoid being buried.

Frej clambered out of the pile. In the dim light of the moon, she could see his scales were shades of white, grey, and blue. He shook the remaining bones from his body and shifted back into his human form.

His wavy brown hair hung to his broad shoulders. His body was built from years of sword work and military training. As usual, he had an air of authority surrounding him. Considering he was both a knight and a nobleman, it wasn't surprising. The only thing that remained the same, in both his human and Dragon form, was his brilliant blue eyes.

"You know," said Darien joining them, "it's pretty nice to have a Dragon around."

Jerrik muttered something, but Laila didn't catch it. Given how short her temper was at the moment, it was probably a good thing. After spending the day stuck in the SUV with Jerrik, Laila was one snide remark away from zapping the prick with her stun baton.

"I'm glad I tagged along." Frej wrapped his arm around Laila's waist protectively. "Whatever that was, it took a lot of manpower to take it down."

Laila didn't miss the cool look the Dragon gave Jerrik.

Jerrik smirked and narrowed his eyes. "Yes, whatever would we have done without you?"

Laila felt Frej tense beside her. Her ex-lover and current boyfriend silently challenged each other like two dogs eyeing the same bone. Laila debated whether she should intervene or allow the males to pummel each other until they came to their senses.

"Where did all these bones come from?" asked Frej. "They look like human remains."

Darien cringed. "They're left over from The Event. There were too many bodies to recover. Most of the abandoned sections of the city still have them littering the ground, where resources ran out to properly bury them." He nudged one of the bones with the toe of his boot.

It was the disturbing reality of this post-apocalyptic world. Laila had seen it firsthand when she passed through some of the towns in the countryside. The shocking number of deaths was overwhelming and tragic.

Darien's phone rang. He pulled it out of his pocket and hit the answer button.

"Hello?"

There was a pause as the person on the other end of the line spoke. Darien's brow gradually creased into a frown as he listened.

"Shit!" he swore, glancing at Laila, "we'll be there soon."

CHAPTER 2

"So, what are we dealing with?" asked Jerrik as Darien sped off towards the more populated west side of the city. Frej had flown back to the house, so it was just the two men and Laila who drove off to the next call.

"What appears to be a homicide." Darien scowled at the road ahead.

"SNP?" asked Laila.

SNP stood for Supernatural Person. It was a term coined by the other members of their team to describe any magical, otherworldly, or non-human individual.

Darien nodded. "The victim was a human by the name of Johnathan Samuel, but it's possible a Vampire killed him."

"With all the pro-human protests, this is the last thing we need right now." Laila cringed and held on tight as Darien pulled around a sharp corner. She would've mentioned something to Darien about his driving if she hadn't noticed how tense the Vampire was.

"We don't know for sure that an SNP was involved," added Darien, "Captain Romero from LAPD homicide division wants us to check it out, just to be sure."

Laila sank back into her seat and watched the dark city rush past them. The Old City was in various stages of decay. It was only five years since The Event, but in that time, many of the structures were left unmaintained. It didn't seem all that long to Laila, but without the regular maintenance, buildings were quickly crumbling.

The government tried to discourage people from living in the unstable buildings. But the option to live rent free tempted many to take their chances. Unfortunately, Laila had experienced first-hand how dangerous living in these buildings could be when a Fire Elemental went on a rampage through a part of the Old City. The death toll was still unknown, and Laila had almost been among them. It was only with the aid of a Goddess that she'd destroyed the Fire Elemental responsible and gotten out alive.

All that remained to remind her of the ordeal were the curious scars that wrapped around her arms. The scars looked like flames in the palest shade of blue that shimmered like moonstones. She had matching scars on her back from a wound she'd received while she and Jerrik were imprisoned by Demons. In both instances, she'd been healed by the same Goddess who had yet to reveal her identity. Laila shuddered to imagine why this Goddess had taken so much interest in her. History was riddled with instances where Gods had interfered with the lives of mortals, and generally speaking, things didn't turn out so well for the mortals.

Darien entered Culver City, the zone where the Old City and the west side met. It was technically habitable. The houses here were old and worn out, but at least they were up to code. Halloween was coming up, and many of the homes had pumpkins decorating entryways, scarecrows, plastic skeletons or other spooky decorations. The holiday was still a few weeks away, but the decorations and candy had started appearing in stores over a month ago. Her roommates had been all too thrilled to pull out their boxes of decorations from the garage, but Laila still didn't get it. In her opinion she had enough interaction with Ghosts and skeletons at work, she didn't feel any burning desire to decorate her house with them.

They pulled up in front of a large apartment complex where police cars were parked. The captain waved them over as they stepped out of the SUV.

"Thanks for coming so quickly." The captain shook their hands.

"No worries," said Darien, "we just finished dealing with a giant skeletal creature lurking in the Old City. This was on our way back."

The captain grimaced. "I don't even want to know."

"Shall we take a look?" Laila nodded towards the building in front of them.

"Be my guest."

The captain led them down a wandering path through the apartment complex, and up a flight of stairs. Yellow tape was strung across the hallway. Captain Romero lifted it for them and beckoned them in.

Even from down the hall, Laila could smell the metallic tang of blood. She glanced at Darien, but he looked unfazed. It occurred to Laila that he probably had the best self-control of any Vampire she'd ever met. Not once had he given in to the bloodlust when she'd been around him. He'd gotten close once when she'd been shot, but even then, all he'd needed was a little distance.

"Gods," breathed Jerrik hesitating in the doorway.

Laila peered around him. The victim, or what remained of him, was lying in the middle of the room. The corpse had been mutilated beyond recognition, and her first impression was that it had been an animal attack, but there was far too little blood soaking the carpet.

She stepped around Jerrik and entered the room. There had clearly been a struggle. A sofa was upturned, and pictures on one wall had been smashed as if someone had been shoved against them, but a quick glance in the other rooms told her that the violence had been contained to the living room.

"What makes you think a Vampire did this?" Jerrik asked the captain. The Dark Elf looked a little shaken, and Laila reminded herself that his law enforcement training was limited.

"There's too little blood."

Darien nodded and crouched by the corpse. "You're right about that, there's nowhere near enough blood left, and at least some of these wounds were made posthumously."

"Why would someone do that?" Jerrik tore his eyes from the body to look at the captain.

Captain Romero shrugged. "Some folk get off on that sort of thing. I've seen serial killers who mutilate as a kind of calling card. But in this case, I think they were trying to send a message. The door was left wide open with the body in plain sight."

Laila crouched down next to Darien. He was right, the wounds did look posthumous. There were also bite marks that looked suspiciously like fangs. Laila exchanged a glance with Darien. So much for hoping it wasn't Vampire related.

"Jerrik," she said finally, "call the investigative team, tell them we've got a homicide and ask them to contact the morgue and prepare for a potentially undead corpse." There was still the possibility the victim could rise under the right circumstances, and she didn't want the medical examiners caught off-guard.

Jerrik pulled out his phone and stepped into the other room.

"So, it *was* a Vampire?" asked the captain.

"We can't be sure until the autopsy is performed," explained Darien grimly. "Do us a favor though, and keep this quiet."

The captain nodded and headed back down the hall looking troubled.

Darien hissed and turned to Laila.

"This idiot Vampire has no idea what he's done." His lip curled showing the tips of his fangs in a snarl.

"Or maybe he does," pointed out Laila as she raised an eyebrow. "It does seem like he's trying to send a message to someone. Maybe revenge?"

Darien waved his hand dismissively. "No way, no one in the Vampire community would risk something like this. We have our own laws and enforce them harshly. The intentional killing of a human is worse than the murder of one of our own because of the risk involved historically. Even if times have changed, our laws haven't. No Vampire in their right mind would risk it."

Laila felt a wave of unease as she crossed her arms and glanced down at the corpse. Of course, the Vampire community had its own rules. Most of the earthly SNPs did. But there was a darkness in Darien's voice that left her unsettled. Some morbidly curious corner of her mind wondered what exactly the punishment would be. Torture? Execution? Perhaps both.

Jerrik reentered, stirring her from the grim stream of thought.

"The investigative team is on their way. They told me someone will have to accompany the body to the morgue." Jerrik glanced from Laila to Darien.

"I'll do it," volunteered Darien, "the two of you have been out since the afternoon. If he does turn, it's better to have a Vampire around to intervene."

He tossed Laila the keys to his SUV.

"We'll see you tomorrow then." She was done for the day.

The Elves headed back to the car just as the investigative team pulled up. Laila nodded to them before driving off.

"That Dragon of yours seems pretty interested in *our* work," said Jerrik after a time.

Not this again, thought Laila. "Colin's agreed that we need the extra help."

"There are others more qualified."

"He's a knight in his own kingdom," irritation crept into her voice.

"Then how do we know we can trust him? What if he's just using us to gain access to information for the Dragons?"

Laila didn't give him the satisfaction of taking the bait.

Before Jerrik had joined IRSA, they'd escaped from a Demon-run fight ring. She and Jerrik had bonded over the ordeal. Laila thought there had been a deeper connection growing between them, that she'd actually meant something to him. After a while, she'd begun to think that there was more depth under his mask of sarcasm and arrogance, that he was compassionate and caring. But after they took down the operation and she'd woken up from her magically induced coma, she discovered that he'd left without a word. It hurt her more than she would admit to him, but she had moved on.

She switched on the radio to deter any further conversation as Jerrik gave her a smug look.

They pulled into the garage at the IRSA office. It was a new building next to the Asclepius Hospital of Supernatural Medicine, in a nice area just north of the Los Angeles International Airport. The IRSA building was large, and the team had yet to fully grow into the space. There were floors for the field agents, like Laila, as well as floors for the investigative team and support staff. There were also additional facilities like specially equipped holding cells for SNPs, a morgue, and a gym. Even though the officials in D.C. had a tendency to turn a blind eye on the troubles of the other cities like Los Angeles, at least they'd built a decent facility to house the agency.

After parking in Darien's usual spot, Laila hastily stepped out of the SUV and hit the button for the elevator. She could feel Jerrik's eyes on her as they stepped inside.

He'd tried speaking to her several times over the last month, but she was not ready to listen to his excuses. He'd made his decision, and so had she.

The doors slid open, and they stepped into the hallway. In the doorway to the first office, Laila paused. Inside, their supervisor rummaged through a pile of papers on his desk, muttering to himself. She couldn't quite understand what he said.

"Colin?" she called, "do you have a moment?"

Colin jumped and spun around.

"Oh, sorry," he mumbled. "I didn't hear you come down the hall."

His curly brown hair was a little disheveled like he'd been running his fingers through it. His beard was a little longer than usual as well, giving him a slightly rugged look and complementing his Werewolf aspect. Otherwise, his appearance was neat and tidy. There was a nervous energy about him though, something she'd noticed often in the past weeks. She was still wary around him, especially since his moods seemed to be worsening lately.

"Is everything okay?" she asked, glancing past him towards his desk.

"Oh, yeah, I was just looking for something. But it doesn't matter, I should get going anyway. Lorel's waiting for me."

Jerrik peered in from the hall. "This girlfriend of yours sure keeps you busy. Are you going on another date tonight?"

"Yeah, we've got reservations." It wasn't an invitation to continue conversation.

"Before you go, we need to speak with you." Laila planted herself in the doorway.

"Can't it wait until the morning?" Colin shrugged into his coat.

Laila bristled, this was too important for him to brush off, so she ignored the Werewolf and continued anyway.

"A human's been murdered by a Vampire. We just came from the crime scene."

Colin waved her off. "People murder each other every day in this city. We'll discuss it tomorrow. I'm going to be late."

Laila remained the doorway, blocking his path. Her annoyance was quickly building, something that happened often recently. This wasn't the kind of issue he could brush aside; it could affect a lot of people and the overall relationships between humans and SNPs in the city.

"I don't think you're taking this seriously," she said coolly. "This is exactly the kind of thing that the humans are afraid of.

If this gets out to the media, these pro-human protests are going to turn into riots."

Colin frowned and crossed his arms. "These problems will still be here in the morning. Don't forget your place Agent Eyvindr," he warned as a hint of a growl escaped his throat.

The threat in his voice was unmistakable. Laila schooled her expression to hide her annoyance and reluctantly stepped aside. Colin brushed past her and Jerrik without another word and entered the elevator.

The two Elves exchanged frustrated glances as the door shut.

"What is going on?" asked a curvy blond woman who strutted down the hall in their direction. Ali looked human, aside from her violet eyes, the hallmark trait of the Fae. She wore a pair of skinny jeans, thigh-high stiletto boots, and a low-cut sweater that showed off her cleavage. She sipped a cup of coffee that smelled strongly of pumpkin. I wasn't sure how many pumpkin beverages Ali consumed daily since October 1st, but she'd insisted it was an integral part of celebrating the season.

Laila tried to shake off her brewing ire from the encounter. "Colin's in a mood. Did something happen?"

Ali rolled her eyes. "He's been like that all day. He claims he's stressing about his date tonight. I don't see what the big deal is. They've been dating for a couple months; I'd think he'd be over the nerves by now."

Laila couldn't care less about Colin's nerves. "Well, in any case, we've got a situation on our hands."

"I heard, there's a Vampire murderer loose in the city."

Laila opened her mouth to respond but yawned instead.

"Come on," Ali chuckled, "you can fill me in on our way home."

"By the way, we found the creature," added Jerrik cheerfully as he headed towards his office. "It turns out that giant, rampaging skeletons are actually a thing."

Ali made a face. "Because that's all I wanted to hear before

I go home to bed." She slipped back into her office and grabbed her purse.

Laila chucked, "Well you can't say our work is boring."

"That's for sure. See you Jerrik." Ali waved as she walked down the hall.

"See you."

His eyes lingered on Laila as he paused in the doorway of his office. She noticed that his black t-shirt was still damp with perspiration from the fight and clung to every curve of his muscular chest. He gave her a wicked grin, and she realized she'd been staring. She glared at him before following Ali to the elevator.

CHAPTER 3

"Okay, spill it," said Ali as she drove. "What happened between you and Jerrik today?"

"Nothing," grumbled Laila in exasperation. "He tried to talk to me about... things. And he expressed his disapproval of Frej's involvement in the team."

"As if he has any say in that," Ali scoffed. "Jerrik's not even a full agent."

Laila couldn't help but feel a twinge of smugness. "In any case, we have more important issues."

She recounted the crime scene and the observations they'd made. By the time she'd finished, Ali's grip on the steering wheel had tightened, and her expression had grown worried.

"By the Morrigan! If we don't get this Vampire in custody soon, the city's going to go ballistic. This is exactly why the SNPs on earth kept a low profile all these years because the humans lash out when they feel threatened. They may not have magic, but there's strength in numbers."

Laila looked out the passenger window at a banner hanging

from a balcony, it read: "Earth is for humans." It had been hanging there for weeks, and finally, someone had vandalized it—or in Laila's opinion, fixed it. They had crossed out humans and replaced it with earthlings. Beneath it was also a spray-painted smiley-face with Vampire fangs.

"How was the protest today?" Laila asked.

Ali had been keeping an eye on a protest outside the Jotunheim consulate. The pro-human protestors were outraged at the acquittal of a Jotunheim man who was accused of killing a woman in a robbery gone wrong.

While the pro-human protestors were a small group, they were vocal, and many of their members were suspected in anti-SNP hate crimes. They'd been standing outside of local businesses owned by or catering to Supernaturals, including the Asclepius Hospital of Supernatural Medicine next to the IRSA offices.

"This one was more agitated than the last," Ali sighed. "They were bordering on the edge of unlawful assembly. It doesn't help that everyone's gearing up for the elections. This will be the first election for Governor since Los Angeles was renamed as the state capital."

It was moved from Sacramento after The Event since the vast majority of the state's surviving population now called Los Angeles home. Sacramento, San Francisco, and San Diego had stable, but small populations, and people were only starting to venture to some of the rural areas now that many of the highways had been cleared for travel.

They arrived home. The building was old but structurally sound. It had once been a business called Fredrico's Automotive Repair. The old sign, in faded paint, was still visible on the street front. There were two more floors above that had once housed other office suites. Ali had converted the top floor into a master suite for herself, while the second floor was comprised of three guest rooms. Laila and Frej currently occupied two of the guest rooms. They'd discussed moving into one room, but between the odd hours Laila worked, and the nightmares that constantly plagued her, it was difficult for Frej to get a decent night's sleep. Erin had claimed the back half of the first floor where she had her own bedroom, bathroom, and an office which was her dedicated study space.

In addition to Ali's renovations, there was also a newly-installed security system with cameras mounted outside the building that sent footage directly to their phones. These were new additions Ali had installed after her sister's recent abduction. They parked in the garage and stepped through the door into the converted interior of the building.

The kitchen and living room were combined in a large and cavernous space, which was filled with a wonderful and homey blend of colorful decor from both Earth and Alfheim, the realm that Ali and Laila were from. Everything in the kitchen was new and up to date, and the living room was equipped with two large sofas and a state-of-the-art entertainment system. But at the moment, the furniture had been pushed aside.

In the middle of the room, Ali's younger sister Erin stood focusing on a spell she was working. A ball of flame whirled around her. It was entrancing, and almost like a dance to watch. Frej watched his pupil from one end of the room intently, looking for any sign that she was losing control.

Laila and Ali paused in the doorway of the kitchen. It had only been a month since Erin had broken through her internal magical barrier, but in that time, they'd seen a lot of growth in her control and ability. There were also physical differences as well as her body started to catch up to its actual age after being stunted by the magical block. She'd grown nearly three inches in four weeks and now looked two years older, appearing to be fourteen by human standards. Ali was concerned that Erin might experience negative side effects from the sudden developmental changes, but Frej assured her that the changes would slow in a few months once her body reached its proper age. Like most creatures in Alfheim though, Dragons aged much more slowly than humans. So while Erin was somewhere in her fifties, that was equivalent to eighteen in human terms.

Erin was not Ali's biological sister. In fact, they weren't even the same species. Erin was a Fire Dragon, whose egg was found after Erin's biological parents were killed. Ali's parents were the ones who found the egg and searched for a living relative, but none were ever found. It wasn't until a couple months ago that Laila's mother had managed to track down a family friend, Sir Frej Ilmarinen, to answer some of their questions. For instance, why Erin had stopped aging in her adolescent stage, or why she had never been able to access her magic or her Dragon form.

It turned out that Erin's lack of exposure to elemental magic had left her growth and abilities stunted. Fortunately, her exposure to Laila and Frej's magic, as well as the training that Frej was giving her, helped her overcome this obstacle. Frej had even moved in with them for the time being to give her his full attention.

Well, most of his attention anyway.

Laila glanced to the side and found Frej watching her. Their eyes locked and she gave him a sultry look as she bit her lip, teasing him. Desire sparked in Frej's eyes, and he looked like he was about to pick Laila up and carry her to his bedroom. Before he could move, they were jerked back to reality.

"ERIN!" Ali screamed.

The young Dragon had let the magical ball of fire stray too far, grazing one of Ali's decorative pillows.

Laila reacted, quickly smothering the fire with a spell, but the pillow was clearly ruined. Its purple silk threads charred brown beyond recognition.

"That's it!" Ali stomped across the room, her eyes ablaze. "No more fire magic in the house!"

"Where else am I supposed to practice?" snapped Erin, sounding every bit like the fourteen-year-old she looked like.

"I don't care, just not in my house!"

"Ugh!" groaned Erin. She glared at her sister before stomping off towards her bedroom.

Frej rushed over.

"I'm so sorry—" began Frej.

"You are supposed to be watching her." Ali glared at him.

The Dragon shrank back.

"The garage," interjected Laila before the situation could escalate further, "I'm sure we could set up a safe, fireproofed space for her to practice in the garage. There's plenty of room in there."

Ali paused for a moment, considering Laila's proposal.

"If that works for you," said Frej slowly, "I would ensure there are proper wards put into place, and other precautions taken."

"Fine," Ali snapped, crossing her arms, "But if anything else catches fire, I'll be holding *you* responsible." She poked him in the chest.

He nodded solemnly. After Ali was certain the Dragon had received the message, she turned down the hall in the direction of Erin's room.

When Ali was gone, Frej released the breath he'd been holding.

"You know," started Laila as she helped Frej move the furniture back into place, "I never thought I'd live to see the day when a Dragon cowered in the presence of the Fae."

A smile tugged at the corners of his mouth. "Accidents happen. And she's right, Erin does need a safer place with better wards to practice her magic. At least until she gets it under control. I just hope Ali isn't too harsh on Erin."

Laila nodded in agreement. She'd set a few wards around the living room to prevent the house from catching fire, but the wards didn't extend to objects within the room.

"Besides," said Frej as he stepped closer, "It was also my fault for letting my attention wander."

He slid his hands around her waist and pulled her in close. She relished the musky scent that clung to him, like old leather-bound tomes and something earthy. Tilting her chin up, she leaned in and kissed him. It was slow and gentle. The tenderness left her wanting more. All too soon he pulled away.

"Are you hungry? Erin and I made dinner."

Laila nodded, she was starving. Frej turned away towards the kitchen, but Laila remained where she was as a thought nagged at her.

"Why did you come along to fight that creature tonight?"

"It sounded like you needed some help." He busied himself with dinner preparations, fetching a pair of oven mitts from a drawer.

"But was that the *only* reason?" she persisted, "or was it because you knew Jerrik would be there?"

She couldn't help but feel there was some sort of rivalry between them.

"Of course not." He paused in front of the oven. "His presence is insignificant."

Laila arched an eyebrow at him. She wasn't buying this act of indifference.

With a sigh, Frej set the mitts down, and took a step towards her, closing the distance between them.

"Look, Jerrik was foolish enough to leave you. He made his choice and left. I stayed. The only thing I resent about his presence is that he makes you uncomfortable."

Frej placed his hands on her hips and drew her close. His lips barely brushed against her own before he said, "I know you don't need my help to deal with him, but I'm here for you in whatever way you need me to be."

A wave of guilt washed over Laila. Frej wasn't the insecure type to feel threatened by Jerrik, and a part of her felt ridiculous for thinking it possible. Perhaps Jerrik's attitude today was influencing the way she interpreted the situation.

"Erin told me dinner is ready," called Ali, appearing from down the hall. "I don't know about you guys, but I'm starving!"

Frej chuckled and removed a skillet from the oven. "Erin

picked the recipe this time, it's a Spanish paella."

"Gods that smells good!" said Ali, looking over his shoulder. "I still don't understand why you're teaching Erin to cook, but I'm all for it."

Both Ali and Laila were terrible cooks. They could handle a frozen pizza, and half the time they managed not to burn it, but that was about the extent of their culinary skill. Before Frej came into the picture, their diets consisted mainly of take-out. But Frej, it turned out, was quite the chef.

"I think it complements her training," he explained. "After all, her element is fire. Cooking just shows her a practical application for her abilities."

Ali nodded thoughtfully and accepted a plate of steaming hot paella. Frej returned to the oven and removed a second, smaller, skillet and placed it in front of Laila.

"This one's vegetarian." He winked.

Laila gave him a grateful look. Elves were typically vegetarian. She'd never mentioned it to Frej, but he'd somehow picked it up. Frej had taken to making vegetarian alternatives for Laila even though she told him it wasn't necessary. It was a thoughtful gesture though, and she truly appreciated the effort.

"Thank the Gods this week is over," said Ali as she got up.

She walked around the counter and to the refrigerator where she removed a bottle of hot sauce. She poured a generous layer on her paella before offering it to Laila.

She wrinkled her nose at the bottle. "I feel like the calls are getting stranger every week."

"At least we have our 'Ladies' Night' tomorrow."

Frej shook his head. "Is it really necessary that I leave for the evening? Couldn't I just stay here and work on lesson plans for Erin?"

"Nope," insisted Erin, "ladies only. Besides, the guys have something planned for you tomorrow."

The "guys" in question were Mato and Henrik, two male SNPs that Laila had met while imprisoned by Demons. Recently, Laila had organized a support group for individuals affected by the Demons. Henrik and Mato had quickly joined the group and expressed their interest in Ali. The Fae wasn't revealing much, but Laila noticed she'd been a little secretive lately, and had made excuses to slip out of the house. It was odd for Ali to be so private about her sex life, but perhaps Frej's presence had something to do with it. In any case, Henrik and Mato had volunteered to take Frej out drinking with them.

Ali talked excitedly about the snacks she was planning to buy for the following evening, but Laila's mind was elsewhere. She picked at her dinner as she thought about the conversation she'd had with Frej.

"Where the hell is she?" Erin impatiently checked her phone again, "The others will be here any minute, and Ali's got the snacks."

"Maybe she's stuck in traffic?" suggested Frej as he put a stack of dishes away.

Laila finished a spell she had cast to collect any dust, it swirled in a circle around the room before it deposited itself into the trashcan. She and Erin had finished cleaning the house while Ali ran out to get the snacks for the gathering tonight. She'd been gone for over two hours though and wasn't answering the phone.

As Laila opened her mouth to speak, the door to the garage opened and in strode Ali, an oversized purse in one hand, and a large pumpkin latte in the other.

"Look who I found!" she announced.

She waved towards Henrik and Mato as they entered the kitchen, their arms full of grocery bags, before disappearing upstairs.

Mato was a Werebear, a human who could shift into a bear form. Weres fell under the general category of Shifters, or SNPs that could take more than one form, but Weres specifically referred to humans with a second animal form. Mato was tall and brawny with dark hair and eyes. He was quick to smile, even when times were tough. On the other hand, Henrik was smaller with pale skin and hair. His eyes were a bright shade of blue that reminded her of glaciers. He looked human but was actually a Mörkö, a form of ice creature. Laila had never pushed him to tell her what exactly a Mörkö was, but she could tell he had some sort of control over ice and water. He was quieter than Henrik and often seemed lost in thought, but the two of them were thick as thieves and always joking around.

"So that's what took her so long," snickered Erin as she glanced impishly at Ali. "I can smell the Werebear on her."

Laila raised an eyebrow at Erin.

"What?" asked Erin innocently. "I can't help it. She literally reeks of it."

Laila shook her head and gave Erin a discrete look, reminding her that this was none of their business.

"Hey!" exclaimed Mato as he placed his bags on the counter. He pulled Laila into a bear hug that lifted her off the ground. "Where were you this week? I thought you were coming to the meeting?" He set her back on the ground.

"Things just got busy at the office." She hastily turned away to unload the bags.

"You said that last week," pointed out Henrik. By the look he gave her, he saw right through the lie but didn't push the matter further.

In all honesty, she just didn't feel like going lately. Sure it was therapeutic, and after the meetings, she felt like a weight had been lifted off her chest, but lately, she didn't feel like talking. Or maybe it was because the things she really wanted to say were the things she couldn't bring herself to talk about.

Frej came over to shake both of their hands.

"We should get going." Mato clapped Laila on the shoulder. "It looks like you've got everything under control here. We just wanted to say hi."

"Don't worry, we'll keep an eye on Frej." Henrik winked at her.

"Thanks," Laila chuckled. Frej gave her a pained look, but she just kissed him on the cheek and mouthed *it will be fine*. It wasn't as if he didn't go out with friends back in the Dragon Kingdom. He just needed time to warm up to the two men, and it would do him good to have some male bonding time.

They headed out the door as Ali returned and helped Laila unload the grocery bags.

"I really think you're overdoing it," said Erin as she emptied yet another bag of candies into a bowl. It was the fifth such bag, and that's not where the junk food ended. There was also a variety of chips, dips, and brownies. Ali mentioned that she would be ordering pizzas later too, once everyone arrived. The candies were mostly in the shape of bats and pumpkins in honor of Halloween, which was fast approaching. More pumpkins decorated the house as well as fall leaves, pointed hats, and black cat cutouts. They didn't have Halloween back in Alfheim, but Ali had quickly grown to love the holiday.

"Yeah, there's only going to be five of us," pointed out Laila. Ali put her hands on her hips.

"Yes, but Erin alone eats as much as two human men."

"Hey!" howled Erin defensively, "I'm in the middle of a magical growth spurt, thank-you-very-much!"

"Go get cleaned up." Ali wrinkled her nose at her sister. "They'll be here soon."

Erin was still dressed in her white uniform that she called a gi. After her kidnapping, Ali had finally given into Erin's wishes to take up martial arts. Ali enrolled her in a judo class around the corner, but Erin was so enthusiastic about it that she started going every day. As much as Ali complained about the cost, Laila knew she was glad Erin was doing something active and more or less social.

While Erin changed, Laila and Ali finished arranging snacks

on the table.

"So, um, you and Mato?" Laila gave Ali a mischievous grin.

Ali barked a laugh. "So you figured it out."

Laila held up her hands innocently, "I'm not judging, he's a great guy."

In all honesty, she was relieved that Ali was moving on. She'd been hit hard by the death of her ex-lover Carlos, who had been assassinated by Demons in front of Ali, although the assassin was never apprehended. The Fae blamed herself for his death. She'd mourned in her own way, by avoiding men. Sure, she laughed and flirted with them, but she hadn't let things go further than that. Even Erin had been concerned, but then Ali met Henrik and Mato at one of the meetings, and things had changed. Both of them expressed interest, but it seemed that Ali had made her decision.

Erin returned in a t-shirt from some obscure metal band Laila had never heard of, and a pair of baggy grey sweat pants. It was the complete opposite of Ali's style with light pink, flannel shorts, and a lacy tank top. Ali had decided on a comfy dress code for the gathering, and Laila wasn't complaining. She had on a pair of brown yoga pants, and a forest green t-shirt.

Ordinarily, ladies' night meant getting dressed up and going out to a club. But this week Ali decided they should try something new. She was going to throw a costume party, but Laila talked her out of it by insisting she had nothing to wear. Instead, they decided on a girl's night in, but it appeared Ali was going overboard with the preparations. In addition to the food, she'd rented a variety of horror movies, and fall-themed rom-coms. There was no way they would make it through half of them. But then again, Ali didn't believe in half-assing anything. Laila silently hoped they wouldn't make it to the horror films. She had enough of that at work.

There was a flash of light in the center of the room. It faded revealing a woman of unearthly beauty. Her skin shimmered with a faint warm light, and from the other side of the room, Laila could feel the overpowering energy radiating from the woman.

"Oh really?" Laila laughed, "The Goddess of the Black Forest likes dinosaur pajamas?"

The Goddess lifted her eyebrows and crossed her arms in mock offense.

"I'll have you know that dinosaurs were quite fascinating creatures," said Arduinna glancing at her blue flannel dinosaur pajama bottoms and their matching top. "I still keep a couple of them around my gardens, but don't tell the other Gods, we weren't supposed to save them."

"Wait a minute," said Erin shocked, "are you saying there are dinosaurs on the black market?" The Dragon had a mischievous gleam in her eyes.

"Don't even think about it." Ali gave her sister the look. "That's not happening in this house. Besides, I can only handle a maximum of two reptiles at a time."

Erin stuck her tongue out.

Ordinarily, Laila would never make fun of a God. Even a minor God could smite her where she stood. But Arduinna was an exception, she preferred the company of mortals to that of the immortals and rarely entered Asgard, the world of the Gods. Instead, she liked to keep an eye on Earth from the relative peace of her forest in Germany.

"It's good to see you," the Goddess said graciously, giving everyone hugs.

The doorbell rang, and Erin left to get the door as Arduinna passed Ali a box of German chocolates.

"Anything new?" asked Arduinna.

"Not really." Ali gave her a glum look. "The protests are getting worse in the city though, and Laila had to take down a giant skeleton last night."

"Oh really?" The Goddess raised an eyebrow at Laila.

"It was made of human bones. They were assembled magically, but the spell binding them felt Ghostly in nature," explained Laila with a frown.

"That's an extremely rare type of haunting," called another woman as she entered the living room. It was Lyn.

Lyn was in her late twenties with her curly, bleached-blond hair pulled up in a messy bun. She wore a pair of flannel shorts and a t-shirt that read "Witches be Crazy!" She had a variety of colorful tattoos and a handful of piercings. The Witch had an easy-going beach vibe about her.

"Did it show itself during the day?" asked the Witch.

"No, I searched all day. I was surprised to find it so quickly at night. I guess we were lucky."

Lyn shook her head, making her messy bun sway.

"Nope, they only assemble during the night. It's a type of Ghostly entity that manifests using the combined energy of many restless spirits. After The Event, I'm surprised we don't see more of them. I attended a lecture on them from a Japanese Witch at my last Witch's convention. He called this sort of creature a Gashadokuro."

"That sounds right to me." Arduinna held out her hand for the newcomer. "I'm Arduinna, by the way."

"I've heard a lot about you." The Witch shook her hand enthusiastically. "I'm Lyn."

Lyn opened her large over the shoulder bag and pulled out a mason jar of shimmery green liquid.

"Look what I found!" She held the jar up triumphantly.

"Troll boogers?" asked Erin with interest as she lounged on a couch.

"Nope, it's the hair-growth tincture I've been looking for. I bought it off a Witch in San Francisco last week."

"Do you think it'll work?" asked Laila as she ran her fingers through her short hair.

After she'd gone charging into a burning building last month, her hair had been badly singed. Laila went to a salon that was able to give it a nice cut, but she really missed her long hair.

Lyn shrugged. "There's only one way to find out. But are

you sure you want to do it? You look super edgy with your hair like this, especially with the tattoos."

"They're not tattoos," Laila muttered, folding her arms self-consciously. "More like scars."

Lyn laughed and motioned for Laila to sit in a chair as she unscrewed the lid.

"So how does it work?" asked Ali. "Do you just pour it over her head?"

Lyn laughed. "No, we just apply a little to the scalp. You never know how potent these spells are. It's probably a good idea to wear gloves too."

Ali nodded and retrieved a pair of nitrile gloves from a drawer. Lyn put them on and carefully scooped some of the green goop out of the jar.

"Here it goes."

Laila resisted the urge to cringe as Lyn massaged the slime into her scalp. It was cold and left her skin with a funny tingling feeling. The Witch muttered an incantation under her breath as she worked, but by the time she'd finished, nothing had happened.

"Definitely Troll boogers," muttered Erin as she flipped through messages on her phone.

"Should we add more?" asked Ali examining the label of the jar with Arduinna.

"Give it a minute," said Lyn stepping back, "sometimes they take a little—"

The tingling of Laila's scalp intensified, and suddenly, her hair started growing.

"Whoa!" Erin held up her phone to record a video.

Laila squawked and glanced around as her hair grew longer and longer. It grew past her waist, then her hips. As it reached her knees, she turned to Lyn.

"Now what?" asked Laila. "It's going to slow down, right?"

"Um…" The Witch looked at the label on the jar.

Then as suddenly as it started growing, the hair stopped.

Laila glanced down at the pool of hair around her.

"Well," laughed Ali. "That might be a bit difficult to manage with work."

"I'll cut it if you want," offered Arduinna.

Laila nodded. There was no way she could keep it this long. It was literally dragging on the floor.

Ali retrieved a pair of scissors from her bathroom, and Arduinna got to work. She trimmed it to Laila's waist, and even put a couple layers in it. Laila washed her hair in the sink and dried it with a spell. As she looked at her reflection in the scrying mirror that hung in the living room, she felt relieved. It looked great, and was it her eyes or did it look fuller than it had been before?

"Thank you!" Laila said to Lyn and Arduinna.

Lyn laughed. "You know, when I was a teenager I used to get together with my friends, and we'd give each other makeovers, but this takes the experience to a whole new level!"

They found seats on the sofas as Ali carried bowls of snacks to the coffee table.

"So," started Lyn, as she sat next to Laila. "How are things going with the handsome Dragon knight?"

Laila thought for a moment.

"Good, I suppose. He's a great guy, but I don't know, I can't help but feel like something isn't right."

"You were doing fine until Jerrik showed up," pointed out Ali.

"Male Dragons are predisposed to being territorial," explained Arduinna, with a frown, "but Frej doesn't strike me as the jealous type."

Laila shook her head. "Frej's been nothing but understanding about the whole situation."

Lyn drummed her fingers on the sofa. "What if Frej's not the problem? Your relationship with Jerrik came to a pretty abrupt end. Maybe there's some lingering feelings, or maybe you just need closure?"

"I've moved on," insisted Laila firmly.

There was silence in the room as the others shifted and struggled to find words for their thoughts. After a moment Ali was the first to speak.

"Just because you're in a relationship with Frej doesn't necessarily mean you've moved on."

Laila sat there in stunned silence. She knew Ali was right. For the last month, she'd been telling herself that over and over, but deep down she knew the truth. There was still a part of her that wondered what would've been different if Jerrik had stayed. If she was back in the Elven Kingdom, she would be expected to walk away from Jerrik and never look back, but she wasn't living amongst Elves anymore.

Laila ran her fingers through her hair in exasperation. "So, what do I do?"

The others gave her sympathetic looks.

"Give it time," suggested Lyn, "or talk to them about it."

Erin gave Laila a devious look. "Maybe Lyn could whip up a love potion for you that would take away your feelings for Jerrik?"

Lyn rolled her eyes. "Love potions don't actually exist you know. Do you think I'd be single if they did?"

"It was worth a shot." Erin returned her attention to whatever she was looking at on her phone.

"I'm sure the right answer will come to you." Ali squeezed her shoulder sympathetically. The others nodded in agreement.

"On a different note," said Arduinna seriously, "when are you going to come out to Germany and train with me? Your power is still growing, and someone needs to guide you through more advanced spells."

Laila frowned. "I had pretty thorough training back in Alfheim."

"Your magic is different. It's not just elemental anymore, I can see it in your aura. I'm not sure how, but it's like your magic is evolving."

"What!?!" Laila couldn't help but feel alarmed.

Arduinna gave her a sympathetic look. "Like I said, I don't know how or why, but you need to be careful. Developments like this can be dangerous, at least until you know how to control these other abilities."

Laila had no idea what other "abilities" she was developing, but the thought left her unsettled.

Arduinna reached out and placed her hand on Laila's shoulder. "For better or worse, there is a powerful Goddess that has taken an interest in you. I'm no closer to figuring out which one it is, but this isn't the kind of thing you can just ignore. Sooner or later it's going to catch up with you, and it'll be a whole lot safer if you take the time to prepare yourself now."

Laila knew she was right, but there was so much else going on in her life. How could she justify taking weeks away from her job in order to train with Arduinna? Even with Jerrik and Frej around, there was more crime than the IRSA team could keep up with. Lately, things had been getting worse, particularly with the protests and increasing tensions between the human and SNP communities. No, now was definitely not a good time to leave town.

"I will," said Laila honestly, "but I can't right now."

Arduinna seemed to read her thoughts. "There will never be a good time. Please don't wait too long."

The Goddess returned her attention to the rest of the group as they debated whether to watch a rom-com or a horror movie. Laila wasn't paying attention though. She leaned against the counter, lost in thought. Glancing at the blue flames that wrapped their way up her arms, she wondered what the anonymous Goddess wanted from her.

CHAPTER 4

Frej sat with Henrik and Mato at a small table while they enjoyed pints of craft beer and listened to a middle-aged man playing the guitar as he sang in the corner of the bar. While Frej wasn't terribly familiar with earthly music, Mato told him that many of the songs were acoustic takes on classic rock songs.

The small bar was packed and had a rustic, industrial feel to it. The tables were made of distressed wood, with black iron pipes for legs. The room was dimly light by the warm glow of old-fashioned lightbulbs, left bare and hanging from cords that were wrapped around heavy wooden beams above. The walls had new wallpaper but were decorated with a variety of antique bikes, old peeling signs, and an odd collection of other old things. If he'd seen it all heaped in a pile, it would have looked like junk to him, but hanging on the wall, it somehow looked artistic. A menu dominated another wall. It was just a large chalkboard where the beverages and dishes available for sale had been listed.

As reluctant as Frej had been to go out tonight, he had to admit that it was pretty enjoyable. Henrik and Mato were amusing guys, and they had an endless supply of stories, each crazier than the last leaving Frej to wonder if there was any truth to the stories whatsoever. But the conversation had taken a more serious turn.

Mato shook his head. "I don't get it. One minute everything's fine and things are going great, the next thing I know Ali's crying. I tried to talk to her about it, but she just changed the subject. I think she used her glamour magic on me because I just sort of went with it."

"Did you say something that upset her?" asked Henrik, frowning.

"We were just making out," sighed Mato. "I wish she'd just tell me, you know?"

Frej picked at the corner of his coaster as he thought. "I don't think I can offer any insight. She doesn't exactly confide in me, that's more of Laila's thing."

Mato opened his mouth to say more when someone over Frej's shoulder caught his attention. The Werebear waved to the newcomer to join them.

"Jerrik! I'm glad you could make it!" cried Mato.

Frej bristled and turned to find the Svartálfr, approaching with his usual smug expression. As the Dark Elf noticed him, Frej noticed a flicker of annoyance cross his expression.

Mato clapped Jerrik on the back before motioning to the empty chair. "Jerrik, this is Frej, he's—"

"Yes, our paths have crossed." Jerrik cast the Dragon a smile that didn't quite meet his eyes. "Frej has a tendency to show up when we're on calls."

Frej ignored the bait. He didn't understand why Jerrik was always trying to get under his skin. He'd done nothing to offend the Elf, aside from his relationship with Laila. If Jerrik would be joining them for the rest of the evening though, this was going to be one long night out. Perhaps he could come up with some excuse to leave.

Mato seemed oblivious to any awkwardness. "Henrik, let's

grab more drinks from the bar. This round's on me!"

Henrik glanced between the two men, sensing the tension growing at the table, but followed Mato to the bar, leaving Frej and Jerrik alone.

Frej ignored him as he sipped the last of his beer, but Jerrik's eyes never left him. Gone was the smugness, replaced by a look cold as steel. The Dragon wondered at this shift.

Frej gave him an exasperated look. "What?"

"I don't trust you."

Something told Frej that this was the most genuine thing he'd herd Jerrik utter, but Frej just scoffed and turned his attention to the singer.

Jerrik's frown deepened. "You can ignore me all you want, but I'm serious. When you break Laila's heart—"

"Ah, but that's your thing now, isn't it? Lucky for her I'm not the kind of man who runs away," the words dripped from his mouth like venom as he gave Jerrik a challenging look.

Jerrik's eyes narrowed, as his expression darkened. "No, but you are the kind of man who beds married women."

Frej froze as Jerrik's gaze bored into him. The Dragon's mind raced as well as his pulse. This couldn't be happening to him, not here.

"How?" he managed finally, the words little more than a croak.

Frej expected the sneer to return on Jerrik's face, but it didn't.

"I was there, or don't you recognize me?"

Honestly, Frej didn't. There had been so many people there on that devastating trip to the Svartálfr Kingdom.

Jerrik continued, "You destroyed your Queen's reputation, and created the largest royal scandal the worlds have seen in the last century. It was the talk of the court long after you left, as everyone wondered how this drama would play out."

Frej gripped his glass to keep his hands from trembling in anger. It was bad enough that the people back in Schonengard still whispered about it when he passed, but here was supposed to be different. A fresh start in a new world, even if it was just temporary. Jerrik's voice pulled him from his thoughts.

"Did you end the affair?"

Frej nodded.

"But you haven't told Laila, have you?" asked Jerrik stiffly.

Frej shook his head. As ashamed as he was, some part of him hoped he wouldn't have to tell her, that he could just leave it in the past. It was foolish and cowardly, but he desperately hoped that this space and this relationship would be what he needed to move on.

Anger burned in Jerrik's eyes. "Why the hell not? You have no right dragging Laila into that political drama you created. She deserves to know the whole story!"

Frej wiped his face with his hands. "You're right."

Genuine shock appeared in Jerrik's expression. He must not have expected Frej to agree.

"Laila does have the right to know, but she deserves to hear it from me."

To Jerrik's credit, he nodded in agreement. "I don't want to hurt her more than I already have."

"If you care about her so much, why did you leave?" asked Frej suspiciously.

Remorse shadowed Jerrik's expression. "I have a lot of enemies. I left to save her from an imminent threat. Even if it made me the asshole, at least she was safe." Jerrik stared at the coaster in between his fingers as if the faces of his enemies were printed there mocking him.

"And what about now? What happened to the threat?"

"I neutralized it. For now, at least." Jerrik glanced at an alert on his phone. "I've got to go. Tell Laila the truth about you and Regina."

As Jerrik disappeared into the crowd, Frej mulled over their conversation. There was a reason he'd avoided telling Laila about his past affair with Regina. While it had been many years ago, there were still complications. He'd hoped there would be more time to prepare himself.

The more he thought about Jerrik, the more the Elf made his blood boil. How dare he involve himself in a private matter like this! The beast within urged him to follow Jerrik and beat the pulp out of him for thinking he could threaten a Dragon. There was a different part of him, the diplomat, that found this conversation intriguing.

It seemed that Jerrik truly cared about Laila in a way. If he had sacrificed a relationship with Laila to keep her safe, then maybe he wasn't as much of a conceited ass as he appeared. This conversation had felt different, more genuine. Frej wondered if arrogance wasn't all some sort of a mask, hiding the true character underneath, especially if Jerrik came from a noble family. But why was he here then? And who were the enemies threatening Laila?

CHAPTER 5

Laila made a cup of tea and slid it across the counter to Ali. The Fae had her head in her hands, hiding from the late morning light that filtered through the windows. She mumbled a thank you as she took a sip.

"Ugh!" she cried, nearly spewing the tea everywhere. "What is this?"

"A special blend," explained Laila, "Elves use it to cure hangovers. Just try it."

Ali muttered to herself but took another sip nonetheless. Laila stepped around the counter to place her hands on either side of Ali's head, tapping into some healing magic to soothe the worst of the Fae's symptoms.

"You're the best!" Ali sighed as her headache lifted. "I swear, this is the last time I take Orin's recommendations on hard liquor."

Laila laughed. "We'll see about that. Besides, you should know that anything from Vanaheim is going to be strong. It's made by some of the oldest creatures in the worlds. Even Arduinna was wary of it."

"It was very good though," sighed Ali.

Laila shook her head and made herself a cup of green tea. The two of them moved to the sofas as Ali switched on the television, mumbling something about a distraction. She flipped through the channels.

"Hold on," said Laila as they reached a local news channel. "Is this about the protests?"

They watched as the footage cut to a human standing at a podium. He was middle-aged with light brown hair and an expensive suit.

"Ugh!" grunted Ali, setting her mug on the coffee table. "It's disgusting how the news crews hang on his every word. They only do it because he's controversial."

"What are you talking about?" asked Laila. "Who is that?"

"It's Fredrik Stacy," said Ali bitterly. "He's like a leader among the pro-human protestors. I've been investigating him lately, but he's slippery as a snake. Every time Colin and I think we're getting close, the trail ends cold."

"What do you mean?"

This wasn't the first time the other side seemed to be ahead of them. They still suspected someone was leaking information, but they'd been unable to locate the source of the leak.

"His name seems to pop up constantly in the recent anti-SNP hate crimes. He's been rallying humans against SNPs for months, encouraging them to take their city back, but we suspect he's done more than just talk."

There were many humans frustrated with the presence of SNPs, but lately things had escalated.

"Is he affiliated with the Di Inferi?" asked Laila, referring to the gang they'd recently discovered has Demonic ties.

"Not that we've found," said Ali sipping her tea, "Maybe it's revenge? His son was killed a couple of years ago in a fight with a Were. It was a part of some frat hazing gone wrong. Long story short, he blamed the entire SNP community in addition to the fraternity and school."

Laila frowned and watched the man. There was something off about him, but she couldn't quite put her finger on it.

"Oh shoot!" She glanced at the clock on her phone. "I've got to go. I need to sort through the evidence from the other night."

"Good luck, we need this murder solved for all of our sakes. I'll see you there later."

"Really?" Laila paused. She'd never known Ali to finish office work on her days off unless there was an ongoing situation. A call was one thing, they couldn't control when an incident would occur, but Ali never spent more time in the office on the weekends than necessary.

Ali jerked her thumb at the television. "He's got some sort of rally. Colin and I are just going to keep an eye on things in case any SNPs show up to protest."

Laila didn't envy Ali. At least Laila wouldn't have to deal with the protestors. She went back to her room to grab her jacket. In the hallway, she passed Frej as he was leaving his room.

"Everything okay?" he asked.

"I have to go in to work for a couple of hours."

"Need an extra hand?"

She shook her head. "It's just evidence from a crime scene. I told the others that I'd meet them at the office."

"Ok, well I'll see you later." Frej gave her a kiss before she rushed off to finish getting ready.

Traffic was light, and she made it to the office in no time. She was the only one there from her team, and rather than going to the third floor where their offices were, she took the elevator down to the basement of the building.

The morgue, like every other part of the building, was a little larger than necessary in order to accommodate a growing population as time progressed. In fact, the agency had recently acquired a second specially trained SNP medical examiner.

Meuric Drisscoll, was an Abhartach, a creature similar to a Vampire but from the world of Svartalfheim. Abhartachs have extraordinarily keen senses, including an ability to sense magic. His associate, Jim Cleary, on the other hand, was human. Jim was late-middle-aged with wispy brown hair that was thinning. His complexion was rather pale, and his skin was smooth like he was rarely outside during the day. With Jim's background and Meuric's abilities, they made quite the team.

Meuric was in the process of examining the victim's hand while Jim entered in notes on a computer when Laila scanned her I.D. and entered the morgue.

"Hey," she said joining them, "is this the victim from two nights ago, Johnathan Samuel?"

Meuric frowned. "Yes, but we aren't finished with the autopsy quite yet. It should be ready by tomorrow."

"Have you determined if this was a Vampire attack at least?" she asked hesitantly.

"Yes. It is definitely a Vampire. Come, let me show you." He waved her closer, uncovering the torso of the cadaver. "If you look at these lacerations on the trunk, they were originally made with a knife—that is before the person who did this reached in and ripped out the organs. This was all done posthumously of course though.

"Now compare these to the wounds on his arm." He pointed. "You see the distance of these puncture wounds on the arm here? They match that of human canines, only the teeth were sharper. Now they look quite a bit different from those other lacerations, but these were also made posthumously."

"What?" Laila looked up at the medical examiner confused.

"Oh yes, that is why this is so messy and violent looking. That's also why there was some blood left inside the body. In addition to mutilating the body, the Vampire was feeding posthumously, which causes an issue for our killer, since the blood is no longer flowing through the body. The real cause of death was the broken neck."

Laila let the information sink in for a moment.

"So why would the Vampire have killed this man first if he knew he wouldn't be able to feed properly?" she wondered out loud.

Meuric shrugged as he stared at the body. "If you want my guess, I'd say you're either looking at a young Vampire who has yet to understand feeding habits or a Vampire who wasn't really interested in feeding. Sure, they had a bit of a snack, but I'd say this was done to shock someone."

Laila nodded thinking the same thing. "Thank you, this information is very helpful."

"You can expect the full report in the morning," said Jim who was still typing notes into the computer. "There are a few more tests we are running."

Laila nodded, as a number of scenarios ran through her mind. She needed more information. From the morgue, Laila headed upstairs to the second floor, where the investigative team was located. Hopefully, they had discovered more about their victim or the attacker.

In the months that had passed since her arrival, Laila had noticed that there was a rift between the various teams in their office; it was rare that the investigative team and the field agents interacted.

In a typical IRSA investigation, SNP field agents like Laila went in, assessed the situation, dealt with people and interviews, and handled any issues and arrests. The investigative team was a collection of humans specializing in forensic analysis that stepped in afterwards, mostly at crime scenes that had been secured, and helped collect and sort through evidence. They also helped with research and ensured that a crew was hired to clean up after the investigations had been completed.

It was a completely inefficient system in Laila's opinion, there was far too much of this passing evidence back and forth for her liking. Then again, the structure of the agency was organized this way for safety reasons. Field agents had an extremely dangerous job, and the qualifications were very high. But with a shortage of agents, they needed to supplement the agency with humans to help with the investigations. It was necessary for the time being, but she always had the feeling the investigative team resented the field agents for giving them the grunt work.

The elevator door slid open. The layout of this floor was nearly identical to her floor above. She walked down the hall to the first office on the right and found a woman sitting at the desk.

"Good morning, Jenn," said Laila stopping in the doorway.

The plaque on the desk read "Jennifer Holdt, Special Investigator." Her clothing was plain, and her brown hair was pulled back in a simple ponytail. She wore no makeup, was physically fit, and had a very no-nonsense attitude about her. She'd once been a detective for one of the police departments but transferred over to their agency after The Event where she now presided as the investigative team leader. Aside from that, Laila knew little of her personal life.

"You're here about the homicide, right?" she asked, not bothering to look away from her computer monitor.

"Yes, I was wondering what your team discovered."

The woman sat there typing away for a minute. She finished what she was writing before she finally turned to Laila.

"The files have been uploaded into the database, so you should be able to access them," she said with a bored tone.

Laila pulled out a tablet from her bag and typed in the code to access the database. Sure enough, the files were there.

"Anything that stood out to you?" asked Laila to the stoic woman behind the desk.

"There was a pretty meticulous calendar on his phone. The guy's a real estate agent, so it looks like he kept his meetings organized in there. There should be screenshots. It looked pretty normal. Some meetings, gym time, and he was supposed to meet a friend for dinner last night."

Laila flipped through the files until she found the screenshot of the calendar.

"I see." She looked at the note that read *Dinner with Drake*. It was scheduled for 7:30pm.

"We did some research into this Drake guy and turned up another real estate agent named Drake Suttner. They worked for different companies, but it looks like they were friends. He'll be at an open house this evening in Malibu."

"Thank you," said Laila putting the tablet away, "I'll start by speaking to Mr. Suttner. I—"

She realized that she had a few hours before Darien would be around. She could take Jerrik, but the idea of sitting in a car with him in nearly an hour's worth of traffic was less than appealing. Then there was that rift between the teams, but what if Laila could help to bring them closer?

"Are you in the middle of something?" she asked Jenn. "Darien's out until sundown, and it's always good to have a second set of eyes."

Jenn's expression remained unchanged, but a light suddenly flickered in her eyes.

"You want me to go with you?" Jenn asked, a little surprised.

"If you're not too busy."

Jenn paused considering the situation.

"Fine. You're driving. I'll see you in the garage in fifteen minutes."

Laila nodded and left for the third floor.

"Oh, hey!" called someone as she passed the conference room. It was Donald.

The male Witch—or Tech Wiz as he preferred—wore a black t-shirt with characters from an old video game on it. He pushed his shaggy, brown hair out of his eyes. He'd been helping to develop new combinations of magic and technology to give their team an edge when dealing with a variety of conflicts, such as magically adapting stun batons.

"What are you doing up here?" Laila eyed the variety of

tools laid out before him. He appeared to be disassembling wires behind the television in the conference room.

"I thought I might be able to hardwire in this new charm I've been working on." He held up a small black box. "It would enable the television screen to also be used as a scrying glass."

The more Laila thought about it, the more useful she realized that could be. They could take video calls from other worlds, or locations where cell service and an internet connection were unavailable. She supposed they could just hang a scrying glass on the wall for the same effect, but Donald seemed so enthusiastic that she didn't want to burst his bubble.

"Is Ali here?" he asked glancing behind her.

"No, she's at home."

"Oh." His shoulders sagged, and Laila caught the disappointment in his voice.

"Why?" Laila watching him suspiciously.

"Oh, nothing." He fidgeted with the black box in his hands, "I just... I fixed her stun baton," he finished lamely.

Laila watched him skeptically, "Right, I'll let her know."

She'd seen the way Donald went out of his way to casually run into Ali. His interest in the Fae was so obvious, but Laila thought back to Mato. Ali had a type, and Donald didn't quite fit the mold.

He gave Laila a small thanks as she continued down the hall. As she reached her office, she felt a presence behind her.

"You're here early," said a male voice behind her.

She spun around and found Jerrik in the doorway of his office. After recovering from her initial surprise, she shrugged.

"There's a lot to do."

His expression was unreadable as he watched her. Today he wore a black boat-neck sweater, the sleeves pushed back past his elbows, something he had a tendency to do when he was working on the computer. How long had he been in the office? The shadows under his eyes revealed he hadn't been sleeping much. Laila was tempted to ask him about it but shoved the thought aside. The last thing she wanted was to encourage conversation. If her friends were right and she did have lingering feelings for Jerrik, then the more distance, the better in her opinion.

She entered her office and unlocked her computer to check her emails.

"So, what's the plan?" He leaned against the doorway waiting for her response.

"I'm leaving to interview a witness, but there's a lot of ground to cover. Why don't you stay here and read through the reports from the crime scene? Maybe something will stand out, or give us more information about this Vampire."

"So, we're assuming it's a Vampire?"

Laila nodded, "I just spoke with the medical examiners, they're still performing the autopsy, but Meuric confirmed it was a Vampire."

"Shouldn't I go with you?" he asked suspiciously.

"I think it's better if you stay here." She deleted an email.

"Are you sure? I—"

"Yes, I am."

"Okay." His expression darkened as he took a step back. "I guess I'll be waiting when you return then."

She opened her mouth to say more, but when she looked up, he was already gone.

CHAPTER 6

"Whoa." Jenn climbed out of the passenger seat and stared up at the house in front of them.

The human wasn't exactly talkative. She'd been relatively quiet on the drive through Malibu, but the three-story mansion was impressive enough to break the silence.

Driving to Malibu was a rare occurrence for Laila, she'd only been out that way two or three times on calls. It was still largely uninhabited, but unlike the Old City, Malibu had remained mostly untouched by the shadier types. It was easier to renovate the homes there, and a number of wealthy people from Santa Monica were becoming more and more interested in the unclaimed beach properties.

"How much do you think they're selling this for?" asked Jenn grinning.

"Looking for a new place?" chuckled Laila as she locked the car and turned towards the front door.

"You and I both know the agency doesn't pay *that* well." The woman smirked and followed Laila.

The door was open and as they entered Laila's jaw dropped.

The view *was* incredible! The wall of windows left her with the feeling the house was open to the beach. She had to drag her eyes away from the beauty of the crashing waves to focus on the man approaching them.

"Welcome! How are you ladies doing today? Please let me know if you have any questions about the property, I can give you a tour if you'd like. I'm Drake by the way."

He offered his hand.

"Actually, we are not here about the house," explained Laila. "I'm Special Agent Laila Eyvindr, and this is Special Investigator Jennifer Holdt. We would like to ask you some questions about Friday night."

"Wait, what?" He took a hesitant step back.

"You had dinner plans that night with a man by the name of Johnathan Samuel, correct?" asked Jenn.

"I-yeah I did, but he didn't make it." He glanced from Jenn to Laila. "Why did something happen?"

"Johnathan was found dead late that night, we believe he was murdered," explained Laila.

"What?" He blinked at them shocked. "No, why? Who would do that?"

"I need you to tell me where you were two days ago," continued Laila.

"Wait, you don't think I have something to do with it, do you!?!" He started to panic.

"Sir, I need you to calm down," said Jenn firmly. "We are doing our best to figure out what happened, but we need your cooperation. Where were you from Friday afternoon on?"

"I-I was here almost the entire day," the words tumbled out of his mouth in a rush, "I was doing some last-minute staging while the cleaning crew worked. You should be able to see it on the security camera installed outside. I stayed until seven or so, and I was cutting it pretty close to our meeting time at eight. I didn't have time to stop home beforehand, so I went straight there, but he didn't show or answer my calls…"

"How well did you know Mr. Samuel?" asked Jenn, motioning for the man to sit on the nearby sofa.

"Well enough to call him a friend." He sunk into the sofa. "We weren't particularly close, but we were considering starting a new business together. That's what we were going to discuss."

"Did you speak to him at all on Friday?" asked Laila.

"No, I didn't. He's good about keeping plans, so I didn't even think to call him until it was clear he was running late. He never answered though, and I assumed he'd gotten carried away with a project or negotiations."

He propped his elbows on his knees and rested his head in his hands.

"Did he mention anything out of the ordinary to you?" Laila asked sitting on the chair opposite from Drake. "Perhaps there was someone following him?"

Drake shook his head and looked up. "No, not that he ever told me."

"Did he have many friends in the Supernatural community?"

"What? I don't think so, just the occasional client. Why?"

"We'd like copies of those security videos," requested Jenn, "and the names and contact information of your neighbors."

He nodded, pulling out a business card and a ballpoint pen.

"Here you go, this is the cleaning crew too. I don't remember the names of the people who were here, but I'm sure it's in their records."

The security footage took a little longer. Laila and Jenn waited in the living room while he went to retrieve it.

"So, what do you think?" asked Jenn, watching the surf through the windows.

"I think he's telling the truth. He seemed genuinely shocked to me. He's not a Vampire so he can't be our perp. We might as well verify his alibi though."

Jenn nodded thoughtfully. "I miss this you know, being able to get out and investigate like this. The agency is great, but I wish I didn't feel so limited in my position."

"I get that." Laila gave her a sad smile.

"I keep thinking I should reapply with the LAPD, but I never seem to get around to it," she sighed.

"It sounds to me like the Norns want you here."

Jenn gave her a blank stare.

"Um, the Fates," explained Laila, "My people believe that if something seems to prevent you from making a change, it's because the Norns don't think you are ready for change, or that there's more to be done where you are."

"Hmm." Jenn watched the sun as it sank in the sky.

"Here they are." Drake Suttner reentered the living room and passed a thumb drive to Laila.

"Thank you," she said, "I don't suppose you know if Mr. Samuel had family in the area?"

He shook his head. "He's got a cousin up in San Francisco, but that's about all the family I know of."

Laila nodded and thanked him for his cooperation. She and Jenn climbed into the SUV and started to make their way back to the city.

As she drove, Laila admired the way the setting sun reflected off the curving waves of the ocean in magenta and gold. She loved living so close to the ocean, especially here in Midgard. Here the sea was wild and untamable, not calm as they were in Alfheim where generations of water Sorcerers had soothed their tumultuous spirits. In the distance, she could see the small silhouette of a sailboat bobbing between the waves. They were alone on the road, and for once Laila found driving to be peaceful.

A blood-curdling scream tore through the serene moment. Laila slammed her foot on the brake, stopping so suddenly that the tires screeched in protest.

"What was that?" Jenn spun toward the hills on their left as another scream echoed through the canyon.

"Let's find out." Laila turned the car around and pulled onto the road leading off into the canyon.

The road was deserted and littered with debris from the overgrown greenery that was closing in on the forgotten street. Laila's eyes narrowed in the fading light as she realized there was another set of tire tracks ahead of them. They looked recent in the otherwise untouched layer of fallen twigs, leaves, and dirt.

"Any idea what's out this way?" asked Laila.

"Some sort of spa retreats and mansions I think, but I hadn't heard of anything opening back up."

Laila frowned. Who would go out of their way to drive all the way out here?

She followed the road, switching on her high beams in order to see the tracks in the fast-approaching gloom. They veered off to the side, up a steep drive and Laila followed. The screams had stopped, but Laila's stomach felt as though it was twisting in knots. Something felt off, she felt as though she was being watched. Jenn was silent beside her, but Laila noticed she gripped the armrest tightly.

The driveway opened up into a large circle drive. An old van was parked out front, but no sign of a driver. Laila and Jenn exchanged glances before slipping out of the SUV. Jenn reached for her firearm and a flashlight as Laila readied a shield spell as they approached the van. The doors to the back were ajar, and Laila cautiously nudged them open. Then Jenn's flashlight illuminated piles of cables, and a couple black cases, but still no signs of life.

There was a loud crash from within the mansion. Jenn jerked her head towards the entrance and Laila nodded. She considered calling for backup, but it would take ages for anyone to reach them. They climbed the steps towards the open door, it loomed before them like the mouth of some great beast. A shiver ran down her spine like an icy finger as they entered the gloom and were immediately swallowed up by the darkness. Perhaps it was all the talk of Halloween in the city that made her feel on edge, or maybe it was something more sinister lurking within.

CHAPTER 7

Ali stood monitoring the situation between the humans and SNPs in her bullet-proof vest and helmet. Checking her watch, she hoped this wouldn't last too long, she had another important meeting to get to. Not that this was unimportant, just the meeting involved a case she was currently working solo.

She and Colin stood in the parking lot in front of a high school gymnasium where Fredrik Stacy was speaking to an enthusiastic crowd of fellow Supernatural-fearing humans. The topic of the rally: the need for more regulations regarding Supernaturals.

He had just concluded the portion of his speech where he insisted that increasing crime rates in the city were due to the influx of Supernatural residents from other worlds. The man had rattled off a list of statistics that were biased and one-sided at best. Ali knew the statistics, over 80 percent of the perpetrators of the crimes committed in the city last year were human. Even then, only a small fraction of the crimes committed by Supernaturals were enacted by otherworldly SNPs—documented or otherwise. Sure, there was a larger human population than SNP, but if he was truly concerned about crime rates, then he should be looking into human-involved crimes, not using the SNPs as scapegoats.

Ali couldn't help but feel disgusted. Back in her kingdom, they welcomed others. There was no discrimination if someone was a Troll, Ogre, or other creature. So long as visitors or new residents respected the laws and the people around them, why would there be a problem? She knew that the Fae, in general, were more free-spirited and less judgmental, but it felt like common decency to her.

She watched the protestors standing outside of the building. In this case, they were mostly SNPs, but many of them were humans. There was a Were holding a sign that read: "this is our city too" while an Elf held another that said: "magic heals." The humans held signs with sayings like "love thy neighbor" and "will discrimination ever die?" Honestly, they had been peaceful so far, and Ali seriously doubted they posed a threat. But with the rally wrapping up inside, there was worry amongst the LAPD officers who stood with her.

As the doors of the gymnasium opened up, the LAPD officers and IRSA agents directed the attendees away from the protestors. It seemed to work, and while many of the humans shot the protestors looks of disdain, they continued on their way to their vehicles. Then there was one man who took a step towards the protestors, causing Ali to groan inwardly. Why did there always have to be that one person?

An LAPD officer confronted the human and told him to be on his way, but he ignored the officer.

"Get out of here!" he shouted at the protestors. "This is our city."

"Yes, it is our city," replied a Vampire, "and I've lived in it since before your grandparents were born!"

One of the police officers told the man to continue on his way. When he turned and left, Ali was relieved, but then he returned with something in his hands, and other humans in tow.

They shouted at the SNPs, growing more heated as a few others who were leaving the gym joined in.

"This doesn't look good," muttered Colin next to her. "We should get these SNPs out of here before there's a conflict."

Ali nodded, and the two of them attempted to persuade the protestors to go home, but they were determined. Ali even used her Fae charm, which convinced a few to head home, but something came whizzing past her head and struck a Were in the face. It was the bottle the first human had been carrying. The Were started to shift, changing into a wolf, but Ali acted quickly and placed her hand on his shoulder.

"You don't want to do this," she insisted, blasting him with charm magic. "They're not worth it, this is what they want."

He paused, and Ali hoped that he was listening to reason. But when a handful of humans forced their way through the police line, all hell broke loose.

Laila conjured a glowing orb of light that floated high above their heads bathing the entryway in a pale white glow. Cobwebs clung to every surface and swirled as they passed like ghostly fingers beckoning to them. By a grand staircase rested a pile of black boxes, cables, and other equipment.

"Looks like film equipment." Jenn examined the pile while Laila surveyed the room. There were multiple sets of footprints from someone loading and unloading the equipment, the dust on the stairs had also been scuffed away.

"Hello?" called Laila, her voice echoing through the house. "We're with the Inter-Realm Security Agency. Is there anyone in the building?"

For several beats of her heart, Laila listened.

"Help me!" a man screamed from upstairs.

Laila unholstered her magical stun baton and charged up the stairs, taking them two at a time. Close behind her was Jenn as she reached the second floor and the hallway beyond. Goose-bumps crawled along Laila's arms, and her hair stood on end. Her instincts screamed at her that something was terribly wrong, but curiosity and duty drew her down the hall as she searched for the source of the scream.

As Laila entered the hallway, she saw a figure pressed against the wall halfway down. It was a man trembling with fear, his eyes were wide, and his hand was clamped over his mouth as if he was trying to muffle his breathing.

Laila opened her mouth to speak, but he shook his head hastily, pointing to the open doorway beside him. She glanced from the human to the doorway and cautiously approached, dimming her light as she went. Behind her, Laila could hear Jenn's quiet footsteps, but she motioned for her to stay back. They had absolutely no idea what was in that room, but that human looked ready to soil his pants because of it.

She reached the closest edge of the doorway and heard a rustling noise from within. The human across from her pressed further against the wall as she cautiously peered around the corner.

The room was some sort of in-home theatre with rows of large leather armchairs. Laila paused a moment to allow her eyes to adapt to the darkness. There was a sucking noise, but whatever was in there was obscured from view by the armchairs. Every fiber of her being cried for her to run, but she had to know what was going on.

She stepped through the threshold and into the theatre, silent as a cat stalking its prey, and took the aisle along the right wall, the shield spell and baton still at the ready. The first row was empty. So was the second, but the sound was growing louder. As she reached the third row, she saw a woman sprawled on her back. Hunched over her was a figure so vile, so repulsive, so *wrong* that the sight of it turned Laila's blood to ice.

Its long, boney limbs poked out from a tattered black robe like the spindly legs of a giant spider. The skin was thick and crusted like a protective scab. Its hands and feet ended in three-inch long, yellowed claws that glistened with fresh blood from where it had pinned the woman's shoulders down. The creature slowly lifted its head revealing the most horrifying sight Laila had ever seen. The creature's face had been ripped away, revealing the bones of the skull beneath. Where eyes should have been was nothing but pits of endless darkness.

"Odin's eye," whispered Laila stepping back, but she bumped into the wall behind her.

Faster than Laila could have imagined, the creature rose and rushed her, only stopping when it collided with the shield that Laila had conjured. Standing face to face with her, the creature opened its mouth and unleashed a piercing shriek. Laila felt her own face contort in a silent scream of terror.

More officers in riot gear rushed in with shields to hold back the humans. Some of the SNPs looked ready to fight, but the others watched in shock.

"Get out of here, now!" she ordered them, pointing towards their cars with her stun baton. Many of them turned to run, but to her horror, the humans were blocking their access to the vehicles.

Ali searched for cover and saw a women's restroom near the entrance to the gym.

"In there!" she shouted at the protestors pointing towards the door. "Now!"

They hesitated, but most of them followed her orders and ran for the door. Ali tried to shove the more stubborn SNPs towards the safety of the restroom, but Colin waved her off.

"I'll deal with them, you guard the door."

Ali nodded and planted herself before the door as a group of police officers created a wall of shields in front of her.

The humans shouted and threw things, some of them

tried to fight their way through the police officers. Ali shook her head, they'd long passed the point of reason. This was senseless violence on the part of the humans. Why didn't they just leave? Why keep attacking like this? Ali wondered if she shouldn't call in the others to help. The Elves could help shield at the very least, but this was primarily a matter of humans, and thus for the LAPD to handle.

Colin rounded up the remaining SNPs and shoved them towards the door.

"This is an unlawful assembly, you must disperse immediately!" called an officer on a loudspeaker. It was their final warning for the humans.

Ali slipped on her gasmask as the LAPD resorted to tear gas in order to deter the humans. The humans choked and gagged, and many of them took off as the screech of sirens echoed through the night.

"What the hell is that!" shouted Jenn from the doorway, her hand trembling as it held her gun.

The creature whipped its head around to face Jenn, and her face paled further. It lunged for her and Jenn fired. The creature cringed, but the bullets had little effect.

Thinking fast, Laila blasted the creature with fire. It hissed and retreated a few steps. Laila took advantage of its hesitation to throw a wall of air in its direction. It shoved the creature down the row of seats and pinned it to the opposite wall.

"Grab the woman!" shouted Laila as she struggled to keep the skull-faced creature pinned. Tendrils of darkness were emanating from the creature, pushing back against her shield of air.

Jenn rushed to the unconscious woman who was quite petite. The agent was able to heft her over a shoulder, and carry her towards the door, Laila falling in step behind. Sweat beaded on her brow as she struggled to maintain her spell.

"Run!" she barked at the man who was still rooted to the spot in the hallway. When he didn't move, she grabbed him by the shirt and shoved him towards the stairs.

The creature screeched with triumph as it broke through Laila's spell. It clambered over rows of seats directly towards her. Laila shoved the doors shut and sprinted down the hall. Over the balcony, she could see the others had nearly reached the exit. There was a bang as the wood splintered behind her, and Laila had the distinct feeling that the creature was gaining on her. The stairs would only slow her, so she leapt over the railing of the balcony and into open space. She rolled to cushion the impact on the hard stone floor and continued running. There was a thud behind her as the creature followed.

She had to stop it, but how? Laila flinched as claws narrowly missed her back. She blasted the monster with flame again and rushed for the exit. Laila dug into a pouch attached to her belt and removed a small glass vial with a glowing orange liquid within. Using a spell, she slammed the door in the creature's face and hurtled the vial at the door. Glowing orange runes exploded from the vial, running along the surface of the building. Within seconds the entire house had been magically locked-down, the creature screeching as it pounded on the door.

The potion was a new concoction that had been created by Donald. It was the first time she'd used it and had no idea how long it would remain active. For now, it seemed to be working though.

"She's not breathing," said the man somewhere behind her.

Laila spun to find the woman lying on the concrete by the van, the other two hovering beside her. Frowning, Laila joined them to examine her. Laila could still sense the woman's life energy within her, so she started a magical version of CPR. After a moment the woman resumed breathing, but Laila knew there was something wrong deep within her. Nothing physical, but that creature had managed to siphon off her energy, nearly draining the life from her.

"Get her in the SUV." Laila grabbed the woman's shoulders while Jenn grabbed her legs.

"What are you doing?" asked the man who was still trembling.

Laila buckled the woman in the backseat. "Meet us at Asclepius Hospital of Supernatural Medicine. An ambulance will never make it in time. I'll keep her alive until the doctors see to her."

He nodded hastily and climbed into his van.

"You drive," she said to Jenn, crawling in the back seat with the unconscious woman.

Jenn nodded and climbed into the driver's seat, switching on the emergency lights and siren as they pulled down the drive. Laila monitored the woman the entire way, but the human was so weak. She stopped breathing twice more, but Laila was able to resuscitate her. Jenn was on the radio, informing dispatch of the situation. They assured her that the hospital would be expecting their arrival in the ambulance bay. They were waiting as promised and quickly moved the human onto a gurney before wheeling her inside, Laila jogging after them.

"What happened?" asked an Elven doctor in the hall.

"She was attacked by a creature outside the city. It took most of her energy. She's hanging on by a thread."

The doctor nodded and rushed off after the gurney, leaving Laila in the hall. She wiped her face with a hand as Jenn appeared beside her, and for a moment they stood there in the hallway, trying to process what had just happened. Then without a word the two of them returned to their building.

Ali watched as another pair of humans were led towards a squad car. In addition to the police, there were also fire trucks and ambulances on the scene, now that the officers had finally convinced the humans to disburse. The LAPD had a handful of humans they'd arrested for attacking the SNP protestors, including the original instigator. All it had taken was that one person to start the riot.

The paramedics and a couple of firefighters were examining the SNPs behind her. The majority of them were unharmed while some were scraped up from tripping in the rush to get to cover. The few SNPs that had jumped into the fray were beaten pretty bad before Colin was able to drag them away from the fight. They were being treated for injuries while one had been transported to the hospital. A few of the humans under arrest were also being treated for minor injuries.

This was nothing short of a mess, and Ali feared there was only more to come. She was torn because people had the right to protest, but when things went wrong like this, lots of people could be hurt or even killed on either side.

The doors to the gym opened up, and a couple of police officers and guards escorted Fredrik Stacy and a handful of others out to where his limousine was waiting. The man was relatively ordinary looking with plain brown hair, and dull grey eyes, but there was something in the way he carried himself that seemed to set him apart from others. Maybe it was his sense of purpose or even self-righteousness, but Ali couldn't help but feel there was more about him. Unfortunately, none of her investigations had panned out. Everything about him was clean, so clean it was suspicious. He had to be hiding something.

Ali watched the humans climb into the limousine and drive off before turning to Colin.

"I have to go, do you think you've got things handled here?" she asked.

He gave her a caustic look. "We're in the middle of something. Whatever it is can wait."

"Oh, I see," chuckled Ali darkly, her eyes narrowing. "It's fine when you have a date, but when I have a meeting related to another case, then I've crossed a line."

"It can wait. That is an order."

Ali's temper flared. If she had elemental magic like Laila, she would've been tempted to blast him with fire, but instead she did the next best thing. She doused him with charm magic until he was practically giggling, he was so drunk off it.

"I'm going to leave now, and you'll wrap things up here," she crooned patronizingly. "Do you understand?"

He had a goofy smile on his face as he nodded. That had been far easier than she'd expected. She thought Colin was made of stronger stuff than this, or would at least try to resist the charm, but clearly not.

"Thanks, Colin. Now, I want you to apologize for being a dick." She smiled broadly.

He mumbled something, but he was so intoxicated with charm magic that his words were slurred.

"Good enough." She winked and dropped the charm magic. By the time Colin had recovered, she was getting into her car. As she pulled out of the parking lot, his angry shouts rang out behind her as she grinned.

CHAPTER 8

"About time!" said Darien as the elevator opened. "What happened? Jerrik said you were just going to interview a witness."

"We were," began Laila as she stepped around Darien and headed towards her office. "We were on our way back when we heard screaming."

"We?" Darien followed her down the hall.

"Jenn from the investigative team."

Darien gave her a smirk as she entered her office and started rummaging through a small wardrobe.

"What?" she asked suspiciously.

"Nothing, just think it's interesting you took a human from the investigative team instead of Jerrik." His eyes glinted in amusement.

She glared at him. "*Anyway*, two humans were being attacked by this living nightmare of an SNP. We got them out and took one of them to the hospital, but the creature is still locked in that building, and we need to take care of it before it breaks free from Donald's lockdown potion."

Laila pulled on her thin black breastplate. It was a gift from Queen Regina of the Dragons. Pegasus leather was covering plates of Dwarven steel, which was incredibly strong. It was better than a bulletproof vest, and lighter, with the ability to protect her from some spells as well. She stuck a couple of throwing knives into her boots, but as she reached for a hand-and-half sword in a black scabbard, Darien stopped her.

"Whoa, easy there," he said glancing from Laila to the sword and back. "Do you even know how to counteract that potion?"

Laila paused. She grabbed her phone and punched in a number, waiting impatiently as the phone rang.

"Hello?" came a male voice on the other side of the line.

"Donald, it's Laila. How do I counteract the lockdown potion?" She drummed her fingers on her desk, ignoring Darien's look of amusement.

"Wait what?" he asked surprised. "The orange vial right? I haven't perfected the counterspell yet. The formula's not quite right. Why?"

"I used it to trap a dangerous SNP up in Malibu."

"Okay, well, you'll have to wait five hours for it to wear off. That or counteract it yourself. When did you activate it?"

"A half-hour ago." She retrieved a protein bar from her desk and bit into it, replenishing some of her strength.

"Okay, well give it a few hours before you try anything. That's one strong spell. Its potency will lessen, and it'll be way easier to break it. Seriously though, you'll burn yourself out if you don't give it at least three hours."

"Okay, thanks." She hung up the phone and found Darien watching her. She knew he'd heard Donald's explanation.

"In that case, I've got a lead I want to look into." He shoved his hands into his pockets. "Our victim from the homicide was a member of the gym *Shape it Up!*"

Laila swallowed a bite of her protein bar. "Aren't those all over the city?"

"Unfortunately, yes," he admitted. "I narrowed it down to one likely location. They're still open, and I wanted to question the staff before they close at nine o'clock. Once we finish there, we can head back to Malibu and take care of that SNP."

As much as Laila wanted to return straight away, waiting an hour or so would allow her to recover from some of the magic she'd used. Reluctantly she nodded and followed Darien into the hall, grabbing her sword and scabbard on the way out. Darien stuck his head into Jerrik's office when voices down the hall caught Laila's attention.

"Ali?" she called.

Ali turned around. The man she'd been talking to arched an eyebrow at the sword in Laila's hand.

He was human and middle-. Laila could tell from the black suit and tie that he was from D.C. No one in their office ever wore a suit. She tried wearing them upon her arrival in Los Angles but quickly realized it how out of place they were in this city. He also had a look of ease that she hadn't seen since D.C. After all, things were very different there.

In Washington D.C., the government officials lived under the impression that everything was under control. Laila hadn't even realized how different the rest of the country was until she'd moved to Los Angeles, which was practically the Wild West these days. Their team had to do whatever they could to keep the peace, even if it meant bending the rules now and then.

The human approached her and extended his hand.

"I'm Adam Johnson. I work for the office of the Inspector General with IRSA."

"Special Agent Laila Eyvindr," she said accepting his hand. "I hadn't realized anyone was coming."

She glanced over her shoulder at Darien, who seemed equally surprised. If an agent sent by the Inspector General was here, it meant that someone was under investigation.

"It was just decided yesterday," clarified the agent.

Laila looked at Ali, who avoided her eye-contact. She had the distinct feeling that Ali knew exactly what was going on.

"We're in a bit of rush," explained Laila. "I'll see you around the office."

She gave them a forced smile as she walked towards the elevator at the end of the hall. Darien and Jerrik were right behind her. Laila's mind had difficulty processing the shock as she realized that Ali had finally followed through on her threat. She had reported Colin.

Ten minutes later Laila, Darien, and Jerrik walked through the doors of *Shape it Up!* They'd left their gear in the SUV so they wouldn't alarm anyone. The entire way there the others had questioned her about the creature they were facing. Neither Jerrik nor Darien had any clue what the creature could be, but just the memory of it sent a shiver down her spine.

All of them avoided the elephant in the room that was the agent from the Inspector General's office. She wasn't really upset that Ali had reported Colin. In fact, they had discussed it with the rest of the team on multiple occasions, but it never seemed like he'd crossed the line far enough to justify it. They had all agreed that when the time finally came, that they would inform the others before reporting him so that they'd all be prepared and aware. It bothered her that Ali had done this without so much as a heads up.

Laila glanced around. The facility itself was big, nearly the size of a grocery store. As they entered the reception room, they were greeted with a blast of cool air. There were a couple of concrete benches, but aside from that, the furnishings were sparse and industrial. Behind a long concrete counter was a male receptionist dressed in athletic clothes and flipping through a sports magazine.

"Oh," he said when he realized they were waiting. "Sorry

guys, uh, do you want to sign up for memberships?" his voice echoed off the concrete surfaces.

"No thank you." Laila showed him her badge. "We're with the Inter-Realm Security Agency. We'd like to ask you a few questions."

"Um, okay…" The guy watched them warily.

"Did a man by the name of Johnathan Samuel visit this gym Friday night?"

"I wasn't working that night, but I'll see if he checked in."

He spent a few seconds searching on the computer before swiveling the screen around to face them.

"This guy?" he asked.

She nodded.

"It looks like he was here from like six to seven Friday evening."

"You're sure?" asked Darien.

The receptionist nodded. "Members have to scan a code on their phones for access to the gym facilities. So, unless someone stole his phone and password, I'd say he was here."

"Is it possible to speak with the receptionist working that night?" Laila snapped a picture of the computer screen.

"Sure, she's teaching an aerobics class in one of our studios. She should be finishing up in about fifteen minutes. You're welcome to hang out and wait. We've got a juice bar through there with more comfortable seating." He pointed to an archway on the left.

"Thanks," Darien gave him a nod before heading in that direction.

The juice bar was tropical with bright colors. The signs were bordered with colorful birds, and the glass that separated the bar from the seating area was decorated with decals of leaves and ferns. Someone had plastered the windows with Halloween decorations though, disrupting the theme. Laila cringed at the skeletal face of a grim reaper that leered at her from a nearby window, looking all too much like the Supernatural waiting back in Malibu. She tore her eyes away. The sweet scent of citrus hung in the air, and an athletic woman in yoga pants and a tank top waited behind the counter.

"Couldn't we just pull the instructor out of the class," muttered Laila as they claimed a table near the door. Jerrik raised an eyebrow.

"You're in a lovely mood, aren't you?" Darien chuckled. "It's fifteen minutes. You heard Donald, it's going to be easier for you to break the enchantment if we wait."

"Not if it finds a way out first." She glared at the Vampire.

It occurred to her that she probably needed something more than a protein bar to fuel her for the fight ahead, and the menu above the colorful bar had a variety of high-protein shakes. She pulled out her wallet.

"Want anything?" she asked Jerrik.

He shook his head, so she placed her order and returned to the table. She noticed Darien was checking out the woman and rolled her eyes as he wandered over to her.

"I can't take him anywhere," she shook her head. Darien was easily distracted by women. The fact they were here to interview a witness was no deterrent.

"I should've gone with you this afternoon." Jerrik watched her carefully. "What would've happened if you didn't have Donald's potion on you?"

"I would have found a way to trap him eventually." At least she hoped she would've.

By his deepening frown, Jerrik seemed to read her mind.

"Look, Laila, I know things are a bit awkward between us, and I know you don't want to talk about it. I feel terrible thinking that this drama put you in a dangerous situation though."

The look of concern he gave her left her with conflicting emotions. She genuinely appreciated the sentiment, and she wondered if it would be better if they talked things through. Then again, she feared that it would stir up feeling best left alone. After last night's conversation with her friends, Laila had decided to focus on the present and her relationship with Frej. Jerrik was still waiting for a response though, so she settled on a simple thank you.

Laila returned her attention to the woman behind the counter, who was now looking more disturbed than anything. At first, she thought it was Darien making her so uncomfortable, but she stormed across the room to a window. She peered into the gloom but returned to the counter.

The Elves exchanged glances then stood and joined the others at the counter.

"Everything okay?" asked Jerrik beside Darien.

The woman let out an exasperated sigh. "I thought I saw someone, just this guy that was hanging around earlier. I think he might be homeless because he sits out front begging for money. He gave me some trouble last week—catcalling and such—and I threatened to call the cops if he didn't leave. He knows he's not welcome here, but you know." She shrugged.

"Annie was just telling me about our victim," explained Darien as he leaned against the counter.

She nodded as she poured the rest of Laila's shake into a cup. "Johnathan stopped by for a shake or smoothie after most of his workouts. He was friendly, and always nice to me. I can't imagine why anyone would want to hurt him."

"Did you see him leave?" asked Laila as the woman passed her the smoothie.

"No, I didn't. He didn't stop by for a smoothie either. I figured he was in a hurry or something."

Darien passed her a card as Laila glanced at her phone. Time was up, and they had another witness to interview. Jerrik was beside her as she approached the front desk once more.

"You're right on time." The receptionist glanced up from his computer. "Just head through the doors and towards the studios in the back. You'll see who I'm talking about. Her name is Diane."

"Thank you," she said, the men following her through the

side door as the receptionist buzzed them through.

They walked past the rows of stationary bikes, treadmills, and ellipticals. There was also a wide variety of free weights and other equipment. Nearly two dozen people occupied the room, many of them pausing to watch as the three of them made their way to the classrooms. Only one of the rooms was currently in use, and they could see through a large glass window that the class was wrapping up.

They waited by the door as the students packed up their equipment and grabbed their bags. The majority of them were women, but there were a few men in the mix. They filed out through the door glancing curiously at the agents as they passed. Laila gave them the occasional nod, or a forced smile as they left. Finally, the last student exited the room.

Laila glanced at the others and entered the room. The instructor was organizing equipment stacked on shelves along the far wall.

"Excuse me," called Laila across the room, "are you Diane?"

The woman turned and examined the three of them approaching for a moment before nodding.

"I'm Special Agent Laila Eyvindr, and these are my colleges Special Agents Pavoni and Torhild with the Inter-Realm Security Agency. We were told you were working the front desk Friday night, is that correct?"

"That's right." The woman crossed her arms. "Is everything okay?"

Laila showed her an image of the victim, "Do you recognize this man?"

"Yeah actually, he's one of our regulars here."

"Do you remember seeing him Friday night?" asked Darien.

"Sure, he came in around five thirty in the evening and left around seven. I remember because I'd been on the phone with tech support for our online scheduling software trying to solve an issue. I'd been watching the clock. He left shortly after I hung up."

"Do you remember if there was anyone watching him, or maybe if someone followed him out?" asked Laila.

"No, why? Did something happen?" She shifted her weight from one foot to the other.

Darien gave her a quick explanation, and her expression morphed from confusion to shock.

"Oh my God!" She covered her mouth with her hand. "Wow, I don't know what to say. I don't remember seeing anything unusual, but I was so focused on that phone call. I'm sorry, that's probably not very helpful."

The instructor shook her head as the agents followed her to the door.

"Thank you for your time," said Laila shaking her hand, "if you remember anything else, please give me a call."

Laila passed the woman one of her cards, she pocketed it with a nod before she turned back to the classroom and to her previous task of straightening the equipment.

They left the gym and returned to the car.

Laila sifted through what they knew about their victim. "So, he was scheduled to meet a friend for dinner a half-hour after he left. Our Victim stopped home, probably to get cleaned up for dinner, and was attacked in his home."

"But no one from the gym saw anything unusual," said Jerrik, "so where does that leave us?"

Darien started the car. "We're still waiting on the security camera footage from the apartment complex across the street from the victim's house."

Laila glanced at the others. "Well if we are done here, we should head up to Malibu and deal with that creature."

"We've got another hour to go before we should start heading that way. I don't know about you, but I'd rather use less energy to break that shield and save it for the following fight," Jerrik reasoned with her.

Laila was about to open her mouth to protest when her phone buzzed. She pulled it out and checked the screen, but she didn't recognize the number. Frowning, she answered.

"Hello, this is Laila Eyvindr."

"Good. This is Captain Romero from the homicide division," said a gruff male voice on the other end of the line.

"What can I do for you Captain?" she asked as the others watched her.

"There's been another homicide. How soon can you get to Playa Del Rey?"

CHAPTER 9

Laila examined the body of the young woman. "She looks just like the other victim."

As before, the corpse was left in an open doorway, mutilated and partially drained of blood. This time the victim was a woman who lived in a small condo near the beach. She'd been discovered by a neighbor who was out walking her dog. Jerrik was taking the woman's statement now.

"I've already called our investigative team," announced Darrien as he returned from the other room. "They'll take it from here."

Laila rose and took a step back from the corpse before poking through the variety of bags and purses resting on the bench by the door. The apartment was tidy, with bright colors. The woman appeared to live alone, but from the pictures on the shelves, she led a very active social life. Laila found a phone with a number of new text messages listed on the locked screen inside one of the purses. She poked through a variety of bags for other occasions that sat on the bench by the door but didn't find anything else of note.

"You know this is going to get out eventually," pointed out the captain. "The witness isn't likely to stay quiet for long."

"I know," said Darien, "but we need to buy some time to figure out what is going on here. Vampires don't attack like this. There's no shortage of blood banks in the city. Someone's trying to scare the humans."

"Well, this will definitely do it," sighed the captain.

Laila closed her eyes and did a quick scan of the magic in the room. In her rush, she almost missed the anomaly. Shifting her weight, she focused on it, then swore.

"Demonic energy, it's faint, but it's still there. I'd say our perp had a recent meeting with a Lesser Demon."

"Great!" Darien threw his hands in the air. "Of course there's Demons involved!"

No one thought to check the other crime scene. Most likely it would've dissipated by now if it was this faint to begin with, but if any Demonic energy remained, she was certain it would be attached to the other victim. Laila pulled out her phone and placed a call.

"Hello Meuric, are you still at the morgue?"

"Yes, I'm finishing up the autopsy on that homicide victim," said the medical examiner.

"Are you able to check the body for traces of Demonic energy?"

"I already have. It came back positive. I was going to give you a call about it when I finished."

Laila thanked Meuric and informed him that there would be another victim in the same condition arriving soon.

Darien shook his head. "I heard what he said. I don't know whether it's more concerning or less."

Jerrik led the investigative team over. They got to work cataloging evidence when Captain Romero left.

"I found her phone." She passed it to Jenn with a gloved hand. "Looks like it's locked though."

"Thanks." Jenn slipped it into a bag before pulling Laila

aside. "Did you deal with that creature up in Malibu yet?"

Laila shook her head. "I've got to go deal with that now. Do you have this under control?"

"Yeah, I'd pick a crime scene over that thing any day." She shuddered and walked over to one of her team members.

"Let's go," said Laila to Jerrik and Darien.

"I'm staying with the investigative team." Darien frowned. "I don't want you two to go in there without backup though."

"I'll call Frej, he can meet us there." Laila removed her gloves, ignoring the look Jerrik gave her.

Darien nodded in approval. "Good, you guys deal with that creature then meet me back at the office."

The Elves nodded and headed for the door.

Traffic was light, and twenty minutes later Laila found herself on the same winding driveway leading to the abandoned mansion. The silence around them was oppressive, and the darkness seemed all the more foreboding. Knowing what horror lie in wait did nothing to ease her feeling of unrest. As she parked in front of the house, she breathed a sigh of relief at the sight of the orange runes that flickered like dying coals on the walls, door, and windows. The spell was still active. She probed it with her magic and noticed that it was significantly weaker than it had been originally, but still held.

She buckled on her scabbard, checked the knives in her boots as well as the other weapons she wore. Jerrik donned a bulletproof vest as a gust of wind buffeted them. Laila looked up to see Frej's winged form above them. He landed gracefully before shifting. Frej wore light armor and an assortment of daggers in addition to a massive longsword strapped to his back. His hair had been pulled back as well, to keep it out of his face when fighting. He looked like a rugged warrior, and Laila realized that this was probably what Frej wore when he was out on errands for Queen Regina.

The gust of wind that had accompanied Frej's landing had thrown Jerrik's hair in his face. The Dark Elf grumbled and brushed the jet-black hair out of the way with a scowl. The men looked at each other wordlessly for a moment, as if some silent conversation passed between the two of them. Something felt different between them, tenser, and Laila made a mental note to ask Frej about it later.

Frej jerked his head at the building. "That's it?"

Laila nodded. There was no sign of the creature, but it had to be in there. She unsheathed her sword and approached the building to peer through the window. Squinting, she didn't see anything in the gloom. Had it retreated to another part of the house?

Bang!

The creature appeared, slamming against the window. Laila swore and stumbled back, nearly tripping over an overgrown bush. Slowly, she backed away while keeping an eye on the hideous face of bone and flesh, her heart beating so loud she swore the creature could hear it. She expected the others to snicker at her, but both of their faces were frozen in looks of shock.

Frej was the first to shake off the surprise. "It's a shadow creature. I'm not sure what kind, but the way it manipulates the darkness is familiar."

"What's that mean?" asked Jerrik, pulling another hand-and-half sword from the back of the SUV.

Frej shook his head. "The other shadow creature I encountered could cross back and forth through the shadow realm, making him vanish and reappear at will."

"Great," muttered Jerrik.

The creature stalked back and forth across a row of windows, waiting for the opportunity to attack.

"Any thoughts on how to contain or destroy it?" asked Laila. "Bullets were useless, fire seemed to have some effect though."

Frej shook his head at a loss.

"Looks like we'll improvise then." Jerrik adjusted his grip on his sword.

Laila got to work on unraveling the spell—not that she felt ready to take on that nightmare for the second time this evening, but they couldn't allow it to escape into the city and terrorize the inhabitants. The spell itself was deteriorating rapidly, likely from whatever magical abilities that creature wielded.

"Here it goes." Laila unraveled the last thread of the spell and the orange markings faded.

Nothing happened.

The three exchanged glances.

A moment later, the doors came flying off their hinges with a thunderous *boom*, and they had to dive out of the way to avoid being hit. A high-pitched screech echoed through the night as the creature stood there in the empty doorway.

Jerrik was the first to lead the attack, blasting the creature with flames. It dodged to the side as it launched towards him on all fours. In a flash it had him pinned to the ground as Jerrik struggled. Laila raised her sword, but Frej was already there, his longsword cleaving in a half-circle through the air. If the creature had moved any slower, it would've been decapitated, but it ducked just in time and rolled off Jerrik.

A throwing knife was already leaving Laila's fingertips. It struck the creature as it fled into the woods, but if it reacted to the knife protruding from its back, Laila didn't see it.

"Don't let it get away." She charged into the woods after it.

The foliage was thick overhead and blotted out the moonlight. Laila longed to conjure a light to see by but knew it would scare the creature away. She needed to lure it back, to get the creature to stalk her. Then she would destroy it, or at least she hoped she could. She'd managed to kill an Elemental, surely she could stop whatever this was. Granted, she had help from a Goddess last time.

There was rustling behind her, but it was just the men flanking her. Frej had replaced his longsword with a wicked-looking knife that would be easier to wield in close quarters. Jerrik's feet made little more than a whisper on the foliage, his pointed ears searching for any sound in the darkness.

Something flickered on the edge of her vision but vanished by the time she'd turned to look. By the dread that clenched her, Laila could tell the creature was here, watching them and planning its attack. She racked her brain for anything she could use against it, but she couldn't risk using fire, not in the dry brush they were surrounded by. It would be suicidal, and could even threaten the city if it spread. The creature was corporeal but reacted like a Ghost. She'd been able to trap a particularly nasty Ghost once, but would the same spell work on the shadow creature?

"Who wants to be bait?" she asked the others quietly. By the way they hesitated Laila knew they'd paused to give her incredulous looks. "You both can conjure shields. I need someone to draw it out so I can trap it in a magical cage. You'll be stuck in there with it though."

"That's insane!" hissed Jerrik.

"I'll do it," said Frej, standing tall. Jerrik rolled his eyes at the Dragon.

"Don't be ridiculous," snapped Jerrik, "I've got more than air magic at my disposal."

"Really?" Frej cocked an eyebrow in the dark. "I thought you said it was ridiculous?"

While the two men bickered, Laila backed away between the trees, watching the surrounding darkness closely. As the men's voices rose, Laila spotted the creature lurking behind a tree, watching the distracted males. Just as she anticipated, the creature rushed them.

"Shield!" she cried at them.

Her own spell was already in progress as she wove a cage of fire and light around them. As she had feared, the creature was moving too quickly to isolate, so she cast her spell to enclose the entire clearing before her. The creature hissed and shrieked at her as it realized Laila's spell had managed to snare it. It wasn't alone though, trapped in the confines of the shield with the creature was Jerrik and Frej, hunched beneath the small dome of Jerrik's shield. There was little room for the two men who glowered at each other.

"You couldn't have made a larger shield?" grunted Frej.

The creature noticed them as well and lashed out at Jerrik's shield with tendrils of shadow that sprouted from its hands.

The creature turned to her and hissed, the sound edged with a high-pitched trill like nails on a chalkboard. The sound made Laila grit her teeth. She didn't need to speak its language to know what it was trying to say: release me or I'll kill them.

Laila forced her shield to grow brighter, the creature shrinking away in response.

"Try to attack it now." Laila was already beginning to sweat with the effort of sustaining the cage. It was more taxing to hold than a shield of air.

Jerrik dropped his shield and blasted the creature with blinding light from his palms. It clawed at the sockets where eyes should have been and took a step back towards Frej. The Dragon hooked an arm around its neck and plunged his large knife into the body with a crunching sound. He stabbed over and over inflicting as much damage as he could, but it still wasn't enough. It unleashed a high-pitched cry as spindly fingers grabbed at Frej's face. He ducked and struggled to pin the nightmarish being's arms, but it was too strong. When Frej couldn't hold on any longer, the air around the Dragon shimmered as he shifted, claws and teeth ripping into the creature.

"Hurry up guys!" Laila groaned as she widened the shield to accommodate Frej's other form. She couldn't keep this up much longer, but if she dropped the spell, the creature would escape, and she knew it wasn't dumb enough to risk another attack.

Something magical within her shifted, like a restless animal in a cage, startling her enough that she almost dropped the cage spell. She'd felt it earlier too. What would happen if she freed it?

Could she use it to destroy the shadow creature? Laila tried to coax it out, but the magic remained where it was. Even a mental nudge was no use, it just slipped away avoiding her intentions.

"Come on!" hissed Laila. She'd used it before, so why didn't it work now? She didn't have the dagger, maybe this magic wouldn't work without it?

After another moment she gave up, frustrated. She'd have to do without.

A skeletal limb went flying as Frej mauled the shadow creature beyond recognition, only pausing when Jerrik blasted the creature with more fire. It was still moving though and slowly healing. Frej had the nightmarish monster pinned, so Laila dropped her cage spell and formed it into an arrow of dazzling light.

"Look out!" she called to others.

The arrow she conjured shone like a star as it burrowed itself into the creature's chest. Light spilled from cracks that ran along its crusty skin. With a final cry, what remained of the creature exploded in a blast of light.

When her eyes adjusted once more, there was nothing remaining of the Supernatural, it had simply vanished, just like the Ghost she'd fought before had. Breathing heavily, she waited in case it reappeared, but the night felt peaceful and tranquil now, and all traces of its creepy magical signature was gone as if it had been sucked through a portal. Perhaps it had in a way if she had sent it to the afterlife.

The two men were alright. Frej shook himself and huffed dust from his nostrils right into Jerrik's face. The Dark Elf swore and spluttered as the Dragon watched with a satisfied smile. He huffed in a way Laila swore was a chuckle. She crossed her arms and shook her head. Clearly, the men were just fine.

"Let's get out of here," grumbled Jerrik. "There was only one of those things, right?"

"As far as I know, but we should search the house." The men nodded and followed her back towards the abandoned mansion.

They'd nearly made it to the edge of the forest when Laila heard a muffled thud behind her. She spun around to find Frej sprawled on the forest floor.

"You've got to watch those roots." Jerrik slid his hands into his pockets and frowned at the Dragon. "I'd be more careful next time if I were you."

Laila shot him a seething look. She knew exactly where that root had magically materialized from. Frej appeared to as well because a gust of wind grabbed Jerrik's long, dark hair and wrapped it around his face. The Elf clawed at it and spat a string of profanity.

"Thor's Hammer, I swear I'll make you two walk home!" thundered Laila. "We're on a call, so act like it!"

The two men gave her sheepish looks as they mumbled apologies. Jerrik even offered Frej a hand up. They followed Laila in silence into the house.

They searched the house room by room but found no signs of other malicious creatures. There was one room that felt all too familiar to Laila, symbols had been drawn onto the floor in chalk around a large circle. There was no corpse in the middle, but otherwise it was identical to the other summoning circles they'd discovered. That explained where the shadow creature had come from.

"There's no sign of a body," muttered Jerrik as he walked around the perimeter of the circle. "Should we call in the investigative team?"

Laila shook her head. "They've got enough to deal with. We'll document it ourselves and add it to the database."

She snapped a photo of the room and wondered how many summoning sights were left undiscovered.

"I'll see you back at the house," announced Frej when they'd finished. He shifted into his scaled form and took off into the gloom as Laila and Jerrik climbed into the SUV.

CHAPTER 10

They returned to the office, and Laila parted ways with Jerrik in the elevator. She would meet up with the rest of the team shortly. At the moment, Laila wanted to check on the two humans the shadow creature had attacked. She walked across the courtyard to the Asclepius Hospital of Supernatural Medicine and found the receptionist waiting behind the counter of an empty lobby. She was an older woman, human, with a pleasant face. She was crocheting something colorful to help pass the time.

"Good evening," called the receptionist as Laila walked through the sliding doors. "Can I help you?"

"I'm here to interview a couple of humans that came in earlier. They were attacked by some sort of Supernatural. I brought one of them in myself."

The woman glanced at Laila's badge and nodded. "I'll see what I can do. Do you know the name?"

Laila shook her head. While the woman searched in the computer, Laila glanced around the lobby that was all but deserted.

"Slow night?" she asked the receptionist.

She cringed. "It's been a slow week with the anti-Supernatural protestors out front. I'm afraid people have been avoiding Asclepius's because of it. They left early tonight though, probably to go to that rally."

It was a shame that patients were avoiding the hospital. The doctors here were helping many patients both with magical and ordinary ailments. Ali had tried talking to the protestors, but there wasn't much they could do at this point, as they were still technically peaceful. So long as they weren't hindering the IRSA agents or the hospital staff from completing their duties, or posing a threat, they were allowed to be there.

"I think I found the patient. A young woman, right?"

Laila nodded.

"Try checking with the nurses on the fourth floor in the intensive care unit, her name should be Natali Atkins."

Laila did as instructed and stopped at a counter. The nurses informed her that the young woman was asleep. Rather than disturbing the patient, Laila decided to speak with the doctor instead, hoping they had some idea of what that creature was. It was the same doctor she'd spoken to earlier: the middle-aged Elf with short blond hair.

"You must be Special Agent Eyvindr." He offered her a hand. "I'm Doctor Elmersson."

"Thank you for speaking with me," said Laila quietly, aware of the resting patients in the rooms around them. "My team dealt with the Supernatural that attacked Natali Atkins. It won't be harming anyone else. I have no clue what it was though, any chance you can tell by the damage it inflicted?"

The doctor thought for a moment. "The creature was siphoning off her life force. There aren't many creatures that can feed off of energy to that degree. What did it look like?"

"Sort of skeletal, I might have mistaken it for a Ghost, but it had a physical form." she fought the shiver creeping down her spine.

"In that case, I believe it was a Nachzehrer."

Laila shook her head, she'd never heard of a Nachzehrer before.

"It's like a cross between a Vampire and a Ghost," he explained, "I've only encountered them once before, and it would've been long before you were born. A Necromancer set one loose upon Ingegard. It killed many Elves before it was stopped. They come from the darker realms of the dead, cursed with an insatiable appetite for energy of both living and dead souls."

The Doctor's words hit her like a freight train. More Necromancy. The summoning circle she'd found looked similar enough to the ones she'd seen before. But was it an old one from the Witch who'd been killed, or had the Demons found a new one, one versed in Necromancy?

"How's Miss Atkins doing?" she asked, shaking off the dark stream of thoughts.

"She'll make it, thanks to you." He motioned for her to follow him down the hall. "She's stable but resting. Her brother came in shortly after, looking for her. He mentioned that he'd seen the Nachzehrer attack her. I'm assuming you'd like to speak to him."

Laila nodded, and he directed her to a room. She knocked on the door and announced herself.

"Come in," called a male voice, and she entered. The man sat up blinking his eyes as he rubbed his face and disheveled hair. He must've dozed off in the chair he was sitting in. He wore the same, dust-covered clothes from earlier. The woman, Natali Atkins, was resting peacefully in the hospital bed.

"Sorry to disturb you," apologized Laila, stepping through the doorway, "I just wanted to ask you a few questions."

"Sure." He gestured to an empty chair. "Ask away."

"What were the two of you doing out there to begin with?" She took a seat.

He gave her a sheepish look. "You see, my sister and I are

paranormal investigators. We investigate hauntings and record them on film."

That explained the pile of film equipment.

"So, you purposefully enter haunted buildings to record Ghosts on camera? Why?" Laila had dealt with enough Ghosts to know that searching them out was foolish. The only times she did so was to prevent bystanders from getting injured.

He shrugged. "Death is a mysterious thing. Maybe Ghosts can give us answers on what happens next. Sure we know Ghosts exist, but we want to document it."

Laila bit her tongue. Hopefully, this experience alone was enough to discourage these siblings from seeking out potentially dangerous hauntings in the future. Otherwise, she worried this would not be the last time she saw them on a call.

"Why that location?" she asked.

"We got an anonymous tip on my phone. They probably found my contact information on my website."

"Does that happen often? These anonymous tips?"

"No." He frowned. "I just figured they forgot to leave their name. I—"

There was a gasp from the woman on the bed. Her eyes flew open, and she sat bolt upright.

"Dr. Elmersson!" shouted Laila, as she hastily opened the door and looked into the hall.

"It was looking for the Elf!" the woman gasped, "They told it—they told it the Elf would come."

Laila froze. "What?"

"They wanted… her dead…" Her eyes rolled back into her head as she collapsed backward on the bed.

"We need a doctor!" shouted Laila down the hall, just as Dr. Elmersson hurried around the corner.

Laila stood back, explaining what had occurred as he rushed into the room to examine the patient. He held his hands above the woman as warm, glowing magic drifted down into her body; gradually her breathing slowed to normal.

"I think that's enough for tonight," said the doctor stepping back, "she needs her rest."

Laila nodded. She took down the young man's information—as well as the number that called in the anonymous tip—before leaving.

Out in the courtyard she paused. The Demons wanted her dead. It wasn't exactly news to her, she'd nearly been killed in a minimart robbery turned trap a little over a month ago, shortly after Frej's arrival. Thankfully she'd survived the gunshot wound, but she hadn't thought much about the occurrence since. Marius had sent them, or at least that's what the Demon who shot her claimed.

This Nachzehrer had been summoned by the Demons and ordered to attack her. Whoever left that anonymous tip—likely a Demon—probably knew someone from her team would be sent to investigate eventually. What if it wasn't the only one? The Fire Elemental had been summoned from Vanaheim. It had been a trap as well, with an audio recorder left to lure rescue workers to their deaths. What if the intention was the same?

The markings on her arms glowed faintly, as if in response. A shiver slithered down her spine, and she continued on her way.

Laila reached the IRSA building and wearily trudged back to her office. If Darien hadn't requested they meet up, she would have gone straight home. As it was, they had a double homicide on their hands and no suspects. She was just putting her sword away when Darien appeared in the doorway.

She jumped before scowling at him. "Gods! Is it really necessary to sneak up on me like that?"

"Can we come in?" he asked, gesturing to Jerrik behind him.

She nodded and waved them in. The office was small, with her desk, bookshelf, and two chairs across from her desk. There was also a window that revealed the glow of the city lights.

Darien paused a moment. "I've decided to involve the local sires from the Vampire community in this."

"What are you talking about?" Laila shook her head. "This is an ongoing investigation."

"Yes, but we need to get this under control, and the old bloodlines have reach and influence that we don't. We need help."

"We have plenty of help, now that Jerrik and Frej—"

Jerrik scoffed. "No offense to your scaly lover, but Darien's right. We need help from the Vampires." He lounged in one of her chairs.

Laila hesitated and glanced at the doorway. She didn't hear Ali or the other agent, but she lowered her voice anyway.

"We're being watched though, the Inspector General's sent that human to observe us. If we're breaking protocol left and right we could get in serious trouble."

"This is more important," insisted Darien, his tone was sharp, and she could tell he was on edge. "The humans are not going to take this quietly. They've treated Vampires with suspicion ever since The Event. We have to deal with this now before we have a civil war on our hands."

He had a point. How could she sit here and worry about her job security when there were lives at stake? She felt a twinge of guilt.

"Fine, what's the next step?"

Darien stood.

"We've got a meeting with my sire."

"Wait, you mean now?" She glanced at the time on her phone. It was nearly one in the morning and considering she'd started her day earlier than usual, she was more than ready to head home.

"Yep, it's in Santa Monica, so we should get going."

CHAPTER 11

A half hour later they found themselves at a high-end apartment building. Darien pulled the SUV into one of the visitor spaces. Inside the elegant lobby was a waiting area with rich furnishings and an antique desk where a receptionist greeted them.

"Good evening, can I help you?" The human was dressed in a nice suit. There wasn't a hair out of place on his meticulously combed head, and even his nails were perfectly manicured. He appeared unsurprised to see them at such a late hour.

Laila glanced at Darien's studded black leather, and Jerrik's plain black t-shirt and jeans that were covered in dust and bits of leaves from the woods. She was dressed in a pair of skinny jeans, lace-up boots, and a gray tank top that revealed the light blue markings on her arms. In the polished marble entryway, she felt more than a little out of place. She resisted the urge to lecture Darien on his lack of warning.

"We're here to see Mr. Veryl."

"Right," the man eyed them with the slightest suspicion as

he stood.

"I know the way," said Darien waving the man off.

He led them to a wall of elevators and took one to the highest floor.

The doors opened, but instead of a hall of condos, there was only one entrance. Outside waited two guards in black suits. They wore sunglasses that helped to conceal their blood-red eyes, one of the identifying traits of the Vampires. Darien never bothered to cover his eyes or hide his fangs, but he wasn't one to hide his identity.

Laila wasn't sure who Darien's sire was, but by the look of things, he was a pretty important and influential man.

A sire is a Vampire who turns a human. By turning the human, they accept a great deal of responsibility for training the newly changed Vampire, which included educating them on the rules of their society. The basic hierarchical structure of the Vampire community was based on age and bloodlines. The older the bloodline and the higher you were within the bloodline's ranks, the more power you possessed, or at least that was what Darien had told her.

Laila realized with interest that this was actually the first time Darien had mentioned his sire. He had a tendency to keep those details of his life private.

They knocked on the door and were admitted by another Vampire guard. Laila nodded to him as they stepped into the penthouse.

It was nothing short of impressive. Large windows offered a panoramic view of the city. It was a combination of Victorian and modern design aesthetics with a black, white, and maroon color scheme. It felt cool and regal. A long dining table of polished black stone was to their left, flanked on either side by a row of black chairs with red velvet cushions. The far corner held a seating area with a white chaise lounge and sofa paired with black leather chairs. The wall to the right was covered in gray and white wallpaper, accented with oil paintings of dark, tortured creatures. Laila didn't know the artist, but she had a feeling they were originals, especially if he could afford a view like this. Something about the penthouse felt familiar to her in a way, but she couldn't remember why.

"Windows are a bold choice for a Vampire." Jerrik nodded to the floor to ceiling windows.

"They're made with a special UV filter," explained Darien. "It's designed specifically for Vampires, but they're currently very pricy. You can also get it put on car windows, which is great so long as you only enter and leave your car in a protective garage."

"Are we early?" Laila asked Darien.

"No, you're right on time," replied a voice behind her. The sound of it was like the deep purr of a wildcat.

He was pale with eyes the color of rubies, and a mane of wavy brown hair that hung to his shoulders. He was dressed in a crimson dress shirt that matched his eyes. The sleeves were casually rolled up, and the top two buttons at the collar were undone. Black slacks and leather shoes finished his look.

Laila turned and couldn't help as a blush crept into her cheeks. Of all the Vampires in the city, *he* was Darien's sire?

Darien bowed slightly.

"Laila," said Darien beside her, "this is Talen Veryl, my sire."

"Yes, we've met before," purred Talen, watching Laila with interest.

Laila nodded, trying to conceal the blush. They certainly had, and it would be hard for her to forget the encounter.

"It was at a Vampire club a few months ago," she explained.

"At *my* club," Talen corrected her as he waved them over to a seating area.

Their previous encounter had been brief, but...intense. It was the first and only time Laila had ever experienced the pull of Vampire charm. It had been similar to a Fae, only darker and more seductive. She received an emergency call from Erin, which pulled her away, but there was no telling how far she would have allowed it to go if it wasn't for that phone call.

"I'm Jerrik," added the Dark Elf stiffly beside her.

"It's a pleasure to meet you," said the Vampire turning to look Jerrik over.

Laila glanced at Darien and found him smirking at her. She rolled her eyes and returned her attention to the pressing matter at hand.

"Mr. Veryl, Darien mentioned you might be able to help us identify a Vampire."

He strolled over to the seating area and motioned to the overstuffed leather sofas.

"Please, have a seat," he crooned. "And call me Talen."

Laila seated herself on one of the sofas, Jerrik sat beside her. Darien occupied the other sofa next to the one his sire took.

"I doubt I can identify your murderer," explained Talen, "but I might be able to help you find him."

"How?" asked Jerrik.

The Vampire grinned, showing the tips of his fangs.

"Our community is very…organized… meaning that we keep close track of Vampires in the area and what bloodlines they belong to."

Jerrik nodded, but Laila could still feel his skepticism.

Apparently, Talen did as well. "While our condition makes us quite powerful, we still have our vulnerabilities. Even though the humans now know of our existence, we still find it necessary to keep a low profile to prevent more mistrust than we already receive. If there is indeed a Vampire murdering humans, I will help you in any way I can to keep this from spiraling out of control."

"What do you think our next step should be?" asked Laila.

The Vampire returned his attention to her. The intensity of it made her want to shift in her seat, but she held her ground.

"One of the local and ancient Vampires is hosting a party this week in the Old City. Rumor has it he's fixed up a historic building, and this little black-tie affair is his equivalent to a housewarming party. He's got his fingers in a lot of pies around the city, so if there's a rogue Vampire on the loose, I imagine he'd know about it."

"Don't tell me you mean Richard," groaned Darien, giving his sire a look. "You know I'm not allowed anywhere near him."

"Ha!" Talen barked. "How could I forget *that*? No, your presence won't be necessary. I intend to bring Miss Eyvindr as my escort."

Jerrik shifted next to her. "I should come too. Just in case there's any trouble."

The Vampire cocked his head ever so slightly. His gaze darting from Jerrik to Laila as a smile tugged to the corners of his mouth.

"Oh no," he said with his velvety voice, "I have the feeling that Miss Eyvindr and I are more than capable of handling ourselves. Besides, my community knows that I prefer the fairer sex." He winked.

Jerrik went stiff as a board as a gentle spark of amusement danced in Talen's eyes. Even Darien smirked. Laila had the feeling that Talen would enjoy messing with Jerrik all too much. Perhaps it would encourage Jerrik to keep his feelings in check, and to himself.

Darien leaned forward to rest his elbows on his knees. "Talen's right, they can handle things on the inside. But we'll be surveying from the van. Backup never hurts."

Laila nodded knowingly. It only took one poorly planned mission to land you in a coffin, or worse.

Jerrik didn't seem pleased with the idea of staying behind. "Well, we need to be careful, especially if there are Demons involved."

Talen looked at him sharply before turning to Darien with a questioning look. It would appear that Darien had left that bit of information out.

Talen recovered quickly though. "Very well, you and your team make any preparations necessary and meet me here in two nights. Laila and I will head over in my limousine." The Vampire leaned back in his chair, folding his arms. It was clear they were dismissed.

They bid him goodnight before returning to the car.

As they made their way through the empty streets and back to the office Laila's thoughts turned towards the party. She wasn't entirely sure what this event was about, but if they could get a decent lead out of it, she would gladly suffer through the pain of heels and a gown. For all they knew, it could already be too late for another human with the murderer still on the prowl.

"We need to watch who we mention the Demons to," said Darien as he drove. "I trust my sire, but I've got a bad feeling that information is still being leaked from the office."

"You're talking about Colin, aren't you?" Laila gave him a wary look.

"I think it's best to be cautious and keep this on a need to know basis. At least for now."

Jerrik nodded, and after a pause, Laila followed suit. She knew Darien was right.

Out of nowhere, Darien started to laugh. It was just a chuckle at first, but quickly he was roaring with laughter.

"What's gotten into you?" asked Laila inching away from the cackling Vampire in the driver's seat.

The Vampire took a moment to compose himself, wiping the tears from his eyes.

"Nothing," he said, "I remember you telling me about a Vampire that tried to seduce you. I just never realized that the mystery man was my sire!"

Jerrik didn't say anything, but Laila could feel his eyes

watching her from the backseat.

"So," shrugged Laila trying to hide her embarrassment.

It wasn't as if Darien didn't have his own share of scandal-ous stories though. He was notorious for flirting with women on the job. Never Laila or Ali of course, but that was where his self-restraint ended. Laila had noticed less of that lately, proba-bly because of how crazy things had been.

"Does Frej know about this?" asked Darien slyly.

"Yes, and it happened before I met him. Ali and I were at Talen's club the night he arrived. In any case, it's none of your business."

The Vampire grinned impishly but kept his mouth shut for the rest of the drive.

Laila leaned her head against the headrest and sighed as she realized that she'd have to explain to Frej that she was going to a party with a Vampire.

"No," said Frej simply, taking a sip from his wine glass.

"Okay," muttered Laila setting down her fork in irritation, "That was a statement, not a question, and you have no idea how inappropriate that is."

"Oh really?"

"This is an assignment Frej! You of all people should un-derstand."

Ali muttered something about bed and beat a hasty retreat to the stairs.

"I don't understand what the big deal is." Laila glared at him across the table where they'd been having a late-night dinner.

"Why do they always have to send *you* into every single dan-gerous situation? You've got an entire team. Let Darien do it."

"He can't, he's not allowed near the place, and it'll be more discrete if a woman accompanies his sire."

"So? Send Ali."

"She's in the middle of something." Laila thought back to the agent from D.C. and their encounter earlier at the office.

"Then I'm coming with you," declared the Dragon stubbornly.

"Absolutely not! I'm not some damsel in distress that needs protecting. I can fight my own battles, thank-you-very-much! Do I need to remind you that *I* saved *your* ass back in Schonengard, as well as your king's?"

Laila stood with her dishes that were left from their dinner and dumped them in the sink. Frej followed on her heels. Ignoring him, Laila added water to the tea kettle and switched on the stove burner. From the cabinet, she snatched a mug and a box of chamomile tea.

"Oh, so it's fine when Darien and Jerrik accompany you but when I—"

"What's going with you and Jerrik?" She spun to face Frej, slapping the box of tea down onto the counter. "You told me two days ago that he wasn't a threat, yet tonight you seemed tense."

"Nothing," he replied hastily as he turned to gather more dishes from the table. She could tell he was avoiding her, and that something was up. Beside her, the kettle pinged and crackled as the water started to heat.

"What aren't you telling me?" she asked frustrated.

He continued to avoid her as he set the rest of the dishes in the sink and began to wipe down the table with a towel.

"Don't you trust me? Or do you think I'm waiting for the first opportunity to throw myself into his arms? Because I'm not!"

The water in the kettle was starting to boil, and the steam escaped from the spout in a small wisp. Normally she would remove it from the heat, but she ignored it, glaring a Frej as he clenched and unclenched his hands. Pressure continued to build until the kettle was screaming. Frej reached over and switched the burner off with a rough snap.

"Gods damn it, Laila! It's *him* I don't trust."

"So what? Let me deal with it," she snapped.

"Fine!" bellowed Frej clutching the dish towel so hard his knuckles turned white, "But I'm going with you. I'm not going to let your own stupidity lead you into another trap!"

He turned on his heel and stormed up the stairs towards the second level. Laila opened and closed her mouth as she struggled to find words.

"Fine, I hope you enjoy sitting in the van with Jerrik because that's where you'll be!" she shouted after him.

There was a sound suspiciously like a roar, then a door slammed shut upstairs.

She propped her elbows on the counter beside the empty mug and rested her head in her hands. She didn't mean for her temper to flare up, but it was true, she'd meant every word she said. Still, she felt like crap.

Soft footsteps padded out from the hall and into the kitchen. There was shuffling as someone opened the box of tea, added a sachet to the mug, and filled it with hot water. Still, Laila didn't move. Behind her, Laila could hear the freezer door open.

"Caramel fudge or mint chip?" asked Ali behind her.

"Mint chip," sighed Laila.

Ali opened a small tub of ice cream and set it in front of Laila along with a spoon. Then, she hopped up and sat on the counter next to Laila before she opened her own tub. After a moment Laila picked up the ice cream and leaned her hip against the counter.

"This is why I don't do relationships," muttered Laila gouging the spoon into the frozen dessert.

She took a bite of the ice cream. It tasted good, and the cold was soothing. It didn't improve her mood though.

"You know he'll come around," Ali insisted gently. "He's just worried about you."

"Maybe, but I think he's hiding something." It occurred to Laila that this was the real reason she was upset.

"What makes you say that?"

"He was avoiding me. He never does that. I don't know, maybe Henrik or Mato said something to him when they were out last night that set him off?"

"I can ask Mato about it," suggested Ali.

Laila nodded. It was frustrating to think he could be hiding something from her. Having an argument on top of that didn't help.

"Laila," said Ali in her older sister warning tone, "don't tell me you're going to sit here and wallow in self-pity."

"I just had a fight, give me break."

Ali poked her in the ribs with her spoon playfully.

"Come on!" Laila swatted the spoon away.

"Frej's just adjusting. He's used to being the hero, and it frustrates him when he has to sit on the sidelines," Ali reminded her.

"We let him help as much as we can."

"I know. He knows that too. But it doesn't mean he agrees with it."

Ali had a point. He was probably used to being more involved when it came to assignments back in his kingdom. But here he had to play by the agency's rules. Even though they bent them as much as they could, there was still only so much they could do. At least for now. Maybe if things got more intense in the city, they could justify Frej's involvement a little more, but at the moment, they were only supposed to call on him when they were in need.

Laila tossed her spoon in the sink and put away the half-eaten tub of ice cream. She decided she was finished discussing her love-life.

"Why don't we talk about the agent from the Inspector General's office?" Laila said, changing the subject.

"What do you mean?" asked Ali innocently.

Laila wasn't buying the act.

"You reported Colin," she said pointedly. "I thought we

agreed to talk about this as a team before reporting him."

"This is… something different." insisted Ali. "I can't talk about it though."

"How convenient," her words were cutting, and a part of her regretted them as soon as they left her mouth. The rest of her stubborn self rejected the notion that Ali had found some-one other than Colin to report.

Ali shook her head incredulously. "Laila, what's gotten into you?"

Laila grit her teeth. It was too coincidental. She didn't un-derstand why Ali was so reluctant to admit she reported Colin. It gnawed at her and did nothing to improve her mood. First Frej was hiding something, and now her best friend. Laila was done. Just done.

Climbing the stairs, Laila retreated to the blissful isolation of her bedroom. She shrugged out of her jacket and tossed it on the bed. She didn't stop, but walked into the bathroom and switched on the water.

She stripped off her clothes, throwing them unceremoni-ously into a pile in the corner before stepping into the steaming hot shower. As the water poured over her head, it washed away what little makeup she wore.

After a moment, she took a deep breath of the warm, misty air, and released it. The breath came out as a sob. She allowed hot tears to roll down her cheeks and mix with the water of the shower, releasing the tension she'd kept balled up inside.

Why was this so hard lately? Maybe it was the lack of sleep? The nightmares were continuous now, and she was struggling to get more than a few hours of sleep at the most.

Then there was the stress of work, but she'd always worked well under pressure. She'd learned that in her training. Work was simple. She went, found the people who were breaking the law, and arrested them. Sure, they attacked her from time to time, but it was a normal and repetitive cycle. It was familiar.

After a long shower, she felt only marginally better. She'd

gone from feeling hotheaded and angry, to wrung out and miserable. A cup of tea sounded kind of good, and she remembered the one that had been left on the counter. She could go get it, but then she'd run the risk of encountering one of her housemates. It was probably over steeped and bitter now, anyway. It was fitting since she'd allow her frustrations to brew within her all evening.

She shouldn't have been so hard on them, but she'd faltered, and allowed her anger with the case and all of these Demon-related issues to get the better of her. She allowed her work life to bleed over into her personal life. If only she could take it back, or find a way to make things right, but it was late, and the others had retreated to their rooms. So instead she dressed in her favorite cotton pajamas, dried her hair with a spell, and crawled into bed, hoping some sleep and a new day would help her see a way to mend things.

CHAPTER 12

Laila ran down the dirt road so fast that the woods were nothing but a blur around her, but still, it wasn't fast enough. Behind her, she could hear the Demonic pursuers racing down the road and gaining on her every second. Their trucks rumbled like thunder, and gunshots rang out in the night.

She needed to get off the road, now. Angling towards the cover of the woods, she almost made it through the tree line when she tripped over something. She scrambled around to see what she had tripped on. It was a body.

"No!" she hissed, struggling to her feet and backing away.

It was like a hole was ripped out of her chest as Jerrik's lifeless eyes stared at her in the gloom. He was riddled with gunshot wounds, and the front of his shirt was soaked in blood.

She turned and ran, weaving through the trees as tears clouded her vision. Laila had no idea where she was going, but she had to get away. The Demons would kill her if they found her.

The forest of oak was closing in on her. The trees grew closer, and their branches lower. She had to struggle through the undergrowth to move.

Suddenly the woods gave way, and she was standing in a clearing, no, a battlefield. She turned taking in the carnage that surrounded her. Bodies were strewn about, missing limbs and heads. The body closest to her had a spearhead protruding from its chest. It was Colin.

Laila trembled as she recognized the bodies that surrounded her. Erin, Ali, Torsten, Orin, Lyn… every single body on the battlefield was someone she knew and cared about.

"Father!" she cried dropping to her knees at his side.

An arrow was lodged deep in his eye socket, and his face was crusted in blood.

"No," she sobbed, grabbing his shirt. "No!"

Her voice echoed through the clearing, distorting her cries like a dozen voices mocking her grief.

"Laila?" said a gentle voice behind her.

She turned. There was Frej standing on the edge of the clearing, his face etched with lines of concern.

She ran to him, wrapping her arms around him as the tears rolled down her face.

Why? How? What had happened here?

"Oh, come now," said a musical voice by her ear, "did you expect anything less?"

She looked up, but it wasn't Frej's face she saw, it was Marius's. Laila shoved him away as he laughed.

"There is nowhere to run," he said with a cocky tone. "No matter where you go, I *will* find you, and destroy everything you love."

Laila woke with a start. Her heart was racing, and she was covered in sweat. For a moment, she sat there trying to ground herself. This was real, the rest had been a dream. She was fine. Everything was fine.

With a shaking hand, she checked her phone, it was five o'clock in the morning. She'd only been asleep for an hour.

Throwing back the sheets, she got out of bed. The thought of sleeping and dreaming made her sick. She needed to move, to do something.

A flash of light in the corner of her eye caught her attention, but when she turned her head to look, all she saw was her dagger sitting on the dresser.

Carefully, she picked up the dagger. It was polished to a high shine with a hilt made of woven silver, and the pommel inlaid with a large, blue-white moonstone. It was a curious object. It appeared suddenly when she had need of it, but she had no idea where it came from. Everyone she'd asked had been unable to identify it for her, but it seemed to have powers of some sort.

She'd never really examined its energy before. Something about the dagger was both mesmerizing and overwhelming. How strong was the magic surrounding the dagger? Would it turn on her if she activated it? At the moment, as her frustrations boiled within her, she felt as though she had nothing to lose. She placed her hand firmly on the grip and concentrated. That magic she'd felt earlier seemed to stir in response.

There was a shift as if someone had shoved her from behind. She glanced behind her and realized that her vision was different. It was as if she'd been in desperate need of glasses and finally put them on. Everything felt more vibrant, details were sharper, and Thor's Hammer, she could actually *see* the magic!

She looked forward into the mirror, but her image was different. Her eyes were bright blue and the scars on her arms were glowing and moving around on her skin. She was so surprised, the dagger slipped from her grasp.

"Shit!" she swore, avoiding the blade as it clattered to the ground.

She looked back up at the mirror, but her appearance had returned to normal.

Cautiously she picked up the dagger. She expected the same

reaction, but nothing happened. After waiting for a time with no reaction, she returned the dagger to its original spot.

"You neglect your training," hissed a voice in her ear.

Laila grabbed the dagger and spun around, but there was no one there. Her heart was pounding in her chest as she reached out to sense the magic around her, but aside from the dagger, there was no unusual energy in the room. She was alone.

How had she done that? Especially when she'd been unable to access that magical energy earlier. Was the dagger the key, or was there some trick?

After struggling to fall back asleep, she slept fitfully the rest of the night. Perhaps she would talk to Lyn about a stronger sleeping charm to keep the dreams away.

Sorting through her closet, she found a pair of black skinny jeans, brown boots, and a green t-shirt. Laila began to braid her hair back when she realized that it was all the way down to her hips. It appeared that the potion Lyn procured had lingering effects. Using a spell, she cut the hair back halfway down her back before tying off the braid. She added a touch of makeup before heading downstairs for breakfast.

Even though it was afternoon, everyone in the house still considered it to be breakfast. Their schedules had become mostly nocturnal, especially since Darien was unavailable during the day. Most of their calls came in at night anyway, so afternoons became mornings.

The others were already up and finishing their breakfast. Only Erin acknowledged Laila's presence as she entered the kitchen.

"How'd you guys sleep?" asked Laila after a while.

There was a pause.

"I slept fine," said Erin through a mouthful of cereal, as she glanced from Laila to the others.

Resisting the urge to confront the others, Laila started another pot of coffee. Perhaps they needed more time?

"I'm out," announced Erin setting her bowl in the sink and

heading down the hall.

"Where are you going?" asked Ali.

"To a judo class."

"No, you have work to do with Frej."

"I'll do it later."

"Erin," Ali's voice was dangerously low

Erin rolled her eyes. "Fine, but don't take out your frustration on me. It's not my fault you're all pissed at each other."

Erin disappeared down the hall before Ali could reply.

Laila watched the other two as she waited for her coffee. Both of them ignored her. She felt like maybe she should talk to them. Then again, they might want time to cool down.

"Do you want to ride with me to the office?" she asked Ali.

"No thanks," said Ali.

Laila waited for further explanation, but none came. Instead, Ali turned to Frej to discuss Erin's studies.

Unsure of what to do, Laila poured some coffee into a travel cup before picking up her bag and heading to work. She needed to blow off some steam, and their office's gym seemed like as good a place as any for that.

When she arrived at the office, Laila realized she'd forgotten breakfast. Locking her car, she hurried out of the garage and across the street to a bakery that was closing for the night. Laila managed to persuade them to sell her a box of assorted pastries even though they were technically closed. As Laila crossed the street, she could see a line of protestors standing in front of the hospital with signs reading "GO BACK TO HELL!" and "SUPERNATURALS NOT WELCOME!" Laila shook her head with disgust. At the very least the protestors could do their research and bother to learn the difference between SNPs and Demons. Pushing aside her annoyance she entered the IRSA building from the street entrance and found a familiar face behind a counter.

"Hey Benning," she called as she nudged the door open with her hip.

"Miss Laila!" The Giant's face lit up when he recognized her.

The Giant had been summoned by the Demons to destroy the city. Luckily, Benning was the kindest Giant Laila had ever met. He helped to clean up what damage he'd caused while Lyn researched a shrinking charm that would allow him to enter the small doors of the Inter-Realm terminals at the Los Angeles International Airport, and cross through the portals back into Jotunheim. But by the time the repairs were made, Benning decided to extend his stay a while longer. He wore the shrinking charm on a regular basis now, helping him to fit in.

When protestors started gathering outside the hospital, Colin determined that they needed someone to work security at the front desk. Even with the charm, Benning was over eight feet tall, and anyone would think twice before messing with the Giant. Plus, his cheerful personality made a pleasant addition to their staff.

"How are you doing?" she asked, leaning against the counter and offering him a pastry.

"Oh, thank you! I'm great!" he said enthusiastically. "Everyone in the office has been very nice." He bit into the pastry with a look of ecstasy.

"That's good to hear."

He frowned as he looked her over. "Is everything okay? You seem a little tense?"

Laila gave him a half-smile. "It's nothing, just roommate drama. I'm off to the gym for a bit. I'll see you around."

She turned away towards the stairwell. Not even Benning with his sweet demeanor was enough to pull her out of the sullen mood she was in.

Forty minutes later she stood before the punching bag dripping with sweat. Left hook, right jab, undercut. Left, right, left. Left, right, left. She found comfort in the sense of repetition and allowed herself to become absorbed in the sequence.

"I was wondering who was here so early," said a voice behind her.

She spun around and found Torsten standing in the doorway. The fatherly Dwarf was only about as tall as her waist, with brown hair, and a scraggly beard that had bits of metal shavings on it. He was wearing his usual jumpsuit and a leather apron to protect his clothes while he worked. There were a pair of goggles resting on his head.

"Thor's hammer, what did that punching bag ever do to you?" He made a clicking sound with his tongue. "I hope you weren't imagining my face on there."

Laila smiled despite herself. "Why would I possibly be upset with you?"

"Hey," he began seriously, "I've got a wife and four grown daughters. I've learned that it's either my fault and I should proceed with caution, or that it's not my fault, but I should still proceed with caution." He gave her a sympathetic look.

Laila shook her head. "I'm just getting some training time in while I can."

"I see." Torsten folded his arms as he searched her face. "But I know your habits, and you like to train with Darien later in the day."

Laila shrugged. Torsten watched her carefully for a moment. She knew he wasn't buying her story.

"Do you want to talk about it?" he asked after a moment.

When she didn't answer, he took a seat on a bench and motioned for her to join him. Laila remained where she was. She wasn't really in a mood to talk about it.

"I haven't seen you at the meetings in two weeks," he pointed after some time had passed. "Why did you stop coming?"

Torsten was referring to a self-help group for victims of Demon-related attacks. The majority of the attendees were from the Demon-run fight ring that she'd been trapped in along with Jerrik and Torsten. But others had started coming to the meetings, even Ali when she was coping with the shock of her sister's abduction. But after three meetings Laila had stopped coming.

"I thought it was helping," he prodded.

"It was…" Laila trailed off.

"So why did you stop?"

He paused as a thought occurred to him.

"Is it because Jerrik's been coming?" He looked over at her. Laila rolled her eyes.

"That's it though, isn't it?" He sighed and leaned against the wall. "Oh Laila, I know things are awkward between the two of you, but that shouldn't prevent you from coming. These meetings are important."

"I know, the dreams are only getting worse. I hardly slept at all last night."

"Do you want to tell me about it?"

She nodded and finally joined him on the bench. After giving him a brief description of the visions of death and destruction. He nodded and listened intently, but didn't interrupt. He had been right, of course, she did miss going to the meetings and the relief they brought her. As she finished, they sat there for a moment in silence.

"I'm working on this Vampire case," she began.

Torsten nodded. "I've heard."

"Faint traces of Demonic energy were found. Whoever it is, I think they've been in contact with a Lesser Demon. It's like the ritual crime scenes all over again."

"You think it's the Snake Shifter?"

"Maybe?" The last time she saw him was when she rescued Erin. He had shifted into snake form and escaped from the building, but no one had been able to locate him since.

"It could be that someone else is involved with these murders," added Torsten.

"That's worse," groaned Laila. "That would mean that there are even more Demons in the city."

Torsten twisted one of the rings on his calloused fingers as he thought on what Laila had said.

"Is that all?" he asked finally, "or is there something else troubling you?"

Laila glanced at him, feeling defensive, but the look of concern on his face made her soften.

"I feel like there's so much drama in the office and at home right now. Colin, the Jerrik and Frej situation, I even got into it with Ali last night, and we never fight."

She peeled off her gloves and threw them into her gym bag then slumped against the wall feeling worn out in a way that had nothing to do with her workout. How could it be that she was this tired and the day had only just started?

Torsten gave her a long look. "Have you tried talking things through with them?"

"I have, it only made things worse." Her shoulders sagged further.

"Sometimes you have to break things in order to fix them. A patch isn't always enough to fix a sword. You need to stick the pieces back in a forge, melt them down, and start again. I think relationships can be like that. You have to give people the time to gather themselves before you can start to grow a relationship again."

Laila nodded slowly. She knew both Frej and Ali needed time to cool down. Hell, she probably needed time too, although she still didn't know what to do about Jerrik. His feelings for her were obvious. In all honesty, though, he wasn't trying to flirt with her, and he rarely brought up the topic of their relationship. But he was still there, a constant presence in her life. Laila didn't know why that left her so frustrated, but somehow it did.

Ugh! She was so not good with this sort of thing. She'd take an angry Troll over this kind of drama any day. There were no Trolls at the moment, but she did have a case to focus on.

Boom!

The sound echoed down the hall, shaking the walls.

"What was that?" Laila leapt to her feet.

"The lab," Torsten groaned and hurried out of the room.

Laila followed him quickly to the room down the hall that had been converted into a workshop of sorts. It was where Torsten and Donald experimented with new equipment for the team. Through the door was a large open room. One side had been left open to use for testing inventions, while the other side held two large workbenches and rows of shelves containing everything from spell ingredients to bits of standard protective equipment, and even a large safe for weapons. Bits of wood, scraps of wire, and metal shavings littered the floor, and every surface of the counters lining the walls was occupied by works in progress. It was a mad scientist's paradise.

Donald stood by one of the workbenches with his back to them, tendrils of smoke curling up from the contraption he'd been working on.

"Thor's hammer!" roared Torsten. "What in the worlds did you do this time?"

Donald coughed and turned around in a daze. His face and goggles were blackened from an explosion. Bits of debris clung to the apron he wore, and the sleeves of his green t-shirt were singed. The mess of his brown hair now stood straight up, and as he lifted the goggles to his forehead, they left rings of soot around his dazed eyes.

"Just a minor miscalculation." The Tech Wiz coughed again and switched on a fan above the workstation. It pulled the smoke out through a vent before it tripped the sprinklers.

Torsten shook his head. "I thought you were giving up on those shield bracers."

"I know I can get them to work," insisted Donald, "I just need to tweak the enchantment a little."

Laila looked past the piece of metal and leather resting on the workbench and examined a diagram. It depicted metallic bracers, from which extended a magical shield that was similar in size and shape to something the ancient Spartans would've used, only formed by magic. The idea was brilliant, and Laila was about to say so when she took a closer look at the woman he'd sketched wearing the bracers.

"Is that Ali?" She peered around Donald to get a closer look. Sure enough, the blond woman had purple eyes. The rather revealing catsuit the Fae wore emphasized her busty nature.

"Well, um, she seemed like the most likely subject, to benefit from the invention," explained Donald hastily, his face bright red. "You know, since she can't conjure a shield on her own."

"Right," said Laila slowly. She'd be informing Ali of the drawing later. Not that Ali would find the drawing offensive, knowing the Fae she would probably find it more amusing than anything. But the amount of detail put into the shape of her breasts and the curve of her butt suggested Donald had spent far too much time focusing on those features.

Laila cleared her throat. "I should probably get cleaned up for work."

Donald reached for something on a shelf. "Here's another one of those lockdown spells, just in case. The blue one is the counter potion so that you don't have to wait as long next time. I finished the formula this afternoon."

"Thanks," Laila accepted the two vials, one orange, and one blue. "I'll see you later."

Torsten nodded and gave her a half-smile, "Don't let your pride get the best of you, and take care that you don't push people away unnecessarily."

Laila nodded, and as she turned to leave, she could hear Torsten behind her lecturing Donald.

"What have I told you about appropriate depictions of co-workers?" he howled.

Laila heard the crumpling of paper. Bits of conversation continued to drift down the hall, but Laila was already lost in thought, mulling over the crime scenes in her head.

CHAPTER 13

A buzzing noise startled Laila, jerking her awake. She'd fallen asleep at her desk. Glancing up at the screen saver on the computer she saw it was almost 7:30pm.

The buzzing continued, and Laila snatched up her phone to check the caller I.D. It was Lyn.

"Hey," said Laila answering the phone, and trying to shake off the drowsiness.

"Hey Laila, I was out surfing, and when I got back, I found this weird voicemail on my phone. It was someone asking for help in the Old City with a nasty haunting. It sounded kind of sketchy, and I tried calling the woman back, but the line's been disconnected. I asked one of my friends in the Old City to drive by and check it out. They confirmed it was haunted pretty bad. Anyway, I have a bad feeling about this, but I don't think it's safe to let a haunting of this magnitude continue."

The drowsiness made it difficult for Laila to focus like her head was filled with fog. It must be the lack of sleep catching up to her. Something about the situation felt familiar, but her sleep-deprived brain wasn't making the connection. She agreed with Lyn though, they needed to deal with the haunting before humans started to grow curious.

There were footsteps in the hall, and Darien stuck his head through the doorway. He motioned down towards the garage.

One minute, Laila mouthed.

"Hold on Lyn, give me just a second." She muted her microphone and looked up at Darien.

"A gun shop's been robbed," explained Darien hastily, "Captain Anderson believes it was the Di Inferi gang."

Thanks to the help of Captain Anderson and the LAPD Gangs and Narcotics Division, they'd discovered a connection between the local gang—once thought to have disbanded—and the Demons. They'd been flying under the radar since IRSA had caught up to the group responsible for the summoning rituals and murders. Captain Anderson was keeping tabs on known members in an attempt to learn more about Di Inferi's antics, but this was the first incident of note in weeks.

Laila drummed her fingers as she debated her choices.

"Lyn needs to check out a haunting in the Old City, and I think it would be a good idea if I go with her. Can you and Jerrik handle the robbery?"

Darien nodded. "Yeah, you could take Jerrik with you too."

She thought about the anonymous tip that had lured the paranormal investigators out to Malibu. It felt all too similar, but she wasn't up to dealing with Jerrik with everything else on her plate. She'd be on her guard—armed and ready for a fight—unlike the victims from the other trap. Since this one was Ghost related, there was no one more qualified to handle the situation than Lyn.

"I think the two of us will manage, but I'll let you know how things look when I get there."

Darien nodded. "I'll grab Jerrik and head to the shop then."

"Thanks," Laila unmuted her microphone. "Hey Lyn, are you still there?"

"Yeah."

"Okay, send me the address, and I'll meet you there. I don't like the sound of this, but I agree. We can't let a haunting get out of control, even if it is in the Old City."

"Cool, I'll send it to you. See you there." Lyn hung up.

Laila pulled on the black leather breastplate that was sitting on her desk from the encounter with the Nachtzehrer. She double checked the holsters for her firearm and stun baton before leaving.

As the elevator doors slid open, she almost ran into another woman. It was Colin's girlfriend, Lorel.

Surprised, Laila took a step back. Lorel's sleek black stilettos made a staccato sound on the floor of the elevator as the woman side-stepped. There wasn't a wrinkle on her bright-white blouse or her black pencil skirt. Her blond hair was pulled back in a sleek up-do. The only way Laila would ever achieve that level of hair perfection was if she went to a salon. Lorel's lips were crimson, and her eyes were masked by a large pair of sunglasses. A designer handbag from this season hung from one arm. She looked like a model who stepped off the page of a magazine. She seemed too perfect.

The only thing about her appearance that seemed out of place was the necklace she wore. Every time she'd seen the woman, Lorel had been wearing it. It was made of silver, handcrafted, and likely very old. On it was carved a woman with wings. Laila assumed it was an Angel, but found the lack of clothing odd. She'd never asked Lorel about the necklace, but she recalled Lyn saying something about it seemed familiar.

"Excuse me," mumbled Laila, feeling grungy by comparison. She wondered what in the worlds Lorel was doing here, and how she'd managed to get up to this floor without an escort.

"Is Colin here?" asked Lorel in a haughty tone. "He left this at my house last night."

She held up a bottle of prescription medication. Laila guessed it was for his headaches.

"No," said Laila, "but you can leave it in his office, the first room on the left."

As Colin's girlfriend strutted down the hall, Laila got an unusual vibe from her. Lorel felt cold and stony. Sure, she was beautiful, but Laila imagined that Colin wasn't all about looks. Then again, what did she really know about Colin?

Laila watched and escorted the woman out of the building. How she'd gotten in there in the first place, Laila didn't know. She would have a word with Benning at the front desk, but it would have to wait until she had dealt with the haunting.

Thirty minutes later, Laila found Lyn waiting for her on a dark street in the Old City. As Laila parked, Lyn stepped from her car and pulled a bag of equipment from the trunk, including a staff carved with runes.

Lyn hefted the bag over her shoulder. "Let's get this over with. I've been watching the place for a few minutes, and there's definitely something strange going on in there. It's not your usual haunting."

"What do you mean?"

Lyn waved her over to a grimy window. "Now when you look inside you can't see the Ghosts, they haven't manifested in their visual form yet. They tend to exist ordinarily in this state because it requires almost no energy. If they started manifesting or knocking things around, they'd drain themselves."

Lyn pulled out an object from her pocket, it was a shard of glass surrounded with a gold frame. Laila had seen it before, at their first encounter when Lyn had used it to see if there were any Ghosts attaching themselves to Laila. She passed it to the Elf.

"Thor's hammer," whispered Laila as she peered through the glass.

The room was literally packed with Ghosts just sort of milling about. But if it required enchanted equipment to detect them, it made the anonymous tip all the more suspicious.

"So, what do you make of this?" Laila gestured through the window. "Why are there so many in here?"

Lyn stared through the window into the seemingly empty space looking troubled. "It's not a naturally occurring haunting, that's for sure. Something must have drawn them here. Something's going on in the far room though. I keep seeing dark shapes moving back there."

Laila followed her gaze to an archway. It was hard to see because of the angle, but there was something glowing subtly back there amidst the shadows.

Shaking her head, she pulled out her phone and sent a message to Darien: *we need backup asap*. Something told her that this wasn't going to be a straightforward Ghost banishing call. When she looked up though, Lyn was heading towards the door.

"What are you doing?" hissed Laila incredulously.

"Relax, I'm just trying to get a better look through that archway. The Ghosts are calm, they won't be a problem unless provoked."

Laila's phone buzzed with Darien's reply: *on our way*.

"Alright, but we're just going to observe," insisted Laila. "The second they start becoming agitated, we get out of there and wait for the others."

Lyn nodded.

"I'll go first and shield us from anything that might come flying at us," suggested Laila.

Lyn nodded. "This staff is enchanted. It's physical on our plane as well as the plane of existence that the Ghosts are on, so it can actually have an effect on them."

They approached the door which was propped shut. The lock had been broken, and someone had placed an old crate filled with rotting garbage in front of the door to make sure no one entered. Or to keep something in.

She shoved the crate aside with her boot and conjured up a shield. Lyn held her staff at the ready as Laila pulled open the door. The hinges groaned and screeched. There was nothing but darkness visible beyond the doorway. Laila conjured up a light and stepped into the building.

The interior was large and cavernous. Cobwebs swayed from rafters and covered old furniture that had been piled to the sides of the room. It had once been a business, a shop by the look of the modular tables and shelves. There was a staircase along one wall that led to a second-floor balcony. Moats of dust drifted lazily through the dim shafts of moonlight filtering through the dirty windows high above them.

They were certainly not alone. While nothing approached, she could feel eyes watching them.

Standing just inside the doorway they still couldn't quite see into the other room. The light was brighter, but the source was obscured by a wall. Reaching out to feel the magic of the space, she could sense some sort of ongoing spell in the other room. With the large amount of Ghostly energy swirling about the room though, it was hard to read any of the other energy signatures. It was similar to searching a room filled with smoke.

The hair of the back of Laila's neck rose as she felt one of the Ghosts brush against her arm.

"Okay, let's go wait for the others."

Laila took a step back towards the door when she heard it click shut behind them. She grabbed the handle and heard the groan of metal bending on the other side. Pulse racing, she tried to force the door open, but it had been barricaded shut. They were trapped.

Lyn took a deep breath. "Okay, we just need to stay calm, so we don't disturb the Ghosts. They won't be a danger until they manifest in their semi-physical form."

Ghosts had three states of being. The first was their transparent state as these Ghosts were now. It meant that the living typically couldn't see or feel them. The second was their manifested form where they made themselves visible. The third was their semi-physical state where they could affect objects and people in the physical plane of existence. They were most dangerous in this form as they could push, throw, and otherwise attack, but it was a one-way relationship. While Ghosts could create an effect on the physical plane such as scratching someone, if the living person tried to fight back, their fists would just pass through the Ghost. Thus, it was difficult to defend yourself unless you had an object that existed on multiple planes such as the staff Lyn carried.

Laila bit her lip as she scanned the room one more time. "Why don't we head to the back room, there should be another emergency exit out that way."

Lyn nodded.

Laila lead the way to the archway. Her shield surrounded them with a faint shimmer, and the dust picked up by their shoes swirled around their feet. Laila couldn't help but notice other sets of footprints that had worn a path through the dust. They hadn't been made by Ghosts, others had been here before them.

With a spell at the ready, Laila peered around the edge of the archway. The room had been cleared, save for a single table and chair. In the center was a circle detailed with a variety of runes that were increasingly familiar to Laila. She groaned it was yet another summoning circle. One was a coincidence, but two?

To make matters worse, a crackling vortex of dark, sickly magic swirled in the center of the circle. Purple bolts of electricity arced around it, and from the dark center, a four-legged form emerged and stepped into the room.

Laila reached out with her magic but recoiled. The magic was contorted and polluted. The ongoing spell that created the vortex felt fragmented and distorted. There were other creatures like it in the room, dark and twisted presences. They were shrouded in shadow and darkness that prevented her from getting a good look at them. They reminded her of the Nachtzehrer, and she didn't need a charmed piece of glass to see them.

"That's another summoning portal," whispered Lyn behind her, "but this one's a Necromancer's portal since it leads to the world of the dead. For some reason, it's stayed open. If I don't stop it now, spirit creatures will just keep coming out."

Laila didn't like the sound of any of this. Black magic was bad, but Necromancy was far worse. It broke the laws of nature and had the ability to wipe out a world in a matter of days like what nearly happened during The Event. They needed backup, but there was no time to wait. The creatures prowling around the portal in the other room hadn't noticed them yet, so Laila pulled out her phone and checked on Darien's GPS location. He was still ten minutes away. Hopefully, they would be here faster. In the meantime, they had a portal to deal with.

She turned to Lyn. "How do we close the portal?"

"It's a similar spell to what I used before, and I have everything I need with me, but you'll have to keep those things busy." Lyn jerked her head at the shadowy quadrupeds.

"Right." She had a feeling that wouldn't be as easy as it sounded.

She readied a fire spell and grabbed her stun baton. After a nod to Lyn, she stepped into the room and knelt by the portal as she began to remove the supplies she needed from her pack for the spell.

Immediately Lyn had the undivided attention of the four-legged creatures from the portal. Laila stepped between the creatures and Lyn, preparing for a fight. From here she could see they were like large hairless dogs, but their bodies were twisted in unnatural ways. Their eyes were dark red and glowed like dying coals. Between their sharp and jagged teeth, flicked a forked tongue. She'd only seen them before in illustrations and paintings; they were Hellhounds, creatures that feed off Ghostly energy. They must have followed the Ghosts through the portal.

The first of the four snarled at her and lunged. She swung the baton which connected with the creature's jaw with a crunch. The Hellhound howled and backed away. At least they were solid and could be impacted by mortal weapons, unlike the Ghosts.

Laila shot a blast of flame towards the group of Hellhounds, causing them to recoil and retreat.

"Come on Lyn!" she yelled over her shoulder. But Lyn was already there, setting up her spell.

The Hellhounds took turns lunging at her. Laila fought back, alternating between her baton and fire to hold them off and drive them into a corner.

"Laila! Look out!" screamed Lyn.

Laila spun to find a Ghost flying towards her. They had manifested now and were growing agitated with the fighting. It knocked her over in its semi-physical shape, and she was immediately swarmed by half-a-dozen other Ghosts. Their icy-cold presence stole the heat from her body as they sapped her energy and pinned her to the ground. They felt solid, yet her arms and legs passed through them. It was completely disorienting. They cried at her in pain and anguish as they pinned her to the floor. She struggled to break free, but they were surprisingly strong.

Nearby, Laila could hear Lyn was caught in the middle of her own Ghost fight. Her enchanted staff kept them at bay, but the monstrous dogs were inching closer, waiting for their opportunity to attack.

She struggled to breathe as the Ghosts pressed against her chest and throat. She clenched and unclenched her hands as she struggled, and as she did, her hand closed around something cool and solid. It was the moonstone dagger.

The moonstone glowed as she raised it and plunged it into the nearest Ghost. It shrieked and fell back. The dagger must exist on multiple planes like Lyn's staff.

She slashed at another Ghost, cutting it across the face. It didn't bleed or show signs of injury, but it screeched and retreated as well. The others backed up, and Laila was able to climb to her feet and fight her way to Lyn's side, who was also occupied by the attacking Ghosts.

The Hellhounds waited while the Ghosts and the women fought as if debating which was the more worthwhile prey. But as they started lunging at her again, Laila wondered if they decided the living energy was more appealing to feed off than the Ghostly energy.

"I'm almost finished closing the portal," called Lyn. "You just have to keep them away a little longer, then we can get out of here and regroup."

Laila nodded, but there was no way she could keep all the creatures distracted. She threw up a shield of fire around herself, Lyn, and the portal. It flickered to life around them, but the Ghosts and the Hellhounds clawed at it, trying to break through.

"I can't hold this for long," grunted Laila. Sweat beaded on her brow, and she struggled to maintain the spell. The Ghosts had managed to steal more of her energy than she'd expected, and holding the shield up was like trying to push a boulder uphill with all the creatures trying to break through.

Lyn worked her magic, referring to a book of spells she pulled out of her bag. She was working as fast as she could, but it wouldn't be quick enough.

One of the Hellhounds leapt at the flaming shield, snapping at her face. The integrity of the shield was weakening, and soon the Hellhound would break through. She tightened her grip on the dagger, she thrust it up through the lower jaw and into the creature's head. It burned up in a blast of blue fire.

The stone pulsed, and the second it pierced the remnants of the shield, it rekindled, the blue flames running over the surface. The Hellhounds and Ghosts shrank back from the blue light.

"Done!" yelled Lyn as the magic of the portal dissipated. "Whatever you're doing, it seems to be working."

"Great, now if only I knew what the hell I'm doing!" said Laila. She stared at the blue shield bewildered.

"Okay, hold on, I'm setting up a banishing spell."

The Witch fished around in her bag. She removed a ceramic dish and a bundle of dried sage. She lit the sage with the blue flame of their shield, and the leaves started to produce a fragrant smoke. She placed it in the bowl and covered it with a lid. Lyn muttered something under her breath, and when she lifted the lid, shimmering green smoke erupted into the room like an explosion, coiling around the Ghosts and Hellhounds. They cried out and vanished as the smoke cleared.

Lyn and Laila stood there panting for a moment, but the manifested Ghosts had disappeared. Lyn searched the room with her shard of glass, checking for any Ghosts in their transparent state, but all Ghosts and the Hellhounds were gone.

"Okay," said Lyn, "that was intense."

Laila nodded. "We should check the front room to make sure we didn't miss anything."

Cautiously they entered the other room, but when Lyn checked, she couldn't find any sign of the Ghosts or Hellhounds.

"Wow, that blue fire you were using was intense. I think it amplified my spell somehow. Normally the banishing doesn't work that quickly."

"It has something to do with the dagger." She held up the blade, which had ceased its glowing. "I definitely left it at home. It just shows up on its own." She didn't include the fact that the blue magic seemed to sleep dormant within her the rest of the time.

"Okay, that's pretty cool though." Lyn led the way back into the front room. "If I could make an enchantment like that, I'd be rich! No more lost phones, or car keys, I—"

There was a blur of movement, and something landed in front of them with a thud. It was a person, more specifically a Vampire. Another one appeared next to him. Both were dressed in black with ski masks, which obscured their facial features.

The first one grabbed Lyn. He wrenched her head back, making her cry out in pain.

"No survivors, he told us." He grinned, revealing his razor sharp canines.

CHAPTER 14

Laila was there in an instant, her dagger lodged into the chest of his companion. Not deep enough to pierce his heart and kill him, but close enough to make him freeze.

"One jerk and I turn him to ashes." She grabbed him by the collar of his shirt. "Let her go."

The Vampire holding Lyn didn't move.

"What are you doing here?" she demanded.

"Cleaning up," he replied, his voice raspy.

"Who sent you?"

"The Demon Marius." He gave her a toothy grin. "He's offering a bounty for your head."

He brought his fangs down on Lyn's throat, but when he was an inch away, there was a loud crackling sound. Magical sparks shot from an invisible barrier along Lyn's skin into his face. He lost his grip on Lyn—who seemed to expect the magical diversion. She spun around and pulled something out of her pocket. It was a jeweled knife.

"You're under arrest," said Laila, as she cuffed the first man.

"Just try," spat the Vampire.

He kicked, shoving the dagger deep into the chest of his companion who screamed as his body erupted in flame. The Vampire became charred like coals, and crumbled to the floor, leaving nothing but a pile of ash behind.

"No!" Laila grabbed for the remaining Vampire, but he was too quick. He shoved past the two of them. He hurdled through a window, shattering the glass, and vanished into the night.

"Ugh!" Laila groaned, looking at the pile of ashes in front of her.

From the center of the pile, she retrieved her dagger and wiped it off on her jeans. She realized that the sheath was at home and she had nothing to carry it in, so she kept it out and at the ready.

"Are you alright?" she asked the Witch.

"Yeah, my neck's a bit burnt, but nothing bad."

"Can I take a look?"

Lyn shrugged and turned around. Laila gently laid her hand on the Witch's neck and worked a small healing spell.

"Better?" she asked.

"Much better, thanks." Lyn gingerly felt her neck as she eyed their surroundings. "So now what? Do we follow the Vampire?"

Laila crouched down next to the pile of ash and sifted through it with a piece of broken glass. "He's long gone. Hopefully, that is the last of the surprises for the evening. Darien and Jerrik should be here soon, and we can call for an investigative team. That's about it for now."

Speaking of which, Laila got out her phone and placed a call. The investigative team would be on their way soon.

Lyn sank into a chair, ignoring the layer of dust that had accumulated on the furniture.

"Well, I'm glad you came, I'd hate to think of what would've happened if I'd come here alone. I'd be dog food."

Laila glanced from the ash to the portal in the other room. "Something similar happened last night. These Demons are pretty persistent." Out of morbid curiosity, she wondered how high her bounty was.

A thought occurred to Laila that made her stomach churn. What if Lyn had been targeted because of her involvement with Laila and the IRSA team?

Since Erin's abduction, Laila couldn't help but think that Erin had been targeted because of her relationship to the team as well. Now someone calls Lyn and tries to lure her into this trap? The Witch might not have made too many enemies over the last few years, but the IRSA team certainly had.

"I know what you're thinking Laila," said Lyn, pulling her from her thoughts, "don't you dare blame yourself for this."

"I—"

"Don't." Lyn's expression grew serious. "I like helping you guys, and I can take care of myself. Don't beat yourself up over this."

Laila groaned as she stood. "How can this week get any worse?"

"Don't tempt fate," warned Lyn, "and what happened? You seemed fine the other night."

"It's nothing, there's just a lot going on in this city right now. Between these bizarre creatures on the loose, people getting attacked, and the protestors…" Laila trailed off shaking her head. Unfortunately, she had a feeling that things weren't about to get any better anytime soon.

"Hey," said Lyn, "At least the portal's been dealt with, and tensions will calm in the city, they always do."

"What was—?" Laila indicated Lyn's neck and the sparks that had erupted from nowhere.

"Ah, a protection spell," she said with a wink. "They're a pain in the ass to make, but definitely worth it!"

Laila thought she might have to invest in one of those. A line of defense that could deploy automatically, without the use of magic, could be extremely valuable in future encounters, especially if she was taken by surprise again.

Outside they heard a car pull up, and Laila bristled, preparing for another attack. There was rattling, and the sound of sliding metal. Seconds later Jerrik and Darien rushed through the door, and she relaxed.

"What's going on?" asked Darien as he looked around.

"It *was* a trap," said Laila. "The Demons opened a black magic portal—"

"A Necromancer's portal," corrected Lyn.

Jerrik and Darien exchanged glances while Laila continued.

"And they left it open for Ghosts and other things to crawl through."

"Then we were jumped by a couple of Vampires." Lyn nodded at the pile of ash in front of them.

Jerrik shook his head. "So, you're telling me that the Demons found themselves a Necromancer?"

"Maybe? But this portal was old." Lyn glanced towards the other room. "It was probably opened by the same Witch that conducted the other summoning rituals for the Demons."

"But that Witch was killed in the fight to rescue Erin, and this portal wasn't on that enchanted map you made." Darien frowned as he noticed the pile of ash by Laila's feet.

"I didn't enchant it to look for Necromancy, only black magic," explained the Witch, "my spell was pretty specific, it wouldn't have identified it. I might have to enchant another map to search for Necromancy now."

"That could explain why the location in Malibu was missing as well," mused Jerrik, disturbed.

Laila nodded in agreement as she waved them through the archway and indicated the circle.

"It's the same as the others," observed Darien.

"Almost," Lyn crouched down to examine the runes. "These are slightly different, and it also looks like he smudged some of the runes. That's why the portal didn't close."

"Looks like they used a Vampire as a sacrifice." Darien motioned towards a pile in the center of the circle. It was hard to be certain, given the amount of dust in the room, but it did indeed look like ash.

"That would make sense," said Lyn thoughtfully, "the death of the undead being a catalyst to open a gate to the world of the dead."

Laila noticed that Jerrik was standing back. He was leaning against the arch with his eyes shut.

"You've been awful quiet," she pointed out, "not enough sleep?"

Jerrik opened his eyes and gave her a grim look. "Demons were here. Definitely more than one."

Laila closed her eyes and reached out into the room. Sensing for energy wasn't like smelling for a scent, you had to actively sort through the magic in the space. Dark, vile magic drifted through the room like smoke. It clung to the space and to anyone who was exposed for too long.

With the overpowering amount of Ghostly energy in the room, she hadn't been able to sense the Demonic energy. Considering that the Demons had opened the other portals, it seemed obvious that there would be some amount of Demonic energy here as well. But this was different, far stronger than she'd felt before.

Jerrik shook his head. "I haven't felt anything this strong since…" he trailed off.

Laila knew exactly what he meant, and she was thinking the same thing.

"A Greater Demon was here," she explained for the sake of the others, "this energy is the same as Marius's."

She looked at Jerrik and could see it in his eyes, all the pain and suffering they had gone through. The things they'd been forced to do while onlookers gawked and cheered. Fear gripped her, but also excitement at the evidence of a Greater Demon in the city. They were close, but there was no telling where the Greater Demon was now.

As Lyn explained in more detail how the portal had worked, and the investigative team arrived to help with the crime scene,

Laila realized that Jerrik had wandered off. She went searching for him and found him sitting on the curb outside, his elbows resting on his knees as he stared at the asphalt in front of him. She considered leaving him to his thoughts in private, but something in her heart told her to stay.

"What are you thinking about?" she asked, sitting beside him.

"What a sick son of a bitch Marius is."

He didn't so much as look at her, but she could see the tension in his body. The same dread and anxiety that gripped her as well. But there was also anger, fear, and remorse. After another moment she spoke again.

"The nightmares keep you awake, don't they?"

He nodded. "When I close my eyes at night, I see their faces. All the men I killed in that Gods forsaken arena."

Laila grabbed his hand and squeezed it. "All night long I have nightmares that the Demons are chasing me, or that I'm surrounded by the graves of the people I love as Marius laughs."

"I dream that I'm back in that arena with you lying unconscious before me, and he's ordering me to kill you. Sometimes I resist, but Marius slits your throat while they force me to watch. Other times my body obeys him even as I try to stop myself." He looked up at her and Laila saw the devastation in his eyes. Devastation at the thought of losing her.

That confession was too much for her, she wasn't ready to hear this. Not from him, and not now. They had endured horrible things, which brought them together, but that had been an extremely emotionally charged time. She couldn't deny that there was a bond between them because of this, but this revelation was more than she could handle.

Jerrik must have seen her bristle because he quickly released her hand. "I'm sorry, I didn't mean to make you uncomfortable."

Laila quickly stood, but seeing him sitting there as damaged as she was, if not more, made her pause.

"We *will* find him, and he *will* be punished," she uttered in little more than a whisper.

He glanced up at her, but she was already gone, stepping through the door of the building to join the investigative team.

CHAPTER 15

The waves rolled lazily along Venice Beach. Laila watched the people walking back and forth along the beach, enjoying the sunset. It had been a beautiful, clear day, but Laila hardly noticed.

She had been out late with the investigative team collecting evidence. She had hoped the extra work might help her sleep, but unfortunately, her nightmares were worse than ever. She slipped from one cruel dream to the next, plagued by Marius and the other Demons. She wondered if Jerrik fared any better.

Around noon she gave up on any notion of sleep and drove over to serve as Lyn's security detail for the afternoon. The Witch insisted she didn't need a guard, but Laila and Darien had both determined it was necessary the night before, worried that the Demons would try to target Lyn again. So, for most of the afternoon, she sat in the back of Lyn's shop. They closed up early—around five—and retreated upstairs, where they sat now.

"Here we go," said Lyn as she held up a charm. "This should help. It's one of the strongest sleep charms I've seen. It should work better than the last one at least."

"Thanks."

She accepted the charm which was a round wooden disk with symbols carved into it. There was a piece of leather cord looped through a hole so she could hang it from one of her bedposts. She was tempted to go home and try it out immediately, but the day was far from over—she still had a Vampire party to attend.

"You should've asked me earlier," pointed out Lyn as she took in the circles under Laila's eyes.

"Probably," admitted Laila, "I just thought the dreams would go away like they did before."

Laila felt like something was missing. Or maybe she was just too stressed out. Perhaps all she needed was a message and a vacation. Something shifted under her skin—it was the blue magic. She still didn't understand why it worked in some situations and not others, but even when it was dormant, she could still feel it as she did now. It occurred to her that maybe this strange magic was affecting her in other ways like draining her energy or causing insomnia? Perhaps she should speak to Arduinna about it later.

"More tea?" asked Lyn as she packed up her carving tools.

"No thanks, I should be going anyway. I have to get ready for that event."

"Right! With Darien's sire. That should be interesting."

"Although both Frej and Jerrik will be there."

Lyn shrugged. "I guess it won't hurt to have extra backup. How do you think they will do in the van together?"

"I honestly don't know. I think they'll be fine, if a little moody about getting left in the van. I mean Darien and that Tech Wiz guy, Donald, will be there too. It's not like they'll be alone."

"Hey! They'll be supervised!"

Laila rolled her eyes. "I mean they don't seem to like each other, but I feel like something happened between the two of them. Frej won't talk about it though."

"Well, there's not much you can do to work through things if he's not willing to talk. Do you think it will be a problem tonight though?"

"It shouldn't be. They make little jabs at each other like a couple of obnoxious schoolboys, but Frej has more dignity than to lose his temper during an investigation." At least she hoped.

They exchanged goodbyes before Laila stepped out onto the street and headed to her car. Lyn's security detail sat in a car parked on the corner of the street. They nodded to Laila as she passed.

She headed home, stopping at a coffee shop to grab a couple of drinks on the way. The house was empty, and there was a note from Frej on the counter saying he'd left for the office to help Dairen prepare for the evening. Somewhere down the hall, Laila could hear Erin in her bedroom playing video games and chatting with people on her headset. There was no sign of Ali, but her car was still in the garage. So Laila carried the drinks up to the third floor, to Ali's room, and knocked on her door.

"I come bearing gifts" Laila called through the door.

After a moment, it opened, revealing Ali with a frown.

"Well, a gift," explained Laila as she passed her one of the drinks. "A large, blended iced, triple shot, pumpkin latte."

Ali accepted the drink and sipped hesitantly, waiting for Laila to continue.

Laila leaned against the door frame. "I also wanted to apologize for the other night. I shouldn't have gotten upset with you. You're my best friend, and you're the one that's always got my back. I'm tired and upset, and I shouldn't take that out on you. I'm sorry."

"And?" said Ali expectantly.

"And I'm sorry I got upset about that agent from the Inspector General's office. If you called him to deal with Colin,

I know you did it for the sake of our team. I know he doesn't deserve to have me defend him, not after the crap he's pulled."

Ali seemed to take her time mulling over what Laila had said. Laila had the feeling the Fae was tormenting her just a little. She might have been annoyed if it weren't for the spark of amusement in Ali's eyes, that she was trying so hard to cover. It was something she'd seen Ali do countless times while giving her sister a hard time.

Ali gave her a calculating look. "Apology accepted on one condition. I get to pick your dress for the party tonight." A smile spread across her face.

"Deal," said Laila relieved, "but can you help me with the hair too? I have no idea what I'm going to do with it."

Ali followed Laila down to her room below.

The Fae started sorting through dresses. "So I talked to Mato about the other night, when they took Frej out. He said Jerrik showed up at the bar and had a conversation with Frej before leaving."

"So whatever Jerrik said to him must've sparked this new source of conflict between them. But did Mato say what they discussed?" Laila was already in the bathroom, applying make-up.

"Not a clue, he and Henrik left to go get drinks, and Jerrik was gone by the time they returned. Frej hardly spoke the rest of the evening."

Well, at least this confirmed her suspicion that something had happened and that she wasn't misreading things.

Ali appeared in the mirror behind her, holding up a dark blue and black dress. It was a high collared, dark blue sheath, with a hem that flared out around the bottom. The back was open and would reveal her skin and scars beneath, matching the scars wrapping around her arms. There was black silk embroidery around the waist in a floral lace pattern. It was one of the dresses Frej had bought for her back in the Dragon Kingdom.

"This is it!" declared Ali triumphantly. "I found black satin pumps to go with it too."

There was nothing Ali loved more than the chance to dress up and go out. She spent the next thirty minutes curling, pining, and spritzing Laila's hair into place as she sipped on her sugary coffee drink. While Ali worked, Laila told her about the drawing she'd discovered on Donald's workbench. Ali just laughed it off.

Things felt like normal between them again, and Laila was beyond relieved.

"How are things going with Mato?" Laila asked after a moment. "You're not the kind to keep your partners secret. Is it because Frej's living with us?"

Ali was silent for a long time, lost in thought. A shadow fell over her expression and Laila worried that she'd crossed a line, but when she started to voice her apology, Ali waved it off dismissively.

"I'm actually not sure, I haven't really thought about it. He's the first man I've been with since Carlos died, and sometimes it's hard."

Ali set the curling iron down and leaned against the counter. Her shoulders sloped with the weight of Carlos's death.

"I broke down crying the last time I stopped by his place. I couldn't help it, I just suddenly had this picture in my head of Mato bleeding out in the street." She looked up at Laila, her violet eyes brimming with tears. "He's such a great guy. I could actually see us being something more than friends with benefits. I might even want that, to actually have a relationship. But…"

She shook her head as a tear escaped the corner of her eye, and she took a rattling breath. Laila stood and pulled her into a hug. She didn't say anything, she didn't need to, all Ali needed was to know that she was not alone. It broke Laila's heart to see her friend so tormented.

Finally, Laila spoke, "Mato's a survivor. He made it out of

the fight rings. He's stronger than you give him credit for."

There was silence for a moment.

"You're right, and I should give him the chance to decide for himself. I shouldn't try to make that choice for him." Ali stepped back and wiped the tears from her face.

Laila passed her a couple of tissues. "We'll get through this—through the Demons and everything else."

"For better or worse, we're in this together," chuckled Ali through the tears. "Okay, now get your butt back in that chair so I can finish your hair."

The rest of their conversation was playful and light. They'd both had enough sadness, blame, and guilt for one day. Twenty minutes later Ali unplugged the curling iron and stepped back.

"There!" announced Ali, with a final spritz of hairspray. "Now you're ready to take on a posh Vampire ball!"

Laila examined her appearance in the mirror. She did look amazing.

"Thank you!" Laila pulled Ali into a hug. "I would never have looked this good without you."

Ali smiled. "Well, I've got to run. I'm late. But make sure someone snaps some photos of you and the sexy Vampire dude." She headed for the door.

"I'm there to hunt for leads, not for prom," Laila called after her.

"I still want pictures!" Ali shouted from the hall.

Laila laughed and shook her head. As she checked her appearance in the mirror one last time, her attention was drawn to the dagger resting on the dresser. She sighed, she might as well bring it. She strapped the knife to her thigh under the fabric of the dress before grabbing her purse and heading out the door.

"Whoa!" exclaimed Erin, nearly dropping the slice of pizza she was eating as Laila reached the kitchen, "where are you going?"

"Oh, just this party for work."

The Dragon wore her white judo gi, and her duffle bag rested beside her.

"Is Ali going with you?" She finished the slice of pizza and stuck a couple of granola bars into the bag.

Laila shook her head. "She's got her own case she's working on."

"What's up with you two?" Erin glanced up at her.

"Nothing, we made up."

Erin gave her a relieved look. "Thank the Goddess! You'd think a Troll sat on her favorite handbag the way she's been sulking around the house."

Erin put a big clownish scowl on her face as she stomped around the kitchen making grumbling sounds. Laila chuckled as she headed out the door.

When the elevator opened on Talen's floor, she was greeted by a pair of stoic Vampire guards. They nodded to her as she approached and knocked on the door. It swung open, but it wasn't one of the guards, or Talen that answered, but Jerrik.

"Wow!" His jaw dropped. "You look amazing."

His eyes took in every detail of the dress. She awkwardly thanked him and gave him a half-smile as she walked into the room. Frej was there as well, glaring at Jerrik.

"You look beautiful, as always," Frej bowed, kissing her hand. The model of a gentleman.

Jerrik rolled his eyes and shot Frej an expectant look. She wanted to question both of them now, to figure out what was going on between them. They weren't the only ones in the room though. Darien and Donald rummaged through the cases that held their audio equipment.

"You know," began Donald, "Laila sort of reminds me of this one character from this movie I really like where—"

"Ok, we get it," said Darien cutting off the Tech Wiz, "it

is—in fact—possible for Laila to dress up and be feminine, but this equipment won't set itself up."

"You're just jealous you're not going with me." Laila gave him a wicked look. Darien just scoffed. He didn't even look at her. It dawned on her that he may actually be upset that he was the one stuck in the van, instead of in the middle of the action.

Aside from their equipment, the apartment was as immaculate as it was before. Laila had no idea how it was possible for Talen to have such a sterile living space. The colors were a little too dramatic and harsh for her taste, but from the little time she'd known Talen, they seemed to fit him perfectly.

It occurred to her that she hadn't seen the Vampire yet. He must be in the back preparing for the evening. Darien caught her looking around.

"Talen had to run out and deal with an issue. He should be back soon, then we can get this show on the road."

He passed her a tiny, in-ear monitor from one of the boxes. It was practically undetectable once it was in her ear.

"Are these new?" she asked, looking at it in the mirror.

"Yup!" Donald beamed. "I just finished them last week. They are charmed to prevent detection and to boost the signal. They have a better range and sound quality too, with a built-in mic."

"Interesting," said Laila, as she double-checked her appearance.

"What happened with the robbery?" asked Laila as she realized there hadn't been time for that the night before.

Darien waved off the question. "Don't worry about it, LAPD has it under control, nothing Supernatural about it. All you need to focus on is the task ahead."

The door opened behind her.

"So sorry about the delay," called Talen as he entered the penthouse flanked by two more guards.

He nodded to the men but stopped in front of Laila giving her the slightest of bows, his eyes drank in her appearance.

"My darling, you look absolutely ravishing!" He walked around her in a slow circle. "Oh yes, I would say you look good enough to eat. This will definitely do."

Both Frej and Jerrik stiffened. It didn't escape Talen's notice, and Laila caught the slightest flicker of a smirk before he turned his attention to Darien.

"So, what's the plan?"

Darien pulled up a map on his tablet and motioned for the others to join him. Both Jerrik and Frej managed to find a way to plant themselves between her and Talen. Laila resisted the urge to roll her eyes.

"Okay, the venue is here." Darien indicated the outline of a building on the map. "The surveillance van will be parked here, down one of the side streets where we can still see the main entrance. Jerrik was observing them earlier today as the setup was going on."

"They have a lot of security," explained Jerrik. "It shouldn't be a problem unless something happens between you and the host."

Talen waved a hand dismissively. "I've known Richard for centuries. Literally. His business dealings may be less than moral at times, but he's never been hostile towards me."

"It seems straightforward enough." Laila folded her arms. "We go in, converse with some Vampires, hopefully learn something useful, and get out."

The risk seemed minimal, so long as Talen wasn't hiding something from them. But Darien trusted him, and that was enough for Laila.

Talen looked skeptically at the map, "I honestly think the surveillance van is unnecessary, my guards will be nearby in the limousine, and we can report anything we hear."

"Back up never hurts," said Jerrik crossing his arms, "besides, this way we'll be able to monitor the conversations you have with the other guests."

Laila had a feeling that included any conversation between

herself and Talen as well, but she kept that thought to herself.

"Well then, we should get going," she announced, turning towards the door.

Talen adjusted his tuxedo. "I'll have my driver bring the limousine around. Is there anything I can get you while we wait?" he asked Laila.

"Bottled water would be great!" Jerrik clapped him on the back as he carried a case to the door.

"Laila," started Frej, pulling her aside, "I still don't think this is a good idea. I have this feeling—"

"We've been over this Frej." She gave him an unwavering look. "I know you hate being stuck in the van with Jerrik."

"It's not just him." He glanced over his shoulder at Jerrik and Talen.

"Really?" Laila rolled her eyes. Jerrik was one thing, but Talen?

"His eyes have been roving all over you. How am I supposed to be okay with that?"

Laila shook her head. "Talen may be a shameless flirt, but he's no threat. Trust me."

"If something goes wrong, I *will* come in there after you." He squeezed her hand, his expression dark.

She struggled with the emotions churning within her, writhing like a pile of snakes in the pit of her stomach. Now may not be a good time, but she couldn't help it, not when it seemed that there was still some sort of conflict between Jerrik and Frej. She hated to think that they were keeping her in the dark.

"Look, I know something happened between you and Jerrik when he showed up at the bar while you were out with Henrik and Mato. I don't know what happened, but I wish you would just tell me."

Frej opened and closed his mouth, searching for the words. "It's nothing, I just told him to leave you alone and he got upset and left."

Maybe she would have believed him if he hadn't turned

away so quickly, or if he'd been able to look her in the eye when he said it.

Talen appeared at her side as a pair of guards helped the men load the equipment into the packed elevator. She and Talen would have to wait for the next one.

"Don't worry gentlemen," he crooned, "I'll keep both eyes on Laila."

He gave them a devilish look. Jerrik's eyes burned while a slight rumbling noise escaped Frej's throat as the doors slid shut.

Talen cracked up and dropped his playboy act. "Are they always like that? So protective?"

Laila shot him an exasperated look. "You have got to be kidding me!"

"How could I resist! I mean, did you see their faces?" He looked all too self-satisfied.

"So, I thought the Dark Elf was your lover? I didn't know Elves were polyamorous."

Thank the Gods the others hadn't switched on their coms yet.

"I'm not—not that it's any of your business." Laila blushed. "Frej is my suitor."

"The Dragon," he said thoughtfully. "Then where does the Dark Elf fall in the equation?"

"It's complicated."

Talen laughed. "Isn't it always?" He looked her up and down as if the answer would appear scrawled across her skin. "I imagine he was your ex-lover."

"Something like that," muttered Laila stiffly.

"What happened?"

"He left."

"And now he's back," added the Vampire, amusement dancing in his blood-red eyes.

"And I am with Frej."

"You could be with both though." He gave her an amused look as he hit the call button for the elevator.

Laila choked. "What?"

"Just food for thought." He gave her an innocent look. "I find it is best to savor the pleasurable things in life. There's more than enough pain and suffering to go around, but pleasure? Well, that's something we could all use a little more of."

Laila shook her head and turned away from the Vampire to check her phone.

"It's a pity, I can see the Dark Elf still cares about you," said the Vampire behind her.

"We're finished talking about this." She didn't want to talk about Jerrik and the way he constantly watched her, yearning for that chance to explain himself. Why should she divulge the fact that she couldn't look him in the eye without blushing?

She'd been thinking a lot about what Jerrik had revealed to her, about those dreams where he had been forced to watch her die. It had been overwhelming, even a bit creepy in a way. But then she realized that similar occurrences happened in her nightmares as well, visions of Jerrik being shot by the Demons while she stood by unable to save him. He had been her ally through an incredibly dark time, so perhaps to each other, they merely represented that hope, desperation, and triumph over the Demons, and the fear that it could be ripped from them again if they couldn't stop the Demons from hurting the people around them.

Talen cleared his throat. "Well, if you ever need someone to talk to, you are welcome at my penthouse any time."

Through the mirror, she saw his expression. It wasn't lecherous, or condescending. If anything it was sympathetic, almost as though he could read her thoughts.

What kind of an invitation was *that*? Despite his interest in the club, he hadn't really made any advances. Perhaps he was genuinely concerned? But why? She barely knew him.

Following Talen, she left the penthouse and headed down to the limousine.

CHAPTER 16

"Everyone in place?" asked Laila, testing out the new coms.

"Yes, and we can hear you loud and clear," said Donald triumphantly in her ear.

"Good, we're approaching the party."

The limousine pulled up in front of a building with a large set of concrete steps and a red carpet leading to the doorway. It was flanked on either side by a row of lanterns and security guards. It was more than unusual to find a formal gathering such as this in the middle of the Old City, but Talen explained that Richard's party theme was inspired by the glamor of old Hollywood. Given the party's location, it was no wonder that there was so much security. The Vampire guards in black suits stationed on the staircase were watching their every move as Talen stepped out of the limousine and helped her out of the vehicle. She accepted the arm he offered and ascended the staircase to the doors above.

Despite the location, the building was the very picture of opulence. Crystal chandeliers hung from the ceiling, and velvet curtains framed the windows. The floor was made of polished marble and priceless antique furniture upholstered with gold silk that had been arranged to create seating areas. Artifacts from different bygone eras bedecked the space, the wealth of their host on display for all to see. There was also a hint of elegant Halloween flair with skulls accenting ornate floral arrangements and other decorative centerpieces that included bats and bones. At least she hoped the skulls were for Halloween and not just a macabre statement.

The building might have once served as a hotel. The main room had a variety of hallways branching off to different parts of the building, and it was several stories tall. There was a large, sweeping staircase on the far end of the room leading off to a corridor beyond.

"Don't tell me he renovated this place just for a party," she muttered to Talen.

"No," he laughed, "This is also one of the properties he operates his various… *businesses* out of."

Laila eyed an ancient Greek vase in a display case as they passed. It was probably worth more than she earned in a year, and IRSA paid their agents well.

"What exactly does this guy do for a living?" she asked skeptically.

"I'm not sure you want to know," he replied with a wink, "let's just say he's a trader of rare items."

So, Richard was a smuggler. That made sense given the number of priceless antiques that were probably better off in museums. She wondered how illegal his activities were, and remembered that Darien knew this Richard well enough to be banned from such events.

"Should I know why Darien is not welcome here?"

He shrugged. "Darien tried to take down his business in the early days of the Inter-Realm Security Agency. That's why I'll be introducing you as a lover I met in my club."

A choking noise came from her earpiece. Laila couldn't tell whether it was Frej or Jerrik and Talen didn't suppress the grin that spread across his face.

Glancing around, Laila noticed that she was not the only living member of the crowd. There were a number of humans thrown into the mix, maybe twenty or so mingling in the crowd. There were about a dozen humans congregating to the right side of the chamber that seemed to be set apart from the rest of the crowd. The gorgeous humans, both male and female, waited by the entrance to one of the hallways.

"Are those the appetizers?" Laila nodded toward the hall.

"Sure," said Talen nonchalantly, "they're for those who prefer fresh blood. I do suspect they serve a variety of purposes though." He winked and gave her a mischievous grin.

"Lovely." Laila rolled her eyes.

"Would you like something to drink?" he asked innocently.

"No thank you."

Talen laughed and guided her down one of the walkways through the tables. He paused from time to time to talk to the other guests, asking them how they've been and how business was. The Vampires watched her with hungry eyes, she could tell they were enticed by the scent of her Elven blood. But as soon as he introduced her as his lover, the others immediately backed off.

From the way the Vampires acted in Talen's presence, she had a feeling he was a man of importance within this community. He was easygoing, but something about his position clearly demanded respect. Perhaps it was his age, or maybe there were other factors, she couldn't say. She'd have to ask Darien about it later.

"Well, well, well," said a woman behind them. "You actually found her, or have you been hiding her all this time to spite me, you selfish bastard?"

Laila turned to find herself face to face with a female Vampire. Fighting back a blush, Laila realized this was the other Vampire from the encounter at Talen's club. She was dressed in a red silk dress that clung to every slight curve of her willowy figure. From the amount of skin that was revealed by the plunging V of the neckline, Laila had the impression that the woman wore nothing but her own skin under the thin layer of silk. It left nothing to the imagination, and the gaze of several men and women alike followed the Vampire with interest.

"Anita!" Talen flashed her a charming smile. "How've you been?"

Anita gave him a look of disdain. "Don't pretend you're happy to see me. I know you better than that." She turned to Laila. "A bit of advice, unless you like sharing your men, I'd walk away now."

"Come now," drawled Talen rolling his eyes, "I invited you to join us."

"*After* I walked in on you!" she hissed. "Seriously, you're about as faithful as a stray mutt."

She turned and stalked away through the crowd, her heels clacking loudly on the marble as she went.

"An ex?" Laila raised an eyebrow.

"Yes…. It's complicated."

It was the first time she'd seen him uncomfortable, fitting payback for his prying questions earlier.

"Will this affect our mission?" she asked amused.

"No." He shook his head. "Anita's presence is an inconvenience, not a complication."

"Talen," said Darien in the coms, "have you spotted Richard yet?"

"Patience Darien," he purred, "all in good time."

A security guard was about to pass them, but Talen stopped him.

"Excuse me, but has our host made an appearance yet?" he asked the guard.

"He will be joining the crowd as soon as he finishes a private meeting," the guard abruptly replied before returning to whatever errand he was on.

After doing a quick glance around the room, Laila felt her

skin crawl. There were far too many people watching them.

"What's with the looks?" she asked Talen.

"It could be that they're gossiping," whispered Talen. "Then again, walking around with you on my arm is akin to carrying a lobster dinner through a hungry crowd. They'd love to dig in, but it would be incredibly foolish."

"Lovely comparison."

He winked.

Laila smirked and decided that she enjoyed his company. He had a dignified, but snarky sense of humor. While he was serious about the mission, he was quick to laugh and find the humor in a situation.

"Don't forget the reason you are there is to speak to Richard," Jerrik's voice was stiff.

"Gee, thanks," whispered Laila sarcastically, "I'd completely forgotten."

"What's wrong?" Talen shot her an amused look. "You boys getting cramped in there?"

"Something like that," huffed Darien. Laila imagined him glaring at the others.

They stopped in a seating alcove that allowed for easy conversation as well as a vantage point to watch the room from. The crowd fell silent as a man approached the center of the room.

"That's Richard," murmured Talen next to her.

Richard was a short and plump man dressed in all the finery she would expect the host of such a lavish party to wear. A variety of rings glittered on his fingers, and it was hard to tell from this distance, but she had the feeling that the large glittering stones on his cufflinks were diamonds. His hair was slicked back, and Laila was reminded of a movie she'd seen about gangsters in the 1920's. He carried a gold goblet, and given the artifacts lying about, she wouldn't have been surprised if it was the holy grail itself.

"Ladies and gentlemen," he said addressing the crowd, "I would like to take this opportunity to thank you for joining me in celebrating the unveiling of my latest project. In these times, where people are so focused on the here and now, I find it important to preserve history. If not for the benefit of the current generation of humans, then for their descendants. After all, we are the ones who have lived the history written in their textbooks.

"Five years ago, when civilization was struggling to reestablish itself, I saw an opportunity. For the first time in a millennium, we are now able to interact with humans openly and freely. Just imagine the ways in which we can tell them about the history of our world. Lost civilizations can be brought to life, forgotten languages remembered, the knowledge that we have collectively is a gift we can now share with the world.

"I am a lover of art and history. I always have been. But in recent years I have realized that the historical architecture of this city is no longer appreciated, but rather left to crumble and fade like an old memory. This is why I have decided to found the Night Angels Historical Society, a foundation of private citizens who care about the city's historic sites and buildings and devote their time and resources to the establishment of privately protected historical sites throughout the Old City.

"Tonight, I ask you to join me in this endeavor. Become a member and donate to the society. Help me bring the city through these dark ages and into the future!"

The crowd erupted into applause. Laila and Talen joined them.

"I was waiting for someone to do this," said Talen thoughtfully.

"What?"

"Claim a monopoly on the historic sites. The pretty speech is just for show, what he really intends to do is claim most of the city for his own and charge outrageous amounts of money to visit pre-Event sites and landmarks."

"He can do that?" Laila watched Richard skeptically.

"He can try," replied Talen with a shrug, "but eventually

other people will start to catch on."

"Like you?" She glanced at him sideways.

"Possibly." He examined his nails with a bored expression.

"Talen!" called Richard as he approached, "I heard you were looking for me earlier. I don't suppose you've reconsidered my offer for the Botticelli?"

Talen stood and accepted Richard's handshake with a smile.

"My old friend, you know I could never part with that painting. He gifted it to me personally."

The Vampire let out a dejected sighed. "Very well, if you change your mind—"

"You'll be the first one to hear about it." Talen gave him a charming smile.

Richard switched his attention to Laila examining her with all the interest of a cat eyeing a mouse.

"Well now, who is this enchanting Elf?"

"Forgive my lack of manners! Richard, this is Laila. Laila, this is our gracious host Richard."

Laila wasn't entirely sure what the protocol was. Did she curtsy? Or shake hands? She offered her hand, and he took it in his own. His skin was cold as ice, and when he lifted her hand to his lips, he lingered a moment too long.

"I've met a handful of Elves," he said, "but none so beautiful as you."

"Thank you." She pulled her hand away and forced a smile. "You are too kind."

His gaze drifted down to her throat, but he quickly returned his attention to Talen.

"Well then, if it's not the Botticelli, then what were you looking to discuss?"

"It's a delicate matter of great importance to our community." He glanced around at the other guests surrounding them. "I'd prefer to discuss it somewhere a little more private."

Richard's dark red eyes glittered with intrigue. He motioned for them to follow him up a staircase, and to the end of the hall that was decorated with elegant wallpaper. Carved statues from a variety of periods stood at intervals between antique wall sconces. Large windows occupied the other walls overlooking the street and protestors below. Halfway down the hall was a door with guards posted outside. They followed their host through the doors and into a large study decorated with a collection of old books. Blending into the shadow of the doorway lurked another pair of guards.

"Please take a seat." Richard indicated a set of chairs.

They seated themselves, and Richard motioned to one of the guards. Laila heard a click behind them as one of the guards locked the door. Laila couldn't help but feel a wave of unease at the sound.

The Vampire propped his feet on his desk. "So, what's really going on here?"

CHAPTER 17

"Straight to business as usual, I see." Talen leaned forward to examine a bobble on Richard's desk, taking his time as the other Vampire waited impatiently. Talen allowed the tension to grow for a minute before continuing, a silent power game between the two.

"Richard, we've got a problem on our hands. I need your help tracking down a Vampire in the city. I've made calls to all my underlings in Los Angeles, but they've heard nothing."

"What's the name?" asked Richard pulling a cigar from a box on his desk.

"We don't have one."

"A picture then?" He twirled the cigar between his fingers.

Talen shook his head. "I have nothing to go off of Richard. The only witnesses who got a good look are dead. They've gone rogue."

Richard paused for a moment, the cigar coming to a stop.

"Is he one of yours?" Talen's eyes flickered up towards the other Vampire.

Richard resumed rolling the cigar back and forth.

"I keep a tight leash on all those I've sired," he snapped. "I'm sure you realize that the odds of you finding this rouge Vampire are slim."

"You're right." Talen cocked his head to the side. "But if this rogue isn't stopped soon, we'll lose what little trust we've gained from the humans. I've been speaking to underlings in the Old City today, and there are rumors spreading of Vampires forcibly feeding on humans, even mugging them with blatant disregard for our laws."

Laila frowned, this was the first she'd heard of that. Was that what he'd been doing when she arrived at his penthouse? She listened as Talen continued.

"You know what will happen if word of this reaches the humans on the west side. These protests will turn into riots, and the persecution will begin." His grave eyes watched Richard intensely, searching for any reaction.

"I see that," said Richard indifferently, "But I don't know what you expect me to do about it."

Laila gave him a coy look as she leaned forward. "Ask around. Surely a man as well connected as you could easily find a rouge Vampire."

"What exactly is your role in all this?" Richard put the cigar back into its box and closed the lid with a snap. "And don't give me that lover bullshit. It might fool the others, but I'm no idiot."

He stood and, in a flash, was looming directly in front of her, but Laila didn't allow herself to be startled.

"Don't tell me you're another special agent. I'd hate to have to fillet a pretty thing like you alive." His expression turned to ice.

"Is that a threat?" she asked sweetly. She heard some sort of a commotion through her earpiece. At first, she thought it was a reaction to Richard's threat, but it seemed something else was going on in the van. She ignored it, focusing on the situation at hand.

Talen opened his mouth to speak, but Laila beat him to it.

"I'm the Private Investigator he hired," she said coolly.

"Hmm," he huffed, "then why haven't *you* found the rogue?"

"Because I just hired her," explained Talen giving Richard a dangerous look. "Now I'd like you to stop threatening my P.I. and take your seat."

Richard reluctantly returned to the other side of his desk, but he remained standing.

"Very well, I'll consider what you've said. But I doubt there is much I can do to help. I'll have my guards show you out."

Laila glanced at Talen, expecting him to protest. Instead, he stood, gave Richard a curt nod, then headed to the door. As she followed, Laila found Richard watching her like a hawk. The door shut behind them.

"Now what?" asked Laila quietly, feeling discontent at their abrupt dismissal.

Talen shook his head as they walked down the hall. "That didn't go nearly as well as I had hoped. I have the feeling he's involved or thinks he may be. He's usually not this prickly unless he's trying to cover his ass. I'll have to—"

He didn't have time to finish the thought.

"Get down!" shouted Jerrik in her ear.

The glass of the window they passed by shattered with the impact of a large piece of steel pipe, shards of glass blasting into the room. Laila pulled Talen to the ground and shielded him as a Molotov cocktail whizzed through the air, where he had stood moments before. It shattered against the wall setting the wallpaper ablaze.

"What the hell was that?" demanded Talen.

"Protests turned into a riot," said Jerrik, "they showed up about thirty minutes ago. Darien's calling it in now."

"Shit!" Laila saw the crowd outside. That must've been the commotion she'd heard over the coms. "We need to evacuate the building."

The door to Richard's office opened with a bang.

"What's going on!" shouted the Vampire.

"Looks like someone found out about the murders." Talen waved at the signs the protestors were holding. "Burn in Hell Murderers," and "Die Unholy Scum" seemed to be the general theme.

Richard ducked as a crowbar came sailing through a nearby window. His eyes were wide, with shock.

"Fine!" he howled. "I'll see what I can find! I'll call you."

He waved to his guards to follow and disappeared through a side door. The immediate danger seemed to have convinced him that the matter was serious. It was unfortunate that the conflict had to escalate this far for him to agree to help though.

"Come on." She snuffed out the flames along their path with a spell as she ran to the staircase, Talen behind her.

They raced down the hallway as another window shattered. She didn't stop to see what caused it.

Reaching the end of the hall, she peered down the stairs as the great hall erupted into chaos. Fires started in various locations as flaming debris smashed through windows. Vampires tried to flee from the front door, only to discover the guards had barricaded them in as they attempted to beat back the human mob out front. Some looked for alternate escape routes while others looked for cover.

"Everybody calm down!" roared Talen, his voice booming.

Silence fell as the panicked crowd turned.

"The sprinklers are not working," he continued, "I need you to find the nearest sources of water. Find hoses, form bucket brigades, do what you have to do to fight the fires. The guards will deal with the humans until the police arrive. In the meantime, we need to stay calm."

He rushed down the stairs in a blur and started barking orders. The wide-eyed Vampires rushed to obey.

"Jerrik, I need an update." She strained to hear the response over the noise.

"Darien went to help restrain the humans. Frej reluctantly agreed to help him. Donald is driving the van around the block to avoid the crowd. We've got your riot gear ready, but we have to find a way to get to you."

A frantic Vampire shoved her aside as he ran up the staircase. She stumbled into a broken display case, hissing as a thick piece of glass cut into her forearm. Three Vampires around her dropped what they were doing and looked her direction, their eyes wide.

"Oh shit!" She backed away as she started a healing spell. "Talen!"

More Vampires were following now, stalking her like a pack unable to resist the temptation of her blood. It appeared the combination of fear and adrenaline only worked to strengthen the bloodlust. Talen turned and swore.

"Up the stairs!" he shouted to her, grabbing the nearest Vampire. "Get out of here, now!"

She nodded and ran, taking two stairs at a time, but the Vampires were faster. Two of them stood blocking her path. Hiking up her skirt, she yanked her dagger from its sheath.

"Back off!" she snarled, threatening them with the dagger.

The Vampires hissed back at her, lost in the haze of their bloodlust. The need to feed was stronger than their fear of the humans. Their eyes shone, and their fangs were bared. The hunt was on.

She feinted right, then stepped left and brought her dagger across the throat of the first Vampire. It wouldn't kill him since he was a Vampire, but blood-loss should slow him down. Laila followed through and stabbed him in the eye. The Vampire hissed and stumbled back. *Disable, but don't kill,* the words echoed through her mind. As an IRSA agent, it was her duty to protect the people, human and SNP. It wasn't the Vampires' fault they had such strong instincts to feed. Luckily, Vampires were hard to kill and fast to heal. So long as she avoided the heart and didn't use fire, they'd recover within minutes.

The other lunged, but she tripped him and shoved him down the stairs into another Vampire approaching behind her.

They collided with a thud and tumbled backwards taking more of the Vampires with them. She didn't stick around. Instead, she sprinted up the final stairs and onto the landing above.

Two sets of hands grabbed her, and drug her backwards. Ramming her head back she bashed someone's face with the back of her skull. He snapped his jaws at her neck, and she could feel his fangs pierce her skin.

She threw up a shield spell forcing him and the others away, then called up her magic and brought crackling flames to life in the palm of her left hand. As she blasted the carpet between them—creating a barricade—the Vampires hesitated. Laila continued to coax the flames upwards, creating a wall of fire.

Most of the Vampires retreated, deterred by the possibility of instantaneous death. There were two that were bold enough to brave the flames. They shielded their skin with their coats and shot through the wall of fire as Laila sprinted down the hallway towards Richard's office. She moved as fast as possible given the pumps she wore, and she tried to heal the wounds on her arm and neck as she went.

"What's going on?" asked Jerrik in her ear.

"I'm bleeding," she panted, "I'm trying to find a back way out, but I've got two Vampires on my tail, and I'm on the second fl—"

Her dress caught on something, and she sprawled on the floor with a grunt. Rolling over she saw the two Vampires above. She blasted them in the face with ice, blinding them as she scrambled away.

Laila wondered at the stupidity of Vampires caught up in blood lust as the Vampires stumbled dangerously close to the burning wall. She reached out with her magic creating a barrier of air. She shoved it at them with all her might, and the two Vampires were thrown out the broken window and down on to the street below. She paused a moment as they climbed to their feet and fled into the night.

Laila coughed as the blaze in the hallway continued to grow, the smoke billowing past her, and toward the broken windows. A spell of wind created a pathway through the flames. When Laila reached another door, the one Richard had vanished through earlier, she ducked inside. After taking a moment to finish healing her arm and neck, Laila glanced at her surroundings.

"Laila! LAILA!" yelled Jerrik in her ear.

"Ugh, sorry, what?" She examined the room she'd entered.

"What's happening? The Vampires?"

"I took care of them." She conjured a ball of light. "I'm still looking for a way out."

The room was filled with crates and boxes piled high above her head. She must have found Richard's goods. It occurred to her that she could probably find a wide variety of stolen and illegal items in there, but now was not the time. She wove her way through the boxes, taking care not to trip over anything.

"I saw Richard run this way. There must be an exit somewhere."

She searched the room looking around the stacks. Finally, along the back wall, she found something. It was another doorway that led to a small hallway beyond.

In the hall, there was another door to the right that was labeled "Exit." She tried the handle, but the door was jammed shut. A spell unlocked it, but Richard must have barred the door behind him. She ran to the window and glanced down into the alley. There was a familiar van with the engine running.

She glanced from the door to the window. "Okay, I found the exit, but the door will take more energy than it's worth. I see you guys in the alley down below. I'm going to jump."

"Wait, what?" squawked Donald.

"Yep." Laila blasted the glass from the window frame.

She took a running leap through the now-empty window frame and landed on the roof of the van with a thud. There was a string of expletives from within as she slid over the edge of the van and dropped to the pavement below.

The door of the van opened revealing Jerrik, who breathed

a sigh of relief, and a very shaken Donald.

"Was it completely necessary to land on top of the van!?!" spluttered the Tech Wiz.

"I would've broken my shoes if I landed on the concrete like that," she managed to say with a straight face. "I might have left a dent on the roof though."

"Seriously?!? This is a new van. It is literally the first time we've used it!"

Jerrik rolled his eyes at the man.

"Here." The Dark Elf tossed her a bag.

She caught the duffle bag with her gear and zipped it open. Without hesitation, she slipped out of the dress in the alley. Donald spun around and hid in the driver's seat, blushing profusely while Jerrik's eyebrows shot up.

"Oh, don't act so surprised," she snapped, "It's nothing you haven't seen before. Hang this up please."

She passed him the gown, followed by the shoes, and pulled on her gear, wiping off any remaining blood from her injuries. In under a minute she was dressed and climbing into the van. Jerrik was already in their standard tactical gear with IRSA stamped across it in yellow, they needed all hands on-deck.

"Okay Donald, take us back to the angry mob." She slid the door of the van shut.

"What is this? I'm a Tech Wiz, not your chauffeur!"

"Do you want to fight instead?" asked Jerrik.

"Fine!" he snapped, "I'm driving."

He turned the van around and back onto the main street. A small band of masked humans were throwing explosives and shooting at the Vampire guards who were doing their best not to seriously harm the humans. A number of guards had already been killed though. Darien was lining up humans as fast as he could cuff them with zip ties while Frej helped him. It looked like he was casting some binding spell to keep the few under arrest from running away.

She and Jerrik climbed out of the van and joined the fray.

CHAPTER 18

"Where's our back up?" she called to Darien as she examined the chaos in front of the building.

"On their way."

He zip-tied another angry human's wrists who was screaming profanities and passed him off to Frej.

"There's a lot of Vampires trapped inside," she explained, as the Vampire guards struggled to keep the humans out. "We've got to contain this before we can evacuate them."

Darien shook his head in frustration. "We can't even get to them. I don't know where this group of humans came from. They're not our normal protestors either, this is definitely pre-meditated."

Something didn't seem right to Laila either, it looked like the humans had been gripped by some sort of frenzy. They pushed onward with little regard for their injuries like they had nothing to lose. Perhaps they were on some sort of drug? But that was a matter to consider later. At the moment, they had a burning building full of Vampires to rescue.

"Okay," said Laila, "If Jerrik and I can reach one of the

doors, we can create a shielded area for the Vampires outside the building. It would help if Frej joined us…"

Darien shook his head. "Not until LAPD arrives. If Frej leaves, the humans will find a way to escape."

"Okay, we'll manage."

It was a good thing she cleaned herself up after that wound. If there were any traces of blood remaining, her gear would cover it up. It should be enough to keep the Vampires from turning on her while trying to rescue them.

Laila called up a shield covering herself and Jerrik as they sprinted into the line of fire. Bullets ricocheted from her shield, but she kept on going. She allowed it to envelop the guards by the doors as she approached.

"We need to get everyone to safety," she shouted over the gunfire, "we'll evacuate as many as we can in one trip and come back for the rest."

They nodded.

She pounded on the door. When they didn't open it, Jerrik forced the door open with a spell. A crowd of Vampires was about to pounce on them, but as soon as they saw IRSA printed on their vests they paused.

"We're evacuating now," she called into the room still holding the spell for her shield in place. "Stay calm and enter the shield slowly. They won't harm you in here."

The Vampires took one look at the fire growing behind them and piled out of the building.

"Wait!" she yelled struggling to cover the wave of Vampires, "slow down!"

Jerrik reached out with his own magic reinforcing her shield as more Vampires shoved into the space. They stretched the shield as wide as they could, about large enough to encompass a tightly-crowded group of one hundred people. By some miracle they managed to keep the shield up, protecting them from the humans on one side and the fire on the other. The larger the shield, and the more damage it took from the attacking humans, the harder it was to maintain. Both she and Jerrik were sweating profusely from the effort.

Talen was the last one into the shield, he slipped into a space next to Laila.

"You okay?" he asked, concerned.

She managed a nod.

Sirens sounded, and red and blue light flashed in the distance. The attacking humans seemed to finally have had enough. They jumped back into several old pickup trucks and sped off into the night.

Even with the majority of the attackers gone, Laila didn't dare drop the shield, not until the police had arrived and secured that section of the street. If only she could access that blue magic as she had last night, but she had no idea how. She still had her dagger with her—now tucked inside her boot—but still, the blue magic wouldn't activate.

Finally, officers poured into the streets. The remaining protestors either fled or were arrested within a matter of minutes. She nodded to Jerrik, and they let the shield drop. Completely exhausted, she fell to her knees, and through the stampede of Vampires, she could see Jerrik was on the ground as well.

"Here we go," said a voice next to her as two sets of arms pulled her to her feet. It was Captain Anderson from the LAPD Gangs and Narcotics division and one of his other officers. Both were dressed in riot gear.

She gave him a grateful smile. "Thanks, I think I can manage from here."

The Vampires were now standing in the center of the street watching in horror as the building burned. That had been close. If it wasn't for the fact that they'd been here, who knows if the guards would have been able to save them. The humans had been prepared to launch an attack, that was for certain. Their weapons and remnants of crudely-made bombs littered the streets.

"Did you recognize the symbol on the trucks?" asked the

Captain.

Laila shook her head, she hadn't even had a chance to look. "Di Inferi."

"Of course," she threw her hands up, "because that's all we need right now!"

"Don't worry, I've got my officers on their tail. With any luck, we'll catch them."

Hopefully, she thought. It was as if every single criminal they'd been after for the last several months was resurfacing at once. They were spread too thin.

"There were a lot of casualties." She looked over her shoulder at the fire, "There were a lot more Vampires in there before…"

He nodded.

"It'll be hard to find the remains though," she continued, "they'll be mixed in with the rest of the ash."

The fire was so loud they had to shout to be heard, and the smoke burned her throat. The fire engines would have trouble putting the fire out in this part of the city where the fire hydrants hadn't been maintained. Not only would the building be destroyed, so would the priceless art within. But the loss of life was worse. She wished there was something more she could have done. Maybe she could have saved them with the help of the blue magic? But she had no idea how to reach it, let alone use it. Every time it happened, it had been on instinct. She couldn't rely on it though, not when she'd been unable to access it multiple times now.

"What were you doing here anyway?" asked Captain Anderson, "It sounded like you were inside."

"I was." She glanced at him. "I was investigating a lead."

"Good thing your team was here." He clapped her on the shoulder before leaving to deal with the humans.

The crowd of Vampires parted as Frej passed through them and approached her.

"Are you alright?" he asked, checking her over for injuries.

"Yeah, just exhausted. Jerrik and I are not going to be of much use to anyone for the rest of the night."

He pulled her into his bone-crushing embrace. "Gods Laila, when the attack started it took everything I had to follow Darien's orders and stay out here."

"It was a good thing you did, they needed you out here." She cupped his face in her hand.

A sound rumbled from within his chest like an exasperated growl.

"Come on," he said, "Let's get you home. You look like you're about to collapse."

"With what?" she asked. "All we have is the van. No, you should stay here and help Darien. Please? I feel bad leaving him alone to sort this out."

"Very well," he sighed reluctantly, "but promise me you'll take care of yourself."

She nodded. Even when he was pissed, it warmed her to know he was still trying to take care of her.

Glancing to the side, she saw Jerrik slumped on the steps a few yards away.

"I'm going to check on him." She slipped out of Frej's embrace.

He nodded and turned towards the spot where Darien and Captain Anderson were in discussion.

Jerrik seemed unharmed overall, but the exhaustion was clear.

"I know that look." She offered him a hand. "Come on, I'm going to find us a ride. We'll only be in the way if we're passed-out on the steps here."

He laughed. "Yeah, you're probably right."

Jerrik accepted her hand, and she helped him up.

An LAPD officer approached. "I'm supposed to give you two a lift back into the city."

"Thank you," they chorused in unison.

The officer led them to his squad car, and Jerrik motioned

for her to take the front seat. They drove through the Old City, which felt eerily quiet after the chaos they just survived. A short while later the officer pulled up in front of Ali's house.

"Thank you!" Laila said to the officer again, giving him a warm smile.

"No problem."

"Laila," began Jerrik from the back seat, "I…"

"Yes?" She waited.

He searched her face for a moment.

"I-I'll see you at the office tomorrow," he finished lamely.

She nodded and shut the door, watching the squad car drive off into the night, and wondering what Jerrik had been about to say.

CHAPTER 19

Laila was just walking through the front door when her phone rang. She looked at the screen and saw it was from Colin. She swiped to answer the call.

"Hello?"

"What the hell is going on!?!" came Colin's voice through the speaker, sounding none too pleased. "Darien told me you're gathering information undercover and the next thing I know you guys are all over the news!"

Laila cringed. "What are you talking about?"

She walked through the kitchen and opened the refrigerator to see what kind of leftovers they had.

Colin must've had her on speakerphone because she could hear more voices trying to get his attention or speak over him, including Ali.

"Turn on the news," explained Ali.

"Which station?"

"Any. Trust me, this is all they're talking about."

Laila found the remote for the TV on the coffee table and switched it on. The screen flashed to life with an image of her shielding Vampires from the attacking humans. The voice of a female news reporter chattered in the background.

"The cause of the fire remains unknown. It is unclear yet what was happening at the scene, but it appears that the agents pictured above were somehow barricading the Vampires within while concerned human pedestrians fought to free the trapped Vampires."

"This is ridiculous!" fumed Laila. "They have no idea what happened. And how in Thor's name did they get these pictures?"

Ali took a deep breath. "Okay, why don't you start at the beginning?"

"Let me know when you're ready." Laila sank onto a sofa.

She briefed them on what had happened and how she was following a lead at the party when the attack occurred— although she left out any mention of Demonic involvement in the case. Laila explained how she had escaped from the other side of the building and came back around to help evacuate the Vampires into the shield to protect them from the humans.

"I can't tell what sparked the attack," added Laila, "but we suspect Di Inferi was involved."

"It was probably the homicide," suggested Colin.

"Yeah, there was another homicide," Ali explained. "It was reported while you were at the party. Colin sent the investigative team in, but—"

"There were news reporters poking around by the time we showed up," finished Colin.

Laila groaned and sank deeper into the sofa, wishing it would swallow her up. She was way too tired to be sorting this mess out.

"Any idea how they found out?" asked Laila as she stood and returned to the refrigerator determined to find something to eat. Perhaps this would all seem like less of a mess on a full stomach.

"No, but we're looking into it," explained Ali. "This is a lot for one night. I'm going to deal with the news stations tonight about the attack on the party. We can't have them spreading shit like this."

Laila poked through the freezer for a frozen burrito. "I'm out for the night. Jerrik and I both used a lot of energy on that shield. I'm home now, and I'm going to get some rest. I'll help sort this out in the morning."

"Tell Erin I'll be home late."

Laila started to nod then realized no one could see her. "Yeah, I will."

Ending the call, she stuck the burrito in the microwave, poured herself a large glass of juice, and grabbed a package of cookies from a cupboard.

"Hey Erin!" she called down the hall. "Ali's going to be home late."

"'kay," she shouted back.

Gathering her dinner, Laila carried it to the bar. Within minutes she'd eaten everything, and was debating whether or not she wanted a second burrito. Deciding she needed a moment to digest, she folded her arms on the counter and rested her head.

It felt like seconds later when a hand resting on her shoulder startled her awake.

"Sorry," said Frej, "I didn't mean to scare you like that. I thought you would've been in bed by now."

She glanced at the clock and realized it was almost four in the morning. She groaned, how in Odin's name had she managed to fall asleep for two hours at the kitchen counter?

"Come on." Frej tugged her elbow.

She nodded and followed him up the stairs.

"Did you get everyone's statements?" she asked, through a yawn.

"Yes, the police helped us, thankfully."

"Did they catch the rest of the gang members?"

"No, they got away."

"Did you—" she started. As they reached the second-floor hallway.

"It's okay." He placed his hands on her shoulders. "There will be plenty of time for questions in the morning. You need rest."

She nodded, allowing him to pull her into his embrace.

"I'm sorry we fought," she murmured into his shoulder. "I know you want to help. I'm really glad you were there tonight."

"I'm sorry too," he whispered into her hair. "I'll see you in the morning."

He gave her a gentle kiss before taking a step back towards his door. She held onto his hand a moment longer before it slipped from her grasp. Reluctantly she turned towards her room alone.

Laila stirred from her sleep as a strong hand ran along her side and came to rest on her hip. Laila sighed and leaned back against the muscular body behind her. She hadn't heard Frej come in. Perhaps he had joined her after she drifted off to sleep.

He pressed against her back and ran his nose along the length of her neck, trailing a row of feather-light kisses as he went. With a pleasant sigh, Laila pressed back against his hips, letting out a low chuckle as she felt his need. In response, he ran his calloused fingers over her stomach, and gently nipped her ear, the warmth of his breath causing her to shudder with pleasure.

He'd gotten her attention, she was awake now and wanted more. Laila twisted around, hooking her leg behind him to pull him closer. The groan that escaped his lips urged her on, and she fisted her hand in his long hair as she brought her lips to his, teasing him, her lips barely grazing his.

"Laila," he moaned, pleading, begging her for more as he wrapped his arms around her, pulling her to him.

She obliged, and kissed him, slowly. Taking time to savor the feeling of their growing need.

In a swift motion, he pulled her on top of him so that she was straddling him, and she pulled away and threw her head back, panting for air. His hands skimmed along her thighs, toying with the hem of her silk shorts.

She ran her palms along the bare silver skin of his chest.

Laila stopped.

She lowered her gaze to his face and gasped. "Jerrik!"

Laila bolted upright in bed, scanning the room. She was alone. It had been a dream.

With a groan, she flopped back down against the mattress. A blush heated her cheeks as she tried to shake the memory of Jerrik kissing her. Why was this happening? Why couldn't she just be happy with Frej?

She sat up and pounded a fist into her pillow as she muttered a string of profanity. When she clenched her fists, there was a tingling feeling in her arms as the magic in the room shifted. The flames on her arms were glowing, but as soon as she realized it, the magic slipped from her grasp and the markings faded. She tried to replicate the feeling—anything to distract her from that dream—but to no avail, the magic was beyond her grasp.

With a huff, she sank back into the bed, pulling the blankets over her head. She drifted off into her usual restless sleep filled with Demons and destroyed cities, but thankfully no more dreams with Jerrik.

The next morning she awoke with a massive headache, a consequence of all the magic she'd used the night before. Between the memory of the dream and her pounding head, Laila was left in a sullen mood. As she wandered down to the kitchen, she was greeted by Erin, who was doing yoga in the living room.

"Want to join?" she asked mid-pose.

Normally Laila would, she liked doing yoga with Erin, but with the headache, she was barely able to trudge downstairs. She shook her head, wincing when the movement worsened the pain.

"Maybe tomorrow," she said gritting her teeth against the pain in her head.

Laila continued to the kitchen and opened a cupboard to find a box of Elven remedies. Healing magic couldn't help this, it would only make it worse. She pulled out a small pouch of dried herbs and poured some of them into a coffee mug. She added water to the kettle and put it on the stove before searching through another cabinet for some cereal.

Erin finished and rolled up the mat.

"You look like shit," the Dragon said pouring herself a cup of coffee.

"Thanks," muttered Laila.

The kettle started to whistle, and Laila switched off the burner. She poured the boiling water into the mug and watched the bits of herbs float around in lazy circles. While she waited, she ate her cereal. Erin poured herself a bowl as well and slid onto a bar stool.

"Did Ali say anything to you about work when she got home last night?" asked Laila.

"No, but she got home pretty late. Frej too."

"Right." The late-night conversation with Frej came flooding back into her mind. She really did need to talk to him.

Feeling impatient, Laila cooled her tea with a spell and took a sip.

"So, they're still asleep?" she asked.

Erin nodded.

Laila wished she could sleep, but even without the dreams, the throbbing of her head made it difficult. Instead, she finished her cereal, rinsed the bowl, and set it in the dishwasher. Then she took her cup of tea over to the sofa and gently took a seat. The remote control was resting on the arm of the sofa, so she picked it up and switched on the TV.

It was still on the same news channel as the night before. Now another reporter sat in a richly furnished living room interviewing a man. It was Fredrik Stacy, the pro-human protestor.

"Ugh! Not this guy again!" Erin flopped on the sofa next to her.

Laila took another sip of the tea as she listened.

"Yes," said the man on the television, "I heard the news last night when I was at home here with my wife. I think it is very tragic the way the government handled the situation last night."

"What do you mean?" asked the reporter in earnest.

"Well, I would venture to say the force used against the humans was extreme. The law enforcement agents allowed Vampires to attack human citizens who were protesting."

"Protesting!?!" spat Laila in disgust, "They were the ones who attacked."

"Wait, is this about last night?" asked Erin looking from Laila to the television.

Laila nodded. "I think you better go get your sister. She'll want to see this."

Erin nodded and ran upstairs.

Laila shook her head as he continued.

"This is our right as Americans. We have the right to protest and to have our voices heard. We were here long before these Supernaturals were, and who are they to come threatening us and murdering us as they see fit? This is our city, and we have a right to live here without the fear of being murdered by one of these creatures in our own homes!"

"What's going on?" Ali descended the staircase.

"Fredrik Stacy's back," grumbled Laila.

Ali stood behind the other sofa and watched the interview.

Fredrik Stacy continued, "I believe the Inter-Realm Security

Agency is truly at fault here. They stood by and took the side of the Vampires. We are supposed to trust that they can keep us safe. They are here to protect us from these Supernatural threats, yet here they are defending them!"

"Seriously!?!" fumed Ali.

"We need to take back our city," declared Fredrik Stacy. "We cannot stand by and be bullied into submission. This is why I've decided to run for governor in the upcoming elections."

Laila nearly dropped her tea while Ali let out a string of profanity in multiple languages.

"What's going on?" said Frej wearily from the second floor. "Why is everyone up so early?"

"This joke of a human being wants to run for governor," spewed Ali.

"Isn't it an elected position?" pointed out Laila.

"Yes," said Ali, "and I doubt he would make it either. The elections are only a month away, not to mention his views are far too extreme. Still though, it encourages the mistrust of SNPs. It's only going to make things worse."

Laila nodded in agreement.

The news station cut away from the interview to give some additional information on Fredrik Stacy's campaign. An image flashed across the screen with Fredrik Stacy exiting a building with an entourage of other humans. One of them looked familiar.

"Who is that?" Laila paused the TV.

Ali shrugged, "Probably a campaign manager."

"Thor's hammer!" cried Laila as the realization hit her. "That's Lorel, Colin's girlfriend!"

"What?" asked Ali sharply, stepping closer to the screen. "Damn, I think you're right."

Erin shook her head. "Why would Colin's girlfriend work for a guy like that? She's dating a Supernatural!"

A funny look passed over Ali's face as she watched Lorel on the television.

"I'll be back," murmured the Fae, "I need to make a phone call."

Laila watched her go, wondering what revelation Ali had just had. It seemed likely that the phone call would be to the agent from the Inspector General's office, but why? And if it wasn't related to Colin, then why wasn't Ali allowed to talk about it? She turned over the thoughts in her head as she watched the rest of the report, wondering who else they could be investigating.

CHAPTER 20

After the excitement of the news report, no one was in the mood to go back to bed. Instead, Ali and Laila opted to head to work. They were the only ones from their team who were there so early, but it gave them plenty of time to get to work. While Ali continued to deal with the media, Laila returned her attention to the homicides.

She hadn't had a chance to see the latest crime scene, but the investigative team had uploaded their photos and evidence files to the database. Taking her time, Laila sorted through everything, searching for some detail that would connect the cases, but turned up blank.

"What'cha doin'?" asked Ali, watching from the doorway.

"Trying to figure out why these humans are being targeted."

"Were they in the same area?" Ali asked, "Maybe it's just a newly turned Vampire that can't control its bloodlust yet?"

The Fae took a seat in the empty chair across from Laila's desk. She still had her half-drunk iced coffee in hand although it was mostly melted. Laila cast a quick spell to return it to its original icy state.

"Thanks," Ali said.

"I really doubt that this is just a young Vampire." Laila shook her head and scrolled to the next photo. "This is far too methodical. Plus, the locations aren't particularly close together. Not close enough to be an easy hunting ground, even for a Vampire."

Ali watched as she scrolled through a couple more pictures.

"How are the phone calls going?" she asked the Fae.

Ali made a face. "Ugh! These conversations would be so much easier in person, but that would take more time. I think I've dealt with most of the large and local stations anyways."

"I don't suppose you were able to track down the person who took those pictures last night?"

"No." She shook her head. "They were submitted anonymously. The message had been routed through multiple servers and was untraceable."

Laila sighed. "Of course it was."

"You know, when I asked you to have photos taken, this isn't quite what I meant." Ali tried to cover up the smile spreading across her face.

Laila face-palmed. "Isn't this a little soon for jokes?"

Ali leaned forward and gave her a mischievous look. "Hey, this is turning out to be one stressful week. We've got to deal with it somehow, and joking is better than arguing."

Laila chuckled grimly. Ali had a point, they'd all been on edge lately with the trouble brewing in the city.

Ali paused for a moment as she glanced at the file on Laila's computer. "What about surveillance camera footage? Or the DNA tests?"

"Thor's hammer," said Laila her heart skipping a beat, "one of the techs was sorting through footage. They haven't entered any notes into the system yet."

"Then let's go upstairs and check," suggested Ali, "maybe they found something."

The two of them hurried up to the top floor and down the

hall to a door labeled storage, above it was a handwritten sign taped to the wall that read "Support Staff." Laila knocked twice before opening the door.

The room was large with no windows. Desks had been arranged in a variety of workspaces where the inhabitants worked away on computers with multiple screens. Their support staff consisted of half a dozen humans primarily specializing in technology. The majority of them had worked for the NSA before The Event. They were usually assigned to anything tech-related, from accessing and decrypting electronic evidence, to research, or in this case, sorting through video evidence.

"Excuse me," said Laila to the nearest man, "I'm trying to find out if there was anything suspicious on some surveillance footage."

"That would've been Steve." The man pointing towards a workstation in the back-left corner. Laila thanked him and wove through the desks to the back of the room, Ali behind her.

"Steve?" asked Laila.

The man spun around and gave her a suspicious look. "Yes."

"I'm Laila Eyvindr. Are you working on the video footage connected to the multiple homicides? I was wondering if you'd found anything yet."

"Oh, right," he turned back to his computer where his fingers flew across the keyboard, "the Vampire killings. I sent the files to you a few days ago."

Laila shook her head, she hadn't received anything.

"Here," he said pulling up an email folder, "oh wait, I sent it to Colin by mistake. Didn't he forward it to you though?"

Laila glanced at Ali. "No, actually, he didn't."

"Huh, well, I'll show you what I found," said Steve as he pulled up a file. "We caught someone following the first victim into his complex."

He played a segment of the security camera footage. In it, the first victim approached the gate and unlocked it. As he disappeared off screen, the gate swung slowly shut. There was a blur of movement, then another person in a worn coat appeared pushing the gate open just before it latched.

"Definitely a Vampire," muttered Laila as she watched the clip a second time, "and probably male by the size."

Steve continued, "Unfortunately, these cameras didn't get a good look at him, and there is no footage of him leaving through any of the gates."

He pulled up a second file.

"This is the footage from the night of the second homicide. It came from the building across the street."

He played the second clip that showed a man in the same worn coat following their second victim along the sidewalk and towards her house.

"We still don't see his face though," noted Ali.

"Not at this angle," he explained as he pulled up a third clip, "but check this out."

This footage was from a different camera. It was angled towards the sidewalk and street, but in the corner was a small, second story window. The same, hooded figure climbed into the window, as he did, he glanced over his shoulder towards the camera. Steve paused the clip.

He glanced up at Laila and Ali. "Don't worry, I was able to enhance the image."

He clicked on another file, a picture of their perp. He appeared to be a middle-aged man with slight wrinkles around his eyes and forehead. There was a dark smirk on his face, and his beady eyes were full of malice. Unfortunately, Laila didn't recognize him.

Steve watched her, trying to cover a grin of triumph. He practically squirmed with excitement.

"Okay dude," said Ali eyeing the human, "just spit it out already."

The human could hardly contain his excitement. "Not only do I have a face, but I've got a name for you too. Your killer is Arnold Koch. He was on death row for seven counts of pre-meditated murder when The Event hit. He escaped prison and has been missing ever since."

"How do you know all this?" asked Laila as he pulled up a file on the man. Sure enough, it was him, but the man in the old mugshot was definitely human.

"Facial recognition software." Steve lounged back in his office chair. "Good old technology! Well, not actually old, but you know..."

"Good work," said Laila as he sent her the evidence.

On their way back downstairs Laila placed a call to the forensic lab the medical examiners had sent the DNA samples to. One of the technicians told her they'd just found a match.

"Let me guess, it was Arnold Koch?" she asked.

"Yeah, actually," the technician said surprised. "I'll send the results over now."

Laila hung up and turned to Ali. "That answers one question, but we still don't have a motive."

"Any idea where they were before their deaths?" asked Ali as they reached Laila's office.

They returned to Laila's office and searched through the files until she found a screenshot of the first victim's phone calendar.

"The first victim was meeting with clients, and showing them properties. Afterwards, he had an hour blocked off at the gym before he went to meet a friend for dinner."

"And you interviewed the friend already?"

"Yep, I think he genuinely had no idea what happened. Plus, the coroner put the estimated time of death at eight o'clock, when the friend was at the restaurant. The alibi checks out. No one at the gym saw anything unusual either."

Ali joined Laila in examining the evidence

"Aren't you supposed to be writing a press release?" asked Laila slyly.

"Hmm, write a boring press release or help you track down a murderer… yeah, I'll go with the murderer." She nudged Laila in the ribs.

"Well," said Laila, "that was the only victim that seemed to have made good use of his calendar. Victim two had a recent breakup, looks like she hadn't been on social media in the last few weeks, and friends were having a hard time getting ahold of her. She doesn't appear to have any connection to the first victim unless he happened to go to the restaurant where she worked."

"Was it the same restaurant the first victim was supposed to meet his friend at?"

"No, that restaurant was in Santa Monica. Victim two worked in Playa Del Rey."

"What about the third victim?" Ali took a sip of her coffee.

Laila scanned over the information she'd found on him.

"He was a computer programmer. Most of his social life was online. Looks like one of his friends got worried when he wasn't online for a game and didn't answer the phone. He was the one who discovered the body and called the police. I'm about to head to this crime scene if you want to join me."

"I really should finish the press release." Ali grimaced.

"Hello?" called Jerrik from the hallway as he stopped in the doorway, "You're both pretty early."

"We had trouble sleeping," explained Laila. "We've got a lead on a suspect though. He's an escaped felon named Arnold Koch."

She pulled up the photo the tech had sent her and showed it to him before continuing.

"I'm about to go to last night's crime scene to see if I can figure out why he's targeting these humans."

"I'll come with you."

He wore his usual attire of jeans and a plain black t-shirt, and his long black hair was neatly pulled back into a low ponytail. He'd done his best to look refreshed and ready for the day, but the shadows under his eyes showed the exhaustion from the previous night. Laila could feel the effects as well, but it didn't seem to bother her as much. Perhaps her stamina was growing since she used a lot of magic on a daily basis.

She was reminded of last night's dream and had to fight the blush that wanted to creep into her cheeks. Going along with him to investigate wasn't exactly high on her list of things she was interested in doing at the moment.

"That's okay," she insisted. "Why don't you stay and—"

"I'm fine," he chuckled, "no need to look so concerned. Let's get going."

He turned back towards the elevator, disappearing down the hall as Laila gave Ali a sideways glance.

"Now what am I supposed to do?" hissed Laila desperately. "What if he tries to talk about, well, us?"

Ali glanced quickly down the hall to make sure Jerrik was out of earshot. "Look, maybe that's not such a bad thing. You can get that closure you need so you can move on with Frej if that's what you want."

Laila nodded.

Ali gave her a sympathetic look. "You'll have to do it eventually. You might as well rip the Band-Aid off now, and get it over with."

"I've never had to rip a Band-Aid off." Laila wiggled her fingers as magical sparks crackled from them.

Ali rolled her eyes. "You know what I mean. Now go! You're a badass, Demon fighting, special agent. You've got this!"

She nudged Laila towards the elevator to the garage where Jerrik was waiting.

As she started driving to the latest crime scene, Laila was completely silent. She focused on anything but the man seated next to her, but even as she drove, she could feel his attention on her.

Something nagged at her, though; Frej still hadn't told her what happened that night at the bar. If he wouldn't, perhaps Jerrik would.

"What happened between you and Frej the night he went

out drinking with Henrik and Mato?"

To her surprise, Jerrik was silent for several moments before answering her.

"I met Frej briefly back in Svartalfheim once, Frej didn't even remember it, but through our previous encounter, I learned something about him. I went to the bar to confront him about it because I feared he would hurt you."

"But why?" Laila shook her head. She didn't understand this secrecy. Did it have to do with one of his past assignments? Was there some connection with the Demons that Frej had failed to disclose to her?

"It's not my place to say more, it's Frej's story to tell."

Laila's head buzzed with thoughts as she drove through the streets bathed in the warm glow of the setting sun. If Jerrik knew there was something dangerous like a Demonic connection, she would think he'd tell her, especially if it affected their work and the team's safety. She became so lost in thought, that it startled her when Jerrik spoke again.

"Laila, I wish you would let me explain what happened. Why I left you months ago."

"There is nothing you need to say. It's done, it's over, and what happened between us is in the past." Laila waited for a pedestrian to cross the street.

"I know you don't want to hear this, but please just listen to me. Listen to my side of the story for once." She could hear the frustration creeping into his voice.

Her jaw clenched as her eyes narrowed.

"We have a case Jerrik, someone *died* last night, and we need to find the killer before—"

"It will wait another five minutes," he insisted through clenched teeth, "just stop being so stubborn and *listen*!"

She remembered Ali's advice, maybe it would give her closure to hear him out.

"Fine!" she snapped, glaring at him. "Go ahead, say what's so Gods-damned important."

"Thank you." There was a pause as he gathered his thoughts. "First of all, I want to apologize for hurting you. You're too proud to admit it to my face, but I know that I hurt you."

Laila continued to stare daggers at the road in front of her, but she didn't say anything.

He took a deep breath and continued, "After you slipped into a coma, I rode back with you to the hospital. While I was waiting, Colin stopped by to visit you and to give me a proposition. He'd heard that IRSA was experimenting with an expedited training program. He asked me if I would apply and come to work for him here. I told him yes, that I was very interested, but he said that I would have to leave right away. The program was starting in two days, and I wouldn't be able to wait for you to recover."

"So, you what? Just left? No message, no calls, nothing?" she asked.

He shook his head, his eyes pleading with her.

"It wasn't like that. I wasn't able to call and tell anyone what I was doing. It was secret, experimental. I had no choice! If I wanted to come back to L.A. with you, and help you track down the Demons, that was what I had to do."

"You could've left a note." She stared straight ahead, refusing to look at him. "You could've told me you were coming back."

She pulled up in front of a small apartment complex and parked her car, activating the camouflage feature to look like a rather worn, and slightly damaged sedan rather than the sleek sports car that it was. Unlocking the door, she moved to get out, but he stopped her.

"I did," he explained quietly, "I wrote you a note, in Elvish, explaining that I would be back in a few months. I gave it to Colin and asked him to give it to you when you awoke."

"But I never got a letter!" she huffed, exasperated.

"Exactly!" His eyes begged her to understand.

"So what? Colin just forgot to give me the letter? I asked

him directly, and he said…"

Suddenly it clicked.

"Colin lied to me." She sank back against her seat. "I-I know he's an ass, but why? Why would he do that?"

"I don't know, Laila." He shook his head. "But it sounds like he's been acting irrationally a lot lately."

Laila pressed her palms against her eyes. None of this made sense. Was Colin trying to hurt her? And to what end, so he could feel in control? Colin had done a lot of obnoxious things like abandoning Ali in the Old City, but why would he keep this letter from her? It didn't make sense.

Then there was the realization that Jerrik hadn't just left. He'd tried to explain to her that he was doing this to come back here, with her. Laila wished the ground would open up and swallow her. What was she supposed to make of all this?

There was a headache brewing behind her eyes. She was starting to feel overwhelmed.

Jerrik reached for her hand, but she snatched it away.

She hastily got out of the car. "I've moved on Jerrik, and you should too."

She slammed the door behind her and walked around the car, but he was right there behind her.

"I know you want me to believe that, but I just don't. Frej is an okay guy, but he's a *Dragon*. They are different Laila, you know that as well as I do. He doesn't understand you like I do. There are things we've been through that he will never understand. Not in the way I do. He wants to protect you. I want to fight at your side."

"Why is it so hard for you to accept that I've moved on?" she snapped. Laila shook her head and walked through the gate of the complex. "This conversation is over, I listened to what you had to say."

She understood what he was saying, but if she accepted it, then what? Perhaps those feelings she'd been trying to suppress would resurface even stronger, and she wasn't convinced that was a good thing. Frej was good for her, he helped her feel grounded. What she had with Jerrik was short and passionate, and while she still felt this connection to him, it would be easier for all of them if they kept their relationship strictly professional.

She unlocked a door on the left and entered the apartment. There was a bloodstain close to the doorway, which she took care to avoid as she switched on the light. Jerrik followed her and shut the door.

"Fine," he said, "but I won't stop fighting for you."

"What part of moving on don't you understand." She rolled her eyes as she pulled on a pair of nitrile gloves and started examining the desk situated in the corner covered with multiple screens, speakers, and other equipment.

"I'm serious Laila, I don't care if I have to wait for fifty years, I'll still be here, waiting for you."

"Why?" she spat.

"Before the Demons imprisoned me, I was already in a dark place. I'd been betrayed by so many people, my family, my friends, my lovers, everyone. I felt so broken that I was convinced that I would never be able to trust again. When the Demons imprisoned me, it seemed that the Fates were just content to make me suffer, but I prayed to the Gods to give me a sign. To show me why I'd been set on this path.

"Then suddenly you arrived. You were compassionate and determined, you were a light in the darkness. You were hope— my hope—that some shred of goodness remained in the worlds. I was attracted to you like a moth to a flame. I knew if I developed feelings for you, the Demons would surely use it against me, but I couldn't help it. There was one day when they took you from your cell—after the night we'd been plotting our escape—and I was nearly driven insane for fear that they would kill you. I realized that I would do anything to protect you, even if I ran the risk of breaking your heart in the process. When we returned, I was afraid, my life was a mess, and I couldn't drag you into that. So instead I left, I took Colin up on his offer and I ran away like a Gods-damned coward."

Laila had tried to tune it out, to tell herself that none of this mattered. But even though she tried to tear her eyes away from him she couldn't, she was rooted to the spot. Perhaps it was morbid fascination, or maybe the need for closure, but she took in every word of his narrative like a shipwrecked sailor clinging to a piece of timber.

"So why did you come back?" asked Laila hesitantly, unsure of whether she wanted to hear his answer.

"I realized I was an idiot for leaving like that, and that I wanted you back in my life. Walking away from you felt like tearing my own heart out because it still belongs to you."

The words hit her like a punch to the gut. She tried to speak, but the words were frozen in her mouth. Why did he have to say that? Why now? Why here? Laila didn't know whether she should scoff, or scream, or blast him with a spell.

She spun around searching his face. "Jerrik, this is ridiculous."

He reached for her hand. "Maybe it is. I just… I need you to know that what we shared wasn't just a fling. We connected on a deeper level."

Laila snatched her hand out of his. There were too many emotions that pulled her in every direction like they were going to tear her apart.

"I'm going to get some air." Jerrik waved towards the door.

Laila nodded absently as he left. She took a moment to clear her mind. She had a crime scene to investigate. So she pushed down those feelings and emotions and locked them away in a distant corner of her heart, as she'd been told to do from an early age. Composure and reserve, that's what Elves were known for. She'd make it through this shift and figure the rest out later. At the moment she was standing in the middle of a crime scene. Lives were at stake, and she couldn't allow her emotions to distract her from the problem at hand.

CHAPTER 21

Laila busied herself with the crime scene. This she could handle. It was familiar, straight-forward. She began systematically searching through the apartment looking for something that would reveal the connection that they so badly needed. After a time Jerrik returned, and wordlessly began to help by searching the bedroom.

She sank down onto a barstool at the kitchen counter. Nothing was jumping out. That's when it caught her eye, a bright blue object that was laying nearly out of sight. She reached back behind the sofa and removed a reusable plastic bottle.

"Thor's hammer, we found it!" She shouted to Jerrik. "We've found the missing link!"

He approached from the hall eyeing the bottle she held.

"*Shape it Up!?*" he asked, reading the label. "Honestly Laila, I feel like this guy's not the type of person we would find in a gym."

He gestured to the gaming and computer equipment on the desk.

"Then why does he have one of their water bottles?"

"Okay then, how about the second victim?" Jerrik folded his arms. "How does *she* tie in?"

"She had a gym bag," said Laila thinking back to the crime scene. "It was by the door next to her purse. I remember searching it."

Jerrik still looked skeptical.

"Look, I know how we can find out."

She did a quick search on her phone and pulled up the website for *Shape it Up!* and located the number for the gym they'd visited the other night. While the phone rang, she searched the apartment for any other evidence the investigative team had overlooked.

"Hello, this is *Shape it Up!* how can I help you today?" Answered a male voice on the other end of the line.

"Hello, this is Special Agent Laila Eyvindr with the Inter-Realm Security Agency."

"Oh, right, you were here the other day."

"I have another question for you. Can you look up two more names in your client lists?"

"Sure," said the man, "What are the names?"

"Claire Summers and Grant MacDonald."

There was a pause, and she could hear the clicking of a keyboard on the other end of the line.

"Okay, Claire Summers is a client. The last time she signed in was Sunday evening. But there's no Grant MacDonald here."

"Are you sure?" asked Laila examining the computer desk, "He would've been there yesterday. Maybe you had someone stop by to sign up last evening?"

"Hold on, let me check with one of the other instructors."

For a few minutes Laila waited, then finally the receptionist returned. "There was a guy here last night who came to inquire about fees, but no one caught his name."

"Did they give him a reusable water bottle with the gym's logo?"

"Probably, we give them to anyone new who's interested in

signing up. Why?"

"I'm going to need to get the security footage from last night."

"Um, sure, I can have it ready for you to pick up in the morning."

"Thank you." Laila ended the call.

She wrote a quick email to Steve about additional surveillance footage then glanced up at Jerrik who continued to search the apartment. It occurred to her that not only was this a new development, but also the perfect excuse to get her off that dangerous topic, and what Jerrik had said.

"How much do you want to bet that the potential client on that surveillance footage is him?" she grinned.

"Even if it is related to the gym, how does that help us really?" he asked. "There was nothing unusual recorded the night the first victim was killed."

"Well, we have a photo of the suspect, why don't we head back to the gym and see if anyone recognizes him?"

Her phone buzzed. It was Darien.

"Hello?" she asked, answering the call.

"Laila, where are you and Jerrik now?"

"At the third crime scene, why?"

"There's been another attack, just now. It must've happened just after sunset, but a witness heard the struggle and called it in. We're on our way now."

"We?" she asked.

"Talen's with me. I want him to see if he notices something I don't."

"Okay, I've identified a suspect. I want to stop at *Shape it Up!* again before they close for the night to see if they recognize him. We'll meet you at the crime scene afterwards if that's okay." She bagged the plastic bottle and headed for the door.

"Sounds good. We'll see you soon."

CHAPTER 22

It was close to ten o'clock by the time they stepped through the doors of the gym. There were still a few late-night fitness buffs finishing up their workouts while a couple of staff members began their closing routine. The same man from before was working the reception desk and waved them over when they entered.

"Didn't you just call?" He gave them a puzzled look as he filed some paperwork.

"Yes, but we have another question for you," explained Laila as she pulled up a mugshot on her phone and passed it to the receptionist. "Do you recognize this man?"

He stared at the phone with a stunned expression.

"Hey Annie! Can you come here?" he shouted suddenly.

From around the corner appeared the young woman from the juice bar. She looked at Laila and Jerrik curiously.

"Weren't you here the other night, with the Vampire?" She approached the receptionist's counter.

He flashed her the picture on Laila's phone. "Isn't that the guy who was giving you problems the other day?"

"Yeah, that's the guy, the creepy guy I was telling you about." She looked up at Jerrik and Laila. "This looks like a mugshot. Is he some kind of criminal?"

Jerrik nodded. "Have you seen him lately?"

"He was here earlier but wandered off a couple of hours ago."

Laila and Jerrik exchanged glances.

"If he comes back, you need to call us immediately," Laila passed her another card. "This man is an escaped convict, and we believe he's extremely dangerous. If you see him, stay inside and wait for us or the police."

Both Annie and the receptionist nodded solemnly. As the Elves turned to leave, they could hear the humans talking behind them in hushed whispers.

Their next stop was the crime scene, but as they approached the block, they could see a crowd had gathered. A few members of the crowd were curious onlookers, but the majority were pro-human protestors. Laila recognized some of them from out in front of the hospital.

"Don't they have anything better to do?" Jerrik scowled as they climbed out of the SUV.

The investigative team was already there at the scene rushing to and from the building. LAPD was at the scene as well, but their attention was focused on the protestors, ensuring they weren't interfering with the investigators. Captain Romero spotted Laila and Jerrik, and waved them over.

"This is happening way too often," he said as she approached.

Laila sighed and nodded. "We were at the previous crime scene when we got the call. We made a new discovery."

She noticed a crowd was beginning to form across the street.

"Is there anything you can do about that?" She jerked her thumb at the humans gawking. Given last night's conflict, the protestors in the crowd left Laila feeling more on edge than usual.

"As much as I would like to, there's not much more to do." He shrugged. "We managed to get them across the street at least, but I'll see if we can't get them to move along."

"Shall we?" Laila asked Jerrik waving at the two-story building before them.

He nodded, and they followed Captain Romero into the building.

This apartment was on the second floor of the building and only shared the floor with four other units. The crime scene was basically identical to the other three. To the right, a wide-eyed couple sat with a police officer, likely the witnesses. The captain motioned towards an apartment.

"I'll leave you to it." The captain returned downstairs to deal with the crowd.

She stepped forward through the doorway, Jerrik behind her, and found Darien and his sire examining something in a bag within the room.

Darien looked up as she entered. "Same as the other crimes, only this time they left the murder weapon behind." He held up the bag which contained a large, bloody knife. "The perp was in a hurry, the neighbors heard the struggle and came to investigate."

Laila glanced at the victim—a man in his thirties. The investigative team had finished photographing the body and was about to prepare it for transport. As Darien mentioned, this murder appeared more rushed than the others. The man had only been partially eviscerated compared to what had been done to the other victims. She also noticed he wore gym clothes and that there was a gym bag resting on the kitchen counter.

"You want to bet he just came from *Shape it Up!*" She glanced at Jerrik.

"What?" asked Darien.

"Yeah, we found the connection," explained Jerrik, "The previous three victims had just come home from the gym when they were murdered."

"So, he's been hunting there," mused Darien.

Jerrik nodded. "Remember that barista who mentioned a man harassing her. That's him."

"His name is Arnold Koch." She passed the phone to Darien. "An escaped convict who's been missing since The Event."

Darien examined the photo carefully. "I'm going to show this to the neighbors. The husband saw a man fleeing the apartment."

Laila nodded and reached out with her magic to search for any magical residue. As she expected, there were hints of Demonic energy clinging to the space, but there was something else, a strange magical stain stuck to the wall in the corner of the room. It wasn't visible to the eyes, but it was like a magical blob stuck to the wall.

"What in the worlds…" Laila trailed off as she approached the anomaly. She'd never seen anything like it.

"Everything okay?" asked Jerrik.

Laila crouched by the wall and ran her fingers over the paint, gasping as two eyes appeared to blink at her as she snatched her hand away. Where her fingers had been only seconds before materialized a set of jagged, lethally sharp, teeth. They snapped shut as the rest of the creature appeared. Its head like that of a large, ugly shark, while the rest of its eight-foot-long body was covered in molted brown scales. To Laila, it appeared like the unholy combination of a snake and a shark as it peeled itself off the wall.

"What is that?" howled Laila as she scrambled backwards across the floor.

"A Bogey," explained Talen, intrigued. "It's a shapeshifting creature. They're pretty docile typically, but not that one." He quickly hoisted her up from the floor.

Laila had no idea what this Bogey was doing at their crime scene, but it was shifting again growing wings, and claws like a cow-sized, hideous Dragon. It screeched and lunged at her, knocking a side table out of its way at it flew through the air.

Jerrik was there in an instant with his magical stun baton, beating the creature away. It lashed out with its tail which connected with his stomach with a painful thud. Jerrik was thrown backwards over the back of a sofa.

Talen bared his fangs at the creature and hissed. It hardly glanced at him before swerving to the side towards Laila. It slammed into her invisible shield with a thud, jaws snapping at her.

"Why is it so interested in me?" snapped Laila, pouring more energy into the shield.

"Witches used to set traps with Bogeys," explained Talen, "they have the ability to be charmed into attacking a certain individual with a blood-binding spell. Someone must've known you'd be at the crime scene and left it here to find you."

Sure enough, it had absolutely no interest in the men.

"Great," muttered Laila. She needed to get it away from the others and out of the crime scene before it destroyed the evidence. Others were starting to gather in the doorway, but Jerrik motioned for them to stay back, away from the thrashing tail of the Bogey.

She took a step back, trying to put some space between herself and the creature and bumped into a windowsill. There was a large alley across the way, if she could make it across the street, she could face the creature there.

"I'll lure it away." Laila shoved the window open and leapt out of it before anyone could protest. The impact of her feet meeting the concrete below was jarring, but she staggered forward towards the crowd.

"Move!" she shouted at the humans. "Out of the way!"

They screamed and dove for cover as the creature clambered out of the window and clung to the side of the building. It screeched at her again before launching into the air, its leathery wings beating.

Shouldering her way through the crowd, Laila sprinted to

the alley, the creature following overhead. It landed in front of her, blocking her path, but Laila realized she wasn't alone, Talen was standing beside her.

She passed him her stun baton and conjured a set of ice daggers, throwing them at the creature. It dodged nimbly and lurched forward towards her. Talen was there beating the creature across the head with the stun baton. The thud echoed down the alley, and the dazed creature shook its head.

Now was her chance, she felt the crackling electricity buzzing within the wall of the building beside her, she reached for it and directed an electrically charged blast at the creature. It shrieked and shuddered before collapsing on the ground. It gradually shifted back, shrinking down into what looked like a large, brown slug, the size of a cat.

"Is it dead?" Laila eyed the creature, watching for any sign of movement.

Talen shook his head. "Just stunned. I'll be back."

Seconds later he returned with a black bin her team used to transport equipment in the back of their vehicles. Laila used her magic to lift the slimy creature into the bin, and Talen snapped the lid shut, locking it in place.

"I know a cryptozoologist that will take it in," explained Talen. "Once the blood-binding charm is removed it'll be fine." He lifted the bin in his arms, careful not to jostle it too much as they returned to the crime scene.

The crowd had finally disbursed, likely fearing an attack from the Bogey. The other members of her team rushed out of the building to see what was going on.

"We've got the Bogey," Laila nodded to the box.

"It shouldn't stay in here too long though." Talen frowned at the box. "It'll get agitated when it gains consciousness and can't get out."

Darien shook his head. "Why don't you and Talen deal with that. You can drop him off at his apartment when you're done. We'll wrap this up and meet you back at the office."

Laila nodded, there was little more she could do at the crime scene anyway. She helped Talen load the box into the back seat of her SUV, watching how carefully Talen handled the bin.

"Animal person?" she asked with a grin.

He shrugged and climbed into the passenger seat, but Laila saw the tenderness in his eyes.

Twenty minutes later they were pulling up to a large apartment building on the outskirts of the Old City. They approached the front entrance, but the wall of glass windows had been blacked out from the inside. Talen rang the doorbell. After several moments a short, older man in his pajama's answered the door. His grey hair was thinning, and he peered through a thick pair of glasses that magnified his eyes.

"Who on earth—" He stopped, as he recognized her companion. "Talen! Well, you're an unexpected surprise!" The man quickly waved them into the room.

The reception area had been converted into a living room, but along the wall were a number of different cages and terrariums. They contained a variety of creatures from Earth and the other worlds. There was a large snake curled up in a blanket on a sofa. It blinked lazily at her and flicked its tongue before resting its head back on the folds of the blanket.

"Give me just a moment," said the man, pulling on an old robe and slippers before waving them through another door.

They entered an atrium, and Laila realized that this was no longer an apartment complex, but a zoo of sorts. The apartments had been converted into habitats for a wide variety of magical creatures containing everything from Unicorns with shimmering white coats to Brownies with their fuzzy brown bodies, and a large swarm of Pixies that lazily drifted freely through the atrium like a swarm of magical, psychedelic butterflies. Calls of every creature drifted through the space like a melodic cacophony as the creatures noticed their caretaker was up.

"What is this place?" asked Laila in awe.

"My sanctuary for homeless creatures," beamed the man as

he led them down a hall. "These creatures are either being reha-
bilitated or have ailments that prevent them from being released
back into the wild. I care for them as best I can. All funded by
Talen of course!"

Laila raised an eyebrow at the Vampire who was carrying
the bin containing the Bogey. He gave her a sheepish grin. He
was clearly more than just a little fond of animals if he funded
a place like this.

They followed the cryptozoologist into a room labeled observation. One wall was made up of cages in varying sizes filled
with creatures that were bundled up in casts, while others sat
watching listlessly through the bars of their cages. Those were
the ones with the worst injuries and illnesses. There was a large
metal counter that Talen set the box on before stepping back.

"So, who's this you've brought to me today?" asked the
cryptozoologist, pulling on a pair of gloves.

"I'm Laila—" she began.

"Nice to meet you, Laila, I'm Dr. Sikora. I was actually
talking about our friend in the box though." He patted the lid
of the bin.

"Right," said Laila taking a step back.

"Careful!" warned Talen, "the Bogey in there has a
blood-binding spell set to Laila."

"I see." Carefully he cracked open one side before shutting
it quickly as the box shook. He retrieved a collar from a cabinet
behind him before returning again. "This'll keep 'em under control until I can remove the spell."

Swiftly, he popped the lid off the bin and scooped up the
creature inside. The Bogey started to grow and sprout fur as
Dr. Sikora pinned it under his arm and strapped on the collar.
The Bogey—who'd started shifting into a large black panther—
abruptly stopped. It blinked at the cryptozoologist as it shrank
back to the size of a little black cat. It rubbed its head against
the man but froze when it spotted Laila. It hissed and spit, as it
clawed at her.

"Oh yes, that is one strong enchantment." The old man clicked his tongue. He muttered something as he reached for one of the many vials on the shelf and dusted the powder on the Bogey. The Bogey-cat froze and sneezed. After a moment, it no longer appeared to be ready to maul her, so he set it on the observation table.

The Bogey-cat walked to the edge of the table and sat down, staring directly at Laila. It meowed at her.

"He wants you to pet him," explained Dr. Sikora. "Go on, it's perfectly safe now that the spell is broken."

It appeared the old man was also a Witch. Laila took a hesitant step forward and stroked the Bogey-cat. It purred and leaned into her hand.

Dr. Sikora watched with interest. "The blood-binding spell has a funny backlash, once broken, the Bogey forms a bond with the person whose blood was used."

"Do you have room to spare for a Bogey?" Talen asked as the cat padded over to him in search of affection.

The old man frowned. "Unfortunately, I've already got one male Bogey, and the males are rather territorial, but perhaps you could take him?" He looked up at Laila.

"Oh no." Laila shook her head. That thing had tried to kill her thirty minutes ago it was not going home with her.

"We can't release it in the city," said Talen seriously, "It wouldn't survive on the streets here."

"It'll stay in that form as long as the collar's on it," added Dr. Sikora. "It would be like adopting a stray cat."

Laila looked from Talen's pleading face to Dr. Sikora's cheerful one. This was ridiculous, she couldn't just bring in a stray Bogey without asking her housemates. It was out of the question.

The Bogey-cat walked back over to her and nudged her with its furry head. It looked up at her before letting out the most pitiful little mewing noise she'd ever heard. *Gods damn it!* she thought, it was awfully cute.

"Just until another home is found?" asked Talen beside her.

Laila threw her hands in the air. "Okay, just temporarily."

Talen grinned, and Dr. Sikora started filling the bin with supplies.

"Luckily, the Bogies are about as easy to care for as a cat. Here's a litterbox for you, some litter, and a couple cans of cat food to get you started."

Laila shook her head. What had she gotten herself into?

Dr. Sikora placed the Bogey in a cardboard carrier and handed it to Laila.

"Now, if that's all, I should be getting back to bed. I've got to get up early for the morning feeding."

They thanked the cryptozoologist as Talen grabbed the crate of supplies and followed Dr. Sikora back to the entrance, parting at the door of his home. Laila and Talen loaded up the supplies.

"Any word from Richard?" she asked as Talen got into the car.

"Not yet, I'll be calling him as soon as I get home. Especially now that there've been two more victims and we've a face and a name to go off of."

Laila nodded. "When we met with him the other night, you spoke of Vampire attacks in the Old City. How long has that been going on?"

"Weeks, if not longer, but because of the nature of the Old City I only just found out before the party. It's a bad omen, if Vampires are brazenly disregarding the rules of our kind, then there is a disruption somewhere in the hierarchy."

"What do you mean?"

Talen shook his head. "It means that there's a sire somewhere in this city who is either completely ignorant or a fool for thinking he can allow this to happen without incurring the wrath of the elders. The question is whether your suspect, Arnold Koch and the Vampires running amuck in the Old City were sired by the same individual."

Laila mulled it over, trying to understand what these Vampires hoped to gain. All they were doing was generating fear, something the rest of the Vampires had worked so hard to fight against. Talen sat quietly in the passenger's seat beside her for a moment, also lost in his own thoughts.

"Thank you," he said after a time.

"For what?" asked Laila as they sat at a stop light.

"For helping to save the Vampires last night. I know it takes a toll on you to use that much magic, even if you are different from most Elves."

Laila glanced at the Vampire.

"What does that mean?" she asked.

"You're not purely Elven, are you?"

"What?" she said, shocked, "Of course I am."

The Vampire didn't say anything, but she could feel his gaze settle on her.

"I mean no offense," he said after a time, "but it is true, you are something more, and it frightens you. Perhaps you weren't born with it, but I can smell it in your blood none the less. It makes you more powerful and gives you strength."

Laila didn't respond. Sure the blue magic was powerful, but what was the use if she didn't know when she would be able to access it. Arduinna would probably know, but Laila wouldn't have time to meet with her until they managed to get this case wrapped up. She'd managed this long, and she could get through another week or so.

"How'd you get those markings, if you don't mind my asking?" He indicated her arms.

"I destroyed a Fire Elemental, but I was badly injured. I was healed by someone… well, a Goddess."

His eyes glimmered with fascination. "You're quite the curiosity."

Laila chuckled and shook her head as she pulled up in front of his building.

"Here you are," she announced, relieved to have a reason to

get off that topic.

"Thank you, I'll be in touch." He paused as he got out of the car, his expression softening. "Just call me if you have any questions about the Bogey. I'm glad you agreed to take him in."

Right, she thought, glancing at the cardboard carrier in the seat behind her. She'd have to find a way to break the news to her roommates.

As Talen walked through the door of the complex, Laila mulled over what he had said. Of course she was fully Elven, but she found it unsettling that this Goddess was affecting her somehow.

There was a shuffling noise behind her, and when she turned, she found the Bogey-cat sitting on the center console.

"*Merf?*" it called looking at her curiously.

"How in the worlds did you get out of there?"

She examined the box, but it was still shut. Apparently, she had an escape artist on her hands. She frowned as the Bogey stepped down onto the passenger seat and curled up in a little ball.

"Fine," she said, "but stay there."

The Bogey yawned and shut its eyes. Laila shook her head as she turned back towards the house.

CHAPTER 23

"You got a cat!" squealed Erin as Laila stepped through the garage door.

The Bogey-cat had woken up from its nap as soon as she parked the car and leapt into her lap. It gleefully purred as she carried the creature inside, rubbing its head against her face. Erin and Frej had been in the middle of a history lesson with maps and books spread across the coffee table in the living room.

Erin practically wiggled with excitement as Laila plopped the Bogey-cat down on the sofa while Frej watched it skeptically.

"It's not a cat," explained Laila, "not really. It's a Bogey trapped in cat form. I agreed to take it for the time being since it magically bonded to me."

"So it's a Shapeshifter?" asked Frej, suddenly more interested.

"Yeah, but the collar keeps it in this form though."

"What's his name?" Erin took a seat next to the cat on the sofa, and it crawled into her lap.

Laila hadn't even thought of that. "I'm not sure, but I have to get back to the office. I've got a box of supplies in the car for him. Erin, do you think you could get them set up in the laundry room for me?"

"Sure." Erin scratched the Bogey-cat behind the ears causing him to purr loudly.

Laila retrieved the plastic bin from the car and left it in the laundry room. On her way to the office, she stopped at a coffee shop to order drinks for the rest of the team. Hopefully, the caffeine would help them get through the rest of the night.

When she arrived at the office, she saw a familiar figure standing on the curb out front, Lorel. She was scowling and appeared to be in a heated conversation on the phone. When she noticed Laila watching, she turned and strode down the street away from the building. As Laila pulled into the parking garage, she wondered what that was about.

Back in the office, she saw that Jerrik and Darien were already there. They must have left the investigative team to wrap-up the crime scene. It seemed strange to Laila since they would ordinarily spend more time there. Ali, Colin, and the agent from the Inspector General's office, Adam Johnson, were in the office as well. Much to Laila's surprise, the entire group was waiting for her in the conference room.

"Good, you're here," said Colin brusquely, "we can begin."

Laila hadn't realized there was a meeting. She gave Ali a quizzical glance. Under the grimace on the Fae's face, she could see her frustration. Colin must be in a particularly foul mood. Darien gave her a small shrug as she passed out the drinks and took a seat.

Colin continued. "Tensions between the human and SNP communities are at an all-time high. I know that we're all tired and overworked, but there are more conflicts every day. Protests are turning into riots, and I expect the number of hate crimes will continue to rise. I need everyone to be extra vigilant. It would be all too easy for one of us to get caught in the crossfire."

The others nodded.

"How is the investigation into Fredrik Stacy going?" asked Jerrik. "Do you have any evidence to support his connection to any of the hate crimes? I know we're supposed to remain politically impartial, but he seems to be at the heart of the pro-human protests. Things might calm down a little if he was out of the picture."

"We're working on a new lead," explained Colin, "this one looks promising too."

Laila suddenly had the urge to ask Colin about Lorel's involvement in Fredrik Stacy's campaign. She opened her mouth to speak, but Ali shook her head slightly as if reading her mind. Laila couldn't be sure, but she decided to keep the observation to herself, at least until she had the chance to talk to Ali about it.

"Given the recent events," continued Colin, "I've been asked by a number of the local and national news stations to give a press release."

Adam Johnson frowned. "I'm not sure that's a good idea,"

"Excuse me?" said Colin, surprised.

"Doesn't Agent Fiachra normally handle these things?" asked the human.

"Yes," muttered Colin, his teeth clenching, "But as the head of this team, I feel it is my duty to—"

"If public relations are one of her specialties, as I've been told, then why isn't *she* handling this?"

Laila watched as Colin fought to keep his composure. He paused for a moment to formulate a reply, then decided to ignore the question. He turned to Laila, Darien, and Jerrik.

"I've left three of you to handle these homicide cases, up to this point, but given the amount of bad press we've been getting, because of this case and the events surrounding it, I think it's time I stepped in to figure out what the hell is going on here."

Next to her Darien sat stiff as a board.

"We're doing everything we can," said Darien slowly. "I'm sure you know that, Colin."

"Yet I'm the one dealing with the media backlash. I—" Colin scowled.

"Agent Grayson," interrupted Adam Johnson, "I think it's unnecessary to continue this meeting. It seems clear to me that your agents' time would be better spent following up on leads."

Colin bristled.

"With all due respect, this is my office," growled Colin. "And I am the one the media is expecting to give a press release, so unless someone here is willing to fill me in on the situation—"

"Didn't you read the case file?" asked Adam Johnson coolly.

The room went silent. Laila braced herself mentally as Colin's face turned bright red.

"Of course I read the file, which seems unusually sparse for a case of this magnitude!"

Laila masked her reaction. Of course it was sparse. They'd refrained from entering the full reports and notes into the file in the event that the information was leaked—potentially by him.

"Who the hell do you think you are?" Colin continued, snarling at the human. "You're not in D.C. anymore, and I'm not going to sit around while you question my leadership. You want to do something useful? Then tell those stuffed shirts back home to open their eyes and see the chaos our country has fallen into!"

Throughout the rant, Adam Johnson merely sat and listened patiently. It was pretty impressive, considering he was facing the rage of a ready-to-shift Werewolf. Either he was confident that Colin wouldn't shift and attack, or just plain oblivious.

Once Colin had finished his rant, he stormed out of the room, slamming the door as he went. Laila glanced around at the others who seemed equally shocked, but none of them made a move to go after him. She'd undoubtedly regret this, and Laila knew she was probably shooting herself in the foot, but she stood and followed him anyway. As suspicious as his behavior had been in the recent months, she still felt like someone needed to talk some sense into Colin and give him that last chance to change before he damaged his career beyond repair.

She opened the door and found Colin heading towards his office.

"Colin?" she called after him. "Can I talk to you?"

He ignored her and stepped through the doorway. Laila gritted her teeth, knowing he would chew her out next, and followed.

"Colin, stop and think, *please*," she pleaded, standing in the doorway. "I know you don't like people breathing down your neck, but he's assessing us. You've got to shape up and quit being an ass to everyone!"

He dug through his drawer until he found a bottle of pills. She didn't see how many he took. As she waited for his response she wondered if he would lose control and shift into his wolf form, but he didn't react, he just ignored her.

"I know you care about this team more than anything." She folded her arms. "I know you'd never forgive yourself if you lost this job."

"I'm not losing my job. I *am* this team."

Laila threw her hands in the air.

"Fine!" she snarled, "I tried, but I can't save you from yourself. Sabotage your career, I don't care."

She turned to leave.

"Always so high and mighty! You think you know everything, don't you? I should've left you to rot with those Demons!"

That struck a nerve as she remembered the cheering crowd, the leering Demons, and the mass grave they'd discovered out back. Oh, he'd definitely crossed a line. Any remaining spark of pity she'd felt for him was instantly snuffed out.

Laila ignored him and walked away. In reality, it took all of her self-restraint to resist the urge to slug him in the face. She imagined the satisfying crunch his nose would make when she broke it. But she knew he wasn't worth it, and he wasn't her problem. She returned to the conference room and gently shut the door. When she turned around, she realized everyone was staring at her.

"He—" Laila started.

"We heard everything," said Darien nodding towards Colin's office. "The walls aren't that thick."

"What an ass," hissed Ali softly. She gave Laila a knowing look that told her they would be discussing this later. Preferably over drinks, or ice cream, or maybe both.

Laila took a deep breath as she took her seat. "Is there anything more to discuss?"

There was a moment of silence, where nobody seemed willing to say anything.

Laila spoke up when no one else did, "Well, I'm positive that our serial killer is following victims from the gym. We should probably survey the area tomorrow night and see if we find anyone following people home. I was thinking it might be a good idea to bring Frej along as well. Having an aerial view might be helpful."

"I'm not sure how I feel about these outsiders helping out in our investigations." Adam Johnson frowned. "It's a liability."

"Unfortunately, we're understaffed," pointed out Darien. "We need the help, and they're willing to offer it. Frej, Talen, and Lyn all know what they are getting into, and I'm confident we can trust them."

Laila nodded in agreement.

"If there was another way, we'd do it," she added, "but with the city in its current state, we can't afford to turn down the help. We'd ask the police, but they're not equipped to handle these things. These contacts are."

There was a pause before the human responded. "Fine, but the agency isn't responsible for any of this."

They nodded.

"Something else is bugging me," mentioned Darien, "Laila, maybe you and Jerrik should contact Captain Anderson in the morning and see if they've found anything new on the Di Inferi. The gang's been quiet up until this point, and I want to know why."

"We'll handle it." Laila glanced at Jerrik who nodded.

"I'll do what I can to handle the media," said Ali. "I'm not sure what's going on with Colin, but I'm sure I can handle the investigation on Fredrik Stacy."

Jerrik stood. "Great, then it looks like we have a plan."

"Why don't we grab our computers and head home?" Ali asked her. "Things seem a little tense here."

Darien nodded. "Go ahead. I'm going to make some phone calls and see what the Vampire community has to say about Arnold Koch. I'll let the rest of you know if something comes up."

The women gathered their things and headed down to the garage. It was early for them, but there wasn't much Laila and the others could do about their cases at this late hour.

"I'm starving," announced Ali, "I hope Erin and Frej saved some food for us."

"I've got a surprise for you waiting at the house." Laila remembered the Bogey-cat. She was sure Erin was giving it all the attention it could possibly want and more.

They were walking out to Laila's car when her phone buzzed in her pocket. It was Lyn.

"Hey!" Laila answered the phone.

"Someone's trying to break in!" Lyn whispered frantically.

"Wait, what?" Laila froze. "Where's the security detail?"

"I sent them home, I-I didn't think there was anything to worry about. Now two Supernaturals are trying to break into the shop!"

There was a commotion on the other side of the line.

"Lyn?" called Laila.

She glanced at Ali who was listening intently.

"Lyn?"

"They broke in," the Witch whispered finally.

"Barricade yourself in your apartment," said Laila jumping in her car, "Ali and I are on our way!"

CHAPTER 24

Laila drove through the deserted city streets. Luckily, no one was on the road down by the beach at this time of night, and they made it to Lyn's house in five minutes flat. The car screeched to a halt as Laila pulled up to the curb. Rushing out of the car, she and Ali sprinted down the sidewalk, stopping at Lyn's shop. The door was ajar, with shards of glass littering the floor. Laila took the lead, unholstering her magical stun baton while Ali readied her handgun.

"This is the Inter-Realm Security Agency!" Laila shouted. "Come out with your hands up!"

"They're on the second-floor landing!" called Lyn above them, her voice muffled from the glass of the window.

"This is your last chance!" Ali called.

The Fae nodded, and Laila advanced. Merchandise and shelves had been knocked over by the intruders. Lyn's beaded curtain that separated the shop from her back hallway had been ripped from the doorway as well. The beads were scattered across the floor, and Laila had to watch her step to keep from slipping.

Above she could hear the intruders trying to force open the door on the second level. As she reached the foot of the stairs, she could see their dark figures facing the door.

"Freeze!" roared Laila.

The figures turned. One of them rushed her, flying down the stairs with superhuman speed, and slamming Laila into the wall. Her head collided with a thud against the wood, and spots danced across her vision.

The sound of gunshots rang out next to her, as Ali shot the attacker twice in the leg. The person, a woman, hissed at her, baring her fangs. She was a Vampire.

The Vampire lunged at Ali, but Laila grabbed her by the hair. The woman shrieked and clawed at her hands, trying to free herself.

Ali reached out, placing her hand on the Vampire's shoulder.

"Easy now," said the Fae, "You don't want to hurt anyone."

The Vampire's eyes grew wide as she was hit with a strong wave of Fae charm. She stood there dazed while Ali motioned for Laila to take the next one.

Laila flew up the stairs, two at a time, as the remaining intruder muttered in a language unfamiliar to Laila and placed something on the floor of the landing. There was a rumbling as the object grew in size until it was towering over Laila.

"Thor's hammer," breathed Laila.

What the hell was *that?* She thought, taking a step back.

The creature swung a lumpy arm at her. She blocked with the baton, which slowly sank into the limb. The creature pulled away, nearly taking the baton with it, but it was released with a smacking sound. The creature was made of clay.

Laila reached out with her magic trying to force the earth to bend to her will, but the spell animating the creature was strong, and it resisted. The earth creature swung again, and Laila reinforced her block with both hands spread wide on the baton, but the force of the blow knocked her off her feet. She crashed through the railing and into the wall, sliding down seven feet to the floor below. If she was human, she probably would've broken something, but she managed to stand, mostly unharmed.

"Lyn!" she shouted, "I've got a magical creature made from clay! How do I stop it?"

"It's probably a Golem," said Lyn through the door, "You have to remove the enchantment charm from its mouth."

"Great," muttered Laila.

She rushed past Ali and the charmed Vampire, then sprinted up the stairs once more. As she neared the creature, she leapt with all her Elven strength, jumping nearly ten feet into the air. She reached out to each side of the narrow walls of the stairwell above, wedging herself in place.

The creature looked around, confused, and took a step forward. One more step and it was directly below her. She shifted so she was facing the other way and dropped down on its shoulders. It grunted and reached for her, but she was already shoving her hand into the creature's mouth.

Struggling to stay on its shoulders, she felt around in the thick, sticky clay for anything that could be controlling the enchantment. The Golem beat at her with its heavy fists, but Laila managed to hold on. Finally, she felt something hard and smooth. She wrapped her fingers around it and pulled. The object came free with a click, and the creature roared. It rapidly disintegrated until Laila was sitting in a pile of dry clay dust.

There was a crash above, and Laila scrambled to her feet to see the remaining intruder break through Lyn's door.

"You have got to be kidding me!" howled Lyn. "Those were my best lock enchantments!"

The intruder approached Lyn with a thin stick in his hand. She swore and dove for cover as the intruder pointed the wand at Lyn, a bolt of lightning shooting out of it.

Laila conjured an ice dagger and threw it at the intruder, the blade lodging deep into the intruder's shoulder. The man cried out and spun around to face her. He blasted her with another bolt of lightning, but Laila was prepared. She redirected the spell, reflecting it back to the intruder. It struck him square in the chest knocking him backwards, to the ground. He didn't rise, and Laila knew the spell had been strong enough to kill him. She approached cautiously none the less, to check for a pulse. There wasn't one.

"Are you okay?" She turned to Lyn.

"Yeah," she nodded. "I knew it had to be another Witch. No one else would know how to get through my wards."

Laila wanted to shake Lyn for dismissing her guards. Instead, she helped her up.

"I'm glad you're okay."

The Witch gave her an uneasy smile. "Just a little shaken."

There was a noise from the doorway, and they turned to find the Vampire standing just inside the apartment.

"Come to him quietly," the Vampire hissed to Laila, "or your friends will pay."

Laila quickly reached out and found trace amounts of Demonic energy clinging to the Vampire. Marius had sent her.

Gunshot after gunshot rang out from down the hallway and the Vampire shook with each bullet that struck.

"DON'T THREATEN MY FRIENDS, BITCH!!!" Ali snarled, emptying the magazine.

By the time she was finished, the Vampire was bleeding from multiple head wounds. She screeched and threw herself at the window. It shattered, raining down onto the concrete below. The Vampire landed in a crouch and took off running into the night. She would heal, but not until she found a blood source.

Ali limped her way up the stairs.

"Is everyone okay?" she asked.

"Remind me not to piss you off," chuckled Lyn darkly. "Thanks for getting here so quickly."

"Of course." Laila gave her a reassuring look.

They surveyed the damage. The room was a mess. Stacks of books and artifacts had been knocked over in the struggle, the door had been broken down, not to mention the wall to wall window that had been shattered. A cool ocean breeze drifted through the opening, rustling pages of open books as sirens in the distance drew closer.

Lyn groaned and flopped down onto a sofa. Ali limped over to join her.

"Why don't I take a look at that?" Laila indicated Ali's leg.

Ali waved her off. "It can wait, the police will be arriving soon, and one of us needs to speak to them."

Reluctantly Laila nodded and went downstairs to wait for the police. When they arrived, she explained what happened and who she was. Since the crime was SNP related, it was in her agency's jurisdiction, but the officers helped her to deal with the couple of bystanders who were gathering on the sidewalk while she called Darien. After that, she returned upstairs to check on the others.

Lyn was still sitting there, with her head in her hands, but Ali had moved to prop her leg up on a chair with an ice pack.

"So what happened here?" Laila gestured to Ali's knee as she knelt beside it.

"The Vampire got me in the knee. I don't think anything's broken, but..." she trailed off.

"Can I check it?"

Ali nodded and removed the ice. Laila placed her hands gently on either side of the knee and reached out with her magic. There was some bruising of the bones, a couple stretched ligaments, and quite a bit of swelling.

"What do you think?" asked Ali.

"I think I can fix it," Laila said after a moment, "I'm just not sure I have the energy left."

"Here." Lyn passed her a rough crystal necklace. "It's a store of magical energy like a magical battery. I use them for enchantments that require a constant source of energy. It should work just fine. Just warm it in your hand to activate it."

Laila did as she was told, and the crystal glowed gently in her hand with a faint pink light. Immediately she felt the energy pulsing. She started the process of healing Ali's leg, and by the time she was finished, Laila still didn't feel the drag of the magic exhaustion.

"That worked great!" Laila passed the necklace back to Lyn. "I think I used it up though."

Lyn shrugged. "No big deal, I've got more of them."

The Witch placed her head in her hands, and Laila knew the charm was the least of her worries. It would take time for her to have the windows and doors replaced, not to mention the rest of the cleanup. There was no way she could stay here with the building in its current state. Laila glanced at Ali and could tell she was thinking the same thing.

"Hey Lyn," said Ali, gently resting her hand on the Witch's shoulder, "why don't you come stay with us until you can get this place taken care of? I've got a guest room I can set you up in, and tomorrow we can figure out what to do about the damage."

Ali's house was probably the safest location aside from the IRSA building at this point. Ali had invested no small amount of money into alarms, cameras, security upgrades since her sister's abduction. They could post guards as well.

Lyn glanced up, looking from Ali to Laila.

"Are you sure?" she asked.

Laila nodded. "It's probably more secure than a hotel room. This confirms that the Demons are targeting you. Until we can put a stop to it, I want you staying somewhere safe." The guilt weighed on Laila, she couldn't help but feel that this was all her fault, and just a way for the Demons to get back at her.

"Okay," sighed Lyn finally, "but I don't want to be a burden."

"It's no trouble," Ali reassured her.

Ali was just standing to test her leg when Darien walked in.

"Weren't you going home for the night?" he asked, observing the wreckage.

"We took a detour," said Laila.

CHAPTER 25

"I'll get this taken care of." Darien gestured to the corpse on the floor. "You guys head home."

"I'll stay," Laila insisted, but Darien shook his head.

"You're exhausted. Go home and get some rest."

Laila didn't argue further. She left with the others and returned home. Frej was still awake, watching a documentary on ancient tombs when they arrived. The Bogey-cat was curled up in his lap asleep, and Laila noticed there were a variety of new cat toys scattered around the room. She wondered whether it was Erin or Frej spoiling the Bogey.

Frej joined her in the kitchen, his expression growing troubled as he took in the grim faces of the others.

"Lyn was attacked in her home," Laila explained to him softly as Ali showed the Witch to the guest room on the second floor, "she's going to stay with us until we sort this out."

"Is she alright?" asked Frej, turning the stove on to reheat dinner.

"Physically, yes, but her house and shop are in ruins."

Laila sighed and slid onto a barstool at the kitchen island.

"This is my fault," she said, "If I hadn't involved her with IRSA, none of this would've happened."

She explained to him about the threatening message from the Vampire. However, she kept her knowledge of the other traps the Demons had set for her a secret. With everything Lyn was going through, it just didn't seem like the time to divulge her own problems.

Frej listened as he heated dinner on the stove.

"What's done is done," he pointed out, stirring the contents of the pan, "don't dwell on it. You have enough stress to deal with right now."

Laila rolled her eyes. "Especially since Colin's lost his mind."

"What did he do now?"

"Yelled at the guy from D.C. in front of all of us, then stormed out of the meeting. I tried to talk some sense into him but…" Laila shrugged at a loss for words.

Frej walked around the counter to stand behind her. Laila leaned back as he massaged her shoulders. The Bogey-cat hopped up into her lap and head-butted her arm. She quickly gave in and started stroking his long silky coat as he purred. Laila felt her tension ease a little.

"Well," said Frej, "if you want, I can go over to the shop with Lyn tomorrow and help her sort things out."

"Could you?" asked Laila. "I don't want her going over there alone, even with the human guards. Marius has targeted her twice now. Maybe she should leave town, at least until all of this calms down."

"Like hell I am!" called Lyn from the stairs. "I'm not going anywhere. This city is my home, and I'm not the only Supernatural being threatened these days. I'd rather stay and fight to protect my home than run like a coward."

"They tried to kill you!" Laila watched her desperately.

Lyn shrugged. "They're not the first, and I can tell you they're not going to be the last."

The Witch glanced down at the ball of black fluff in Laila's lap.

"You're new," she pointed out with a hint of a grin. "When did you get a cat?"

"You got a what!?!" howled Ali from the stairs.

"Surprise!" Laila gave her a sheepish look.

The Fae stalked over, preparing for a speech on taking in stray animals, but as soon as she took one look at those bright green, feline eyes, the words died on her tongue. He nuzzled her with his head and gave her a questioning meow as her eyes grew wide.

"Oh my Gods!" squealed Ali picking him up. "You're the cutest little fur ball I've ever seen!"

Ali continued to coo over the Bogey-cat while Laila explained how it had come to be in her care.

Lyn watched the creature with fascination. "Bogeys are very loyal and protective. They make good guard dogs, so to speak. This one also seems particularly affectionate."

"Don't crowd Mr. Whiskers," chided Erin as she entered from down the hall.

"Mr. Whiskers?" asked Frej skeptically.

"Well, he needed a name, and he looks like a Mr. Whiskers to me."

The others shook their heads, but since no one else could come up with an alternative, Mr. Whiskers seemed to stick.

After dinner, Laila wearily climbed the stairs with the others. She parted ways with Lyn and Ali in the hall, but as she was about to enter her room, Frej caught her hand.

"Can I come in?" he asked.

Laila nodded. She sat down on the corner of the bed as he shut the door behind him. He took a seat next to her on the bed.

"How are you?" he asked.

She leaned her head on his shoulder. "I'm worried that I can't stop them."

"Who?"

"The Demons, the Di Inferi, this rogue Vampire, all of

them. What if I'm not strong enough to protect the people I care about?"

"Hey." He wrapped an arm around her shoulders. He used his other hand to tilt her chin until she was looking at him.

His bright blue eyes were gentle and warm. They filled her with a sense of calm, and through the swirl of emotions and guilt, they grounded her.

"There will always be another criminal or another battle. Life doesn't give you the chance to slow down and breathe. Not for people like us. That's why we need to make time for ourselves and the people we care about."

She allowed him to pull her onto his lap. He kissed her briefly before pulling away.

"I've missed you, Laila," he said resting his forehead against her own, "I miss kissing you, and falling asleep in your bed. I miss waking up with you in my arms. I know there's a lot going on right now, but please, let me be here for you."

Laila lifted her face and met his lips with a slow, lingering kiss. After several long moments, she leaned back to look at his face.

"I've missed you too," she admitted. "I'm sorry we've been fighting."

"I am too."

He leaned back onto the bed, pulling her down with him.

Laila lay there awake resting her head on Frej's bare chest. It felt good to have his company. It was comforting. But still she feared the dreams that would come in the night, full of blood, loss, and death. They were getting worse despite the new charm Lyn had given her.

She sighed. It appeared she couldn't escape from the troubles of this world, even in her dreams. Shifting, Laila wondered when she'd last had a peaceful, pleasant dream. It had been months, probably, but it felt like years, unless she counted the dream about Jerrik.

She thought over what Jerrik had said about his feelings for her. Not only that, but it appeared he hadn't left without a word after all. Instead, it had been Colin who'd mislead her. Buy why? Why would Colin do that? Or was Jerrik lying about the whole thing?

This was all so confusing. She was over Jerrik, she had moved on, and there was no going back. But still, there was a part of her that wondered what would be different if she'd received that letter.

Then there was that dream… that traitorous, seductive dream. She hated her mind for showing her that. The guilt weighed on her even as her head rested on Frej's chest. Should she tell him? Or would it make matters worse? Frej was already suspicious of Jerrik, and she didn't want to give him another reason to suspect there was anything going on—not that there was.

As her mind swirled with thoughts, she gradually drifted off to a troubled sleep. In her dreams, she walked from one scene of destruction to another both in Midgard and the other worlds. She was crossing yet another battlefield covered in carnage when a musical but terrifying voice startled her.

"Don't ignore the call!"

Laila awoke with a start. Her phone was buzzing on the nightstand beside her. She grabbed it and saw she had a new message from Jerrik.

I've got a lead on Di Inferi from LAPD. New location. When can you be ready for surveillance?

She glanced at the time, it was already ten o'clock. She needed to get going.

I'll pick you up at the office in an hour, she wrote.

"Who's that?" asked Frej groggily.

"Jerrik," she said.

"What does he want?" groaned the Dragon.

"We've got surveillance this morning." Laila got up and

headed towards the bathroom.

"Should I come along?" asked Frej, following her.

"No, we can handle it. Besides, you were going to go help Lyn today."

Laila could tell there was more Frej wanted to say, but he hesitated.

Laila took a deep breath. "I spoke to Jerrik yesterday, and he told me about his confrontation with you. He didn't tell me what, only that there's something that I don't know. I don't like the fact that you're keeping something from me, but it bothers me even more that you're willing to lie to me about it."

Frej looked at her stunned but still remained silent. She didn't have time to deal with this. She had to get ready for work. She started to shut the door to the bathroom, but he stopped her.

"I'm going to tell you. I swear to you I am. I-I'm just not ready, not yet." His expression was pained and conflicted. There was something deeper there, possibly remorse? But for what? Maybe for lying or keeping this from her.

She nodded as she shut the door, she could live with that, especially since he'd been so understanding of her. It was the least she could do.

Jerrik handed Mato and Henrik their coffee orders as he took a seat at the table of the little seaside café they'd met at for breakfast. It was a sunny morning, and they were sitting outside as they waited for their breakfast. Jerrik didn't have much time, he'd have to leave for the office in thirty minutes to meet Laila for surveillance.

"So, you told Laila everything," clarified Henrik.

"Well, almost everything," admitted Jerrik. "I didn't tell her about my father. Or about his bounty hunters. She's had enough people targeting her, thanks to the Demons. I didn't want to worry her, especially since the problem has been dealt with."

He'd noticed the bounty hunter sniffing around the hospital when he'd gone to visit her. It wasn't entirely surprising considering that their story had made news headlines around the country. He'd already accepted Colin's offer and only had a few days before he was supposed to leave. If he didn't deal with the bounty hunters and get them off his trail, they'd find out about Laila. His father couldn't know about her, not after what he'd done to his mentor, Master Kyvik. The thought of what his father would do to her made his blood boil.

So he'd left, and hopped his way through a couple of portals with a fake I.D. Somewhere in Jotunheim he lost the bounty hunters. But he didn't have time to return to L.A. before his training program started. He wanted to contact her, but he couldn't risk it, not until he knew for certain that he was no longer being followed. By the time he had finished the expedited training program, there was still no sign of the bounty hunters, so Jerrik determined it was safe for him to return to L.A.

Henrik frowned. "And what about the fact you left without a word?"

Jerrik shrugged. "I told her I left a letter with our boss, but he didn't give it to her. She seemed skeptical, but I guess his obnoxious behavior has been strange enough to justify it in her mind."

Mato shook his head. "I don't like this, man. A half-truth is the same as a lie. I know your life is one big dumpster fire—"

"Gee thanks," muttered Jerrik sarcastically.

"But seriously bro, you should just come clean with her." Mato gave him a pleading look.

Henrik nodded in agreement.

Jerrik sighed. "Maybe I should, but the less she knows, the better. What if the bounty hunters show up and I have to disappear again? No, it's safer this way."

As much as it broke his heart, he knew that it was entirely possible he'd have to leave again. He hated that he had to live this way, but as long as his father wanted him dead, he didn't see any other option.

CHAPTER 26

"I think this is it." Jerrik nodded as they drove past a non-descript building.

Laila pulled down a side street and parked her camouflaged car where they had a clear view of the building in question.

That morning Jerrik had spoken with Captain Anderson from the LAPD Gangs and Narcotics division. When Jerrik asked about any leads on the Di Inferi, he was surprised to find that the captain was in the process of placing an undercover officer amongst their ranks. While the officer was still mostly in the dark on the gang's proceedings, he'd managed to track down a hideout of sorts that was located in the Old City. It was that building that Laila and Jerrik were observing now.

"So, what exactly are we looking for?" asked Laila.

"Captain Anderson mentioned they've been stockpiling weapons. I guess the shop they robbed the other day was just one of such incidents, the others were in the Old City though. His officer believes one of their weapons caches will be moved this afternoon, but they're not sure where they'll be moved to or why."

As suspicious as it was, it seemed like a waste of their time. She wanted to snap at Jerrik for volunteering them, but he was only trying to help. Laila supposed a couple of hours away from the homicide investigations couldn't hurt.

She cast a spell of light on the windows. Anyone passing by would only see sunlight reflecting off the windows, not the agents within. It wasn't as good as a glamour, but it would do for now.

The hours ticked by slowly. Finally, in the late afternoon, an old pickup truck pulled into the alley across from them. A couple of men stepped out of the building to chat with the driver before they rolled up a garage door and started loading bundles into the truck.

"What is that?" asked Jerrik.

Laila grabbed her binoculars.

"Guns," she said, "mostly, I can't tell what's in the crates though."

She passed the binoculars back to Jerrik.

"I'm calling Frej." She pulled out her phone. "Just in case we need some aerial surveillance."

Jerrik muttered something under his breath as Frej answered the phone. She explained the situation, and he told her he was on his way. With that, she returned her attention to the Di Inferi members.

The gang members finished loading the truck, then one of the men joined the driver in the cab as he prepared to drive off. Laila waited until the other man was back inside the building and the truck had pulled around the corner before starting the engine. Frej would have to catch up with them later if he could locate her car.

Laila followed a few blocks behind the truck as it wound its way through the streets of the Old City. About five minutes later the truck took a right, but by the time they made it to the street, the other vehicle was out of sight."

"Crap," she groaned, looking around. "Do you see it anywhere?"

Jerrik scanned the street as they drove, but there was no sign of the vehicle. There was no sign of Frej either. They drove around the streets searching for any sign of the truck. Finally, after twenty minutes of weaving around the southern section of the Old City, they spotted something.

"I think that's it," Jerrik indicated an old pickup truck pulled up along the curb.

The occupants were nowhere in sight though. Laila headed down the next street and parked. They got out of the car and peered around the side of the building, but there was still no sign of life. All the buildings along the street had been boarded up, preventing access. It was as if the men and weapons had just vanished.

"Maybe it's a different truck," said Jerrik, "There are so many old cars out here, it's hard to tell."

Laila shook her head. "It's the same license plate. That's it."

After double-checking to make sure they were alone, they crept closer towards the truck. Laila checked for enchantments that might conceal a hidden entrance to the nearby buildings, but she didn't detect anything.

Jerrik walked around to the back of the truck.

"What's this?" asked Jerrik as he looked at something on the ground.

Laila walked around the car and saw a large metal panel on the ground. It looked old, and the paint was chipping away exposing rusted metal.

"I'm not sure," she said.

They tried to lift it, but the metal didn't budge. A faint noise within caught her attention though. She pressed her ear to the metal and could faintly make out voices below.

There was a sudden groan of metal, and the panel started to shift.

Move! she mouthed at Jerrik.

They ran as quietly as they could across the street and dove behind a broken-down car just as the two men emerged. Laila shifted, peering over the hood of the car as she tried to get a better look, but she was all too aware of how close Jerrik was beside her. His arm brushed against hers, and she bit her lip, trying to focus on the armed men in front of her rather than the one crouching beside her.

The gangsters were standing on some sort of a lift. Once the men stepped off of it, the panel creaked shut once more.

"Well that's different," she muttered.

One of the men looked in her direction, and she crouched down further behind the car. Laila exchanged a glance with Jerrik, hoping the man hadn't seen them. They waited, hardly daring to breathe as footsteps approached.

A roar echoed through the street as a pale, winged figure swooped into view. He dove down between the buildings and caught the gangsters' truck in his back claws, flipping it over.

It was the distraction they needed. Laila grabbed Jerrik's arm and hurried back to their car as the gangsters shook off their surprise. The engine rumbled to life, and Laila took off down the street as the Di Inferi members opened fire. Jerrik conjured up a shield to protect the car from bullets as they sped away. Above, Frej banked right, back towards the west side and they followed.

"Should we double back and try going down there?" asked Jerrik.

"No," she said firmly, "not until we have more information. We should head back anyway, it's almost sunset and Darien will want to hear about this."

Frej peeled off once they'd left the Old City in the direction of home, while she continued to the office. The sun was just setting by the time they pulled into the parking garage, but Darien's car was already there. Laila realized that it had been parked there earlier as well. It appeared Darien was sleeping in his office.

As the elevator door opened, she could hear Ali's frustrated voice.

"Seriously?" Ali fumed. "After all that, Colin's a no-show?"

She was pacing back and forth while Adam Johnson watched with a furrowed brow.

"What's going on?" asked Jerrik as they approached.

Ali planted her fists on her hips.

"Apparently Colin doesn't want to do the press release after all," she huffed. "We're supposed to leave in two minutes, and he's nowhere to be found!"

"You can do it though, right?" asked Laila.

"Sure, but it's just… you know!" Ali waved at Colin's empty office.

Laila understood; it was just another instance of Colin being Colin.

"I should go," Ali stalked off towards the elevator.

"See you later!" Laila called after her.

She glanced at Adam who was still standing there in the hallway.

"Are you going with her?" Laila asked him.

He shook his head.

Laila shrugged and continued down to Darien's office with Jerrik on her heels.

"Hey," she called from the doorway.

The Vampire glanced up from his computer.

"Any luck?" he asked.

"Looks like they're storing the weapons underground or something. They used some sort of old-fashioned lift set into the sidewalk."

Darien leaned back in his chair. "Could it be from the old subways? They haven't been in operation since The Event."

"What?" asked Jerrik and Laila in unison.

"Sure," he shrugged, "They had tunnels below the city, no one ever saw a need to reopen them since the city's no longer as spread out and overpopulated as it once was."

"Really?" Laila gave him a disbelieving look. "We are investigating a rogue Vampire, and you didn't think to mention the underground tunnels?"

It sounded like the perfect place to hide in her opinion.

Darien shrugged. "I think they're sealed up pretty good. At least the ones on this side of the city."

"Is there a map?" asked Jerrik.

Darien typed something into a web browser and turned the laptop to face them. There was a map of the city crisscrossed with multicolored lines.

"This is where we were." Laila pointed towards the location where they'd found the trapdoor. It wasn't anywhere near the old tracks. So much for that idea.

"It would've made sense though," said Jerrik, "Vampires hiding in old underground tunnels."

Darien shrugged. "Anyway, we've got to head over to *Shape it Up!* It's nearly dark, and we need to be there before our serial killer starts hunting."

"I'll come with you," said a voice behind her, startling Laila.

It was Adam, who had apparently followed them down the hall.

"Are you sure?" she asked.

He nodded. "I'd like the opportunity to ask you a few questions and seeing as you're usually out of the office…" he trailed off.

Laila wasn't sure how great of an idea it was to take a human along with them, but she could tell he was determined to go.

"Okay, let's go find us a Vampire."

They took a moment to prepare and gear up. Laila pulled on her breastplate and met the others down in the garage.

They took two SUVs with Darien and Jerrik in one, and Adam and Laila in the second. The last rays of sunlight had just vanished on the horizon when they pulled out of the garage.

"Now that we have a moment," began Adam, "There's something I need to speak to you about."

CHAPTER 27

Laila knew it would only be a matter of time before he approached her, but it still gave her a hint of anxiety. Was this about Colin? Or was it about the long list of protocols and procedures that were constantly ignored? The list in her mind grew as she waited for the human to continue.

"I've read your file, and you have a pretty impressive record. Not just with your work at the academy here, but in your training in Alfheim as well."

"Thank you," she said following Darien's SUV.

"I believe I can rely on you to give me a truthful response to my next question."

"Go on."

He crossed his arms and leaned back into the seat.

"I know this office operates a little differently than the agency would hope. Do you think this affects the efficiency of the office?"

"No," insisted Laila firmly, "the agents in this office, myself included, do what we have to in order to effectively handle the situations that we face in this city. It is our intention to keep the largest number of Los Angeles' citizens safe. We don't operate the way we do out of convenience. The way IRSA would like us to act is modeled after agencies that existed before The Event. It doesn't take into consideration the new challenges this world faces, and it definitely doesn't take into consideration how chaotic the city is. We are understaffed. Period. Maybe if we had more field agents, we'd be able to follow protocol to the extent you would like, but right now, it's just not possible."

"I see," he mused after a moment, "is Colin functioning in his role as supervisor?"

She hesitated. "I know that he personally has dealt with a lot. Honestly though, no, he's not."

Adam nodded and waited for her to elaborate.

"I know this job is… well, was his life, but lately, he treats it like a joke. Something's changed since I was abducted. Something feels off, and his behavior's been inconsistent with what I came to know before the incident, or maybe I'm just starting to get to know him."

"Yes," said Adam, flipping through his tablet, "I've read the reports on your abduction. Is there anything you'd like to elaborate on with regard to this?"

Laila shrugged. "It's all in the reports."

"Do you trust Colin?"

She thought of the times he'd left Ali behind on calls. Laila recalled how he'd been unwilling to listen to her input and belittled her even after she gave him far more chances than he deserved. Then there was the letter that Jerrik had given him explaining why he'd left….

"Not anymore."

Adam watched her closely.

"Ali's told me that she and the rest of your team has felt it necessary to exclude him from certain investigations, is this true?"

"Yes."

"Why?"

"We recently became suspicious that there was an information leak in the office."

"Which you believe is Colin," finished Adam.

"We haven't found any evidence."

Adam typed a note into the tablet before speaking again.

"I have one more question for you. If you were to select an acting supervisor on the team to step into Colin's position for the time being, who would it be?"

"Probably Ali or Darien." She certainly didn't see herself in that position, and they had the most experience.

Laila pulled into a parking space on the street. From there they could see the doors of the gym and keep an eye on the parking lot. They could also quickly follow any suspicious vehicles leaving. Laila didn't see where Darien parked, probably along the side street up ahead.

By the entrance of the gym, there was no sign of anyone loitering. Scanning the cars in the parking lot, she didn't see anyone waiting. She turned her attention to the building across the way but didn't see anyone watching out of windows either. Perhaps it was possible that their killer wouldn't be hunting tonight.

She put one of the com devices in her ear. Darien already had his in.

"Are you in position?" he asked.

"Yes, we're parked on the street by the parking lot entrance. Where are you?"

"Parked in the lot next door."

"How long do you think we should give him?" she asked.

"No more than two hours. He only seems to follow people who leave shortly after dark."

"Okay," she said, "I'll let you know if we see anything."

They sat for about thirty minutes in silence. After their previous conversation, Laila wasn't in a talkative mood. Luckily, Adam didn't appear to be the talkative type. A few cars drove into the parking lot, their occupants heading for the gym.

It occurred to Laila that it was a little silly to drive your car to the gym, especially since many of the members seemed to be riding stationary bikes or running on treadmills. Why not go for a run on the beach? Or ride a bike to the gym at the very least?

Another fifteen minutes passed when movement across the street caught her attention. A car parked on the opposite side of the road. A figure in a shabby grey coat sat in the driver's seat.

"Hey Darien, I think we've got something. It looks like there's a man that just parked on the street. I can't get a good look at his face, and he's not getting out of the vehicle."

There was a rustling noise before Darien's reply came. "I'm sending Jerrik over that way to see if he can get a better look."

They watched and waited as Jerrik strolled down the street. He was wearing a pair of jeans, and one of Darien's old black leather jackets that was scuffed from past fights.

Leisurely, he walked down the street, stopping by the passenger window of the other car. Laila watched as he pulled a pack of cigarettes and asked the guy for a light. He ignored him the first time but snapped at him the second. Jerrik put his hands up and took a step back before walking away.

Her cellphone buzzed, and she looked at the screen. It was a message from Jerrik.

It's him.

There was a picture as well that Jerrik had managed to snap.

"Darien, did you get the message?"

"Yeah, I—"

A car pulled out of the gym, and immediately the suspicious Vampire started up his engine, following the car.

"He's on the move," she said, following them.

"Right behind you," Darien replied.

They followed the cars for a few blocks through a series of turns. Laila switched on the emergency lights to pull the Vampire over, but instead of slowing down, he peeled off to the right and down across street.

"Great," muttered Laila, following him. "Darien, he's running."

The suspicious Vampire turned right again.

"I think he's heading back towards the gym."

"Okay," said Darien, "I'll see if I can cut him off."

Laila and Adam followed the car through a series of streets, Darien caught up with them, but the Vampire turned down another street and into a parking garage. They pulled in, winding up to the third floor just in time to see him ditch the car and make a run for it.

"Here." Laila cut the engine and passed the keys to Adam as well as the com device so he could communicate with Darien in the other vehicle.

She opened the driver's door and sprinted after the perp. He was slow for a Vampire, and Laila remembered Darien mentioning that younger Vampires were slower than older ones. Still, he was faster than her, and she struggled to keep him in her sight.

He raced up two more flights of stairs and across the parking structure. Reaching the end of the level, he didn't stop. Instead, he jumped from the railing. The Vampire sailed over the walkway below and onto the roof of the next building. Laila followed suit, launching across the space between the buildings. She landed in a roll on the flat roof of the building next door. As she rose and continued her pursuit, Laila saw the Vampire scramble over the far edge of the roof.

Racing across the roof, she peered over the edge and saw a twenty-foot drop. Below was a dumpster where the Vampire had landed, cushioning his fall with the garbage within. He was quickly climbing out of it though, so Laila jumped, casting a spell as she fell. The air below her became solid like one of her shields, and she slid down the slope. The second her feet hit the ground, she kept running.

A blur of movement intercepted the fleeing man in front of her. Darien slammed into the other Vampire like a semi-truck, and the two Vampires crashed into the wall of a building, which shook from the impact as cracks grew in the stucco surrounding them.

Darien stumbled back, something protruding from his chest. Laila realized in horror that he wasn't wearing his bullet-proof vest.

"Darien!" she screamed.

Knife wounds would heal, but this one was horrifically close to his heart.

"I'm fine," he gasped.

Darien carefully backed away from the other Vampire, careful not to make any sudden movements. The other Vampire kept running.

"Just get him!" Darien added.

Laila formed ice daggers from the water vapor in the air and paused to throw three of them at the Vampire. All three sank into the backs of his legs. The Vampire stumbled and hissed but kept running. He grabbed the back of a trashcan and hurled it at Laila. Throwing up a shield, she plowed through the debris. Much to her dismay, she was quickly losing ground. Even with the blood trickling down his legs as the daggers continue to shred his flesh, he was still running faster than she was.

Something about it was just off. Vampires could still feel pain, so either he had an insanely high pain tolerance, or there was something else at work like magic or drugs. But there was no drug to her knowledge that affected Vampires.

She was beginning to tire and starting to feel desperate. Reaching into the ground, she opened a crevice just in front of the Vampire. It was about six feet long, and the Vampire didn't have time to avoid it. Even so, it only took seconds for him to crawl out of it.

Laila leapt over the crevasse and turned a corner after him. He was only ten feet in front of her by now, but when she followed him around the next corner, he'd vanished. She searched the street, but he was truly gone.

A car pulled onto the street a couple blocks away. It was Jerrik.

"What happened?" he called through the window as he approached.

"I don't know," she said, "he's just gone."

"What?"

"I turned the corner, and he had suddenly vanished. He had a second or two at the most."

The Dark Elf parked the SUV and got out.

"See if you can figure out where he could've hidden." Laila turned back the way she came.

"Where are you going?" he called after her.

"To check on Darien."

She retraced her steps, closing the gap she'd made in the earth as she went. In the distance, she saw Darien leaning against a wall. If it was possible, he looked even paler than usual, his breath came in short gasps, and the knife was still lodged in his chest. Blood continued to soak the front of his shirt. He glanced at Laila as she approached.

"I can't," he said shaking his head. "It's close, I can feel it."

For the first time since she'd met Darien, she could see fear in his eyes.

"It's going to be okay," she insisted, "we'll get it out."

He nodded, then his gaze drifted away from her.

"Do it." He grit his teeth.

Laila approached and placed both hands on his chest, feeling for the dagger. He'd been incredibly lucky, it missed his heart by a quarter of an inch, but any movement could bring the knife closer to his heart. She didn't dare touch the knife; she'd use a spell in order to be precise.

Taking a deep breath, she felt the strings of magic attached to the blade, carefully, she drew it straight out towards her. Seconds later the knife clattered to the ground as she released the spell.

Darien coughed and sank to the ground.

"I-I need blood," he stammered shakily, "Call—"

"Don't be ridiculous." She peeled off her leather jacket. "You're drinking from me."

"No, I don't feed from coworkers... or friends."

"We don't have time," she said, unwavering, "the Vampire got away. He basically vanished into thin air. We need to figure out where he went."

Darien shook his head.

"Oh, for Thor's sake!"

Laila conjured an ice dagger, sliced her wrist, and shoved it in Darien's face.

"Drink!" she hissed.

A strange look came over Darien's face as his self-control—that was normally as strong as steel—was overwhelmed by his need to feed. He held her wrist to his mouth and drank for several long seconds before she pulled the arm out of his grasp and healed herself.

"God," he breathed, "that's different."

He leaned back against the wall for a moment, Laila's blood still smeared across his mouth. Darien wiped it away, and Laila offered him a hand up.

"How are you feeling?" she asked.

"Incredible, actually." He looked down at the hole in his chest that was healing faster than usual. "But never do that again."

"No promises." She pulled him into a hug. "I thought I was going to lose you for a second there."

He nodded in agreement.

"So, what happened? What do you mean he vanished?" he asked, following her back to the street.

Laila and Darien returned to the street where she had lost the Vampire. Jerrik was talking with Adam, who'd found his way over. Both of them were frowning.

"No luck?" she asked.

Jerrik shook his head.

"Hold on," said Darien, "Did you think you lost him somewhere around here?"

He indicated part of the alley.

She nodded. "Why?"

"He went into the storm drain." Darien blinked in surprise. "This is going to sound crazy, but I can sense him. It's like I can practically see an energy trail, but it's faint."

From the way Jerrik and Adam exchanged glances, they were more than a little skeptical.

"It must be the Elf blood," Darien mused.

"What?" Jerrik glanced from Darien to Laila. "Was he feeding on you?"

"He'd nearly been staked, and he'd lost a lot of blood. He needed more quickly, and I didn't give him a choice," she explained.

"And she's not doing that again." Darien cast her a dark look.

"Are we going to follow the magical Vampire trail or not?" she asked, waving at the drain.

Laila crouched down by the storm drain and pulled the grate up.

Jerrik shook his head. "If I've learned anything from American horror films, it's that you're *not* supposed to go down those things."

"Our job is literally to go after the creepy crawly things that go bump in the night and kill people," she reminded Jerrik.

Adam didn't seem particularly thrilled to climb down a storm drain either.

"Okay," she said, "Well why don't you two stay here and watch to see if anyone else enters the drain. You can give us a heads up."

She wanted to add that she didn't think it was a good idea to bring a human into a potentially hazardous situation, even if he worked for the same agency. Jerrik looked like he was about to protest, but she gave him a small shake of her head. She didn't want to leave Adam out here by himself in the Old City either. Having Jerrik there would be safer.

Adam nodded. He and Jerrik returned to one of the SUVs

to wait and watch. It was either that or climb into an old building and hope it was uninhabited. As they went in, Laila conjured a faint light and led the way down into the abyss.

CHAPTER 28

Laila jumped down from the last rung of the ladder bolted to the wall, her feet landing with a light crunch on the debris below. Turning, she saw Darien peering through the dark tunnel ahead.

Thanks to the magical light she'd conjured, Laila was able to watch her step as they made their way down the passage. The only other source of light were the faint shafts of moonlight that filtered through the occasional grate above them.

There was no water in the drain of course. It had been many months since the last rainstorm had passed through the area, but there was a layer of trash and dirt covering the ground that crunched underfoot. A pathway was worn through the middle of the debris as if someone had walked this way often.

The agents watched for any flicker of movement, or sign of life, but there was none. They relied on the strange energy trail that Darien had picked up on, and Laila hoped it was leading them in the right direction. After following the tunnel for a short distance, something ahead caught Darien's eye. Flickering light filtered through the hole and across their path. As they approached, they could see it was a hole broken through the wall of the storm drain and large enough for them to easily step through.

Laila dimmed her light as they approached, straining her ears for noises on the other side of the hole. Darien unholstered his gun and edged closer to the opening. Laila readied a shield to cover him as he peered around the edge of the hole, but he shook his head. No one was there.

Laila climbed through the hole after him, and what she saw made her jaw drop. Illuminated by a row of enchanted torches was a passage. The walls were not made of concrete, but stone blocks. She brushed her fingers against the solid rock of the tunnel. There was no way this had been made by humans. She could sense the magic that bound the stone together, it was stronger than concrete. Only a team of Sorcerers could have accomplished this. But why go through such lengths when there were so many abandoned buildings that could be inhabited instead?

Darien motioned that he was moving ahead. Laila followed in step behind him, watching their backs in case someone entered the tunnel after them. As they neared the other end of the passage, they reached a series of tunnels that branched off in various directions. They could hear distorted voices echoing from a number of the tunnels.

"What is this place?" she whispered to Darien.

"I don't know," he said shocked, "I had no idea anything like this existed down here."

She reached out to test the energy of the area and found faint traces of Demonic energy, similar to the traces found on the bodies.

Laila motioned towards one of the passages. "Should we continue?"

Darien shook his head. "No. Other Vampires have been through here, and I'm afraid your scent would draw too much attention. We should head back and tell the others."

Laila nodded, and they quickly retreated the way they'd come. When they crawled out of the storm drain, they found Adam and Jerrik waiting in the SUV down the street. They crawled into the back of the vehicle.

"Did you find him?" asked Jerrik from the driver's seat.

"No, someone's been busy building magical tunnels down there," explained Laila. "I also found traces of Demonic energy."

"We went as far as we could," added Darien scowling, "but it looks like there's a whole network of tunnels and we can't go charging in there blindly, not without taking some precautions first."

The others nodded.

"We should keep an eye on this entrance then," suggested Jerrik, "and find out if there are any more like this."

She doubted they'd be able to track down more unless they crawled down every storm drain in the city. They could use surveillance teams to monitor Vampire activity in the area, Frej could even do it from the sky, but that would consume a lot of time and resources.

Laila looked at the others. "We need some way to camouflage ourselves so we can explore deeper into the tunnels without drawing too much attention."

"How do we do that?" asked Jerrik.

"I'm not sure." Laila glanced at the tunnel uncertainly. "Lyn might know a spell, or even Donald. We could give him a call and see if he could meet us here with the surveillance van."

Darien nodded. "Okay, let's get Donald and a member of the investigative team to bring the surveillance van out here until morning. Jerrik and I will keep an eye on the entrance until they arrive."

"What about you two?" asked Jerrik looking at Laila and Adam

"I can take Adam back to the office," she offered, "I'm sure he has work to do. And I'll see if Lyn has any ideas regarding a charm of some sort. Ali's got some good contacts in the Old City as well, so I'll reach out and see if they know about any tunnels."

"Sounds good." Jerrik pulled out his phone and flipped through his contacts.

Laila and Adam left the others and climbed into the second SUV. Something troubled Laila about the discovery. They hadn't been able to see much of the tunnels, but she had a feeling that they extended for quite a distance. Someone had gone through a lot of trouble to build this network, but how was it that they hadn't heard of these tunnels before? And who built them? It reminded her of the Demon's gladiatorial ring all over again.

Ali had finished dealing with the media by the time they arrived back at headquarters. She had a growing headache, so she opted to head home early with Laila, who filled her in on their discovery on the way.

Ali shook her head. "That's pretty sketchy. Any idea where the tunnels lead?"

"No, not yet, but I thought your contacts might know something." Laila pulled into the garage of the house and cut the engine and changed the subject. "Any idea where Colin went?"

"Nope," grumbled Ali climbing out of the car, "No one's seen him since yesterday. I honestly don't know what I'm going to do when I see him next."

Laila was at a loss for words as well, all she knew was that she was done defending Colin.

As she climbed out of the car, something caught her attention. In one corner of the massive garage, a room had been roughly walled off. It hadn't been like that this morning.

Ali noticed her gaze. "Henrik and Mato came over this evening to help Frej with that. It's a fireproofed practice space for Erin."

They entered the house and heard the sound of voices drifting around the corner. As they entered the kitchen, they saw Frej and Erin cooking while Lyn watched from a barstool, Mr. Whiskers cradled happily in her arms. Mato and Henrik sat at the counter as well.

"You're home early," Erin pointed out as she stirred a pan.

"Well, we did go in early today," said Laila, "and I've got a problem that I'm hoping Lyn can help me with." She slid onto the stool next to the Witch.

"Oh?" Lyn gave her a sly look.

Ali set her things down and helped herself to a glass of water before joining them.

"Do you know a spell that would help conceal me from Vampires?" asked Laila watching as Erin magically adjusted the flame beneath the pan.

"That's oddly specific," said Lyn glancing sideways, "but I've got a spell that will help dampen the way people perceive your magic, it should help to mask the magic in your blood and make you less identifiable."

"How much time do you need? And can you make two of them?"

"Sure, it will probably take an hour or so, but I can have it ready in the morning."

"That would be great." That was one less thing for her to worry about.

"Wait a minute." Ali narrowed her eyes at the stove, "Erin, is the stove even on?"

"Nope," said Erin proudly, "This dinner is brought to you by Dragon fire."

"It's pretty cool," said Lyn, watching with interest, "and it's practical. It makes me wonder if there is money to be made from enchanting self-heating frying pans."

"I imagine that going wrong in so many ways." Laila laughed as she was wondering how such a device could even be stored.

Ali frowned. "I thought the point of building a safe practice space was for you to, well, practice there."

Erin made a face at her.

Frej carried a pot over to the table. "Well, I hope you're hungry because we're going to have lots of food."

As they all pitched in to set the table, Erin finished cooking the last dish. They had a variety of grilled vegetables, mashed potatoes, salad, and pork chops for those who ate meat.

"Wow," said Mato as he scooped another pile of mashed potatoes onto his plate, "this is really good."

"Thanks!" Erin beamed.

There were so many things that Laila knew she should be thinking about. From the Vampire attacks and the underground tunnels, to the human-SNP conflicts, and the search for those responsible for breaking into Lyn's home. But in the moment, there was little Laila could do about any of it, so she allowed herself a moment to relax with good food and great friends.

When they finished eating, Henrik and Mato helped to scrub and dry dishes while Lyn and Frej discussed recipes and cleared the table. Laila and Ali retreated to an office down the hall while they made some calls to Ali's contacts. An hour and a half later, they hadn't discovered anything new. The contacts were able to confirm that there was an increasing number of Vampire attacks and that there appeared to be more Vampires than usual roaming the streets. None of them mentioned anything about known Vampire hangouts above or below ground though.

Ali yawned. "Whatever's going on, the Vampires are doing a good job of keeping it secret."

Ali moved to leave, but Laila stopped her. "Can I talk to you for a minute?"

Ali nodded.

In the privacy of the office, Laila told her about the conversation she'd had with Jerrik yesterday. Laila told her everything from the secret between Frej and Jerrik, to Jerrik's explanation for his abrupt departure, and his feelings for her.

"Seriously?" snorted Ali, "Sounds more like an obsession to

me, and that excuse just doesn't seem to cut it. Even if he was in some super-secret training group, he still could've called to check in on you."

Laila rolled a pen back and forth between her fingers as she mulled over Ali's thoughts.

"So, you think there's something else going on?" asked Laila after a time.

"Maybe? Maybe not? I have a hard time reading Jerrik. I could ply him with Fae charm and get him to confess the whole story. If you aren't planning to go back to him though, I don't really see the point."

Laila nodded pensively. "What about Frej and his secret?"

Ali frowned. "That I don't know, but I think your instincts at the moment are probably right. He's an understanding guy, and I genuinely think that he puts your best interests first. I'd say give him time and let him tell you when he's ready."

"How do you always seem to know the right thing to do?" chuckled Laila.

Ali winked, "It's just one of my superpowers, like my incredible good looks, or my killer sense of humor."

Laila laughed. "Come on, let's see what the others are up to."

They rejoined the rest of the group but found Henrik had already left. Mato, however, was sitting on the sofa watching television with Frej. Mr. Whiskers dozed on a barstool, and there was no sign of Erin or Lyn.

"Okay," Laila said stifling a yawn, "I'm going to bed. It's been a long day."

The others nodded in agreement, but Laila saw the way Mato and Ali quickly climbed the stairs and had a feeling those two weren't getting to sleep any time soon. She was glad that Ali had decided to continue things with Mato, especially since it sounded like she was happy with him.

When she and Frej reached the second landing, he paused in the hall and wrapped his hands around her waist.

"Hey," he murmured, "do you want to talk about this investigation with the Vampires?"

Laila opened her mouth but hesitated.

"It's okay," said Frej gently, "you don't have to. Just don't forget that I'm here to help."

Laila nodded and rested her head against his shoulder, breathing in his musky scent of leather, books, and something herbal.

"Thank you for distracting those gangsters earlier." She lifted her head to look at him.

"Of course."

He leaned forward to kiss her, his hand pressing against the small of her back to pull her closer. Laila lost herself in the tenderness of his mouth. His tongue brushed along her lower lip playfully as she wound her fingers in the rough cloth of his shirt. He backed her up against the wall, the frenzy of his passion increasing.

Traitor.

The word echoed through her mind as she remembered that dream, the feel of his bare skin under her fingertips...

No, it was just a dream. It didn't mean anything. That was just a cruel trick of her restless mind. This was what she wanted, to be here with Frej. She wanted his arms around her, holding her close. To feel Frej's lips pressed against her own, his—

"Is everything alright?" asked Frej. Laila hadn't even realized that he'd stopped.

"I—yeah."

His brow creased with concern.

"I'm just tired." She forced a smile.

His expression softened as he hooked a stray strand of hair behind her ear.

Liar, hissed some part of her, in a dark recess of her mind. Laila ignored it.

"Will you stay with me?" she asked, nodding to her room.

"I would, but I'm expecting a scrying-glass call from Isaac

updating me on how things are going back home. I'm not sure when he'll be calling, and I don't want to disrupt your sleep."

Lord Isaac Mavrik, was one of Frej's closest friends back in the Dragon Kingdom. Laila had made his acquaintance when she visited the kingdom for a ball in honor of the king's birthday. Frej had found the level of crime in the city more than a little concerning, and he was working with Lord Mavrik and the queen to find a solution. She knew the call was important, but she was still a little disappointed.

"Another night." He rested his forehead against her own. She nodded and stepped out of his embrace.

"Goodnight," she said with a half-smile before returning to her room.

She shut the door behind her and tried to shove aside the vortex of emotions swirling inside her. When she crawled into bed after a long shower, Laila wasn't feeling much better. She moved to switch off the lamp on the bedside table when something landed on her bed with a thump.

"*Mert?*" A set of bright green eyes watched her from the corner of the bed.

"How did you get in here?" asked Laila as Mr. Whiskers padded across the bed.

She remembered that it had found a way out of the cat carrier as well. Perhaps Bogeys were escape artists?

It stopped beside her and butted her ribcage with its head before kneading her with its little paws. Laila smiled.

"Okay, just for tonight."

She switched the light off and settled into the bed, Mr. Whiskers curling up in a ball against her stomach.

Quickly she fell into a restless sleep, plagued by nightmares of hellish creatures crawling out of storm drains and attacking the city. She tossed and turned, but every time she shut her eyes, another nightmare began.

Finally, she threw the covers back and sat up. Rubbing her eyes, she checked the clock. It was only a little after 5am.

Mr. Whiskers let out a little squeak in protest as she climbed out of bed and started pacing. Why was this happening? She was using the sleeping charm from Lyn, but if anything, she was sleeping less than ever.

Stopping before the mirror on the dresser, she ran her fingers through her hair and stared at her reflection. Laila was so tired she felt like breaking down and crying, but how was she supposed to sleep like this?

She rested her arms on the top of the dresser, leaning her weight against the wood. Her hand brushed against the moonstone pommel of the dagger resting on the dresser. Suddenly the moonstone started glowing.

Immediately she snatched her hand back, but a crackling sensation had started in her fingertips and continued up her arm, like electricity coursing through the limb before continuing through the rest of her body. The scars on her arms started shifting and crackling and wound around the length of her arms. It felt like she was being electrocuted and burned alive while being torn limb from limb.

Laila screamed, the sound echoing through the house followed by the thunder of footsteps rushing to her door.

"Laila!" shouted Frej pounding on the door, "Laila, what's going on?"

CHAPTER 29

Laila tried to respond to Frej, but all she could do through the blinding pain was to choke out a sob. Mr. Whiskers yowled at the door.

Frej came barging in and stared in shock for a moment before rushing into the room.

"Gods," breathed Frej approaching her, he reached out, but hesitated, unsure if the magic would lash out at him.

Lyn entered the doorway sleepily. "What's going—holy shit!"

The Witch rushed to join Frej, who was trying to lower Laila onto the bed.

"What's happening?" asked Frej desperately.

"I don't know!" said Lyn shaking her head.

Laila had lost consciousness, but uncontrolled magic continued to crackle through her body.

"Did somebody scream?" called Ali from the doorway, Mato beside her. She stopped, horrified, when she saw Laila unconscious. The blue magic continued to crackle uncontrollably up and down her body.

"We need help!" said Frej, whipping his head around to look at Ali.

Trying not to panic, Ali rushed over to Laila's dresser and rummaged through it, looking for something. In the corner of a drawer sat a quartz crystal. She snatched it up and hurried over to the bed.

"Mato, stay here, everybody else hold on to me!" She held the crystal in one hand and Laila's arm in the other. In an instant, they vanished.

Ali glanced around at the magnificent forest surrounding her. Sunlight filtered through the canopy, and a variety of creatures milled about, but the wild beauty was lost on her. She scanned the area looking for the only person that Ali was sure could help Laila.

"Where are we?" Frej looked at the forest around them.

"Arduinna!" Ali cried, untangling herself from the others.

The Dragon watched the surrounding area cautiously while hovering protectively by Laila who was still unconscious as the blue magic crackled and snapped around her. The scars on her arms were writhing along her body like two flaming snakes.

Lyn was sorting through a variety of charms she wore around her neck and wrists, desperately searching for a spell that could help Laila. Ali had no idea what was happening, she'd never seen anything like this. She suspected it had something to do with Laila's growing magical abilities and hopefully, Arduinna would know what to do.

There was a rustle in the bushes to Ali's left, and she turned to find Arduinna stepping onto the path dressed in a long-sleeved white shirt and a flowing brown skirt. The Goddess's expression morphed from delight to horror as she took in Laila's condition.

"Oh dear!" the Goddess said kneeling by Laila's side, "This is bad, very bad."

"Can you help her?" asked Ali and Frej simultaneously.

"I believe so," said the Goddess, "but I have to find some

way to release the magic."

"What do you mean?" asked Lyn, glancing up at the Goddess.

"Laila's been suppressing this magic, and she doesn't know how to control it, so it's burning her up from the inside out. We need to redirect the magic out of her body before it destroys her." The Goddess shook her head. "This is why I've been trying to convince her to come train with me."

"How do we release the magic?" asked Ali.

Arduinna rolled up the sleeves of her shirt. "I'm going to try to access it and use my body to conduct the magic and harness the energy. But I need all of you to stand back and take cover." She pointed towards an ancient stone wall a short distance away.

Ali grabbed the others and ushered them over the wall. Frej hesitated.

"Arduinna's got this," insisted Ali, shoving him towards the wall.

The Dragon clenched his teeth before following suit. Once the others were safely behind the wall, Ali followed and peered over the rough, moss-covered stone, the others watching beside her.

Arduinna reached out and placed one hand on Laila's chest. The Goddess began to chant. Ali couldn't understand the language, but somehow she could tell it was ancient and powerful, and Arduinna spoke it with authority.

Ali became aware that they were not the only ones watching. Birds stopped their chirping in nearby trees, smaller woodland creatures poked their heads out of burrows, and even larger creatures approached from the surrounding forest to witness the Goddess at work. Not all of the creatures were ordinary either, many of them were magical.

As the Goddess continued to chant, the magic was slowly drawn up her arm. It arced across her skin like an electrical current. The Goddess began to glow as the magic surrounding her intensified, her divine energy forcing the unruly magic to bend to her will. Ali could see Arduinna's jaw clench against the pain, but she continued to allow the magic to flow into her body.

Just when Ali thought the Goddess couldn't take anymore, there was a blinding flash of light. Ali and the others dropped behind the stone wall shielding their eyes, as the creatures surrounding them took cover as well.

The light persisted for several beats of Ali's heart. It seemed like an eternity to her, but when the light slowly faded, she cautiously glanced over the wall, fearing what she might find.

Laila rested peacefully on the ground in the sun. She appeared unharmed, and Ali could see the gentle rise and fall of her chest, and nearly cried with relief. Arduinna was still seated beside her, but her shoulders sagged, and she used her arms to prop herself up.

"It's safe to approach," called the Goddess, as she lifted her head to look at the others.

Ali exchanged glances with her two companions before climbing back over the wall.

"Are you okay?" Ali asked as she approached.

"I'll be fine," said the Goddess waving her hand dismissively, "and I think Laila will be too, but she needs rest. Let's bring her inside."

A carved wooden staff appeared in Arduinna's hand, as Ali helped her up. It was covered in carvings of deer, wolves, rabbits, and a variety of other animals. Arduinna used it to steady herself as Frej carefully picked Laila up. The Goddess led the way down one of the paths through the forest, and the rest of them fell in line behind.

Ali glanced behind her at Lyn who was taking up the rear. She seemed a little in shock, but otherwise, she appeared okay. Ali didn't blame her. This was a lot to witness. Arduinna had said Laila's powers were growing, but Ali hadn't expected it to be so dramatic, or life-threatening for that matter.

CHAPTER 30

Laila awakened to the sound of crickets chirping, and a cool breeze playing across her face. She opened her eyes and sat up, realizing she was definitely not in her bedroom anymore.

The bed she'd been sleeping in was tucked in the corner of a cozy room with two large windows overlooking a forest. The room was decorated with a large wardrobe of dark, carved wood and a matching dresser. The four-poster bed had a canopy above her that mimicked branches of a tree.

Laila pulled back the blankets, walked over to the open window and peered through it, into the night. The forest felt old and sleepy to her, like a grandmother watching her grandchildren play on a warm summer night. Laila felt safe and at home in a way she hadn't felt so far in Midgard. In fact, she wasn't sure she was even in Midgard anymore.

Where in the worlds was she? And how did she get here? The last thing she remembered was waking up from a dream and being unable to go back to sleep. As sleep deprived as she had felt then, she felt fully rested in a way she hadn't been in months. It felt wonderful.

Searching for some answers, Laila left the window and wandered through the house. She found a living room where a woman sat in front of a fire.

"Arduinna?" asked Laila surprised.

A smile spread across the Goddess's face. "I'm glad you're awake. How do you feel?"

Laila rested her hands on the back of a plumb-colored, antique chair "Surprisingly well, but what am I doing here?"

Arduinna stood. "Come, let's walk through the forest, and I will answer as many of your questions as I can."

Laila followed her out through a door to a plain dirt path that led through the woods. As much as Laila wanted answers, and to get back to Los Angeles, she knew better than to pester Arduinna. So instead she used the time to enjoy the peace of the forest. The night was cool, and all Laila wore were a thin set of green silk pajamas, but she hardly noticed the cold.

"So how do you like my forest?" asked Arduinna.

Laila turned her head to find the Goddess watching her pensively.

"It's beautiful, even in the dark."

The Goddess nodded. "It's a sanctuary. Not just for me, but for the creatures that look to me for protection, so long as the creatures do not wander beyond my wards, they are safe from the prying eyes of humans."

They reached a fork in the road, and Arduinna turned left before continuing.

"My territory stretches beyond the wards, and through the forest. It used to stretch far beyond that, but the humans developed the land and chased the wild creatures away. So, my focus remains here in the forest."

Laila frowned. "Do you resent the humans?"

Arduinna was silent for a moment as she considered the question.

"No, I don't, I know that it is the way of things. In the forest, I watch over them, just as I do with all creatures. Most of the humans love and respect my forest, and so I help them when they are in need."

Laila nodded and watched an owl fly over-head.

"Laila," said the Goddess seriously, "you've put off my offer for too long."

Laila froze. This was not the time, not with the new developments in the case. "I know I keep putting it off, but I—"

"No more excuses. You *need* to start training. Your magic has grown far beyond your control. I've never seen this happen as fast as it's occurring with you, but if you don't take measures to gain control, it *will* destroy you. It nearly did today, but luckily Ali thought to bring you to me."

Memories drifted back to Laila in fragments. The moonstone dagger, her scars glowing, the magic scorching her, it all seemed surreal now.

"What's happening to me?" whispered Laila.

The Goddess stopped and turned to her. There was pity in her eyes.

"To be honest," said Arduinna sadly, "I have no idea. If I didn't know better, I'd say you were a Demigod, but I know both of your parents are Elves. One thing is certain: you're developing powers of the divine."

"What?" asked Laila, shocked. She put her hand against the trunk of a tree to steady herself. How could she have magic of the Gods?

Arduinna gave her a sympathetic look. "I know this is a lot to take in."

"How does this happen?" asked Laila as she stared at the earth.

"I'm not sure. I suspect this other Goddess is the one causing these changes, but I have no idea how or why." She sighed and looked up through the branches to the starry sky above. "I have the impression that we're merely pawns in a bigger game."

"Is there a way to stop this?" Laila asked desperately. The last thing she wanted was to get caught up in some game the

Gods were playing.

Arduinna took her hand. "Unfortunately no, but you can learn to control it, and I can show you how."

Laila shook her head. "I'm in the middle of an investigation, I can't afford to split my attention like this."

"I know," said Arduinna gently, "your Witch friend Lyn is preparing a spell to help suppress some of these new abilities, but it is only a temporary solution. You must start your training with me soon."

Laila nodded, but even as she did, she questioned her ability to follow through.

"It's not all bad," added Arduinna with a half-smile, "this could prove invaluable in your line of work, particularly with the Demons."

Arduinna was right, but it was still overwhelming. It frustrated Laila that she had no say in the matter. Laila just wanted to live her life and help people. How was it that things had become so complicated?

"I think it is time for you to return to L.A." Arduinna released her hand and took a step back. "I know this seems like a lot to process, but just take it one step at a time. I'm here for you, and your friends in Los Angeles are here for you too. We'll help you through this."

Laila nodded, not trusting herself to speak.

"Okay," said Arduinna, "I'm going to send you home. Hang in there, and I'll talk to you soon."

Before Laila could react, there was a shift in the ground beneath her feet, and suddenly she was standing in the middle of Ali's living room.

"Laila!" Frej exclaimed, rising from the sofa, "How are you? Are you okay?"

He stepped around the coffee table to pull her into his embrace.

"Yeah, I'm fine, thanks to Arduinna." She wrapped her arms around the Dragon.

She glanced at the clock, it was four in the afternoon. There was no sign of the others, aside from Mr. Whiskers who meowed at her from his perch on the back of the sofa before hopping down to rub against her legs.

"Where are the others?" she asked as she released the Dragon and scratched the Bogey's head.

"Erin's at her Judo class. Lyn realized she needed some supplies from her shop for the spells she's working on, so she and Ali went to go find them. I told the others I'd wait for you here and text them when you returned."

Laila nodded. "I should probably find my phone, I'm sure Darien's been trying to get a hold of me."

She was just turning to leave when the door to the garage opened. Ali and Lyn came walking into the kitchen. It took a second for it to register that Laila was back. In that moment Ali's expression morphed from relief to fury, and back.

"By the Morrigan!" howled Ali throwing her purse on the counter and stomping over to Laila. "You scared the crap out of us!"

Ali pulled her into a big, bone-crushing hug.

"Don't do that again!" said Ali.

"You know," gasped Laila, "I didn't exactly intend for that to happen."

Ali took a step back and planted her fists on her hips. "No, but if you'd started training with Arduinna sooner, this wouldn't be an issue."

"Are you sure you two aren't related?" asked Lyn with a grin. "If I didn't know better, I'd think you were sisters."

Ali huffed and muttered something about stubborn Elves before returning to the kitchen to make some coffee. Lyn fished around in her bag before pulling out a collection of items and setting them on the counter.

"I've got two potions for you and Jerrik. They should help dampen your scent, but it won't totally remove it. If a Vampire were to start sniffing around, they'd still smell you. Also, it only lasts two hours max, so you'll have to keep an eye on the clock."

"Thanks," Laila accepted the two glass vials that Lyn passed her. The liquid inside was murky brown. "Do we drink it?"

Lyn nodded, a funny look on her face. "It tastes pretty nasty, but that's the only spell I've got for that sort of thing at the moment."

"Don't tell me you're still planning to go after those Vampires tonight," groaned Frej with a disapproving frown. "You were nearly killed by your own magic this morning."

"I'll be fine," Laila insisted, firmly, "I actually feel better than I have in weeks."

"Plus, she'll have this." Lyn held up a woven hemp bracelet. "It's a spell to help her suppress the newer abilities she's developing. So long as Laila keeps it on, she shouldn't have another episode like last night."

Laila looked at the bracelet skeptically as Lyn tied it to her wrist. There were a variety of beads woven into it that had tiny symbols carved into them. Some were glass, others were metal or wood.

"But it won't affect my ability to use elemental magic, will it?" she asked, concerned. She couldn't go charging into a den of Vampires not knowing whether she could rely on her magic or not.

Lyn shook her head. "I was discussing it with Arduinna earlier, she explained that these new abilities are different from your elemental magic. I focused this spell to only affect the divine magic."

Laila cringed. It appeared that the others knew.

Ali passed her a cup of coffee, "Don't worry, we won't tell anyone, but it does explain a few things."

"Like what?" asked Laila bitterly.

"Like the fact you were able to destroy a Fire Elemental."

"Or the reinforced shield you conjured when we were fighting the Ghosts," added Lyn as she looked through their boxes of tea.

"I know you're not thrilled about this," said Frej, stepping behind her to rub her shoulders, "but maybe it's not such a bad thing."

Ali gave her an optimistic look. "Maybe this gift is that Goddess's way of helping us keep the people of Los Angeles safe."

Laila knew the others were right. The divine magic had already helped her in a number of different situations. Even though it seemed unreliable now, maybe Arduinna could show her how to access it, and the full extent of how it could be used. If she'd known how to use it, maybe she could've saved more of the Vampires during the fire, or stopped the Snake Shifter who'd abducted Erin. Still though, with the divine magic came more responsibility, and at the moment she had no idea what that responsibility was. Helping to fight the Demons was one thing, but what if there was a catch?

"Thank you, Lyn," Laila glanced down at the charm around her wrist.

"No problem," said Lyn smiling "and don't you even think about paying, this is on me. You guys gave me a safe place to stay, making a couple of charms and potions is the least I can do."

Laila gave her a half-smile before retreating to her room. She needed some space, and to think about something else for a while. She found her phone resting on the nightstand exactly where she'd left it last night. There were dozens of new emails, alerts, phone calls, and messages. Many of them were from Darien. He'd stayed at the office through the day researching and preparing for the night ahead. She sent him a message telling him that she had the potions from Lyn and that she was leaving for the office soon. The rest of the messages could wait.

CHAPTER 31

Laila sat in the back of the surveillance van with Jerrik and Donald as it rumbled down the streets of the Old City. She was dressed in dark skinny jeans, black combat boots, and a black hoodie that would help her hide her face and eyes, just in case they encountered any Vampires underground. Underneath was her leather armor. Jerrik had on a pair of jeans and a black hoodie as well. Darien was dressed similarly, but with a leather jacket.

Torsten drove the van, and there were a couple of plain-clothed police officers stationed near the tunnel entrance in case they needed backup. Ali was on standby, but something had come up with Colin. The Fae didn't elaborate, and Laila had more than enough to think about at the moment, so she didn't question Ali further. Frej and Lyn had also volunteered, but Laila was determined to keep them out of danger.

Laila double-checked her weapons. She had a gun concealed under her jacket and a couple of knives in her boots. She'd opted to leave the dagger at home, especially after the incident last night. She didn't want another episode like that occurring while in the tunnel underground.

Donald shifted in his seat beside her. "Laila, could I ask you something?"

"Um, sure," said Laila as she pulled her hair back into a braid.

"Do you think Ali would give me a chance?" he asked, avoiding eye contact.

"What?" Laila lifted an eyebrow.

Donald had watched Ali with big puppy-dog eyes since the day he started working in the office. Laila could never tell if he was more frightened of Ali, or in awe of her. If the drawing at his workbench was anything to go off of though, she would have to say that it was more than likely an awkward infatuation that bordered on creepy.

The Tech Wiz shrugged. "I know I'm kind of out of her league, but—"

Jerrik snorted, and Laila elbowed him in the ribs, glaring at him.

"Look Donald," she began, searching for a way to word her thoughts, "Ali's not exactly the kind of woman who wants your average relationship, not to mention that she's sort of taken at the moment."

"I-I know," stuttered Donald as he fiddled with a piece of equipment, "but I've never met anyone like her before. She's so strong, and intelligent, and beautiful. I don't know, she'd probably never be interested in someone like me."

She gave the Tech Wiz a sympathetic look. "I'm not saying you wouldn't stand a chance, but I would think about the consequences of that kind of action. You work together after all."

Donald looked from Laila to Jerrik. She knew rumors of their past relationship had made their rounds through the various departments within the office. She avoided the urge to grit her teeth.

Jerrik rolled his eyes. "If you want to ask her out, you've got to be able to handle a basic conversation with her. Maybe that's a good place to start?"

"Right." Donald sank back in his seat meekly.

"Jerrik has a point," Laila said, not bothering to look at the Dark Elf, "perhaps it's better if you try to get to know her as a friend first."

"And you should definitely do something about that." Jerrik gestured at Donald's appearance.

Laila poked her finger into Jerrik's thigh and zapped him a small jolt of electricity. Jerrik flinched and gave her an innocent look.

Donald glanced down at his wrinkled graphic t-shirt. It had a picture of a superhero on it and was far too big for him. The old jeans he wore had oil stains splattered on them from work and were short enough that Laila could see his mismatched socks beneath them. His beard was also looking pretty shaggy, and his brown hair was in desperate need of a trim. Laila couldn't help but think that Jerrik was right, but that didn't mean he needed to point it out.

The van lurched to a stop before she could form a reply, and Darien turned around in his seat.

"Alright, let's rock and roll."

Laila pulled out the glass vials from the pocket of her jacket and passed one to Jerrik. "Drink up."

"Ladies first." Jerrik eyed the brownish substance with distaste.

Laila drank it in one gulp, the taste wasn't as bad as she expected though, more like a bitter tea than anything. Jerrik followed suit before he opened the door to the van.

"We're going pretty far underground," Laila explained to Donald. "Even with your enchantments, you still might lose us. If we're not back in two hours, call Ali."

She was about to add another word of advice for Donald, but thought better of it and stepped out of the van. Laila slid the door shut and followed the others over to the storm drain. Darien removed the grate and motioned for Laila to descend into the dark abyss. Once they were down there, Jerrik pulled out a flashlight and switched it on, shining the beam down the path. It appeared they were alone.

They retraced their steps from the other night back through the hole in the concrete and into the stone passageway.

"Whoa," said Jerrik examining the stone, "this is held up by a spell."

He switched off his flashlight and shoved it into his pocket. There was light from torches burning along the walls to light their way.

Laila could feel the magic holding the rock in place like mortar. It would need an energy source, but she had no idea where the source was located. The magic didn't seem to be drawn from anywhere in particular as she would expect.

"Hopefully we'll get some answers further down the tunnels." Darien continued onward, down the sloped tunnel.

"Testing coms," said Laila, but no reply came through the earpiece. "Shoot, we already lost the connection."

Jerrik shook his head. "That guy doesn't stand a chance."

Laila scowled at him.

"Who?" asked Darien.

"That Tech Wiz, or whatever he calls himself," Jerrik chuckled. "He wants to ask Ali out."

Darien snorted and shook his head.

"Mato makes sense," continued Jerrik, "but Donald?"

"Be nice!" Laila hissed.

"You can't be serious!" moaned Jerrik. "You're the one that found his sketch of Ali in the lab. That's a bit creepy and desperate in my opinion."

She gave Jerrik a pointed look. "Maybe it is, but do you think shutting him down is really helping? Yeah, he's kind of awkward, and sure he has trouble expressing himself, but making him feel bad about that is just plain shitty."

Jerrik barked a laugh as he stopped and turned to face her with a cocky look. "And what do you suggest I do?"

Laila narrowed her eyes and jabbed a finger against his chest.

"For starters, you could show a little compassion and give him some productive advice. So what if he and Ali wouldn't work? I'm sure there is someone out there he would be right for, and he doesn't need an asshole like you convincing him to never try."

Laila shoved past him and headed down the tunnel.

Darien chuckled. "And that, Jerrik, is what we call a roasting. You might want to ice that later."

Jerrik struggled to find an appropriate response, but Dairen motioned for them to be quiet. They'd reached the place where the tunnels branched off in different locations.

Laila put her hood up, and Jerrik followed suit. Darien listened at the mouth of the tunnels before motioning them towards one on the right.

"There's more noise coming from here," whispered Darien, "just be on your guard, we'll probably encounter someone soon."

They followed the tunnel for a ways without incident, after five minutes they heard voices approaching. Laila and Jerrik ducked their heads, hoping that Lyn's charm would work. It appeared to, because the other two Vampires passed them without a second glance. Laila breathed a sigh of relief as they kept moving.

Gradually the tunnel began to widen, allowing for boxes and crates to be stacked along the walls. Jerrik walked over to one of the boxes and used a knife to open it. He silently held up a box of ammunition, and Laila exchanged a concerned glance with Darien. They searched a few of the crates and found cases of guns and other weapons. It was essentially an armory.

"This has Di Inferi's symbol on it," muttered Laila, running her fingers over the three-headed skull spray-painted on the side. "I guess we know where they were taking the weapons."

"Do we head back now and report this?" asked Jerrik quietly.

Darien shook his head. "They'll just take the weapons and run into the far reaches of the Old City. We need to find out who's in charge of this." He jerked his thumb at the tunnel wall.

More voices echoed down the tunnel in front of them, and they quickly took cover behind the crates of guns. Laila tried to still her breathing as the footsteps approached. The footsteps stopped just in front of the crate.

"Hear that?" asked a male voice on the other side of the crates. "Sounds like a heartbeat."

Laila glanced sideways at Jerrik who stiffened.

"I don't hear anything," whined a woman's voice, "come on, let's go, I'm hungry."

The footsteps left in the direction of the exit. They waited until the sound faded into the distance before emerging.

"Are you sure about this?" Jerrik whispered to Darien.

Darien led the way down the tunnel, "Relax, that potion works well enough, just a little further."

They followed him down the tunnel and Laila stared in disbelief as the passage seemed to widen into what felt like a street. There were doors and windows on either side, and the occasional arch leading down yet another path. They encountered more Vampires and tried to blend in, but no one seemed to question their presence.

Up ahead the sound of voices grew louder as the passageway opened up to a massive, domed chamber. It was like a courtyard or a town square. Laila's jaw dropped as she saw a crowd of Vampires gathered before them surrounding a circular stage in the middle of the chamber. A single man stood on the platform dressed in a long leather duster, a black top hat, and chunky black boots. His eyeliner was thick, and he wore a variety of large rings. There was blood crusted around his mouth and staining his shirt. He made Darien look like a charming schoolboy.

She glanced sideways at her partner and saw his brow furrow. Jerrik seemed equally disturbed.

Glancing up, she heard the Vampire's voice echo above the crowd.

"We are close, so close, soon the time will come for us to

rise and claim this city as ours!" He thrust his fist into the air, and the crowd of rebels cheered. It took some time for the other Vampires to quiet down so their leader could continue.

"For now though, I need your patience. There are a few more pieces in the puzzle that must fall into place. We will strike when the time is right, when the humans can no longer ignore our superiority. For now, we must walk the streets peacefully, drawing others into our circle and lulling the humans into a false sense of security. But soon, we will rule this city."

The rebels roared with enthusiasm, shaking the walls of the chamber. Darien nudged Laila and nodded towards the far right side of the stage. In front was a familiar face watching the leader with a dark grin. There—in a shabby grey coat—was Arnold Koch, their murderer.

They'd seen enough, now they had to get out before someone noticed them. Laila checked the time on her phone. They'd been down there an hour and a half, they'd need to get moving if they were going to make it out before the potion wore off. She turned, motioning the others to follow her, but stopped in her tracks as she nearly walked into someone standing right behind her.

"Watch where you're going," hissed the Vampire in her face.

"Sorry," she muttered and tried to step around him. He blocked her path.

"What do we have here?" the Vampire said turning to Jerrik, "You don't look like any Vampire I've ever seen."

"He's an Abhartach," explained Laila hastily, thinking of their medical examiner, Meuric. His skin was similar in color to Jerrik's, and they were similar in nature to Vampires. "Our cousins from that other world."

The Vampire stared at Jerrik intently for a moment before stepping aside and allowing them to pass.

As they hurried down the tunnel, Laila realized how badly that could've gone. They tried not to attract too much attention, but they were quickly running out of time, and the tunnels stretched for miles under the city. They had just passed the box-es and crates of weapons and were approaching the narrower part of the tunnel when a voice boomed behind them.

"Stop there!" called a male voice behind her, Laila spun to find the same Vampire holding Jerrik in a choke hold. They'd been followed.

"Stop there, or your Svartálfr friend dies," he sneered squeezing his arm around Jerrik's throat.

CHAPTER 32

"Easy now." Darien took a step forward.

The Vampire retreated, dragging Jerrik with him. Jerrik gave Laila a questioning look, and she knew he was asking her if he should attempt to fend off the rebel Vampire. Laila shook her head slightly, this was their chance to get some answers.

Laila saw Jerrik throw up a subtle shield protecting his windpipe from the crushing pressure of the Vampire's arm, while Laila examined the Vampire for weaknesses. He was fairly tall, perhaps a little over six feet. As a Vampire, he was clearly stronger than most men, but he wasn't well grounded. Even as he held Jerrik, she could see him wavering to keep his balance.

"What do you think you're doing, bringing outsiders in here?" spat the other Vampire, "I should report you to Sire Ashford for this."

"Just let him go, and I'll explain everything," said Darien spreading his hands in surrender.

"The real question is why didn't we hear about this meeting?" Laila snapped.

"Ask your sire, they sent word through the network." He

paused, eyes narrowing. "You've got a pulse too."

Well, there went her plan.

"Dodge left!" hissed Laila in Elvish as she pulled a knife from her boot.

Jerrik obeyed, and Laila's aim was true, the knife lodged itself deep into the rebel Vampire's eye socket with a sickening thump. Jerrik threw the Vampire forward, over his shoulder, and backed away from his attacker who hissed and clawed at the dagger in his skull. Laila retrieved the second knife from her boot and held it at the ready.

"Kill him," ordered Darien, watching the side of the tunnel that led to the underground complex.

Laila hesitated. He was down, it would take time for his wound to heal.

"Do it!" hissed Darien. "Someone's coming, and we can't risk him talking."

Jerrik yanked the knife from the Vampire's eye-socket and thrust it directly into the Vampire's heart. Before the Vampire could scream, flames erupted from the wound and consumed the body in a matter of seconds. All that remained was a pile of ash and the knife.

"We need to go," said Darien quietly, "more of those rebels are coming, and the potion is wearing off."

Laila grabbed her knife as Jerrik used a spell to sweep the pile of ash off to the side of the tunnel where no one would notice it. They took off back through the tunnel at a sprint.

Up the sloping passage, and around twists and turns they ran. Laila didn't bother to sheathe the knives but kept them ready in her hands. Another set of Vampires had heard the commotion and caught up to them baring their fangs. This time Laila didn't wait for Darien's command, she stabbed one in the chest while he shot the other through the heart. Jerrik once again disbursed the still smoldering ashes as they continued to run for the exit.

They encountered no one else in the tunnels, and before

long they reached the hole in the wall that lead back to the storage drain. They hurried through it as Laila conjured a light for her and Jerrik to see by. When they reached the ladder, they rushed up it and onto the street. They didn't slow their pace until they'd returned to the surveillance van down the street. Laila's heart pounded as she tried to catch her breath.

"What's going on?" asked Torsten looking them over from the driver's seat. "Donald lost connection with you about ten minutes after you entered the tunnels."

Darien shook his head in disbelief, "I never would have expected that. There is practically an entire city built beneath the streets, and it appears the Vampires that live there are planning to launch some sort of rebellion."

Torsten's jaw dropped.

"We encountered three Vampires as we left," added Laila grimly, "they won't be talking, and I don't think anyone else followed us."

"I want a word with Talen," said Darien running his fingers through his hair. "This seems way too big to have passed his notice. I want to know why he didn't tell us about this place, and I want Laila with me as backup."

"Should we head back to the office?" asked Torsten starting the car.

"No, I want you two to stay here with Jerrik and keep an eye on the entrance. It's unlikely this is the only way in, but we need to keep an eye on it at all times. At least during the night. I left a car in the area yesterday, just in case. Laila and I'll take that."

He opened the door to the van and stepped out. Laila followed him while Jerrik pulled out his phone to make the calls.

They walked down the dark, abandoned streets as Darien led the way to the car he had planted, keeping an eye out for any sign of life as they went.

"Do you think Talen knew about this rebellion?" asked Laila as they reached a nondescript sedan and climbed in.

Darien hesitated before starting the car, his expression dark.

"I want to trust him, and I want to give him the benefit of the doubt." He glanced at Laila. "But when it comes down to it, Talen will put his own interests above anything else. He wouldn't have survived this long otherwise. I intend to find out exactly what he knows. This isn't just about a murder investigation, this puts the entire city at risk."

Laila stared at the empty road ahead as he started the car and drove off. She agreed with Darien, as helpful as Talen had been, it seemed unlikely that this sort of development within the Vampire community would be beyond his notice. That place was massive, and there had to be nearly a hundred Vampires present. In all honesty, she knew nothing about Talen. What if he'd been leading them on a wild goose chase? Then again, Talen was the one who mentioned the rising number of Vampire-involved attacks in the Old City. What if this underground group of rebels was responsible for them?

"Let's not make any assumptions here, okay?" She watched her partner closely, but if he was listening, she saw no indication.

Darien pulled up to the apartment complex. He slammed the door of the car, walked through the entrance, and past the receptionist without a glance. He headed straight towards the elevator, Laila directly behind him.

They reached Talen's floor, and the elevator doors slid open. As usual, two guards waited on either side of the door eyeing them as they approached. Darien ignored them and pounded on the door.

"Open up!" he roared.

The guards turned to seize him when the door opened, revealing Talen.

"We need to talk," hissed Darien, shrugging off the guards. "Now!"

Talen raised an eyebrow at Darien, and Laila had the feeling this was not the way Darien should be speaking to his sire.

"We've made a disturbing discovery," added Laila over her partner's shoulder hoping to defuse the situation a little.

"Very well," spat Talen after a moment. He slowly turned and motioned for them to follow.

"Easy," Laila mouthed at Darien as they entered the lavish penthouse.

"Please take a seat." Talen showed them into the living room. Laila sat on one of the armchairs, opposite of Talen, but Darien remained standing.

"For heaven's sake," groaned Talen, "what's got you so upset Darien? I could punish you for the way you spoke in front of my guards."

Laila stiffened, hoping Darien could keep himself in check. When it came down to it though, Darien took his role as a protector of the peace very seriously.

"What do you know about the underground city?" demanded Darien, his fangs were showing."

"What are you talking about?" asked Talen, annoyed, "do you mean the Old City?"

"No," hissed Darien, "the one *under* it."

Talen shook his head and looked a Darien as if he'd lost his mind. "What the hell are you talking about?"

Laila sensed the tensions rising. Darien looked ready to pounce, and Talen's lip was beginning to curl, exposing his fangs in response. Not wanting to be caught up in the middle of a Vampire fight, she interrupted their stare-off by clearing her throat.

"Let's just talk this through like reasonable people." She cast her partner a warning look. "Darien and I discovered an underground city of Vampires. They were holding some sort of rally and discussing plans to take over the city in a rebellion."

"What?" snapped Talen.

"Someone called Sire Ashwood is leading them," added Laila.

"Never heard of him," mumbled Talen, frowning. "When you say city—"

Darien cut him off, "We mean a full network of tunnels, it

was like walking down the street of an old village, except everything was underground. There was plenty of space to house the crowd of Vampires we saw."

"How many?" asked Talen troubled.

"Nearly a hundred," said Laila, "but it's hard to say."

She glanced at Darien who was still staring daggers at Talen, he didn't seem to be convinced of his sire's ignorance. Laila on the other hand, was inclined to believe that Talen was truly shocked.

Talen stood and began to pace back and forth in front of the massive window overlooking the city, hands clasped behind his back.

"You said they were plotting to take over the city?" asked Talen as he paced. "Was there anyone you recognized there?"

"No," answered Darien stiffly, "aside from our suspect in the multiple-homicide case."

"But you suspect I'm involved?" Talen froze and turned to face Darien.

He didn't respond, instead, he stared blankly at his sire. Talen sighed and returned to sit on a sofa. He looked from Darien to Laila.

"This is as much of a surprise to me as it is to you," he said seriously. "There've always been whisperings between younger Vampires of taking over the human population, but as I'm sure you know, the laws of the Vampire community are designed to prevent this. The only reason we were allowed to stay here in Midgard was that we agreed to keep our presence unknown from the humans."

"What about now?" asked Laila keeping a close watch on Darien standing beside her.

"Even though the humans know of our existence, the elders of the Vampire communities throughout the world have agreed that we should keep a low profile for the sake of peace. Could Vampires take over the world? Yes. Should they? No. It would only breed mistrust and resentment from the other Supernaturals and our otherworldly allies." This news seemed to weigh on him like a load of chains. His shoulders were hunched, and his handsome, immortal face seemed to age as he continued to process this new development.

Laila turned to her partner. "I believe him."

Darien's jaw was still set, but Laila could see his resolve soften. The anger was still there, but he seemed to reach the same conclusion: Talen wasn't involved.

"So now what?" Laila asked the others. "There are too many of them for our team to arrest. We'll have to involve other branches of law enforcement, but that'll be risky."

Talen shook his head. "This is a matter for the local Vampire counsel. These rebels cause a threat to the structure of our community. We need to assemble an emergency meeting."

He rose and pulled out his phone before stepping into the other room.

"Wait, what?" Laila asked Darien quietly.

"These rebels have broken sacred Vampire law," explained Darien, as he finally relaxed enough to take a seat. "The Vampire community has the ability to punish these Vampires however they deem fit, but the most powerful local sires must discuss the matter first."

Darien scratched the back of his head and looked at the doorway his sire had exited through before continuing.

"It's possible that they could give us the necessary reinforcements to dismantle the rebellion before more harm comes to the city. We'll just have to hope the other sires are willing to help. Otherwise, we'll be on our own."

CHAPTER 33

Ali's elbows were propped on the desk before her, her head cradled in her hands. She'd suspected this. It shouldn't come to her as a surprise, but the knowledge still hit her like a blow to the stomach.

The evidence was spread out before her, the result of nearly two weeks spent subtlety investigating with the help of the Inspector General's office. They'd spent time searching through emails, and chasing down leads, even following her coworkers, trying to make sense of it all. But finally, they'd found their leak.

For a couple of months, she'd been convinced someone was feeding information to the Demons but had no way of proving it. It occurred to her that if someone in her office was leaking information on cases, what was stopping them from going further and sabotaging investigations? That's when she had contacted her superiors in D.C. and informed them of her suspicions. There was a traitor among them, and she needed to find out who, but she also needed help.

Adam was a relief to have around. He was impartial and had never met anyone in the office before his arrival. That meant that he had no previous relationships or experiences with the others that would affect his ability to examine the situation objectively.

Prior to The Event, he'd worked for the FBI but later switched over to IRSA when the organization was getting started. As a human, he'd been discouraged from investigating cases in the field, but IRSA kept him on to handle the agency's internal affairs. Sniffing out liabilities was his specialty.

"We'll have to make the arrest," said Adam, as he sat across the desk watching her.

"I know, but we have to be strategic about this. It needs to be done as quietly as possible. If the media catches wind of this, they'll have a field day. Then there's also the rest of the team…"

He nodded. "Even so, it must be done as soon as possible. We'll wait until he returns tonight."

Laila sat in the corner of Talen's living room observing the Vampires that had gathered. There were seven sires who comprised the local council. They were of varying shapes, sizes, and ethnicities, and each council member arrived with their own entourage of advisors and guards. Some appeared young, barely reaching adulthood, while others were old and wrinkled. But age was always deceptive with Vampires, as their physical appearance remained the same as when they were changed.

To Laila's surprise, Talen was not a member of the council. It was odd to Laila because the Vampire seemed to have a great deal of power and influence, but Darien explained that only the most ancient Vampires were allowed a place on the council. While Talen was quite old, even by Vampire standards, the Vampires who gathered in the room had lived even longer.

A number of them cast curious glances in Laila and Darien's directions. Laila noticed that Darien was unusually quiet beside her and made no move to approach the elders. She followed his lead and waited for the last of the council members to arrive. Laila caught Darien's eyes on one of the elders more than once, a woman who looked younger than the rest in sleek black business clothes. When the Vampire noticed Darien's attention, she gave him a wolfish grin. Beside her, Darien stiffened.

Laila glanced at her phone. She'd heard nothing from Jerrik, or from Ali. But perhaps no news was good news. After all, she was not being called out for another emergency, but an emergency might be preferable to her current situation, surrounded by a small crowd of powerful Vampires. Hopefully, they were as willing to help as Talen was; they needed all the help they could get.

The last council member arrived, and they seated themselves at the massive dining table of polished black stone. Laila and Darien watched as Talen cleared his throat from the head of the table.

"Esteemed council members, you have my deepest gratitude for agreeing to meet on such short notice." Talen bowed, and from his ease, Laila could tell he was clearly an experienced diplomat.

"You mentioned that this meeting was urgent," said a woman, her skin was old and wrinkled. The long gown she wore was a gothic style with opulent gold jewelry. Laila imagined she must have belonged to some sort of human nobility during her living years. Darien had mentioned her name was Aalis.

A middle-aged man with dark hair and a crimson suit watched shrewdly. "What is this threat to our society you spoke of?"

Talen glanced at Laila and Darien. "One of my underlings is a special agent with the Inter-Realm Security Agency. He and his partner have been working a series of troubling cases in which the suspect is a Vampire."

"Of course," sighed the young woman as she examined her perfectly manicured nails. "The reports have been all over the news."

"What the news hasn't spoken of is the increasing number of Vampire attacks or the connection these murders seem to have with a Vampire rebellion that is literally hidden beneath the streets of the Old City," explained Talen, as he watched the reactions of the council before him. There were hushed whispers and exchanged glances between the council members. Some appeared surprised, while others were skeptical.

"What do you mean 'rebellion'?" asked the councilman in the crimson suit, doubtfully. "I've heard nothing of any rebellion since shortly after The Event. Surely, we would have heard whispers and rumors."

"Dagan is right," agreed Aalis sharply.

"You would think so," said Talen as he circled around the table slowly, "but earlier this evening a hundred or so Vampires gathered below the city in a system of secret tunnels."

He paused for a moment to allow his words to sink in before continuing.

"I've invited my underling, Special Agent Pavoni, and his partner, Special Agent Eyvindr, here tonight to give a first-hand account of their findings." He stopped beside Darien and Laila, motioning for Darien to address the council.

Darien took a step forward and bowed. "Esteemed council members, what my sire has spoken is true. My partner and I discovered this gathering accidentally as we followed a lead in one of our cases. Their leader, a Vampire by the name of Sire Ashford, addressed the crowd and spoke of plans in effect to take over the city as their own. He also spoke of allies that have been working with them in this cause."

"I've never heard of this 'Sire Ashford,'" drawled another council member in a black suit with blond hair slicked back from his face.

The others nodded in agreement.

"Nor have we," explained Talen darkly, "but we know someone who does."

He waved to the guards, who opened the door to the apartment. In stepped a familiar face, the Vampire, Richard, from the ball. He'd managed to escape the fire completely unscathed. It had taken Talen's resources some time to track him down, and apparently, he'd found some interesting information. After a long phone call, Talen managed to convince Richard to make a reluctant appearance.

"Many of you know Richard." Talen indicated the newcomer.

The majority of the council nodded, and Laila noticed mixed expressions. She had a feeling that Richard had a couple of enemies among the crowd.

"Please tell the council what you told me earlier," instructed Talen.

Hesitantly, Richard addressed them.

"One of my underlings overheard a couple of younger Vampires discussing Sire Ashford." He watched the council warily, as if afraid that one of them might lunge at him and rip his throat out. "The rumors on the street say that he was changed during The Event by an anonymous Vampire. Sire Ashford supposedly killed his own sire and rejected the rules of our society, then set out to create his own by changing his followers. He's been discrete about this, but as his numbers grew, the underlings started to talk."

"And how did you come across this information?" The blond male stared at him venomously, "How long have you been waiting to sell it to the highest bidder?"

Richard's throat bobbed as he swallowed hard. "I caught one of his followers trying to steal from the wreckage of my building in the Old City. My guards brought him to me, and he begged for his freedom dropping Sire Ashford's name."

The council watched Richard's explanation like a pack of wolves eyeing a scrawny deer. He stood his ground though—barely—and continued.

"I didn't think much of it until I received Talen's call. When he mentioned the name, I had my guards haul the thief from his cell and question him. He didn't have much aside from a brief explanation."

"Where is the thief now?" asked Aalis.

Richard nodded to one of his guards who approached with a jar full of ash. He set the jar on the table in front of the young woman who smirked. Laila shifted where she stood, even Darien's frown deepened as he watched Richard. Vampires certainly had their own way of dealing with things, but Laila wondered if this was one of the reasons Darien had been investigating him.

"One of my guards got a little too rough with his torture," Richard explained. "He nicked the heart by mistake."

The young woman unscrewed the lid of the jar. She scooped up a handful of ash, allowing it to run slowly between her fingers with a pleased look that left bile creeping up Laila's throat. The woman's eyes glazed over as if lost deep in thought.

"He tells the truth," she mused, shaking herself from her trance, "the ashes have confirmed it."

Laila didn't want to know how the ashes supposedly confirmed the story, although she imagined the Vampire had some sort of ability that allowed her to communicate with the dead. The Vampire dusted the remaining ash from her fingers, screwed the lid back on the jar, and passed it to the guard.

Richard glanced sideways at Talen, who dismissed him since the council had no further questions.

"What of the crowd?" asked Aalis, "Were there any faces you recognized?"

"No one, except for a suspect in an ongoing case," said Darien stepping forward again. "The majority appeared to be newly changed. I could still smell the scent of human blood in their veins."

"So, someone is raising an army of the recently undead," mused the young woman, with a faint smile, "Do they really think they can succeed?"

"I do not know, councilwoman," said Darien with a stiff

bow, "but I am equally surprised they've gotten this far without our notice."

There was a pause, as the council considered the information they'd been presented. A few of them quietly whispered back and forth with their advisors or each other, their expressions troubled.

"We should wait." Dagan picked a speck of dust off the arm of his crimson suit. "This isn't much information to go off of. I'll send spies into this group and have them report back. In a month's time, we can reconvene."

Laila's jaw clenched, it seemed that these Vampires didn't have the same sense of urgency she felt. Perhaps it was a result of their age, but Laila worried how far this rebellion would proceed in a month alone.

Laila took a step towards the elders. "With all due respect, we need to act now."

"Hold your tongue Elf," snapped Aalis, "this is a matter for Vampires."

"I beg to differ," insisted Laila, refusing to back down. "While the issue lies within the Vampire community, it affects all of the citizens in this city, both Supernatural and human."

Darien grabbed her arm, but she shrugged him off. Laila had the feeling that she put her own life in danger by continuing, but she'd seen their kind in the courts of her own world. They were comfortable and virtually untouchable, their lives would probably not be at risk if they waited, but the lives of the common people would.

"We brought this problem to you here today because we are looking for your support. There are stacks of crates packed full of guns, ammunition, and explosives waiting in that tunnel. You can go hide away in your mansions and estates, but don't think they won't come after you too. They're out for power, and you stand in their way. You can wait and see what happens, or you can take control of this situation and help us stop this rebellion before innocent lives are lost."

"I should cut that tongue from your mouth for your inso-lence," spat Dagan, his eyes narrowing. From the look on Darien and Talen's face, she had a feeling that the Vampire would likely follow through on the threat.

"It's the truth," finished Laila simply, as she folded her arms.

"I like her." The young woman on the council gave Laila a bemused look. "She's direct. It's refreshing."

The woman stood.

"I'll give you my support. I'd prefer to see this rebellion crushed before it becomes more problematic."

"I agree," said the blond Vampire, "I say we make an exam-ple out of them and show any others that this insolence will not be tolerated."

There were more members of the council that nodded in agreement.

"Then let us debate this matter amongst ourselves," declared the noblewoman. "Talen, please give us privacy to discuss."

Talen nodded and waved for Laila and Darien to follow him out of the room and into the kitchen. Laila glanced over her shoulder at the council one more time before Talen shut the door to the kitchen.

The kitchen was a much smaller space by comparison. Ev-erything was updated and new, but Laila had the feeling that it had never been used.

She waited impatiently as she leaned against the counter. Darien watched the dark city skyline through the window, while Talen waited by the door.

"What the hell were you thinking?" spewed Darien sudden-ly. "These aren't Elves we're dealing with."

"No, they're not," said Laila pointedly, "but I didn't come here to play political games, I came here to protect this city."

Darien shook his head.

"Don't be so harsh." Talen's eyes twinkled with fascination. "I think it was a good move. Laila was truly the only one who *could* get away with being blunt. They can forgive her ignorance of our ways. We've managed to persuade a few. Hopefully, the rest will follow."

Darien paced restlessly; Laila could tell the council made him uncomfortable. Perhaps it was the ruthless hold they had over their people, or maybe it was something more. She remembered the way he'd watched the young councilwoman and wondered what their connection was.

They waited a few minutes longer in silence before there was a knock on the door. Talen opened it to reveal one of the advisors who had accompanied Aalis.

"A decision has been reached," announced the man solemnly.

CHAPTER 34

"Colin?" Ali knocked on the door to his office. It was shut, but she knew he was in there.

Benning had informed them that Colin entered the building fifteen minutes ago looking agitated. They'd given him more than enough time to make it to his office and sounds of shuffling within only confirmed his presence.

"Colin, we need to talk."

Still no response.

Ali glanced sideways at Special Agent Johnson whose frown mirrored her own. He stepped forward to give it a try.

"Colin, this is Adam Johnson. I need you to open this door—"

"What the hell do you want?" snarled Colin as he flung the door open.

Ali noticed he was looking worse than before, almost sickly. Ali could all but feel waves of anger and aggression rolling off him. Something was certainly wrong, and this wasn't the most ideal way to start this sort of encounter. Had he known they were looking for him?

"Colin Greyson, you're under arrest," she began as she reached for his arm, and intending to charm him into submission.

"This is ridiculous!" he snapped and shoved her away, breaking Ali's concentration. "On what charges?"

"Conspiring with Demons, exposing confidential government information, treason…" Adam Johnson continued the list.

Ali saw the muscles in Colin's body tense. She pushed Adam Johnson out of the way and into the hall. Planting herself between Colin and the human, she tried to talk Colin down.

"You don't want to do this, resisting arrest will only make things worse, you know that."

Something didn't seem right about this. She knew Colin would be upset, but this was something else entirely, as if any grasp on his self-control had been lost. Maybe it was the drugs he'd been taking for the headaches?

Colin growled and tackled Ali, shoving her against the metal doorframe. She felt something crack as pain exploded in her chest, she imagined it was a rib breaking. Colin seemed to hesitate at the look of pain on her face. Ali knew he'd be more vulnerable in that moment, so she smothered him with charm magic.

"Freeze, hands behind your back." Ali grimaced as every movement of her chest sent new bursts of pain echoing through her body.

Colin did as she commanded, his eyes slightly glazed.

Adam Johnson quickly cuffed Colin. "I'll take it from here."

Ali shook her head. "Without the glamor, you're toast. I'll manage."

Every breath was torment, but walking seemed to be okay. She led the way down to the holding cells and waited as Adam locked the Werewolf up, although the trip left her unusually short of breath.

"Someone will be by soon to transport him, but we should get you to a hospital." Adam watched her carefully.

"Call Asclepius and tell them I'm on my way over, you stay and deal with him."

She glared at Colin who was beginning to recover from the charm. To his credit, he looked horrified and was mumbling apologies. They fell on deaf ears though.

Slowly, Ali made her way back to the elevator and to the ground level where Benning fussed over her and insisted on escorting her to the hospital. Hopefully an Elven doctor was on staff and could patch her up. Otherwise, she'd have to call Laila. Given everything her friend had been through last night with the divine magic overload, she'd rather not involve Laila unless it was necessary. She didn't know how drained her friend would be from such an ordeal, and how bad could her injury be? She was still standing after all.

As she walked with Benning, she tried to keep her mind off the pain. She thought of Colin and the way he'd reacted. Something had set him off before they arrived, but what? Maybe it was something to do with Lorel, or even those pills he was popping for his headache? At this point, it didn't matter all that much, he was in custody now, and that was a huge weight off her chest.

Ali was so consumed by her thoughts that she didn't even notice the ground rushing up to meet her as she passed out. Or how the staff from the hospital came rushing out as Benning caught her and carried her toward the door.

Laila and Darien followed Talen back to where the council waited. If the council voted against them, there would be little their team could do alone to stop the rebellion, and they'd have to find aid elsewhere. They approached, flanking Talen where he stood at the head of the table.

"Against my better judgment," started Aalis, "the council gives you their support to end this rebellion."

"Thank you," said Talen graciously, bowing his head.

The woman continued, "The council members will determine individually how many of their underlings will be offered for the cause. It is nearly sunrise, so if there is nothing further to discuss then, the council is dismissed."

Talen nodded, and the sires rose from their seats.

The younger woman approached Laila with the grace of a tiger on the prowl. "Congratulations, I will ready thirty of my finest warriors to aid you."

"Your help is much appreciated." Laila inclined her head.

"My name is Sarnai, by the way." She offered Laila her hand, which Laila shook.

"You can call me Laila."

She gave Laila an appraising look that felt as if she was peering into Laila's soul. "She's a fascinating specimen isn't she Darien?"

Sarnai glanced sideways at Darien, but he pretended not to hear. She rolled her eyes at Laila.

"A casual fling over a century ago and he still can't face me." Sarnai clicked her tongue and shook her head.

Laila raised her eyebrows at Darien.

"Keep an eye on him, will you?" asked the Vampire quietly with a wink before sauntering away through the crowd.

Laila turned to question her partner but found herself face to face with the blond Vampire instead.

"Excuse me." She made to step around him, but he stopped her.

"Tread softly, Elf," he whispered in her ear. "Not everyone on the council appreciates you meddling in the affairs of Vampires."

"Is that a threat?" she asked, narrowing her eyes.

"No," he said simply, "a warning. Be careful, some of these Vampires wouldn't think twice about killing you or using you for your blood." His eyes flickered to Dagan.

Laila fought the shiver that was creeping down her spine.

She knew Talen had powers beyond the ordinary Vampire thanks to his age. One of those was a type of charm magic that could be used to influence others. How strong would the abilities of these other Vampires be? She was about to question him further when she realized that he was gone.

Laila shook her head and strode over to Darien and Talen as the last of the council departed.

"It's almost sunrise," she pointed out glancing at the faint glow on the horizon through the UV filtering glass.

Darien nodded. "I'll stay here with Talen until sundown."

Laila sank into a seat beside him. "We need more information, to figure out what exactly we're up against."

From what they had seen, the network of tunnels was pretty vast. There would be multiple points of entry. They also needed to determine how many Vampires were among these rebels, and Laila suspected there were more weapons than the one cache they'd found.

Talen joined them at the table, taking the seat across from Laila. "It'll take a few days for the council to ready their forces. That will buy us some time to get the answers we need."

"We have to be careful though," said Darien, "from now on only Vampires should be sent in to spy. That was a close call with Jerrik and Laila tonight, even with the potion from Lyn."

Laila reluctantly agreed. They needed someone on the inside who wouldn't draw attention.

Talen nodded. "I may have someone who will work. They're newly turned, so their scent will blend in nicely. I'll contact them today."

"We should also contact the other government agencies and bring them up to speed," added Laila. "They'll want to know about this, and we'll need all the help we can get to take down these rebels."

Darien typed notes into his phone. "Alright then, I'll give them a call and fill Jerrik in. I'll also coordinate shifts to monitor the tunnel entrance. You should get some sleep though, I have a feeling there are more long nights ahead.

"Sounds good," yawned Laila.

She told the others that she'd meet them at the office after sunset, then headed back to the house, not even bothering to swap out Darien's sedan for her car back at the office. Traffic was horrible, she'd managed to leave right in the middle of rush hour. By the time she pulled into the garage, the sun was well over the horizon.

The house was silent and empty as she entered. The others would be in bed for sure, so Laila quietly picked her way up the stairs and to her room. Mr. Whiskers stirred from his sleep on the sofa as she passed and meowed before following her. He curled up in a ball at the foot of the bed. Laila was asleep before her head hit the pillow.

It was late afternoon by the time she awoke. She'd slept pretty well, and it was a good thing too because it was going to be a long day.

She took her time getting ready, tugged on a pair of sturdy combat boots over her jeans. She wore a royal blue blouse with her black leather armor and pulled her hair back into a braid. After applying a bit of makeup, she headed downstairs in search of the others.

Down in the living room, she found the others occupied by a variety of pastimes. Erin was in the middle of a lesson with Frej, Lyn was reading a book on advanced protection enchantments, and Ali was typing away on her computer. They all looked up as Laila entered.

"You were out late," pointed out Ali as she shut her computer.

"Darien and I were trying to get the support of the Vampire council." Laila filled the kettle with water and switched on a burner. "Last night we discovered a Vampire rebellion that our murder suspect is involved with."

"Geeze, that's intense," said Lyn, setting her book down.

"I'll be out helping with surveillance or tracking down entrances. It'll be another late night."

"Why don't I come with you?" asked Frej. "I can help scan the area from the sky."

Laila added a teabag to a mug. "Sure. We'll meet Darien back at the office after sunset."

Still, something didn't feel quite right, the others shifted in their seats and kept glancing at her. Laila couldn't shake the feeling that she was missing something. Finally, Ali pulled her aside.

"I need to tell you something." She motioned for Laila to follow her into the laundry room for some privacy.

Laila followed with uncertainty. Whatever was going on sounded serious. Ali shut the door and leaned against the doorframe.

"Something happened yesterday," said Ali avoiding Laila's gaze, "well, technically today. I got home even later than you did. The others already know, but I wanted to be the one to tell you in person."

Ali hesitated and fidgeted with a ring she wore. It did nothing to ease the tension building in Laila's muscles. After a moment the Fae took a deep breath and continued.

"I mentioned before that I hadn't reported Colin. The reason I called the Deputy Director was because of a leak, that's what I've been investigating with Adam. I couldn't tell you because everyone was under investigation. It turns out our suspicions were correct, and someone *was* giving information to the Demons."

Laila nodded as her stomach twisted and turned into knots. She desperately wanted Ali to say it, to just get it over with.

Ali lifted her head to look Laila directly in the eye.

"Colin's been arrested for treason."

"For *treason?*" The words hit Laila like a train. She didn't know what to say. It was one thing to suspect something like this, but another matter entirely to hear that your supervisor has been found guilty of treason. Laila blinked several times as she tried to wrap her head around the idea.

Ali continued. "He was transferred over to a pre-trial detention center and is scheduled for his initial appearance in court tomorrow. There'll be a bail hearing early next week."

Laila nodded absently and leaned against one of the machines. He'd been an unreliable jerk for the last two months, but a traitor? Her mind raced as she wondered what information he'd given up, and to whom. She had a feeling it would be the Demons, and she wondered how long that had been going on.

Ali rested her hand on Laila's arm. "As frustrating as Colin's been lately, I sincerely hoped that it wouldn't come to this. But the evidence points to Colin."

"What evidence did you find?" asked Laila still in shock.

Ali hesitated, "I can't discuss the details, not until Adam's finished sorting through the evidence. To be safe though I'd just assume that any information he had access to has been compromised, including our personal information."

"Right." Laila pushed her self away from the machine and took a deep breath.

She understood where Ali was coming from, it was just protocol. Still though, she wondered how much information about their team had been leaked. Had he led the Demons to their doorstep when they abducted Erin, or when they attacked Lyn?

"He was agitated when we went to arrest him," continued Ali. "I was able to sedate him with charm magic, but he managed to break a couple of my ribs before we apprehended him."

It was at that moment that Laila noticed the band around Ali's wrist, she recognized it from the patients at Asclepius's. God's above, how did she miss that?

Ali noticed her gaze on the wristband, which she promptly ripped off an threw into a trashcan.

"It's okay, they discharged me late this morning with a clean bill of health," insisted Ali.

Laila opened and closed her mouth, the words refusing to form on her lips. Colin had attacked Ali, not only that, but he'd sent her to the hospital! For the last month, Laila had been reluctant to act, hoping he would turn around and find some way to redeem himself. She'd imagined Colin could do something stupid or reckless that placed the rest of the team in danger but to attack Ali, his partner? The thought made Laila sick.

"Can I check?" Laila asked gesturing to Ali's body.

Ali nodded. Laila reached out with her magic searching for any source of pain but found nothing. The elemental magic from the doctor still lingered around the left side of the rib cage and the left lung, residue from the healing.

"You should've called me," said Laila hoarsely, "I could've been there—"

Ali shook her head. "It's fine. You had enough to deal with."

Laila didn't know what to say. She felt horrible. If only she'd been there to help.

"Next time, we do this together," insisted Laila, pulling Ali into her embrace.

Ali smiled and nodded. "I won't argue with you on that. The important thing is that our office is once more secure."

Laila took a step back shaking her head. "The important this is that you're safe!"

"Hey, it takes more than one pissed off Werewolf to take me out of the action." Ali gave her a sly look that left Laila exasperated.

Ali opened the door, and Laila followed her out of the room. Ali was right. Even if the news was unpleasant, at least the Demons were no longer privy to their investigations. There was more than enough to do today that would require Laila's full attention. She'd have to think over this new development later, after handling the Vampire rebels.

CHAPTER 35

Laila stepped into the conference room with Frej in tow. Irritation flashed across Jerrik's face as he saw the Dragon, who replied with a look of disdain. Laila ignored the silent exchange, focusing on the Vampire seated between Darien and Talen. His clothes were plain and nondescript, his hair slightly messy and he seemed hyper-aware of everything around him.

"Meet Jason," Talen gestured to the Vampire. "He's the one I mentioned last night. He'll attempt to infiltrate the tunnels for us and report back before dawn."

The man gave her a half-smile, and she nodded in greeting. As she and Frej found their seats, Darien gave them a rundown of the situation.

"I've been in contact with the LAPD and FBI about the situation. They've agreed to help if necessary, and the FBI is trying to track down any information they can about the rebels through their own channels. The council members are making their selections tonight, so we'll be able to meet with our reinforcements and fill them in tomorrow."

"Any new information regarding the rebels?" asked Frej.

"He's getting to it," drawled Jerrik.

Laila shot him a look, wondering what could've put him in such a foul mood.

Dairen ignored them. "Torsten's currently there with two members of the investigative team. They've been keeping an eye on the one access point we've identified, but with the daylight, there's been little activity. We'll relieve them and take the night-shift to watch for any activity.

"Frej, you'll take the sky and rooftops to see if you can find any indication of other entrances. I'm going back into the tunnels with Jason. We'll split up so we can cover more ground."

"Are you going in too?" Laila asked Talen.

He shook his head. "I'll be there for backup and to help monitor things from the exterior with you and Jerrik."

"I want extra hands on deck in case something happens," explained Darien. "There's a possibility that we'll catch Arnold Koch leaving the tunnel. Someone needs to be available to make the arrest, and Talen will be able to help apprehend him."

"Sounds good." Jerrik rose from his chair. "Let's load up."

They divided themselves amongst two SUV's before driving to the fringe of the Old City. They parked a couple blocks away before gearing up. Laila showed Jason how his magically enhanced com device worked.

"You won't be able to contact us up here, but you will hopefully be able to communicate with Darien." She passed the ear-piece to him.

"Got it."

She stuck one in her own ear as well, to communicate with Frej and the others who would be above ground before climbing out of the back seat after Jason. Darien pulled her aside though, away from the others.

"I want you to keep an eye on Jerrik," he whispered, concerned. "Something happened today. All he'd tell me was that it has to do with his father, but he seems ready to blow a gasket. I don't want him to do something reckless on account of that."

Laila didn't know much about Jerrik's father, only that he was pretty horrible. Cruel enough to slit the throat of Jerrik's beloved Sword Master, while Jerrik was forced to watch. Whatever this new development was, she imagined it was something awful.

"Sure," she replied before rejoining the others.

Frej shifted into his scaled form and took off to circle the area above. Darien and Jason headed directly to the storm drain that hid the tunnel entrance while Jerrik and Talen headed to an abandoned building where two members of the investigative team had been stationed to observe the alley below. Pulling on a black hoodie, Laila hung back for a minute or two before entering the alley that Darien and Jason had vanished into. She walked past the storm drain to where a van was parked next to a dumpster, tapping on the door before she entered.

"About time!" said Torsten, as Laila climbed inside. "I'm starving."

He and Donald had spent the majority of the day monitoring things from the surveillance van. They were relieved that their shifts were finally over for the day, and they could go home.

"Anything new?" she asked.

"Nothing, not even a hit on the radar." Torsten waved at a screen in front of him. "This here will show you if the undead are approaching. You can see where Darien and that other Vampire are."

He pointed to two red dots on the edge of the screen. Laila watched as they vanished from sight.

Torsten continued, "This way you know if they're approaching above or below ground. It's another one of Donald's inventions. These four screens show the outside of the van, and the fifth is a camera I mounted in the storm drain earlier today. If anything starts acting up, just call me or Donald. We'll walk you through it. There's also security features built in like a shield, but hopefully, you won't need those."

"Thanks." Laila swapped keys with him. Torsten and the other agents would take one of the SUVs back to the office.

He paused, "I heard about what happened with Colin. How are you holding up?"

Laila shrugged. "I haven't had much time to process it. I just can't believe that he's been feeding information to the Demons or that he'd hurt Ali like that. He's been a jerk lately, but this?" She shook her head at a loss for words.

What hurt more than anything was the sense of betrayal. She had given him her trust, but now she didn't want to think about how he'd potentially exploited her. Ali hadn't been able to say what information had been compromised or how long this had been going on. Eventually, Laila would find out, but she would have to assume the worst, that the Demons potentially possessed any information from case files to personal information.

Torsten clapped her on the shoulder and exited the van leaving Laila alone.

"Testing coms." She settled into her seat.

"I hear you loud and clear," said Jerrik.

Talen's voice came next. "We're in place one floor above you to the right of the van. The room with the broken window. We've got a good view of the entrance."

"Good," she replied. "I'm in the van. I'll let you know if any Vampires are approaching."

Frej wouldn't be able to communicate until he landed somewhere and switched back into his human form. According to Donald, his earpiece should be fine. It would just be tucked into the sub-dimensional pocket where his clothes existed when Frej was in his scaled form. Donald had tried to explain the physics of it to her, but she hadn't followed much of the explanation.

The good thing about tonight was that she, Jerrik, and Frej were all separated, cutting down on any drama. Unfortunately, it also meant that Laila was left to her own thoughts as she stared at the magical radar screen.

She looked at the bracelet charm she wore that kept her newly discovered powers in check. There hadn't been much time to dwell on this new development. If she was being honest with herself, Laila would even admit that she was terrified. What did it even mean? Was she morphing into some sort of Demigod, or some other divine being like an Angel? It made her head spin just thinking about it.

These new powers were coming from somewhere, probably the mysterious Goddess, and perhaps she could persuade her to take the power back. But was that truly what she wanted? As intimidating as this all was, the reality of the situation was that the Divine magic made her stronger. These powers could be what she needed to stop the Demons, but she needed to learn how to use them first.

A couple hours later her thoughts were interrupted by a voice in her earpiece.

"Hello?" called Frej. "Can anyone hear me?"

"Unfortunately, yes," muttered Jerrik.

"I wasn't asking you," snapped Frej.

"Enough!" Laila hissed. "Frej, we can hear you loud and clear."

"Good. I've managed to find a couple of possible entrances. Vampires were either coming or going. I'm going to snap some photos and keep looking."

"Okay, we'll see you soon."

As Laila sat there, a few Vampires left through the storm drain, but Arnold Koch was not among them. If he'd gone out to search for another victim, he must've used a different exit. The minutes ticked by slowly though, and Laila wished she'd been able to go down into the tunnels with Darien. She hated being left behind to wonder what was happening down there.

Something moved on one of her monitors, it was Frej at the mouth of the alley.

Laila spoke through the coms, "Frej, you can head up to

the second floor of the building on your left. That's where the others are."

He nodded and vanished around the corner of the building.

"Here's what I found," Frej explained as he reached the others. "I've recorded the location for each, but if there are entrances that are accessible from any of the buildings, hopefully, the others will find them. Laila, I'm sending them to you now."

"There's only a few hours left until dawn," Talen pointed out. "Darien and I will have to leave before then with Jason, but there may be more activity just before sun up as they take cover for the day."

Laila's phone buzzed as she received the photos. She picked them up and started flipping through them.

"I'll get back out there in a few minutes and continue until sunrise."

"What's the matter? Tired?" sneered Jerrik.

"I haven't been sitting on my ass for the last six hours," the annoyance was creeping through his voice.

"Maybe you should go home?" suggested Jerrik.

"Jerrik, watch the attitude," warned Laila, suddenly regretting her decision to send Frej up there.

"Or better yet," continued Jerrik in a cutting tone, "why don't you go crawling back to your queen?"

"Jerrik," growled Frej in a warning tone.

Jerrik scoffed. "Her infamous ongoing affair with her knight that the king tried so hard to cover up. You couldn't even bring yourself to tell Laila—"

There was the unmistakable sound of a fist connecting with flesh, and a loud thud as someone hit the floor. Laila felt as though it had been her as the words sunk in. This was the secret that Frej had been so reluctant to tell her about.

Frej and Queen Regina? Was it true? It felt like the floor had fallen out from underneath her, and she was in freefall. Her lungs wouldn't work, and her head swam with confused thoughts. Sure, it seemed that the two were close, but was there something more? It made sense though, the more she thought about it. He always spoke of her fondly, like their relationship was more than professional.

She was pulled from the poisonous thoughts by the sounds of the fight raging in the building above her.

"Stop!" She yelled into the earpiece. "Stop it! Both of you!"

But they weren't listening. Laila flung open the door of the van searching for some way up to the second floor. There was a metal drain pipe from the rain gutter. She scrambled up it climbing as fast as she could. As she pulled herself up onto the window sill, shards of glass cut deep into her hands like daggers. Pushing through it, she climbed up through the window and dropped into the room where Frej broke through Talen's grip. He tackled Jerrik again, rolling on the floor. Frej pinned him there punching him once, twice, three times. Laila could hear the crunch of his nose break before Jerrik shoved the Dragon off him with a blast of air. Frej slammed into the wall behind, groaning as he staggered to his feet.

"Enough!" Laila stood between the two of them as she froze them in place with magic, the two men glaring at each other. She stood there breathing heavily with her arms outstretched, blood dripping down her palms.

"Enough," she rasped, shaking. "Frej, I want you to go. Now."

She released him from the spell, and he stumbled forward.

"Laila, I—"

"*Go!*" she hissed.

His expression was pained as he staggered backwards through the door. Laila waited a few moments longer before she turned to face Jerrik. She just gave him a disgusted look before jumping from the window and storming back to the car, slamming the door behind her.

Within the dark privacy of the van, she shut her eyes and leaned against the door. Hot tears of frustration and anger and uncertainty rolled down her cheeks. Something dripped down on to the floor of the van, but it wasn't her tears, it was blood from her injured hands. Laila summoned the magic to heal her bleeding hands, wishing it could heal the ache in her chest.

Talen removed his earpiece as he watched the Dark Elf. His petty comments to the Dragon were even starting to grate on his nerves so he couldn't imagine how Laila felt. But this was something else entirely.

"You're not doing yourself any favors, you know."

"What?" Jerrik snapped his head up. He removed his earpiece as well as he cast a spell to mend his wounds.

"Look, I know you don't like Frej. He knows, Laila knows, *everyone* knows! You don't need to remind us all the damn time," snarled Talen.

Jerrik shook his head and looked out the broken window.

"You can ignore me all you want, but I've got nearly two thousand years on you. Pissing Laila off isn't going to help your situation with her. Hurting her is going to help even less! I take it you've told her how you feel?" He crossed his arms his eyes never leaving Jerrik

Jerrik nodded stiffly.

"Then there's nothing more you can do."

The Elf gaped at him, and Talen could hear the beating of his heart hasten as his temper flared. Once he'd been like that as well, but age and experience had taught Talen control. He'd seen enough war, hate, and bloodshed where sensitive egos and broken hearts were concerned. Laila was a fascinating woman, and Talen genuinely liked her. She didn't deserve this, not when there were so many other problems on her mind.

"I revealed the truth, something Frej would have done if he cared about her!" Jerrik spat.

"No you didn't, you took a jab at Frej. You knew it would hurt Laila. Did you think you'd look like some sort of hero?

That she'd come running back to you? You're just an asshole who revealed a secret that wasn't any of his business!"

Jerrik's face twisted into a snarl.

"Cool it," Talen hissed. "You can't force her to be with you, and antagonizing Frej will only push her away. Now I suggest you find some way to make amends because we have far bigger issues than your ridiculous feud!"

He glared at Jerrik until he backed down.

"Now clean up the blood before someone smells it," added Talen. "You'll blow our cover."

CHAPTER 36

By the time two red dots appeared on Laila's magical radar screen a couple hours later, she'd regained her composure. Sure, she was still furious with the two men for choosing to settle their differences during surveillance, but she pushed the rest of it as deep as she could beneath her cool Elven mask of indifference.

She watched on the monitors as Darien and Jason climbed out of the storm drain and back towards the street.

"Jerrik," Laila said into the coms, her voice as cold as steel, "you're taking my place in the van. Just observation, no arrests. That's an order."

She ghosted past him in the alley, ignoring his presence as she followed the Vampires back to one of the SUVs. Riding back with Jerrik was too much for her at the moment, and he'd survive on his own in the van for an hour.

Reaching the SUV, she climbed into the back seat with Jason, as Darien and Talen took the front. Darien gave her a quizzical look, but she shook her head, putting a stop to the question on his tongue. Instead, he started the vehicle and left.

On the way back to the office Darien and Jason told her

what they had discovered. It was hard to get an estimate on the number of Vampires involved since they were coming and going. They were able to confirm four of the five entrances Frej found led into the tunnels and added another three to the list. There were more tunnels left unexplored though.

"They've got humans down there," said Darien with disgust. "They're feeding off them, and they're all so drained they can hardly walk."

Laila shook her head in disgust. "Was there anything you could do for them?"

"Not without drawing attention to ourselves. We also found more weapons. They're definitely preparing for a major conflict. They must've plundered the countryside to come up with this many."

If only they could just march in there and raid the place, but it wasn't that simple. It would mean one hell of a fight. If it was at all possible, they needed to find a way to contain the violence. She had the feeling that Sire Ashford was probably not open to negotiation though.

She wanted to ask if there was any sign of the Demons. If there were traces of Demonic energy back at the crime scenes, then the Demons had to be involved in some way. But the Vampires didn't have the ability to sense Demonic energy.

Turning to Jason, she thanked him for his help.

"It was nothing," he insisted, "I'd do anything to help my grandsire, especially after…" The Vampire trailed off.

"You don't have to tell me," said Laila as she watched his haunted expression.

He smiled. "It's okay. I married one of his underlings, Eric, after The Event. He and I helped each other rebuild our lives, but when I got the cancer diagnosis earlier this year, I knew I only had months to live at the most. Even the Elves at Asclepius had little they could do other than make my passing easier. I wasn't ready, but Eric didn't want to turn me, to make me a monster. Talen spoke to him on my behalf and eventually wore him down. I don't regret it, not for a minute. I wasn't ready to leave Eric after such a short time."

Something stirred in her heart as she listened to his tale. It was beautiful if bitter-sweet, and she was happy for him. She felt honored that he was willing to risk his happy ending by putting himself in danger to help them.

When they reached the office, Laila parted ways with the Vampires and headed home. She wasn't looking forward to going home and the impending conversation with Frej. There had been no communication from him after the fight, so she didn't even know if he was home or still out in the Old City. As much as she dreaded it, she needed to hear the explanation from Frej's lips. Perhaps it was nothing, just some misunderstanding. As diplomatic and grounded as Frej was, that had struck a nerve in him. It left her wondering what feelings he still harbored for his queen.

She parked in the garage and entered the house. It was completely silent, and the other women in the house would be asleep. Frej sat at the counter alone, a mug cradled in his hands. Laila steeled herself as she took a step closer.

His eyes rose to meet her own, and she could see the pain. He rose from his chair like he wanted to go to her, but she took a step back, her stony composure slammed down, strong as a wall of bricks. It was a wall of protection from him, from what she feared he'd say.

She watched as he struggled with that void of emotion. He knew she was pissed, and hurting.

"Explain yourself," she said stiffly.

For a moment he struggled to find words. "Why don't you sit down?"

"No," the word slid out her mouth cold as steel as she stood her ground.

He ran his fingers through his hair in frustration. "It's not what you think. I didn't—I wouldn't do that to you. What happened between Regina and I…"

He waited, but Laila made no move to approach him, so he continued.

"Regina and I were lovers before she met the king. We were both young and in the army, but life pulled us in different directions. She was sent to work at the castle while I was sent to one of the forts in the North. I'd hoped that she'd be waiting for me when I came back, but another had captured her heart. I tried to tell her that the king—he was the prince at the time—would have to marry for power, but she didn't care.

"They did eventually get married, but after some time I saw her start to fade away. The king had many duties, and while he tried to make time for her, there was also a kingdom to rebuild and connections with other monarchs to strengthen. It was on a diplomatic trip that we slipped up. It destroyed me to see her like that and Regina was terribly lonely. We told ourselves that it was a mistake, that it wouldn't happen again—"

"But it did." Laila crossed her arms.

He cringed and nodded. "We were on a trip to Svartalfheim for a week for trade negotiations. The night before our departure home I was caught leaving her bedchamber by one of the noblemen. By the morning it was clear that word of our transgression had spread through the court like wildfire. When we returned home, we managed to hide it, but Regina knew she had to tell the king.

"That was the last time I accompanied her on a diplomatic trip. After that Regina was determined to put some space between us. I was sent away on mission after mission, each one longer than the last, and Regina found a way to mend her marriage. That was nearly twenty years ago, and nothing has happened between us since."

As he finished, he sank back into the chair, watching her with a pained expression, willing her to say something.

Jerrik must've found out about the affair from someone at the Svartálfr court, or perhaps he'd been present that morning. For a while she had suspected he was the son of a lord so the information would not have been terribly hard to for him to uncover.

"Why didn't you just tell me Frej?"

"I was waiting for the right time. I just wanted to be sure that… That I really was…" he trailed off. There was something in his eyes, a longing.

It occurred to her that twenty years was not all that long in the span of a Dragon life, perhaps only five years or so in human terms. How long had he been holding onto those feelings before that? Another twenty years or so? If he hadn't gotten over Regina before, then was he really over her now?

"Do you love her?" The words felt like ice as they left her mouth. Frej didn't meet her gaze. He opened his mouth, but the words escaped him. Finally, he nodded.

She gave him a disgusted look and stormed off to the stairs.

"Laila—"

She ignored him.

"Wait!" He grabbed her arm as her foot reached the first step.

"Don't touch me." She didn't bother to look at him, around her the air crackled with energy like an electrically-charged storm. He released her and retreated a step.

After a moment she continued to her room where she locked the door and leaned against it before sliding down to the floor. Once more the warm tears rolled down her face, and she hated every one of them. How had she been so blind? She'd seen the way they looked at each other, she had known there was something more between them, but she was a fool for mistaking it for mere friendship.

"*Mert?*" meowed a shadow in front of her. Mr. Whiskers blinked his bright green eyes at her and approached.

With no respect for boundaries, he crawled under her arm and into her lap, his boney feet digging into her stomach. He rubbed his head against her cheek, blotting away a stream of tears as he purred loudly. She didn't know how long she sat there with the Bogey-cat, but gradually his presence began to soothe her. It felt good to have him here, this way she wasn't completely alone with her anger and hurt. Perhaps she needed Mr. Whiskers as much as he needed her.

Laila descended the stairs, each step jolting her aching head. How could it be she felt so worn out after six hours of sleep? Mr. Whiskers batted at her feet playfully as he raced past her, shooting under the sofa where all that was visible were his eyes.

At least someone's in a good mood, she thought as she headed to the kitchen.

To her relief, Frej was nowhere in sight. She wasn't ready to see him at the moment. Perhaps in time she would be, but for now, she needed space. Ali, Lyn, and Erin were there though and silently watched her approach.

"Is everything okay?" asked Ali as she got up to make a cup of tea.

"Where's Frej?" Laila croaked.

"Out. He said he wanted time to fly." She lowered her voice, "A fight?"

"More than one," snorted Laila wryly. "He beat the snot out of Jerrik."

Laila felt the others turn to look at her as she explained what had happened the night before. She still didn't know what to make of it, but she felt raw and emotionally exhausted.

"Shit." Ali leaned against the counter. "I really didn't expect that from Frej."

"Me neither, but he still loves her, he admitted it."

Ali wrapped an arm around her and Laila leaned into her embrace.

"What do you need?" the Fae asked gently.

"I-I don't know. I don't want to deal with him right now. Either of them."

She felt ashamed. If she was back in the Elven Kingdom there was no way she could show her face like this, her emotions so exposed, but the pain of betrayal was pulling down her Elven composure brick by brick.

How could he do this? Why would Frej lead her on like this when he knew he was still in love with another woman? Was he just so Gods damned lonely? Laila knew that there were similarities between her and the queen, but were those likenesses the reason Frej was with her?

"Hey," said Ali, "it's your day off. Surely the others can handle the investigation tonight. Why don't we go out and blow off some steam? Mato found this club that's got great reviews, we could check it out."

Laila nodded slowly. She wasn't ready to face Jerrik and Frej as she would have to at the office, but she also didn't feel like pining away at home. Perhaps a night out would be nice. Tonight would just be more surveillance and preparation anyway since the Vampire council was still readying their forces.

Lyn sauntered over to them with a wicked grin. "You know, I've got this lovely little hex that will make his favorite part fall off. Temporarily of course. It'll eventually grow back. Just in case you want a little revenge on either of them."

Laila choked a laugh and shook her head as Lyn winked.

"You're only just now telling us this!" howled Ali incredulously, "What do you think you're doing keeping a perfectly good spell like that to yourself?"

Laila shook her head at the Fae.

Lyn shrugged. "Well, I think a night out sounds like a great idea. Personally, I could use a distraction as well, and you Fae know how to party."

"You've got that right!" Ali started dancing to a phantom rhythm, shaking her butt in a ridiculous dance. Lyn quickly joined in.

"You guys are so weird." Erin rolled her eyes. "Guess I'll have to go along to keep you out of trouble." She gave Laila a meaningful look that left a smile tugging at the corners of Laila's mouth.

"It's settled then!" cried Ali, "Grab your heels ladies because we're going out!"

CHAPTER 37

Lights flashed, and bodies writhed to the beat of the music, the bass pulsing strong enough for Laila to feel the music through her entire being. It was steady, and hypnotic and helped to ground her in the moment.

Her friends were in short, slinky dresses of varying styles: Erin in dark blue velvet, Lyn in white satin, and Ali in a violet dress that matched her eyes. Laila was clad in a tiny black dress that tied behind her neck, and a pair of platform stilettos that increased her height to an intimidating seven feet. That left her towering over the rest of the crowd, including Henrik and Mato, who Ali had brought along to deter any men from hitting on them. As skeptical as Laila was of whether Ali's plan would actually work, she didn't mind. The goofy men kept her laughing, so she didn't dwell too much on Frej.

The club was near the pier in Santa Monica and had a beachy, tropical theme with a nearly endless list of cocktails. Laila and Ali refrained from drinking on the off-chance they got called in to deal with an emergency, and Erin wasn't drinking since she was already getting enough strange glances from the surrounding humans for looking so young.

Laila danced with her friends, content to let loose and not care, even if it was just for a few hours. Eventually, Mato challenged Henrik to a dance-off, which drew the attention of a small crowd cheering them on. Even the D.J. was getting into it and pumping up the crowd.

Buzzing drew Laila's attention away from the battle, and she pulled out her phone to see who in the worlds would be calling her right now. When Jerrik's name popped up on the caller I.D., she rolled her eyes and shoved her phone back into her pocket. Whatever he wanted could wait.

Laila returned her attention to the men and found Mato spinning around on the ground. This kind of dance was nothing like Laila had ever seen in her homeworld. It occurred to her that the guys were actually quite good at this though, and she wondered how often they practiced these tricks. Mato's spinning came to a sudden stop as he stalled, his feet twisting in a pose.

"Yeah!" screamed Lyn next to her, totally invested in the battle.

Henrick stepped up, determined to outdo the Werebear. He performed a handstand then started hopping around on his hands, his feet kicking back and forth. He sprung back up to his feet, but liquid had sloshed out of one enthusiastic bystander's drink. Henrik's foot slipped on the slick floor, and he landed with a painful thud. Laila cringed with the others but quickly rushed to help him up.

"You okay?" she shouted over the music.

He rubbed the back of his head. "Nothing a drink won't fix."

Laila shook her head and followed him over to the bar. "Come on, let me take a look."

He reached the bar and stopped, allowing her to examine his head. With a quick spell, she put an end to the concussion he'd received.

"Thanks," he said, probing the back of his pale blond head

with his fingers. "Can I get you something?" He waved at the bar.

Laila gave in after a moment and allowed him to buy her a fruity drink that was alcohol-free. They stood there waiting for their drinks as the others danced with the crowd.

Her phone started buzzing, and she glanced at the screen again. It was a call from Frej, and two voicemails from Jerrik. She hit ignore. Henrik arched an eyebrow, but she just shook her head.

A bartender passed them their drinks, and they headed back onto the dance floor to join the others, but it was hard to enjoy the dancing when her phone was buzzing nonstop.

Ali noticed her irritation. "What's wrong?"

"*They* won't stop calling!" she muttered. "Can't I enjoy a night out without them getting in the way?"

Ali stopped dancing suddenly as she removed her own phone from where she'd tucked it in her dress. She paused to read something before leaning closer. "I think something's going on. You'd better give Darien a call."

Laila whipped out her phone again. Amid the list of missed calls from Jerrik and Frej was a text message from Darien.

Call ASAP. New development.

Laila swore and stomped off through the crowd to the back of the building. She stepped into the relatively quiet hall where the bathrooms were located before calling Darien.

"Where the hell have you been?" grumbled Darien, "Why haven't you been answering the phone?"

Laila ignored his questions. "What's going on?"

"Fredrik Stacy's been kidnapped by the Vampires."

"Wait, the protestor-politician?" Laila's frown deepened.

"Yes! There was a break-in at his home tonight, his wife found a note."

"Oh Gods!" This was so not good. Of all the people the Vampires could kidnap, he was by far the worst.

"News reporters are swarming the place and his supporters

are starting to find out. LAPD's on the watch for potential riots, and the Vampire community as a whole is under suspicion."

"Okay, I'm on my way."

"Bring Ali too. She knows more about this guy."

"Alight." She ended the call.

As she neared the archway, she realized that something was drowning out the sound of the fast-paced music. Screaming.

"What in the worlds—" She hurried through the archway as humans rushed past her towards the emergency exit.

There at the far end of the building were three hulking figures, two Bubac that flanked a massive Ogre.

"Where's the Elf?" roared the Ogre. "Her head is mine!"

"Shit," Laila swore. This was so not how she planned to spend her night.

CHAPTER 38

"Everybody out!" shouted Ali from somewhere amid the crowd.

Laila fought her way through the stampede of terrified humans to where her friends waited. She reached out with her magic to the three intruders to find hints of Demonic energy stuck to their beings.

"Lesser Demons," she spat, finally arriving at the others.

The crowd was quickly thinning, but not fast enough. She needed to keep the Demons away from the humans.

"Erin and Lyn, get the humans out of here. Ali, Henrik, and Mato, we need to keep the Demons occupied."

"On it!" Mato started shifting, his body sprouting long brown and gold fur as he grew in size. Humans paused, staring at the grizzly bear, but Erin and Lyn quickly herded them towards the door.

Ali rushed to the bar, searching for some sort of a weapon while Laila and Henrik approached the Demons. Laila could feel waves of mist and freezing air rolling off Henrik, and she heard the crackling of ice. Beside her, Henrik had become coated in a layer of frost, his pale blond hair had turned into spiky shards of ice while his fingers grew icy talons. Laila had never actually seen the Mörkö in his magical, icy state before. Behind them loomed Mato.

"Looking for someone?" called Laila, electricity crackling at her fingertips. "Leave peacefully, and I'll let you walk away. Stay, and you're under arrest."

The Ogre grinned, his yellow tusks protruding from his cracked lips. His hide was like thick, greenish leather and he had a rank odor about him. His clothes were made of scaled skin, and she really hoped it wasn't Dragonhide. He was about nine feet tall, and his head nearly hit the lighting equipment above him. In his hand was a large, well-worn club made of wood.

The Bubac beside him had tan skin that was rough like bark, and jet-black eyes that were sunken deep in their skulls. There was little hair visible on them, and their nails were lethally sharp like daggers.

"Take the ice creature," ordered the Ogre. "I've got the Elf!"

Laila didn't wait for him to prepare an attack before blasting him with electricity. Had he been a human, the Ogre would've been dead on the spot, but Ogres were tough. He clenched his teeth through the pain and hurtled a chair at Laila who dodged it, but the distraction was enough to break her concentration, and she dropped the spell. The Ogre continued to throw chairs at her, and Laila had to conjure a shield to protect herself.

The Ogre was so distracted that he missed the grizzly bear lumbering through the shadows behind him. Mato stood on his hind legs and sank his teeth into the Ogre's neck. Screaming, the Ogre clawed at the grizzly. Mato retreated and growled, challenging the Ogre.

Nearby, Henrik was struggling against the two Bubac. He blasted one in the face with a cloud of ice while he slashed at the other with his claws. The other Bubac was backing him up though, closer to one of the fallen chairs.

"Look out!" Laila shouted as the Bubac shoved him back.

There was a loud thump, and the Bubac crumpled. Above him stood Ali brandishing a fire extinguisher. She blasted the other Bubac in the face with the foam, who spluttered and backed away. Henrik recovered and grabbed the Bubac's shoulders. From his hands spread ice, coating the creature's body until he was encased in a thick block of ice. The Mörkö left the Bubac's head exposed to allow it to breathe. It started howling expletives, but Ali shot him in the face with more foam, shutting him up.

Mato and the Ogre circled each other, the Ogre swung its club, and Mato tried to avoid it, but it caught him in the shoulder. The Werebear roared in pain, and Laila threw up a shield, protecting him from the club that was ready to descend on his skull. Laila conjured a pair of thick ice daggers and dove. She sliced through the skin and flesh on the back of the legs, severing the hamstrings. He crumpled backwards in pain.

Laila quickly disarmed the creature, kicking the club out of his reach, and forced the Ogre's hands behind his back with magic. Lyn appeared behind him with a length of rope that Laila had seen before. They'd used it to tie up a Minotaur that had gone on a rampage through a shopping mall. The rope had been soaked in a powerful binding enchantment. Hopefully, it would be strong enough to hold him.

With the Ogre taken care of, Laila assessed the damage to Mato's shoulder. The bone was fractured badly, and there was extensive damage to the joint. In Bear form, Mato cried out and gave her a desperate look.

"Mato, you're in pretty bad shape," Laila explained quickly. "I know it'll hurt, but I need you to switch back into human form."

He huffed a gust of warm air through his nose in response. After a moment he growled and started to shift. He was screaming by the time he'd finished. Laila placed her hands above the wound and reached out with healing magic to dull the pain.

"By the Morrigan! What happened!" exclaimed Ali, rushing over.

"The bone is shattered, it's too complicated for me to heal," Laila explained to them both. "We've got to get you back to Asclepius. They'll be able to help."

Mato nodded as a couple of EMTs wheeled a gurney through the doors.

Beside her, Laila could see the horror in Ali's eyes. Mato cupped her chin with his good hand.

"I'll be fine, I want you to stay here with Laila though. Don't make her sort this out on her own."

Ali opened her mouth to argue.

"Please Ali?" he asked wincing at the pain.

The EMTs started loading him onto the gurney.

"He's a Supernatural, he must be taken to Asclepius," she told them.

The EMTs nodded and loaded the Werebear onto the gurney. Even with the magic, Mato cried out in pain.

Laila cringed. "Okay Mato, I'm going to release the magic. Hang in there."

He nodded. Laila released the spell, and he groaned and clenched his teeth as they wheeled him out. Ali paled beside her but stayed as Mato asked.

"Don't bother with him," Laila said to the other two EMTs that were trying to figure out how to transport the Ogre.

She used her magic to weave the severed tissues back together in the Ogre's legs. The clean cut was far easier for her to mend. It was straight forward where Mato's injury would be difficult due to the number of the fragments. A part of her wished to leave the Ogre to suffer for what he'd done to Mato, but that wasn't how they operated, so she finished the spell and turned back to the others.

"What the hell was that about?" Ali shook her head.

"They must be following me." Laila collapsed on a chair.

One of the Bubac was just starting to gain consciousness as a paramedic checked his head wound. The other had managed to spit the foam out of his mouth and was making threats.

"Shut it," growled Erin holding a flame coated hand in front of the Bubac's face. "Or I'll give you a little taste of fire and ice." She watched him with an evil grin.

"Erin!" snapped Ali, "Don't threaten the perps!" She rolled her eyes.

A middle-aged man came stomping over to them. "What the hell is going on? Look at my bar!"

Laila glanced around and the damaged floor and broken chairs. The Ogre's club had shattered a number of the lights hanging above, and there was foam floating in a growing puddle of water around the Bubac.

"I'll handle him," muttered Ali as she pulled the man aside.

"Now what?" asked Henrik joining them. The ice had melted away, and his appearance was back to normal.

Laila shook her head. "Ali and I will have to ride in the ambulance with them." Laila gestured toward the two Bubac. "I'll see if the police can handle things here. Lyn and Erin, you should probably head home."

"I'll start driving to the hospital," added Henrik. "I want to check on Mato."

Laila nodded, she was about to say more when a familiar face walked through the door. It was Special Investigator Jenn Holdt.

"Well, you certainly made a mess here," she nodded to the destroyed tables and chairs as well as the dented floorboards. "The transport vehicle for the Ogre is outside. I'll take it from here."

Laila thanked her and headed towards the waiting EMTs, grabbing Ali along the way.

By the time they had transported the two Bubac back to the hospital, defrosted the one, and had both of them cuffed to the beds and under the supervision of the SNP security guards, over an hour had passed.

Now that her duties were handled, Laila could see the distraught look on Ali's face. Laila suggested they check on Mato, and the two were directed down the stairs to the ICU. He was still in in the magical operating room.

They were about to search for Henrik in the waiting room when Laila's phone buzzed, it was a text message from Darien.

Where are you?

"Thor's hammer!" Laila groaned. "We've got to go."

"What?" snapped Ali. "What about Mato?"

Laila understood the outrage in Fae's eyes. Of course Ali wanted to make sure that Mato was okay, especially after what happened to Carlos, but they also needed her help regarding this new development.

"I was on the phone with Darien before the Demons showed up. Fredrik Stacy's been kidnapped."

Ali swore up and down. After hesitating for a moment, she followed Laila to the elevator.

CHAPTER 39

There was a row of police officers standing in front of Fredrik Stacy's home working crowd control as Laila and Ali approached. There were multiple news vans there and reporters speaking to cameras in addition to a growing crowd of humans.

The officers cast skeptical looks at the agents' dresses but allowed Laila and Ali to pass. They headed up the front steps.

"This place must've cost a fortune," murmured Laila. Houses this large, in this part of the city, were hard to come by.

"He claims it's from the lawsuits he filed after his son's death," Ali explained quietly, "But there's something more to it. I've been trying to figure where the money's coming from, but I've been too distracted to focus on that investigation."

Laila knew Colin was the reason for the distraction.

Darien and Jerrik were waiting for them in the parlor.

"Took you long enough," huffed Darien.

"We had a run-in with some Lesser Demons," explained Laila. "Looks like they're still after my head."

"They're in custody though, so maybe we can get some information out of them." Ali checked her phone nervously, waiting for any news on Mato's condition from Henrik. Laila pulled her eyes away from the phone and back to Darien.

"So, what happened?" asked Laila.

The situation was fairly straight forward. The Vampires had broken through a window downstairs while the homeowners were asleep. Mrs. Stacy had waited in the bedroom with the door locked while her husband went to see what the noise was, but her husband never returned. After the police arrived, she came downstairs and found a note in an unmarked envelope on her husband's desk.

"Where's the note?" Laila glanced around.

Jerrik passed it to her from a side table. It was encased in a plastic bag and read:

Now's the time for change. A new era begins: the fall of the humans.
Sire Ashford

Ali shook her head. "Why abduct him? I mean, why now?"

"I think I can explain that" called a voice from the entryway. They turned to find Talen walking through the door.

"How'd the police let him through?" Ali frowned.

Talen shrugged. "I told them I was a consultant."

Laila stepped forward. "Ali, this is Talen. Talen, Ali."

"A pleasure," he replied quickly. "Anyway, I just heard that the council decided to take matters into their own hands. They captured one of the rebels and used her to send a message earlier this evening."

"So, this could have been retaliation." Darien glanced over the letter once more.

"Possibly." Talen shoved his hands in his pockets looking troubled.

Ali paced back and forth. "We have to do something. The city's going to lose its mind when it wakes up. They don't know about the rebels, they'll blame everyone in the Vampire community."

"That's exactly what Sire Ashford wants," said Jerrik. "He's trying to tear a rift between the humans and Vampires. If the Vampires think their lives are in danger from the outraged humans, it puts him in the perfect position to lure them over to his side and start a war."

"Goddess," breathed Ali. "I hate to say it, but it looks like we've got to rescue this SNP hating bastard."

"What kind of message did the council send?" asked Laila hesitantly.

Talen flipped through his phone before passing it to her. The others crowded around to see. There was a video clip of a woman, a Vampire, being shoved down the storm drain. Her hands were bound behind her back with chains. Wrought iron stakes had been shoved through multiple parts of her body then bent to prevent their removal. Several knives had been thrust into her chest, lethally close to her heart. One of them had a note stuck through it.

Bile raised in Laila's throat, and she had to look away to keep from vomiting.

"I was told the note ordered Sire Ashford to surrender, but knowing the council, I'm sure it involved additional threats," added Talen.

Ali squinted at the screen. "Wait a minute, we've seen her before. That's the Vampire that attacked Lyn in her home, the one that fled the scene."

Laila's disgust lessened slightly.

"Sarnai sent this to you?" asked Darien.

Talen nodded. "Looks like her methods too."

Darien flinched. Laila wondered what he'd witnessed as her lover, nothing good by his reaction.

After a moment Darien spoke, "I agree with Ali. We've got to get Fredrik Stacy back and convince him to talk his supporters down. They'll listen to him."

Laila ran her fingers through her hair as she thought. "We can't just march in there and demand him back. We'd be walking right into a trap."

Darien glanced around, there were news crews trying to talk their way into the house. "This isn't the place for this discussion. We'll leave the investigative team and the police to wrap up here."

They left the scene and headed back to the office on the other side of the city. They gathered in the conference room around a map the support staff had generated based off of the team's observations. It had the identified entrances and exits marked as well as a rough map of the tunnels.

In all honesty, they had no idea where Fredrik Stacy was being held, or if he was even in the tunnels at all. It seemed to be the most likely location though. Even though Darien had spent the better part of the previous night exploring the tunnels with Jason, they'd only been able to access portions of it without drawing suspicion. There were too many unknowns for Laila's liking.

The team debated what the best course of action would be. They could try to arrange a meeting with Sire Ashford and request the politician be returned, but that was unlikely. If they launched a raid, the Gods only knew what they would do to Fredrik Stacy, not to mention the humans that were being held underground. There was no telling what kind of a trap the team and their reinforcements would be walking into either. If the rebels were smart, they'd have layers of defenses to protect from a direct attack.

They determined that the safest way to extract Fredrik Stacy would be to send in two small teams from different entrances to discreetly locate the human and return him to the surface. In the event things went south, their reinforcements would be waiting to raid the tunnel.

"I should go in there," insisted Ali. "I can use my glamor on myself and others."

Darien shook his head. "We'll need you to handle the media this morning, and entering those tunnels bone weary would be suicide. I'll take one entrance with Jerrik, then Talen and Laila can take the other. If Lyn can whip up more of those charms from last time, they'll have to do."

"Who's going to lead the raid if Talen's in the tunnels with us?" Jerrik asked. "Would one of the council members be in charge?"

"No," Darien spoke firmly. "We need someone that knows how our team operates, that we trust to make decisions on our behalf. I think Frej would be perfect. He's commanded units back in the Dragon Kingdom."

Talen nodded in agreement.

They spent the better part of the next hour working out details and preparing contingencies. Laila could feel Jerrik's eyes on her constantly but refused to give him the satisfaction of acknowledging his presence.

It was nearly five in the morning before they solidified their plan and decided to break for the day. Ali would have a long day ahead of her and needed to return home to change for her meeting with the press. Laila and Jerrik would return home to rest before the night's rescue mission, but as Vampires both Darien and Talen didn't require sleep. They'd spend the day putting their plan into motion.

"I want to stop and check on Mato," declared Ali as she stood. For the last hour, Laila had noticed that the Fae had checked her phone constantly, waiting for news.

"You'll be late for your meeting," insisted Laila.

Jerrik frowned. "What's wrong with Mato?"

Laila cringed. "An Ogre sent him to the hospital with a shattered shoulder. Henrik's with him at Asclepius."

Jerrik's expression grew worried.

"I'll check on him and send you an update," he told Ali. "You've got enough to worry about with news of Fredrik Stacy's abduction being announced."

Ali reluctantly agreed. Laila was about to follow her to the garage when Jerrik stopped her.

"Can we talk?" His eyes begged her. "It will only take a moment."

There was a very long list of things she would rather do than talk to Jerrik, but this would be one hell of a night. The logical part of her brain insisted that they needed to get along if they were going to make it in and out of the tunnels in one piece. Hesitantly, she nodded and followed him down the hall.

He stopped and took a deep breath. "What I did was completely inappropriate."

"Yes." Laila gave him a sharp look. "Yes, it was."

He grit his teeth. "Look, I didn't mean for that to happen. I couldn't shake the feeling I'd met him somewhere before. I was worried the affair was still ongoing, but that's why I confronted Frej about it in the bar. I honestly intended for Frej to tell you on his own terms, but yesterday I received news from a friend about my father's latest atrocity. It's got nothing to do with Frej, but I was so angry that I lashed out. I'm so sorry Laila, I truly didn't mean for that to happen."

Laila didn't think it was a particularly good excuse. What news would justify that sort of behavior? But she held her tongue as he continued.

"I feel horrible, I really do. I spoke to Frej about it earlier, and we came to an understanding. We've agreed to be civil, but I wanted to tell you myself that I'm truly sorry, and regret losing my temper."

"I get that you're sorry, but you crossed a line." She could feel her nails digging into her palms and forced herself to let it go. "We've got bigger issues at the moment, so I accept your apology. But if you ever do something like that again, don't expect me to intervene and save you from being beaten to a pulp."

"Fair enough." He relaxed ever so slightly.

Before he could say another word, she left.

"Are you okay?" asked Ali as they climbed into one of the SUVs.

Laila nodded. She wanted more time to process Jerrik's

apology though. "How about you? How are you holding up?"

"I don't know." She shook her head.

Laila glanced over to find Ali's expression haunted. Given everything the Demons had put her through with Carlos, her sister, and now Mato getting caught in the crossfire, Laila couldn't help but wonder if this was all too much. She waited for Ali to say more, but Ali remained silent.

There was a sick feeling deep in Laila's stomach. She felt responsible for what the Demons had done to Mato. They had gone to that club looking for her, and Mato was the one caught in the crossfire. Likewise, Lyn had been attacked by the Demons twice now. She needed to find a way to stop this, to keep the people in her life safe, but how?

The question plagued her long after she arrived home and slid into her bed. Once more her dreams were filled with death. Her friends were slaughtered in front of her while Marius laughed and the city burned.

CHAPTER 40

It was afternoon when Laila awoke. She pulled on her usual jeans and boots and strapped on her leather armor over a black tank top. In order to disguise her appearance, Laila applied some heavy eye makeup and pulled on a black hoodie.

Downstairs she found Mr. Whiskers curled up on the sofa beside Erin, whose eyes were glued to the television watching a news reporter with angry protestors shouting behind her. Lyn and Frej sat at the table while Lyn worked on a potion.

"Did Ali make it home?" Laila asked Erin.

She nodded. "She got home about an hour ago and went straight to bed. They're expecting her to give an update in a couple hours though."

Frej watched her with a desperate look as she made her toast. Laila tried to ignore it, she really wasn't ready to talk to him yet. It was just too soon. Luckily, Lyn spoke up before Frej could.

"I'm bottling the potions for you and Jerrik hopefully they'll work better than last time, but don't forget they'll only mask your scent."

Lyn corked the two vials and set them on the counter.

"I also want you to take this." She removed a ring and placed it on the counter. "It's my Vampire repelling spell. Just in case."

Laila thanked her and slid the ring on her finger before pocketing the vials.

"Has anyone heard how Mato's doing?" she asked.

"Healing but still in the hospital," called Erin. "They're hoping to release him in the morning though."

Laila considered stopping to check on him, but there was so much to do. She needed to get back to headquarters and prepare for the night ahead.

She turned to Frej. "I'm assuming Darien spoke with you?"

He nodded. "I told him we'd leave as soon as you were awake."

Lyn watched closely, and Laila could tell that she wanted to help too.

"Are there any security spells we could add to the house?" she asked the Witch after a moment. "I want to make sure the rest of you are safe if…"

As Laila trailed off, she realized there was a good possibility that if things went wrong, this could be the last time she saw them.

Lyn seemed to understand her unspoken thoughts.

"I set my strongest wards around the house the first night I was here. I'm tracking down some additional ones, but I think that's why the Demons waited to attack until we left the house."

"What do you mean?"

Lyn gave her a mischievous grin. "Anyone who approaches the building with ill intent forgets what they were here to do. I've got some other spells on the doors and windows."

Laila breathed a little easier. Hopefully, that would be enough, at least for now. She quickly ate her toast before heading out the door with Frej.

He was silent as Laila made a stop at a Halloween store to pick up some supplies for the night ahead. Some red-colored contacts would hopefully help the Elves blend in with the crowd.

Even as they pulled into the garage below IRSA, Frej was quiet. But as Laila parked the car, she knew there was something she had to say.

"Frej," she began, "if I don't make it out of there tonight, take care of the others. Please?"

He started to speak, but she cut him off.

"I want to forgive you. I do forgive you. But I-I just need some time."

He nodded. "I know."

There was a hesitation before he said the following words, "Please come back to me."

Laila could see the heartbreak in his eyes. It wasn't just that he wanted her to forgive him. Frej knew the risks that would be taken tonight. She could see the internal battle raging within him. There was that part of him that wanted to be there by her side, protecting her as Jerrik had said, but Frej knew that they both had their roles to play tonight.

She wouldn't allow herself to comfort him, to say it would be okay. That felt too much like a lie. All she did was take his hand briefly and squeeze it before quickly turning away.

Laila spent the rest of the early evening preparing equipment, scanning a few new reports, and checking in with Talen and Darien. She was loading cases into an SUV when her phone buzzed. It was Jenn.

"I know you're heading into the Vampires' lair tonight, but there's something you need to know."

"Go on." Laila absently scanned through her inbox. There was an email from Steve with more footage placing Arnold Koch at the more recent crime scenes. It was just more evidence to put him behind bars.

"I just got the results back from a vial of liquid you found when you shut down that Necromancer's portal. It's some sort of an adrenaline-enhancing drug. It's incredibly strong though, and powerful enough to kill a Troll."

Laila paused for a moment. "What's the purpose of creating a drug like that?"

"You found it on a Vampire, right?"

"Yeah, but you don't think it would actually work on one, do you?" She hadn't heard of any substance having an effect on Vampires, save for magically affected blood from Supernaturals like Elves.

"I think it only makes sense that it's intended for them. It's too strong for any other SNP, with the exception of a Giant."

Considering Benning was the only documented Giant in Midgard, it seemed unlikely that the Di Inferi were cooking up drugs for Giants.

"Any idea what it's effects are?"

"The lab wasn't entirely sure what sort of reaction it would cause in the body of a Vampire, but they might appear stronger, and may exhibit unusual behavior. Be extremely careful, and assume they're more dangerous than the run-of-the-mill Vampire."

"Great," muttered Laila, "this is all we need. I'll warn the others."

"Good luck," she said, "we'll be on standby. The FBI and LAPD are ready too."

"Hopefully it won't come to that, but thanks." Laila ended the call and went to find the others. It was time to go.

She parked on the street and pulled up her hood before slipping into the alley. She glanced around but saw no signs of Vampires, so she knocked on the door to the van. Torsten opened the door and waved her in. He and Donald had continued to monitor the activity of the Vampires throughout the afternoon.

"That's just wrong." Donald indicated her red eyes. She wore one of the sets of red-colored contacts that she'd purchased for both herself and Jerrik on her way to the office earlier.

"The reinforcements are ready to move into place," she explained, ignoring the comment.

Torsten gave her a short nod. "Tell them to move in to their positions. The tunnel is clear."

Donald rolled his eyes. "Are you sure you have to rescue Fredrik Stacy? Couldn't we just let the Vampires keep that racist dick? It's not like he's done the SNP community any favors."

A part of her agreed, but that would do more harm than good.

"Be safe." She clapped Torsten on the shoulder.

"We'll be fine," he replied with a smile, "it's you I'm worried about."

Laila hoped for all their sakes that the Gods would be on their side.

The Vampires from the council quickly moved into place near the several entrances they'd located. Slightly further away were police barricades, and teams of human law-enforcement officers at the ready. Darien and Jerrik were on their way to one of those other entrances while Talen would be meeting her here at this one.

Laila entered the building beside them and climbed the stairs to the second floor where Frej was already waiting, the same spot where he and Jerrik had fought the other night. Frej wore a pair of thick canvas pants and boots he'd brought from the Dragon Kingdom. His long-sleeved tunic was partially obscured by the bullet-proof vest she'd given him. They stood there in a heavy, oppressive silence, neither of them knowing what to say.

It was only a matter of minutes before Talen appeared in the doorway flanked by heavily armed Vampires. He wore his usual suit in black. The Vampire appeared sharp as ever but didn't exactly look ready for a fight. Then again, Talen was ancient and powerful, definitely not someone to underestimate.

Laila on the other hand, had knives sheathed in her boots and her hoodie helped to conceal her firearm and the two small-swords strapped to her back. She hadn't brought the magical dagger. Even though she had Lyn's charm tied to her wrist, she hadn't wanted to chance another sudden outburst of magic.

"These are the representatives sent by the council members." Talen indicated the Vampires filing into the room. "Six of them will accompany us in the tunnels, the rest will remain here with Frej."

Frej's earpiece would allow him to communicate with the council's reinforcements in the other locations as well as the humans. He stepped forward as Talen introduced him to the Vampires. They turned to look at him, but that was the only reaction they had. Their stony expressions were more difficult to read than Elven nobles at a court event. It was unsettling in a way, but all that mattered was that the Vampires had their backs.

Talen watched the Vampires closely. "Sir Ilmarinen will give the orders in my absence. I expect you to follow his command as you would mine."

"Yes, sir," they chorused in eerie unison.

It was as if they were more robotic than flesh and blood. Laila had a feeling that the council members took their discipline very seriously. These weren't guards or soldiers, they were brutally trained killing machines.

Frej had orders to wait until midnight. If they had yet to emerge, then he would give the command to initiate the raid. That would give Laila and the others about four hours to retrieve Fredrik Stacy.

Talen gestured, and six Vampires clad in black tactical gear approached. They were a blend of men and women who were armed to the teeth with knives, guns, and even crossbows.

"Time to go," announced Talen grimly as he headed for the door.

"Be safe," whispered Frej grabbing Laila's hand as she passed. Their eyes met, and Laila could see the fear in his eyes.

"I'll come back."

His eyes lingered on her before she followed the Vampires out of the room.

Down in the alley, she removed the metal grate of the storm drain.

"Let's go." She nodded at the entrance.

Talen plunged through the hole and into the darkness below. One by one they followed him down into the abyss.

"Is that your lover?" a stoic female Vampire asked Frej from their vantage point. They were watching from a large broken window on the second floor of a building. It was the perfect spot to view the entrance to the tunnels without being exposed on the street.

Frej nodded as a cool autumn breeze played at his face and stirred his hair.

"And you're just letting her walk into a den of rogue Vampires?" asked the woman with mild interest, it was the first hint of emotion he'd sensed.

He snorted. "I couldn't stop her if I tried."

The Vampire thought over the information silently.

"Besides," he added, "I'd do the same thing if I was her."

Nonetheless, it was killing him to wait here while Laila entered the tunnels, but she also needed someone she could trust out here. If it came to it, he would tear those tunnels apart stone by stone until he found her.

He glanced to his right, where the nondescript surveillance van was parked.

"Donald," he said into the coms, "is everything set?"

"Yes," replied the Tech Wiz in the earpiece. "I've got magical trackers on them. We'll lose the signal soon, but they're walking away through the tunnel now. If nothing else, it will notify us of their approach when they return."

"Okay, keep me informed." The Dragon glanced around at the Vampires waiting behind him.

"Will do," said Donald.

Frej pulled up an old wooden chair and straddled it backwards, facing the storm drain. He had a feeling it was going to be a long night.

CHAPTER 41

The tunnel felt cramped with their large group passing through. Laila and Talen led the way, the others following. The purpose of the accompanying Vampires was to have strategically placed reinforcements along the exit route in case they ran into trouble. The Vampires would remain hidden and help cover them during the escape. In the meantime, they'd lie low in concealment.

The first pair broke off at the entrance to the main tunnel, stationing themselves near the hole in the wall of the drain. The rest stepped through the opening into the tunnel beyond as Laila retraced her footsteps through the magically-created stone tunnels.

She sensed Talen beside her, growing more tense. His jaw was clenched, and he shook his head from time to time. He caught Laila watching him and gave her a sad smile.

"How do you imagine these tunnels were built?" he asked her as they descended deeper underground in the torch-lined tunnel.

"Elemental Sorcerers of some sort." She could feel the magic that held the stone up. "It would require a baffling amount of energy, but I can't identify the source. I'm not even sure if a dozen Elves or Dragons would be strong enough to cast a spell of this magnitude."

A shadow crossed the Vampire's face.

"With age, Vampires gain certain abilities," his voice was barely audible, even to her keen ears.

"Like the charm magic?"

"Precisely, but not all of them are as pleasant. Another of my abilities allows me to hear the voices of the dead."

That sounded nothing short of horrifying in Laila's opinion. All of the encounters she'd had with the dead had been unpleasant. She couldn't imagine hearing their restless voices constantly.

He read her expression. "It's not so bad. Usually it's faint whispers. But these walls are practically screaming."

"You mean..." Laila trailed off looking at the walls around them.

He nodded. "The walls are held by Necromancy."

Laila's blood ran cold. She reached out to feel the magic once more, and deep within the spell, so deep that she'd overlooked it before, wove dark, smoke-like strands of magic. Talen was right, it was indeed Necromancy.

The Sorcerers who had created these tunnels hadn't just cast a spell to hold a wall in place. It was their spiritual energy that continued to hold it up. A Necromancer had forced them to cast the spell, then bound their life-force to the walls. Their bodies had likely been killed while their spirits were trapped within.

Laila's mouth gaped; she had no words to describe the horror. She was trembling with anger, so many lives had been lost. How could this many Sorcerers go missing without anyone noticing? They hadn't had enough reports of missing persons lately to explain where they had gotten the Sorcerers from.

Then a second thought occurred to her. If the Vampires were hiding in tunnels created by Necromancy, and receiving weapons from Di Inferi, then how were the Demons involved in this? And why?

They reached the stacks of crates, and two more Vampires faded back into the shadows behind them. There was no sign of the rebels yet, so they proceeded with caution. A short while later, the murmur of voices approached from around a corner. She spun to tell the remainder of their escort to take cover, but they had already vanished, tucking themselves into the shadows of one of the dark alcoves.

She stuffed her hands in the pockets of her hoodie and kept her head down as she walked past the approaching Vampires. They didn't so much as glance at her, although they scoffed at the suit Talen wore.

"You just had to wear a suit," she muttered once the Vampires were out of earshot.

He shrugged. "Think of it like this. If they become suspicious, at least it won't look like you're with me. You'll have a head start to run." He winked.

Laila shook her head, but continued on, encountering more Vampires as they went. They reached the large, open chamber with the raised dais. Vampires hurried back and forth, and the excitement was palpable. Perhaps it had something to do with Fredrik Stacy? She scanned the crowd carefully, but he was nowhere to be found. There was also no sign of Darien and Jerrik either, but supposedly their coms would work if they were in close range underground.

"Darien, we've reached the central chamber," she said just loud enough for her com to pick it up.

She breathed a sigh of relief when his reply reached her ear. "Jerrik and I are heading down to a lower level. I'm seeing more armed guards down this way, and they've got to be guarding something. There's some sort of gathering in a chamber off to one side of the dais—it's through the set of large doors. Why don't you see what's going on in there?"

Across the chamber, she saw a hallway leading away with a set of open doors a short distance through it.

"I think I've found it."

Her eyes darted to Talen, but he was leaning against the arch of the tunnel they'd come from, looking bored. He would stay there to watch the courtyard.

Laila trudged her way around the dais and towards the hall, blending in with a small group of rebels. A pair of guards waited outside, who hardly glanced at the group as they entered.

The chamber within was massive with large wooden tables and benches lining the hall. They were occupied by numerous Vampires laughing and talking boisterously. There were multiple couples making out with hands on asses or other parts of the anatomy. Laila avoided looking at the lewd displays, but she couldn't tear her eyes away from the humans present—if you could say they were present. Their eyes were glazed over, and they stared off into the distance. She couldn't tell what they'd been drugged with, but perhaps the drugs were a blessing, considering the way the Vampires were treating them. Despite the cold of the tunnels, they wore so little clothing that Laila couldn't help but blush. Vampires passed the humans back and forth to feed, with total disregard for any personal boundaries. Some even used the humans in other ways. Bile rose in Laila's throat.

She forced her horror aside as she split off from the group and slid onto a b.nch in the corner. Removing one of the knives from her boot, she pretended to clean dirt from under her nails as she made observations.

Laila focused on the far end of the room. There was no furniture occupying that wall, except for a single chair. It was a massive throne made entirely of human bones. Seated upon the gruesome monstrosity was a man in a top hat, and long leather duster—Sire Ashford.

His face wasn't the only one she recognized, near the throne Arnold Koch lounged against the wall, eyeing one of the human women that another Vampire fed on. The young Vampire that had been tortured by the council was present looking rather drained as she sipped a goblet of blood. There were no signs of her injuries though, thanks to the rapid healing ability of the Vampires. Traces of Demonic energy clung to many of the room's occupants.

"No sign of him," she whispered. "Sire Ashford's here though."

Through the earpiece, she heard some sort of commotion.

"What's going on?" she asked, but for several tense moments, there was no reply.

"I'll check it out," said Talen in her ear.

She was so focused on the radio silence that she didn't notice the Vampire approaching her.

"Have I seen you before?" His shrewd eyes looked her up and down. He crossed his thick, muscular arms across his grey shirt which was flecked with blood. In general, he stank of stale sweat. His red eyes lingered on her body though, and Laila smirked.

"Probably. I guess you were so fixated on my other parts you didn't bother to look at my face." She gave him a dark, feral look. "Now move before your smell makes me vomit."

She went back to cleaning her nail as if he didn't exist. He still watched her closely, but the corner of his mouth twitched in amusement. He wandered off to find someone else in the crowd.

"Talen, what's happening?"

No response.

"Talen!" she hissed.

Movement by the door caught her eyes as several Vampires entered and Laila's heart sank. It felt like someone gripped her heart with an ice-cold hand. They shoved Darien, Jerrik, and Talen forward towards the throne. Darien spotted her in the crowd and gave her a small shake of his head, warning her to stay where she was.

Laila clenched her jaw but remained in place, shifting to get a better view.

As they neared the throne, she noticed Talen falter. It was a reaction to the spirits whose remains formed the throne of bones, no doubt.

"Guests!" cried Sire Ashford as a crooked smile spread across his face, bits of crusted blood flaking away from around his mouth, "what a pleasant surprise!"

The room became silent as a grave as every pair of red eyes focused on them. Their sire took his time examining them as well. Once he was finished, he shifted in his seat to hook one of his legs over the arm of the throne as he lounged sideways. Clearly, he didn't perceive them as a threat.

"And who have I had the pleasure of pissing off?" asked the Vampire as he continued to watch them with mild interest.

"The council," said Darien stepping forward, "not to mention the state and federal governments."

The Vampire shifted his attention to his nails as he picked flecks of blood out from underneath them.

"Oh dear! Is this about that politician? Or those humans that died? They're so delicate, these humans, so easy to break."

Arnold Koch walked over to the woman he'd been eyeing, drawing the attention of the others. He caressed her face before snapping her neck in one, sharp movement. The body crumpled on the stone at his feet. He flashed them a toothy grin as the Vampires in the crowd roared with laughter.

Laila gripped the knife in her hand so hard it trembled. She took a forced breath and reined in her emotions. By the throne, she could see Jerrik shaking with rage. On his face was etched the pain of a distant memory. He'd told her once that his father had executed his beloved Sword Master in front of him. Was this how he'd done it?

"We've come to make a deal," said Darien, his eye's never left the rebel leader's face.

"Oh really?" said Sire Ashford in an annoying, mocking tone, "I don't think you're in a position to bargain."

"A hundred Vampires trained in combat and handpicked by

the council wait for us outside." Darien's voice echoed throughout the chamber.

"I have more than two hundred."

"Plus, there are the multiple law enforcement agencies. If you surrender now and hand over Fredrik Stacy, we'll see to it you are given a fair trial in a federal court."

"And if I reject your offer?" he asked in a bored tone.

Darien's voice took on an icy quality. "Then the Vampire council will enact their punishment as they have for millennia. Death to you, and all your followers."

The room froze, even the drugged humans didn't dare to breathe. The focus was entirely on Sire Ashford as he contemplated his options. Seconds passed like hours as the Vampire picked at a loose thread in his shirt.

"You'd be a fool to refuse," added Darien. "You may have an army of Vampires at your disposal, but they're young and slow. They wouldn't stand a chance."

Slowly, Sire Ashford directed his attention back at Darien and stood. The smile vanished, replaced with a snarl.

"You come into *my* domain to threaten me and my people," he spat, "then you expect us to go with you quietly?"

He prowled back and forth in front of his macabre throne. His expression shifted suddenly.

"How about a demonstration?" he leered.

There was movement around them as a handful of Vampires drank from small vials with white, three-faced skulls imprinted on them. Sire Ashford watched them with all the intensity of a viper who has cornered a mouse.

"Attack!" he snapped.

The room erupted into chaos. The rebels leapt into action hissing and snarling while her companions defended themselves, keeping their backs to each other. Around her the Vampires stood and cheered, egging on their fellow rebels. The attacking Vampires were vicious and showed no sign of pain as Jerrik stabbed one of them with a knife, it only faltered when

Jerrik twisted the knife, shredding its heart. The Vampire crumbled to ash as another one attacked, punching Jerrik in the face before he could block. Darien and Talen were struggling with their opponents as well, who seemed unusually strong, even for Vampires. It was the work of the drugs Jenn had mentioned.

Laila's companions cut, thrust, fired and beat back the onslaught of Vampires, but there were just too many of them. Even when Jerrik resorted to magic, it wasn't enough to turn the tides of the fight without the risk of Talen and Darien getting caught in the blast.

Laila watched helplessly. If she moved to aid them, her cover would be blown, and there would be no one left to help them. Instead, she stood by and watched the others struggle. Her eyes met Darien's, and they both realized that the only option was surrender.

Jerrik cursed as Vampires pinned his arms behind him, but he didn't blast them with fire. Knives were thrust into Darien and Talen's chests. Not through the heart, but close. One jerk and the Vampires would be dust.

Sire Ashford approached, kicking up piles of dust in his wake from the fallen rebels. Their leader scowled at Darien and his sire.

"You're the fools," spat the rebel leader, "obeying your ancient elders like a flock of terrified sheep. For too long we've hidden from the humans like rats in the shadows, but not any longer. We are the predators, and we will take this world and make it our own! The time has come for Vampires to rise and claim what is rightfully ours."

He looked from Darien to Talen. "Your council and their ancient rules will fall, and a new order will be established. Too bad you won't be around to see it."

"Think about this," Talen reasoned, "you're not the first to try. Every one of your predecessors has failed miserably. You can't defeat them."

"Oh, trust me," snarled Sire Ashford, "they never had allies like mine."

He winked and patted Talen on the cheek, making him flinch. But Sire Ashford's attention quickly turned to Jerrik.

"*Elf*," the word dripped from his tongue like honey as hunger burned in his eyes. "We'll have fun with you."

He picked up one of Jerrik's knives off the floor. Laila could hardly breathe as he grabbed a fist of Jerrik's hair and thrust his head back. Gently he ran the edge of the blade along Jerrik's neck. Even though it barely scraped the skin, and no blood was drawn Laila could feel the terror and anger welling within her, the blue magic fighting to break free even as Lyn's spell kept it in check. What would happen if she removed the charm? Would she be able to control it and stop the Vampires? Or would it burn her alive?

Sire Ashford shoved Jerrik away.

"Take them to a cell," he hissed, "I'll deal with them later."

He returned to his throne of bones as her friends were led through the massive doors once more. Jerrik's eyes met hers, and she could see the faintest glimmer of fear as he was led away to a cell. A prisoner once more.

"I will get you out," she whispered into her com, praying the others still had theirs. "I swear to you Jerrik, I will find you."

Her own dread seized her as she remembered the sound of cheers echoing through a stadium. She would get them out, no matter the cost.

CHAPTER 42

Frej paced back and forth as he waited, the Vampires watching wordlessly. There was no sign of Laila, and while only two hours had passed, he couldn't shake the feeling that something was wrong.

"Hey Frej," said Donald through the earpiece, "I'm getting a reading here on the magical radar. There are two undead figures approaching underground."

"From our team?" Frej watched the storm drain for any sign of movement.

"No, they don't have our trackers on them. And they've stopped right at the grate."

"Scouts," bristled Frej. He turned to the others, "If the rebels are sending scouts through the tunnel, then something's gone wrong."

The female Vampire approached. "Easy now, give them some more time. If we attack before they are ready, it could make the situation more dangerous for those inside."

A soft growl escaped Frej's throat, but he knew she was right. Reluctantly he turned away from the Vampire to watch the storm drain.

He grit his teeth. "Fine, but I want everyone in place and at the ready. That's an order."

Laila waited, but no reply came through her earpiece. Around her, Vampires started to argue over Darien's threat, their voices climbing to a roar.

"Quiet!" shouted Sire Ashford over the crowd.

Silence fell immediately.

"I want everyone to ready themselves," he spat. "We're going to take this fight to them before they can bring it to us."

He rolled an empty vial of the Vampire steroids between his fingers, an evil grin spreading across his face.

"They may have age and experience of their side, but we've got something stronger." He crushed the vial in his hand and allowed the powdered glass to slide between his fingers. "Go now, ready yourselves."

All around her the Vampires rose. She followed suit and filed through the door and into the hall. She nearly stopped in her tracks when a voice came through her earpiece.

"Laila," called Darien, "are you still there?"

She breathed a sigh of relief.

"Hold on." Laila glanced around. Most of the Vampires were heading back to the square with the Dias to her right, so Laila turned left, down the hall. There was another door a short way down the hall that she pressed her ear against. When no sounds drifted through the wood, she tried the handle but discovered it was locked. A quick spell took care of the lock, and she slipped into the room and relocked the door before anyone noticed her.

The room she entered was some sort of an office. There was a desk with a lamp and a computer, as well as two sofas gathered around a coffee table. Tapestries and fabric draped the walls in some effort to cover the bare stone.

"Darien? Is everyone okay?" she asked.

"Yes," he said, "they've locked us in a cell one level down from where you are."

"They've cuffed me as well," added Jerrik. "They're identical to the ones the Demons had to prevent the use of magic."

Laila swore, so much for Jerrik being able to use magic to get them out. "Alright, I'm coming to find you, you'll have to help direct me though."

She was about to mention the rebels' preparations for a fight, but the scrape of a key in the lock silenced her. Swiftly, Laila slid behind the fabric gathered along the corner of the wall; it would conceal her as long as she didn't move. With a spell, she quickly cut a small hole where the fabric was gathered together. It would allow her to see into the room but kept her hidden by the shadows to prevent detection.

The door of the office swung open and in stormed Sire Ashford, Arnold Koch hurrying after him.

"We're surrounded," hissed Koch. "Our guards that found those men trying to break the politician out of his cell sent scouts to check the entrances. They just reported back to me."

"And?" Sire Ashford paced back and forth.

"The majority of our exits have been discovered. What the intruders said was true, they've got support from the council and the government." He shook his head. "We should consider evacuating while we still have time."

"You coward!" snapped Sire Ashford as he threw a chair across the room. It flew beyond her field of view, and she heard the wood splinter against the wall.

Koch flinched but didn't cower. Laila had the impression Sire Ashford was often volatile. Koch stood there and waited while Sire Ashford continued his rant.

"This is your doing! I warned you to be careful with your victims. I told you to make it look like random attacks with no connection. We needed to scare the humans, to make them fear us like they once did so they'd know what to expect if they refused to submit when we took over the city."

He grabbed the other Vampire by the collar of the shirt and thrust him against the wall. The fabric obscured Koch from her view, but she could hear the crunch of his skull hitting stone.

"Instead you brought the authorities and the council straight to us!" He had a look of pure malice in his eyes. "You literally led them to our door!"

"I'm sorry!" snapped the other Vampire. "But we've still got the politician. If we take him—"

Sire Ashford snarled.

The door opened and in walked another Vampire.

"Easy now," purred the newcomer.

Laila recognized him as well. He'd been at Talen's house with the other council members, and Laila recalled that his name was Dagan. The traitor had worn a crimson suit at the time, but now he was dressed in a white button-up shirt and black slacks. As Dagan stepped into the middle of the room he grinned and pulled out a small vial with the three faced skull stamped on it.

"You know we've got the upper hand here. These drugs are potent, and your underlings will attack like rabid wolves. The Vampires from the rest of the council won't stand a chance. Then, when you approach the council with your offer, I'll be there to persuade the others to bow to your demands."

He pocketed the vial as Sire Ashford released the other Vampire.

"You knew about this didn't you?" Sire Ashford turned on Dagan.

The Councilman shrugged, "I was being watched. Besides, I know we're ready for this."

"And what about the others?" asked Sire Ashford "What about Caine Ubel?"

Something about the name was familiar, but why?

The door opened once more.

"Mr. Ubel!" said Sire Ashford with a slight bow. "Thank you

for meeting with us on such short notice."

The man gave the Vampire a threatening look as his fangs extended. They weren't those of a Vampire, but a snake.

Laila's vision turned red with rage as she saw the Snake Shifter. The Lesser Demon was dressed in one of his suits as usual, but Laila noticed something was different about him: one of his hands. During their last encounter, it had been ordinary, but now it appeared to be made of some metallic substance that moved and reacted just as an ordinary hand would. The silver color and the faintly glowing runes revealed it as an extremely clever enchantment. Had he somehow lost the hand? Or perhaps he had just chosen to give himself a magical upgrade.

She had to force herself to remain still.

"It was difficult to find an entrance that wasn't being watched," hissed Ubel, "I sacrificed Sorcerers for you to build these caves, and my gang provides you with weapons and steroids, yet look at this mess you've made!"

"Yes," said Sire Ashford, giving Koch a withering glare, "we are sorry about this. But this just means we'll have to move up our plans."

"This isn't the kind of thing you rush!" snapped Ubel. "Di Inferi's not ready. Not for a coup like this."

"We need to act now." The Vampire's temper was rising once more. "We start our attack tonight, whether you are ready or not. The humans are outraged at Fredrik Stacy's abduction. The city will fall into chaos and be ripe for the taking."

The Demon didn't respond.

Sire Ashford circled the Demon slowly. "Look, you were the one that came to me. You told me it was time to build an army and that you had the resources to make it happen. Don't tell me you're backing out now."

The Demon was quiet for a long time as he stood there leaning against the back of a sofa as he thought.

"Fine," he spat eventually, "have it your way. If you survive the night, meet me at the warehouse. We'll plan our next step then."

Without another word the Demon left, slamming the door behind him.

Sire Ashford swore viciously and threw a vase of dead flowers at the wall. Laila couldn't see where it struck, but by the ripple of the fabric, and how loud it seemed, she imagined that it had only been a foot or so away.

"That wasn't so bad," reasoned the councilman.

"He's not sending his men," roared the Vampire, "how the hell is that okay?"

"We don't need them," insisted the councilman in a soothing tone. "All we need are the drugs, and we have plenty to get us through the night. Now go prepare your army."

Sire Ashford gave Dagan one last begrudging look before leaving, Koch following at his heels. Laila froze as Dagan approached the broken vase of flowers next to her. He was only feet away, and beyond her small field of view. Laila feared he would pick up on her scent, or perhaps her beating heart. She hardly dared to breathe.

Ali yawned as she entered the kitchen and tossed her purse on the counter. Even though she'd taken a nap in the afternoon, she still felt the strain of the all-nighter.

She'd spent the morning and the evening trying to convince the people of Los Angeles that IRSA was handling the investigation into Fredrik Stacy's disappearance and already had a lead. Much to her frustration though, someone had leaked word that Vampires were somehow involved. It was still unclear who had spread the rumor, although she suspected it was either the Vampire rebellion or someone close to the victim. In any case, the humans were outraged, and several humans had already been arrested for assaulting Vampires.

"Any news from Laila?" asked Lyn from the kitchen table

where she and Erin sat. Mr. Whiskers sat on the table sniffing something sitting in front of Lyn.

Ali started a pot of coffee and shook her head. "She's probably still in the tunnels, I doubt we'll hear from her for a few hours at least."

Lyn shuffled a deck of cards. "I've got a bad feeling about this, I can feel it deep in my bones. I think something's gone wrong."

Ali was about to protest, but she couldn't shake the feeling that something wasn't right either.

"These are tarot cards," explained Lyn. "This particular deck belonged to my great-great-grandmother. She was a priestess and a very powerful Witch too. I can feel her presence nearby guiding me when I use them, and they've never failed me."

"Okay," Ali joined the others at the table. "Do you think this deck of cards can really show you what's going on?"

"Oh yeah." The Witch nodded and finished shuffling the deck of cards, and spread them into a long arch, face down. Carefully, the Witch selected three cards. She set them in a row in front of her, facedown.

"These three cards represent the past present and future events that Laila is currently facing," Lyn explained.

She picked up the first card and flipped it over.

"The Tower," she said as the other two leaned in to look at the stone building painted on the front of the card.

"What does it mean?" asked Erin, looking up at the Witch.

The color drained from Lyn's face. "Something bad has already happened. The rescue mission probably didn't go according to plan."

"Is she okay?" asked the Dragon, "is she hurt?"

"Let's find out."

Lyn flipped over the second card. There was a painting of a skeleton hanging with a noose around its neck.

"The Hanged Man," explained Lyn, her frown deepening. "This would explain why we haven't heard from her. Laila hasn't left the tunnels yet, she's been captured, or feels trapped. Somehow, she's stuck."

"But she's still alive, right?" asked Ali fearfully.

Lyn nodded. "Despite the card's appearance, it represents an inability to move. This can be psychological, but in this case, I'm sensing that Laila is physically trapped."

The Witch hesitated and Ali imagined the Witch was debating whether they truly wanted to see was the future. After a moment, Lyn flipped the card over.

Ali gasped, she didn't need an explanation for this card. Painted on the final card was a skeletal figure in a black robe with a scythe. It was a Reaper.

Lyn looked up at the others and whispered, "Death."

CHAPTER 43

"No," said Ali, shaking her head, "that can't be right."

She slid out from the bench trying to put some distance between her and the table, and the card resting upon it. Death. The skull grinned up at her, jeering as she went.

They were just cards, just old bits of paper and paint, nothing more. So how could something so small and insignificant make her feel so scared and helpless?

"These things are representative, right?" asked Ali, her hand trembling as she poured more coffee into a mug.

"Yes," began Lyn slowly. "Death can represent a lot of things. For example, the end of a cycle and the beginning of a new."

"Then why doesn't that comfort me?"

Lyn didn't answer.

Ali wanted to throw something. This was not supposed to happen. Laila was not supposed to be killed by Vampires.

Erin stood. "We have to do something! We can't just sit around here waiting."

Ali shook her head. "If Laila's trapped by a small army of Vampire rebels then what can we do that the reinforcements aren't already?"

Erin folded her arms and gave her sister a pointed look. "We've got magic! The Vampires and humans don't. We also know plenty of other people in this city who can help us too."

"Like who?"

"Benning," suggested Lyn. "If he takes off my charm, he'll grow again. The Vampires won't be able to stop him."

"Don't forget about Henrik and Mato," added Erin. "The others from the meetings would probably help too. So would Orin."

"We can't ask civilians to launch an attack with us!" howled Ali as she paced back and forth. "And look what happened to Mato last night. No, we are not dragging anyone else into this."

"Why not?" asked Lyn.

"I've already got one friend in the hospital. I'm not letting anyone else get hurt!"

Erin gave her an incredulous look. "If we don't do something, Laila's going to end up six feet under! You can't protect everyone, but maybe we can make enough of a difference to save Laila!"

Lyn nodded. "I for one am not going to sit at home when I know I can help."

Ali knew they were right. They needed to do something and if the others wanted help, who was she to say no? By the Morrigan, Laila needed them, they couldn't sit around and argue if she was fighting for her life.

"Alright, we'll pick up Benning on the way. Just give me time to change."

"I'm coming too," declared Erin.

"Absolutely not!" Ali shot her sister a look. That's where she drew the line. Erin scowled at her as she rushed upstairs to change.

❖

There was a clinking sound as Dagan examined a shard of the broken vase. He suddenly appeared back in her sight before turning on his heel towards the door. As it shut with a click, Laila breathed a sigh of relief, but waited before leaving her cover to ensure the Vampires weren't coming back. She crossed the room and listened at the door.

"You're stubborn, aren't you?" said a voice behind her.

Laila gasped and spun but was nearly blinded by dazzling pale light. There stood a Goddess in a billowing white gown that floated on some phantom breeze. Her hair and skin glowed like moonlight, and her piercing blue eyes watched with a mixture of frustration and furry. It was the Goddess that Laila had met before, the one that was giving her access to the divine magic that nearly destroyed her.

Seeing her, Laila forgot the urgency of her current situation.

"What is happening to me?" demanded Laila. "Why are you giving me these powers?"

The Goddess watched her closely for a moment as if determining how much to say.

"There is a great imbalance in the universe. It threatens not only the existence of mortals but of immortals and even magic itself. I cannot act on my own, it is not the way, but it's possible for me to act through a proxy. You have been chosen for this role."

"I don't understand!" Laila took a step closer, "I'm just an Elf. I'm an ordinary person, with an ordinary life."

"I've watched you since the day you were born," said the Goddess, her voice drifting through the silent space. "I chose you out of all other possible choices because of your ability to sense balance, both in magic and amongst the various creatures that inhabit the worlds. You also understand the balance of right and wrong, and of giving and taking. This is key to the journey before you. All things do not exist independently in the universe. Magic binds us all, and when the magic is disrupted, it echoes throughout the worlds."

Laila shook her head. "So you want me to fix this imbalance by stopping the Demons?"

"Precisely." The smallest hint of warmth crept into her eyes. "These Demons are no small threat. Their reach is expanding every day as they feed off of instability and fear in Midgard. They must be stopped."

"What will happen if they aren't?" asked Laila tentatively.

The Goddess placed her hand on Laila's head, and suddenly visions swam before her eyes. Death and destruction, the same as the nightmares that plagued her sleep.

"Those are not nightmares but premonitions," explained the Goddess. "These are the possible futures that will come to pass if you continue to ignore your destiny."

"What are you talking about?" asked Laila incredulously, "All I've done the past months is try to track down the Demons!"

"You're ignoring your power!" thundered the Goddess, her eyes glowing with blinding white light. They flickered down to the charm on Laila's wrist, which dissolved to dust under the intensity of her gaze.

Laila opened her mouth to protest, but the Goddess cut her off.

"You must train and prepare."

"There's no time—"

"There will never be time unless you make it!" The ground shook as she spoke. Mist appeared, swirling around them in a frenzy. "Make time for it. If you don't, then you'll be too weak to prevent this!"

In the mist, Laila saw rows of corpses covering an endless expanse. Everyone she knew, everyone she held dear, dead. Then slowly the bodies turned into mist, obscuring her vision once more.

"Start your training with Arduinna once you finish here. Learn to use and control your new powers." Her voice was firm, and magic crackled around her form. Laila knew she must obey.

"What if I can't control it?" Asked Laila after a moment.

"What if the magic destroys me instead?"

"This will help you." The Goddess waved her hand and a necklace formed around Laila's neck from the mist. Its chain was silver and short with no clasp. A moonstone pendant hung from the chain about the size of her fingernail. It was surrounded by an intricate circle of woven silver. It matched the dagger she had.

"The necklace will help you control the magic, but it's time for you to go."

"Wait!" cried Laila suddenly, "Who are you?"

The Goddess smiled faintly. "All in good time."

She vanished in a flash of bright light, leaving Laila standing there alone in the room.

"Laila?" called Jerrik's voice through her earpiece. "Laila, what's going on?"

She grimaced. "Nothing. I'm on my way."

Jerrik sighed. One moment Laila had been talking to them, then suddenly there was silence. Then static crackled through their earpieces, but as suddenly as it began, the static stopped. Even if he didn't know the cause, the relief of knowing that she was okay was overwhelming.

He sat in the back of a cell with Darien and Talen, but they weren't alone. In the cell beside them was the human they had been sent to retrieve, Fredrik Stacy. He still wore a pair of long cotton pajama pants and a shirt matching the description his wife had provided after his abduction. Far from the proud and confident presence he was on television, he now sat hunched in the corner of his cell as he trembled from the cold. He ignored their attempts at conversation and cast them dirty looks. So much for gratitude.

He and Darien had gotten as far as the holding cells, and Jerrik had been working on a spell to open the lock when they'd been captured. When Talen had come looking for them, the rebels apprehended him as well. Now Laila was on her own if she managed to stay undercover.

Jerrik looked down at the familiar cuffs strapped around his wrists, identical to the ones he'd worn for months. He shook his head, trying to keep the memories at bay, all the blood, pain, and death he'd witnessed. He had so much blood on his hands that some days he wondered if he was beyond redemption.

Then there was the matter of his feelings for Laila. He had been so focused on trying to convince her that Frej wasn't right for her, he'd hurt her in the process. He regretted that more than anything at the moment. He knew he'd crossed a line, but he wasn't sure how to fix it. He'd been so furious at what had happened in his absence back home, that he'd lost control.

"That Vampire's out of his mind," muttered Talen, pulling Jerrik from his thoughts.

"Laila will be here soon," said Darien. "Hopefully without getting caught as well."

Jerrik shook his head. He'd known this was a stupid idea. Now they were locked away deep underground in a network of tunnels dominated by a psychopath Vampire and his newly turned army that was pumped full of drugs. Reinforcements would come eventually. Maybe. But he had a bad feeling about those drugs the Vampires were taking. Whatever was in that steroid put them in a freakish battle rage. It wasn't that the drugs were making them that much stronger, but it dulled any pain, making it harder to stop them. What if they lost? What if there were too many? Even if Frej made it into the tunnels, would he be able to find them? What would happen if Sire Ashford decided to kill them? He wanted to lash out and hit something, he felt like the darkness was swallowing him up.

No, he told himself firmly. Laila had gotten them out of the Demon's fight ring, she'd get them out of this as well. If he could survive months in there, he'd survive an hour in here.

Laila peered around the corner where four armed guards patrolled the corridor. By Darien's descriptions, the cells should be located through the door at the far end, she just needed to find a way to disable them.

She called up her magic to her fingertips, feeling the crackle of electricity. Stepping around the corner, she approached the guards.

"What do you want?" one of them hissed.

She brushed her fingers against his shoulder, and he shuddered as the electricity shot through his body. He collapsed, stunned. Laila grabbed the arms of two more, but the final guard pointed a gun at her as the two collapsed.

Laila superheated the gun in his hands, which he dropped, hissing. Before he could reach for another weapon, she shocked him as well. They'd only be stunned for a minute at the most though, so she'd need to act fast.

She threw open the door and unlocked the cells.

"About time," drawled Darien, but he gave her a grin of approval as he passed her.

"Throw them in one of the cells." She jerked her head at the stunned Vampires in the corridor.

Jerrik passed her with those cuffs. For a moment she remembered the pain of the metal chafing her wrists and shuddered. Quickly, she removed the cuffs with a spell and Jerrik's eyes connected with hers as his body relaxed, but underneath she could still sense the panic he was trying to keep at bay.

"I told you I'd get you out," she said quietly.

"I know." He nodded towards the cell where Fredrik Stacy cowered. "We found him."

Laila entered the cell and hauled the man to his feet.

"We work for the Inter-Realm Security Agency." She flashed him her badge. "Are you injured?"

He shook his head.

"Then we need to get moving."

"Why should I trust you?" He pressed his back against the rough stone wall as if he might become a part of it if he tried hard enough.

Darien gave him an incredulous look. "Seriously? This is our job. That's why we're here. But if you want to stay behind and take your chances with the rogue Vampires, then be my guest."

Darien stormed away, and the human seemed to reconsider. He hastily followed as Laila turned on her heel and lead the way back down the hall with the others.

CHAPTER 44

Frej crouched down by the open window as he watched the storm drain. Torsten had just informed him that a large group of Vampires was headed this way. The Vampires he commanded were already in place, awaiting his signal.

The rumble of a car engine neared, and Frej cautiously peered out of the broken window. An SUV parked in the alley below, and out climbed Ali.

"Back up has arrived!" she announced.

"By the Gods!" exclaimed Frej, "What are you doing here?"

"We're here to help," said Lyn, opening the door of the passenger's seat.

Frej shook his head, he was about to open his mouth when the back of the SUV opened, and the vehicle shook as a large lumbering figure crawled out.

Benning stood and straightened his uniform, frowning at his pants. "Oh dear, these trousers are horribly wrinkled."

Frej gave the Giant a skeptical look. Benning was the definition of a gentle Giant. What were they thinking bringing him along?

Ali seemed to read his expression.

"When Lyn called, he volunteered to help. She's going to take the charm off of him. When he's at his full size, the Vampires won't be able to hurt him, and I have a feeling we're going to need all the help we can get."

She pulled out a couple of cases from the back of the SUV with the help of the Giant, while Lyn shouldered her pack and retrieved her quarterstaff.

Frej fought the urge to roll his eyes as he motioned for them to join him quickly on the second story of the building.

"Torsten, how close are they?" he asked.

"About a hundred yards from the entrance."

Ali and the others had just sprinted into the building when the back of the SUV opened once more. To Frej's horror, out stepped Erin. She flashed him a cocky grin in her t-shirt, ripped up jeans, and boots.

Before the teenaged Dragon could take a step, Frej used his air magic to pick her up and deposit her on the floor in front of him.

"Care to explain?" His expression was severe, but Erin kept her chin up, a defiant look on her face.

The door opened behind him, and the others entered the room. When Ali saw who stood beside him her jaw dropped.

"By the Morrigan," howled Ali, "I told you to stay at the house!"

"I can help though!" insisted Erin, conjuring up a ball of fire.

Ali shoved the cases into Benning's arms and stormed over to her sister, but a Vampire in tactical gear appeared in her path.

"It's too late," said the female Vampire, glancing at Frej. "They're here."

Sure enough, he looked out the window and saw the grate shift.

❖

Darien handed out the weapons he'd taken off the guards. Jerrik accepted two knives and a gun, but Talen declined and passed the handgun to Fredrik Stacy.

"You know how to use one right?" Darien asked the human.

The man blinked at him. "You point and shoot?"

"Considering we're in a stone passage, don't use it unless you really have to," grumbled Jerrik, "and don't shoot us."

Lucky for them, most of the rebels would now be at the surface facing the others. The most important thing was to ensure that they kept Fredrik Stacy safe. Hopefully, their escorts were still lying in wait.

Into her com device, Laila said, "I need all members of the escort to check in."

She waited, but only six of them responded.

"I need all available units to meet us at the platform in the center of the complex in ten minutes. Avoid the rebels and stay hidden if at all possible."

The confirmations came through, and she returned her attention to their current situation. The others had been stripped of their bullet-proof vests when the Vampires had apprehended them. The only one left with any form of armor was Laila, but Fredrik Stacy needed the protection more than she did.

"Hold on," she whispered to the others as they reached a bend in the tunnel.

Quickly she pulled off her hoodie then removed her breastplate. Standing there in her black tank top, she motioned to the human to come over. She helped cram him into the awkward fitting armor as the others watched in mild amusement. He was quite the sight in his pajamas with the clearly feminine curves of the armor, but it would give him some protection at least. She unsheathed the two small swords she'd strapped to her back.

They continued onward, retracing Laila's steps, and keeping Fredrik Stacy between them.

"Why do you hate Supernaturals?" Jerrik asked the human.

He scowled. "A monster like you *murdered* my son! You're violent creatures that want our world for yourselves."

"That's literally what we're trying to avoid!" said Darien. "Why else would we risk our own lives to save yours?"

"Because you're paid to do it," snapped Fredrik Stacy.

Talen scoffed. "I'm not."

"Quiet," hissed Laila, "someone's coming."

As they rounded another turn, they ended up face to face with six Vampire rebels. Laila didn't hesitate as her twenty years of Royal Guard training took over. She kept Fredrik Stacy behind her as she skewered the nearest rebel, the Vampire crumbling to ash.

Another attacked her with a piece of metal pipe nearly as long as her small swords. She caught it with the sword in her left hand and expulsed it away with a flicking motion, disarming the man. The other sword in her right hand was chambered and at the ready. She cut across the Vampire's throat, steel cutting through flesh to debilitate, before thrusting her other sword through his heart. He crumbled as well.

Nearby Talen struggled with his armed opponent.

"Talen!" she shouted and tossed him one of her swords.

He caught it before decapitating his opponent.

One of the Vampires had skirted around her towards Fredrik Stacy. She conjured an iced dagger that impaled him through the heart before he could reach the human.

"Stay close," she ordered him as she sheathed her remaining sword and reached for the two daggers in her boots instead.

Darien and Jerrik had managed to take down their opponents as well, but more appeared from around the corner behind them. Laila placed Fredrik Stacy behind her as she turned to face the newcomers, two of which raised their guns at her.

With a twist of the magical threads connected to the guns, she cast a spell that bent the weapons in half. There was a groan as metal contorted and snapped, rendering the guns useless. After a split second's recovery, the first Vampire threw his useless firearm to the ground and lunged for Fredrik Stacy. Darien intercepted him, knocking him into one of his comrades. Laila didn't stop to watch but readied herself for the two rebels approaching her.

They were faster, but their attacks were direct and clear, and Laila was able to anticipate their every move. She took a quick step to the side as the first Vampire rushed her. She cut sideways at his neck as he passed, surprised to find air instead of an Elf. He screamed and clutched at his neck where she'd cut him. Clearly, he hadn't taken those drugs. Perhaps there wasn't enough to go around?

Her other attacker was now armed with a handgun. Her Vampire friends were on the other side of the passageway, so she blasted the attacker with a stream of fire. There wasn't time for him to cry for help as his body was incinerated.

She turned to find the first Vampire had recovered from the shock of his wound. She was too slow to stop him as he reached for her throat, his hands clamped around her in a vice-like grip. Her body slammed into the stone behind her. As she tucked her chin to protect her windpipe, there was a split second where she made eye contact. Malice and bloodlust burned in his bright-red eyes. He thought he had her, but she was still armed.

Laila pinned his hands down to her chest with her left hand as she thrust her knife down into his chest. Eyes-wide, he tried to pull himself away, but Laila had his hands trapped. She plunged the dagger into his chest over and over, Blood splattering from his wounds, but she didn't stop until metal finally met heart, and he crumbled into a pile of ashes.

Beside her, Fredrik Stacy stared wide-eyed. The remaining Vampires were occupied fighting her friends, but they needed to end this and keep moving.

Talen grappled on the stone ground with his attacker. The rebel pinned him to the floor, but before he could make another move, Laila hooked her arm around him and plunged her dagger into his heart.

"Thanks," said Talen as she helped him up.

Darien shoved the final attacker in the chest. The rebel stumbled back down the hall as Jerrik blasted him with fire as well.

"Let's go," she ordered as more voices bounced off the walls of the tunnel in the direction they'd come from.

They sprinted down the hall, Laila keeping herself between the human and the fast approaching Vampires behind them. They needed to create a barricade or something to cut the rebels off.

"Keep going," she told the others. "Jerrik and I will deal with them."

Laila worked her magic, calling flames to her fingertips, Jerrik quickly catching on. As the Vampires rounded the corner, the two Elves incinerated the entire group with a blast of fire. Once they were certain none of the Vampires would follow, they turned and ran to catch up with the others.

They quickly caught up and continued without another encounter until they reached a large set of double doors.

"Careful," warned Laila, "Sire Ashford is probably nearby."

The others started to move forward, but Talen stopped them and pointed through the massive double doors to the throne of bones at the other end.

"You've got to destroy it." There was a haunted look in his eyes. She remembered him telling her that he could hear the voices of the dead and the initial reaction he'd had to the throne.

"You have to set them free," he pleaded quietly.

Laila nodded and ducked into the room. She worked the strands of magic in the room, calling up flames to ignite the throne of bones. It caught fire immediately, and Laila fed the flames with additional magical energy to incinerate the bones as she sent a silent prayer. Perhaps the Gods would listen and guide their spirits onward into the afterlife. The empty sockets of the skulls seemed to watch her from the inferno. As the bones crumbled to ash, she turned and joined the others at the doors.

She started to reach for her knives again, but just as the thought came to her, the cool metal of a hilt materialized in her hand. Blinking at the moonstone dagger, a shiver crept down her spine.

The group cautiously approached the large square where the dais stood and found three members of their escort waiting in an archway shrouded with shadow. Laila had the feeling that they were all that remained. The Vampires stepped out from the cover of the archway to join the rest of the group in surrounding Fredrik Stacy, who struggled to catch his breath.

"Come on!" she shouted to the others, charging towards their way out.

Three figures stepped in, blocking her path. It was Sire Ashford, Arnold Koch, and the Snake Shifter, Caine Ubel.

CHAPTER 45

Frej continued to frown as Ali ordered her sister to stay back with Benning. What was the girl thinking coming here? He'd be having a long talk with her by the time this was all over. Then again, he was sure Ali would have that part under control.

Vampire rebels crawled out of the storm drain and into the street. They looked feral and wild as they hissed and snarled. Something wasn't right, he'd never seen Vampires act like rabid animals especially compared to the calm, cool Vampires he commanded.

"Hold your positions!" shouted Frej to the Vampires below before turning his attention to the others. He was about to demand that they surrender, but they lunged at the council's Vampires. There was no reasoning with these creatures.

"Fire at will!" he shouted instead. "Force them back."

The Vampires didn't so much as hesitate. Immediately they fired into the oncoming surge of rebels. But they were spewing out of the storm drain at an alarming rate and began to surround the surveillance van.

"Torsten," said Frej into the coms, "You're surrounded. You and Donald need to get out of there."

"I've got it covered," Donald replied. Seconds later an orange shield appeared around the van. It looked similar to the lockdown spell Laila used on the mansion in Malibu.

Frej turned to Ali, Lyn, and the handful of Vampires that surrounded them preparing their guns. The Witch was pulling something out of her bag as well. It looked like a feather, but his attention was drawn back to the storm drain.

His Vampires attacked, firing at anything that emerged from the grate. But the rebels pushed forward, only stopping when they took a bullet to the heart.

There was definitely something off about these Vampires. They charged directly into the line of fire in a way he could only describe as suicidal. Despite the casualties, the rebels were starting to gain ground and break through the first line of defense. The Vampires with him on the second-floor opened fire, trying to keep the rebels back.

There was a crackling of fire behind him, then suddenly a blazing object soared over his head and into the alley. It beat its wings and circled around before diving towards the emerging rebels. It moved like a bird and left a trail of flame as it dove, taking out six rebels in one pass.

Frej tore his eyes from the flaming bird to glance at Lyn. The Witch watched with wide, staring eyes. The brown irises were gone, replaced by a circle of flame. Somehow, she was controlling the bird.

"I'm going to get an aerial view," he shouted to Ali sprinting for the stairs.

He took the stairs two at a time and threw the door to the roof open as he started to shift. Within seconds he was airborne.

He soared above the building watching as the battle raged below. The council's Vampires fought the majority of the rebels emerging from the tunnels, but other rebels were already in the streets, fighting the law enforcement officers.

He dove with his claws outstretched and plowed through rebels trying to break through a barricade of shields that a group of police officers had formed. The Vampires cried out as they were tossed about. Beating his pale wings, he pulled up and landed on another building.

He shifted back to human form. "Ali, are you there?"

"Yes."

"It's not looking good from up here. I'm going to help our human allies. You handle things over there."

"Got it."

Frej shifted once more and took to the sky, roaring as he dove back into the fray.

"This is so not good!" howled Donald as he double-checked the ward enchantment he'd installed on the dash of the van.

"What do you mean?" huffed Torsten. "I thought you said the shield was fully operational?"

"It was until a Vampire just broke one of the crystals off the dash! It must've happened just before I activated the shield."

Torsten groaned. Without a shield, they'd be sitting ducks, and there was no way to move the van. Aside from a knife in his belt, they had few weapons that would be of any use against Vampires. He glanced around hastily for anything they could use. A thought occurred to him, and he dug through his toolbox in the corner until he found a blue can of propane he used for soldering. The flame would work, but the current attachment was too small to be of any real use.

"Donald, where's the can from the energy drink you had earlier?"

The Tech Wiz pulled it out of a bag and held it up. Torsten took the can and cut the top part off, then added a small hole to the bottom before handing it back to Donald.

"Now I need you to enchant it, so it's impervious to heat," he explained.

"Why exactly?" asked the Tech Wiz skeptically.

"I'm going to make an attachment for the propane tank that will create a larger flame, kind of like a weed burner."

"A what?"

Something hit the side of the van with a thud as a hole flickered in the shield.

"Just do it!" ordered Torsten as Donald hastily got to work.

Within minutes, Torsten's creation was complete. It was rough, and there was no way to test it, but it would have to do.

Torsten braced himself as something else hit the door of the van. He checked the cameras, but there was still no sign of the Giant and Vampires would soon find a way to break through the windows of the van.

"And whatever happens, *do not* leave this van," said Torsten gripping Donald's shoulders.

Donald gave him a bewildered look. "Why are you saying this?"

"I'm old, I've lived my life, but this team needs you and your inventions."

"No Torsten!" Donald begged him. "You can't go out there."

Torsten grabbed a hammer to smash through the moon roof, but Donald caught his arm.

"This is insane!" he shouted at the Dwarf. "Just stay here, we'll be fine."

"By the Morrigan," breathed Ali as she picked off rebels one by one with her rifle. "Where did they all come from?"

The Vampires stared in shock as well.

There was nowhere to retreat, and the rebels kept coming. The Vampires sent by the council were good, but the rebels were determined. They needed help.

The flaming bird dissipated, and Lyn shook herself from the trance.

"That works a hell of a lot better on Vampires than Zombies," said Lyn pleased.

"We're losing ground," Ali shouted to her over the noise. "We need Benning."

The Witch glanced at the Giant, watching with wide eyes from the corner.

"Come on!" Lyn rushed past him and through the door. "You heard Ali."

Ali watched as the rebels attacked the van below. She aimed at another one, but it was hard to get a clear shot at their hearts. Some of them even wore bullet-proof vests.

"Torsten, I don't like this," she said as the shield around the surveillance van started to fail. "We've got to get you two out of there. Just hold on, we've got one Giant distraction coming."

The shield died completely, and she heard Donald swearing. Clearly, the shield hadn't worked as well as he'd anticipated.

"Then I'll hold them back in the meantime," grunted the Dwarf.

"No, Torsten, stay where you are!" she ordered.

The sound of shattering glass drew her attention as the moon roof of the van broke. From it crawled Torsten with a torch, it had some sort of long attachment fixed with a partial energy drink can. His contraption put off a large flame, which he aimed at the Vampires surrounding the van, and took out five in one sweep. The others started to retreat, but one of them raised a gun.

"Look out!" she screamed.

She fired at the rebel, but his gun had already discharged. Torsten stopped what he was doing and looked down at the entry wound in his chest. He grit his teeth and returned to his task of keeping the Vampires back. He took down two more before he stumbled, another gunshot wound to the chest.

Ali tried to take down the rebels, but she just couldn't stop them fast enough. Her eyes clouded with tears as she looked through the scope.

"Frej! I need your help!" she cried.

There was no response.

Torsten was on his knees now, but he wasn't finished. Fire shone in his eyes as he continued to fight. He coughed and slick blood coated his tongue, but he would not let them get to Donald, not as long as there was breath in his lungs and blood in his veins. Rough hands wrenched the weapon from his grasp. He reached for anything he could use, and his hand found the handle of the knife in his belt—a gift from his father many years ago. He unsheathed it and plunged in down into one of the Vampires that crumbled away in ash and flame.

He felt another bullet, and another pierce his abdomen. He knew he was a dead man, and a tear escaped the corner of his eye as he realized he wouldn't see his wife and daughters again in this life. Their beautiful faces flashed before his eyes, they felt close, and he leaned forward as if he might be able to touch them.

Somewhere in the distance he heard someone cry his name. He was falling from the van but didn't feel the impact of the ground below, only warmth and light enveloping him as he released his final breath.

Above, Ali knelt in the window, frozen. All around the skirmish continued, but Ali couldn't hear it. She and Torsten were not terribly close, but it felt so similar to the night when Carlos had been gunned down in front of her. The memory of his warm blood coating her hands and the sirens wailing in the distance flooded back to her. Ali couldn't stop it then, and she hadn't stopped it now.

How many more people around her would die? Carlos, her parents, and Torsten were gone. Mato was in the hospital. Erin and Lyn had been attacked. Laila had faced near-death experiences multiple times now. How much more could she take?

CHAPTER 46

It was as if everything around her vanished. All of Laila's focus was drawn to the men standing in front of her. Anger raged within her, and she could feel the magic at her fingertips.

"Get him out of here," Laila shouted over her shoulder. "I've got this."

Darien was about to protest, but Talen shoved him towards the door.

"I'll help her," insisted Talen, "just take the human."

Darien grabbed Fredrik Stacy and hefted him over his shoulder. He and the remainder of the escort ran for the other exit, faster than Laila's eyes could follow, while Talen and Jerrik stayed behind.

"Deal with the others," Laila said to the men behind her, "these ones are mine."

She could honestly care less about Sire Ashford and Arnold Koch. They were threats to the city and needed to be neutralized, but Caine Ubel was another story. There was a personal score to settle, and this time she wouldn't let him get away.

He was the Lesser Demon who'd sent her to the fight rings,

along with countless others. Then he'd been in charge of the illegal summoning rituals and kidnaped Erin to use as a sacrifice. With the help of Frej, Darien, and Lyn, she'd saved Erin, but Caine had once again escaped. This time would be different though, he would not escape.

Sire Ashford was the first to approach. With her magic she sent a blast of lethally sharp icicles at the Vampire. He dodged, but the icicles embedded with a thud on his right side. Arnold tried to rush her, but Laila unleashed a blast of fire. Both Vampires dropped to the ground as Laila had hoped they would. Beneath them, the stone shifted and rolled until the Vampire's bodies were entirely encased in stone. They struggled to move and escape, but the magic Laila used to bind them was strong, and while they were in the stone, it was partnered with that of the dead Sorcerers whose spirits were forced to hold these walls up. Laila sensed they were all too happy to help her trap the men. The Vampires howled from within as Laila stepped over the mounds of stone. She would handle them later.

Caine stood there watching her approach with a grin. The magic crackled around Laila's fingertips as she prepared another spell. She could try to talk him down, try to convince him to come quietly with her, but that would be pointless. The enchanted right hand morphed into a long, wicked blade.

She blasted him with a bolt of electricity, but he held something up. Some sort of amulet with carvings that caused the spell to be redirected away. It was a charm of protection against magic. He put the chain around his neck as he continued to smirk. The Shifter thought he had the advantage, but Laila continued her approach, dagger at the ready.

She might not be able to use magic directly, but there were other ways to use it against him. Laila shut her eyes as she summoned a blinding white light. It lasted for a second, but Caine flinched and shielded his face. With her dagger, Laila cut towards his stomach. He was barely able to parry with his normal arm before the tip of her dagger met flesh. Already his blade was descending towards her shoulder. Hastily, she intercepted his knife arm with her left hand. She wrapped her fingers around his wrist and pulled him towards her. He stumbled off-balance as she thrust her dagger into his side.

As he screamed in pain, he lashed out with his free hand. Laila didn't see the backhand coming, the blow collided with her mouth. There was a crunching sound as bone shifted, and pain blossomed in her jaw as she spun sideways.

In that split second before she regained her senses, Caine wrapped his left arm around her shoulders and thrust his blade, under her ribcage. It slid easily through the soft tissues as pain tore through her body.

"We *will* conquer Midgard," the Demon whispered to her.

Laila opened her mouth to reply, but coughed, choking on her own blood. As the Demon twisted the knife into her flesh, her eyes locked with Jerrik's on the other side of the chamber.

I'm sorry, she mouthed.

Jerrik cried out, or at least he thought he did, yet no sound reached his ears. He shoved his way through the growing number of Vampires, but time had slowed and every second felt like an eternity.

As he fought his way through the crowd, he never once took his eyes from hers.

The Demon holding Laila gave him a triumphant look, as he twisted the knife in her body. She coughed up blood.

I'm sorry.

Her voice echoed through his mind. Hands grasped his arms as the pain of his heart breaking overwhelmed him. It ripped him apart like a thousand serrated blades. He teetered on the edge of insanity, pleading with the Gods. He could save her with his magic as he had before, but there were too many Vampires in his path now.

"*NO!*" he screamed as the light faded from her eyes.

The Demon released her, and Laila's body crumpled to the ground. He stepped over and approached Jerrik as he was restrained by the rebel Vampires. He was numb, too consumed by what he had just witnessed to try to fight back. Somewhere next to him Talen fought fiercely, desperately trying to get to Laila's side, to turn her in order to preserve her life, even though he knew it was already too late—her heart had stopped.

CHAPTER 47

Frej shook his head as he watched the battle below. Nearly half the council's forces were dust. Humans and Vampires alike were on their phones calling for reinforcements, but it would be too late by the time they arrived.

He shifted back into his human form and heard Ali's voice speaking to a hysterical Donald through his earpiece.

"What happened?" He rushed to the edge on the building he was standing on and tried to get a visual on Ali's location.

"Torsten's dead," Ali's voice was strained.

"Listen to me," his voice firm. "I need you to pull yourself together. We've got to push forward."

From where he stood, he could just barely see her nod as she took a breath to steady herself. Ali rose and fired round after round of bullets into the Vampires, but he could tell she was running low on ammunition. Erin hung back, watching from the shadows with a scowl. Lyn and Benning were nowhere to be found, he just hoped she had some sort of plan.

He tried not to think about Laila trapped somewhere below. If it was this bad up here, what could she possibly be facing underground? As much as he wanted to go in to search for her, Frej knew he had to handle this situation first.

Something flew through the broken window and into the room where Ali stood.

"Grenade!" someone screamed.

Ali's eyes widened with fear as Erin ran towards it. Frej cried out, but it was too late, the explosive deployed. Instead of bursting outward, the explosion was magically redirected out the window and away from the building. When the flames and debris cleared, Erin was still standing. The little Fire Dragon's quick thinking saved the lives of everyone in the building.

Frej sagged against a vent behind him. Erin punched her fist into the air. Her voice was picked up by Ali's mic.

"This is clearly why you need my help," declared Erin triumphantly.

Ali looked torn between relief and rage for her sister's brazen act of heroism. There was no time to celebrate this little victory though, as the battle raged on around them.

Finally, Lyn returned to stand by Ali, but she was alone.

"Where's the Giant?" asked Frej.

"He's coming," explained Ali, her voice now steady, "As docile as he is, Benning sure doesn't like it when someone harms his friends."

Lyn held something up for him to see. It was the shrinking charm she'd given the Giant.

"What does he plan to do?" asked Frej with a frown. They had Vampires of their own out there. They couldn't risk losing more of their forces.

A thunderous sound in the distance announced the Giant's approach. There was a crunching sound as he the asphalt cracked underfoot. A trail of dust from crushed rebels floated in his wake.

"I'll show you!" muttered the Giant, as he stomped on Vampires left and right. Each time he lifted his foot, a trail of ash fell from it. It was strange watching a Giant squash the rebels like bugs, and Frej was glad this Giant was a friend instead of a foe.

Within minutes the Giant had demolished a quarter of the rebels on the street. From there he made his way down the alley, crushing any rebels in his path. He was making progress, and the stream of rebels exiting the storm drain had come to an end, but a loud crack resounded as the ground beneath the Giant gave way. The tunnel caved-in, leaving the alley full of rubble.

"No!" shouted Frej, as the tunnel entrance was buried. Laila and the others were trapped.

This wasn't real, it couldn't be real, thought Jerrik trembling all over. Laila couldn't be dead.

Her red blood glistened on the stones beneath her body. As her eyes stared lifelessly at him. Physical pain tore through his body, and he continued to fight with every ounce of strength he had left, but someone had restrained his hands again with a pair of those Gods-damned cuffs.

"Your pain is intoxicating," said the Demon, watching him while trying to apply pressure to his own wound. "It truly is priceless. But I have other issues to deal with."

The Demon leaned a little closer. "Don't worry, you'll join her soon," he sneered.

Out of nowhere, a bright light appeared, leaving everyone to stare in shock.

Laila floated along a current, it was warm and pleasant at first, like a hot bath. She allowed her body to be carried along with a peculiar feeling of lightness as she bobbed and swayed. But suddenly there was a change, the water became frigid, and she was surrounded by an oppressive darkness, it was like nothing she'd ever experienced.

Struggling, she tried to fight her way to the shore, but she couldn't see it, only darkness. Amid her flailing and thrashing, someone offered her a hand. There was no other choice, she grabbed it, and it pulled her out of the water and into the light. Kicking and clawing, she scrambled over the wooden side of a small boat.

Her savior was a small, older man in a grey, hooded robe. He sat on one of the benches and watched as Laila coughed and spluttered.

"Easy now," he said, patting her on the back, "you're alright."

"Where am I?" asked Laila, confused.

"This is the river Styx," explained the man with a warm smile, "and I'm the ferryman."

Laila started to panic. She couldn't be dead. There was so much left she needed to do.

The ferryman continued to speak with a soothing tone, "Don't worry, it's normal to panic. Never fear, the afterlives are wonderful places, for the most part. There's no need for worry there."

Laila clenched the sides of the boat in shock. She was dead. She was actually dead.

"Here now," said the Ferryman giving her a gentle smile. "Let's see your payment. The directions as to which afterlife awaits is usually on there. Check your pockets."

Laila patted down her pockets. Something was in her left pocket. Reaching for it, she pulled out a large, round, coin. She passed it to the Ferryman.

"Alright, let's see…" He studied the coin, the lines on his forehead deepening as he frowned.

"I see," he murmured at last, glancing up at Laila solemnly. "It's been a long time since I've seen one of you."

"An Elf?" asked Laila confused.

The man chuckled and shook his head. "We'd better get you back to the mortal worlds."

He picked up a long pole that rested against the side of the boat, then he pushed off and propelled them up the river Styx, which was now calm and still. They were in a long tunnel with stalactites far above and shorelines on either side. Along the shore were portals of shimmering magic, which helped to illuminate the cavern.

A second boat passed propelled by a man identical to the one beside her. Were they twins? The boat also contained another passenger. Laila gasped.

"Torsten!" she cried.

He noticed her and waved with a blissful expression.

The Ferryman placed a hand on her shoulder. "He's off to a better place. I can tell that he's going to Valhalla."

"If you see my family, tell them I love them more than they'll ever know!" shouted Torsten as his boat passed them and drifted further away.

Laila could feel her throat closing up as she shook her head. She wanted to scream but froze when she saw the look on his face. He smiled in a way Laila had never seen him do before, free of care or worry. It was the first time she'd truly seen him relaxed and at peace.

"Ah yes, you see it, don't you?" The Ferryman watched her with a gentle expression. "It's not truly the end, just a new beginning."

"But what about me?" she asked confused. Why was he sending her back?

"Fate is a strange thing, woven from magic itself. It commands Gods and mortals alike."

"So, it's my fate to go back to my life?"

He chuckled. "It's far more complicated than that. Now remember, you can let fate control you, but you are also powerful enough to control your own destiny."

Laila shook her head. The man was speaking in riddles, but he was probably just happy to have someone to talk to. In any case, Laila filed the thoughts in the back of her mind.

"You really should be more careful next time," the Ferryman suggested as they continued on their way. "But I can see that you're new at this."

"What?" asked Laila confused, "What are you talking about?"

He ignored her question. His lack of straight forward answers was starting to grate on her nerves.

"Here we are," announced the man as he beached the boat along one side of the shore. "The portal will take you to your destiny."

Yet another cryptic message. Laila climbed out of the boat though, not seeing another option.

"Good luck!" he called, pushing away from the shore.

Laila turned to thank him, but the Ferryman had vanished.

"You're welcome," mumbled Laila as she turned to face the portal. She took a deep breath and stepped through.

Laila blinked. She was laying on the hard, stone ground in a pool of her own blood, but the wound was gone. Thor's hammer, she'd been dead! Then the Ferryman had returned her to life. Gods, this was a lot to process.

She lifted herself up off the ground, and her necklace started to glow. There was a shift in the magic within her, and it felt like she was seeing the world more clearly. Everyone in the chamber turned to watch in shock and horror. The crackling blue magic surfaced, but this time she was its master. Ancient knowledge flooded her mind, and suddenly, she understood what to do, her divine magic had been fully awakened.

Reaching out with one hand, the blue flames wrapping around her arm suddenly crackling to life, they shot forward through the room like a shockwave, blasting every Vampire in its wake. Only Jerrik, Talen, and Caine were spared.

"It's not possible!" The Demon backed away, terrified.

"Y-you were dead. I killed you!"

"Caine Ubel!" her voice shook the room. "I damn you to Muspelheim as punishment for your crimes."

"No, please!" begged the Shifter, but she had no sympathy for the Demon.

At her command, a portal opened up behind him, crackling with the hostile red energy of Hell. It pulled him backwards into the opening as he screamed. His cries were futile though, his sentence had been given. When the last of Caine Ubel was sucked into the portal, it snapped shut, leaving no evidence behind.

"Well," said Talen staring at her. "That was intriguing."

Laila had no idea how she'd done that, but it was certainly the divine magic at work since only a God could banish someone to Hell without access to a portal. She could see the markings on her body were still glowing and knew her job was not done.

"Come on, this isn't over." She turned and started walking through the tunnel, Talen and Jerrik following behind.

CHAPTER 48

Laila followed the tunnel towards the exit. Not a single rebel passed them, but they could hear distorted noise of the battle echoing through the tunnel ahead.

"Hold on a second." Jerrik grabbed her arm. "What happened? He *killed* you."

They had more pressing matters to deal with, but when she turned to look at Jerrik, the shock and confusion in his eyes stirred something in her.

"I'll explain later, but now's not the time." As she spoke to him, she could see the glow of her eyes reflected in his own. Her red contacts were gone, perhaps they'd been burned up by the magic she wielded.

What the hell was she? Laila turned away quickly and proceeded through the tunnel. She didn't want to think about any of this right now, she just needed to act while she maintained a shred of control over this new magic.

Up ahead was the arch where the other tunnels branched off. They didn't have much farther to go, but she noticed movement beyond the archway.

"Laila?" the voice echoed down the chamber.

Ali approached them at a sprint, only something looked off. Her skin was pale and deathly, and her eyes were red. She must've disguised herself with her glamour magic to make it past the rebels.

"What are you doing here?" asked Laila, surprised as she eyed Ali's fangs.

Talen glanced at Ali amused. "Well, this is interesting. Nice Vampire glamour, but I can still smell you."

"I look interesting?" Ali shook her head in disbelief. "Laila is glowing. Literally."

"Long story." Laila picked up the pace once more.

"Hold on." Ali stopped her before they reached the hole in the storm drain wall. "Benning caused a cave-in, we can't get out the way you came in. This way."

Instead of turning left in the storm drain, Ali led them to the right. After a short distance, they reached a ladder.

"Up there." Ali motioned to the ladder. The others started climbing, but she pulled Laila aside. "I want to warn you, something happened. Torsten—"

"Is dead," Laila finished for her. There wasn't time to process it though, she had to finish this before the divine magic slipped from her grasp.

Ali gave her a bewildered look. "How'd you—?"

"There's no time." Laila started climbing, Ali right behind her.

When they reached the surface, Laila could hear sounds of a battle raging in the distance. They cautiously approached, fending off the occasional rebel. When they reached the street, Laila paused, taking in the fight before her.

Humans from multiple law enforcement agencies fought side by side in the street as the rebel Vampires continued their attack. They skirted around the skirmish in the street and towards the worst of the fighting back in the alley. Rebels and Vampires from the council battled on, led by Frej who was in the thick of it. Benning was hard at work shifting the rubble away to expose the tunnel. Above them on the second floor of a building Lyn was dropping potions on rebel Vampires.

"Take that you piece of shit!" called a figure beside Lyn as she hurtled fireballs at the rebels.

"Is that your sister?" asked Jerrik, with amusement.

"Erin!" howled Ali before she stalked off, muttering something about too many videogames.

Laila waded into the fray, as Vampires stopped to stare.

She felt the magic building within her. If she didn't release it soon, it would destroy her. In one massive wave, she unleashed the energy.

Blue fire tore through the battlefield. As it reached the rebels, they were incinerated. Her allies, on the other hand, remained untouched as if the magic could tell the difference. It rippled outwards to the street beyond and into the city. When the ripple of energy faded away, ash was raining down as silence settled in the alley.

"Whoa," said Erin, breaking the silence, "that's new."

Ali appeared beside her sister, and one by one the others started moving.

Trucks could be heard in the distance as more reinforcements arrived from the council. They were surprised to find the rebels had been annihilated.

"Laila!" called Frej, climbing over rubble to get to her. He embraced her in a hug that lifted her off the ground. Laila felt the last of the blue magic leave her as the markings on her arms faded back to their normal color.

"Are you alright?" he asked, his nose pressed against her ear, "I was so worried. The rebels attacked, and no one had heard from you."

"It's okay," she said, holding him to her. "I'm alright. We're alright."

As she stood there in his arms, she saw Jerrik watching. He turned away to speak to one of the Vampires.

"I'm sorry. I'm so sorry I didn't tell you about Regina."

"I know." Laila couldn't think about that. Not now, not when Torsten...

She pulled away. "Where is he?"

Frej looked towards the surveillance van, and she followed his gaze. There, lying on the cracked asphalt, was Torsten's body. Donald was hunched over him, sobbing. Tentatively, Laila approached and knelt beside him.

"Stupid, stupid idiot!" screamed Donald, beating the side of the van.

"What happened?" asked Laila gently.

He shook his head, tears staining his face. "I told him—I told him n-not to go. I told him to s-stay, that the shields would hold. He didn't listen. He climbed out to fight, but there were too many—" He choked on a sob.

Laila could feel the tears rolling down her cheeks.

"He thought he was protecting me," Donald choked out. "This is all my fault."

"Look at me." Laila grabbed his arms. "Donald, look at me now."

He did, his eyes red and swollen.

"This is not your fault, okay? Torsten knew what he was doing. If he left the van to protect you, then that was his choice to make."

"But why? What would he do that?"

Laila thought for a moment. "Because that's who Torsten was."

She thought back to those weeks when she had been trapped by the Demons. Torsten had given her food and water. In a place where she had never imagined compassion could survive, he showed her that it could thrive. Torsten was kind, and fatherly, and had been there every step of the way. Even when they returned to Los Angeles, he was the one who listened to her troubles and helped her think things through.

She glanced up at Ali who placed a hand on Donald's back.

"Hey, let's take a walk."

Donald's breathing came easier as Ali used her charm magic to help lift some of the grief. He nodded and allowed the Fae to lead him away.

"Oh Torsten," Laila sighed, looking down at his bloodied face. "I hope we meet again one day in Valhalla."

She grasped the handle of the worn knife lying beside him. It had Dwarven runes on it, and the blade had been well cared for. Laila placed it in his hand over his chest before rising.

In the distance, sirens announced the arrival of the investigative team and the paramedics. Laila answered as many questions as she could until finally she and the others were released.

The battle was over. They'd won, but at a heavy cost.

CHAPTER 49

"Tea?" asked Laila holding up the kettle of steaming water. A few of the others nodded their heads.

After being released from the crime scene, it seemed odd to just go their separate ways. Now they gathered around in Ali's kitchen. Darien and his sire spoke quietly at the kitchen table where Mr. Whiskers had crawled happily into Talen's lap. Lyn, Jerrik, and Erin sat at the island on the barstools while Frej and Ali sorted through menus, trying to find a restaurant that was still open at four in the morning. Lyn had offered to restore Benning's shrinking charm, but he insisted on staying to help shift the debris for easier access to the tunnels.

Laila poured the water into four mugs. She passed one to Ali, saved one for herself, then passed the remaining mugs across the counter for the others as well as a box of assorted tea. She would've offered them something stronger, but tea was the only thing they had on hand.

"Looks like there's a pizza place open." Ali glanced over the menu to the others. "Will that work?"

Wearily they nodded. At this point, Laila didn't care what

they ordered, she just felt numb. While Ali placed the order, Laila wandered over to the Vampires.

"What happens now?" Laila slid onto the bench, cradling the mug of tea in her hands.

Darien folded his arms. "I received word from the investigative team that both Sire Ashford and Arnold Koch survived, thanks to your tomb of stone. Arnold and Sire Ashford will be handed over to Talen and the council for questioning."

Laila opened her mouth to protest, but Talen cut her off.

"It's alright," said Talen, "it's legal. It's also the only way to prove which council members were involved in the rebellion. I'll get Sire Ashford to talk and relay any information to Darien. Then he will be punished as the council sees fit."

Laila cringed. Whatever methods Talen used, she had a feeling she was better off not knowing. Cruel and unusual came to mind, but then again, the Vampires had their own way of handling their problems. Even if it conflicted with federal law. Eventually, this would have to change, but until then the Vampires were allowed to punish their own as they had for millennia.

"Do you think Dagan will try to run?" she asked, propping her elbows on the table.

"If he's smart, he will." Talen's expression was dark. "We'll eventually find him though."

"There'll be at least one opening on the council," pointed out Darien, "you should apply."

Talen gave him a smirk. "That's a lot of drama I'd rather avoid, but I'll think about it."

It occurred to Laila that something didn't seem right. How had those rebels so easily apprehended Talen when he was so strong? Couldn't he have used his charm magic against them? She voiced her concerns.

Talen chuckled and scratched Mr. Whiskers behind his ears. "I realized that being caught was the fastest way to get to Fredrik Stacy. Sire Ashford wanted to kill us the moment we were presented to him, but I used my charm abilities to convince him to lock us up instead. My plan was to charm the guard into giving us the keys, but you showed up first."

"Why didn't you just charm the Vampires into submission in the first place?" she asked.

"My charm doesn't work like that. I can only influence one individual at a time." He gave her a wicked look. "If you'd like me to give you another demonstration…"

She laughed. "That won't be necessary."

He shrugged.

Laila grinned and patted him on the shoulder as she stood and returned to the others.

"Pizza's on its way!" Ali announced as she took a stack of paper plates from a cabinet and set them on the counter.

"While we wait," said Jerrik, looking directly at Laila with his intense gaze, "I'd love an explanation for what happened down there."

Laila shifted, as all eyes settled on her.

"What?" asked Ali looking around, "am I missing something?"

Laila took a deep breath. "Well, I managed to control the divine magic."

"How did you keep it from destroying you?" Lyn frowned, noticing Laila's missing charm.

"I think this helped." She tapped the necklace she wore. "The Goddess gave it to me. She said that I have to start my training with Arduinna soon. Otherwise it will be too late to stop the Demons."

Jerrik watched and waited for her to continue, but she didn't. She wasn't ready to talk about what happened. First, Laila needed to process the fact that she'd died. There were so many questions of her own that cycled through her head, she didn't need to add their questions to it. But by the look on Jerrik's face, he wouldn't be ready to drop the topic any time soon.

"Well," said Frej, wrapping an arm around her waist affectionately, "we survived this battle. Even if there are more ahead, tonight we can rest knowing that there is one less group the Demons can use against us."

"Said like a true soldier!" Talen gave him a faint smile. "I want to thank all of you. You didn't have to come fight for us tonight, but you did."

"You're welcome!" said Erin brightly.

Ali shot her a withering look. Laila knew the lecture was yet to come and imagined it would involve the confiscation of a videogame console or her computer.

Ali rested a hand on Talen's shoulder. "Of course we'd be there, we don't leave four of our own to suffer at the hands of some psycho rebel leader."

Talen looked confused. "You mean three."

"She meant four." Lyn winked.

Talen threw his head back and laughed. He rose from the bench, causing Mr. Whiskers to meow in protest.

"Well, I better get going. I've got a lot of phone calls to make. Certain council members will want to hear about this from me directly. Come on Jerrik, I'll give you a ride."

Laila could've kissed him from gratitude. At some point or another Jerrik would confront Laila about her death, but Talen had bought her some time.

He and Darien said their goodbyes before stepping out into the night. The Dark Elf hesitated before sliding off the bar-stool.

"Take it easy." Frej offered him his hand. Jerrik accepted it with a surprised nod. He glanced back at Laila one more time before reaching the door.

The pizzas arrived a short while later and quickly vanished. With everyone's appetites satisfied, they wandered off to their rooms one by one until all that remained were Ali and Laila. Mr. Whiskers napped peacefully in her lap.

"Can I talk to you for a minute?" asked Ali, sinking onto the couch next to Laila.

The Elf nodded, yawning.

"Look," began Ali uncertainly, "I know something else happened down there. I could practically cut the tension between you and Jerrik with a knife."

"Oh." Laila stared down at her cup. "Yeah, something did happen, but it wasn't anything between the two of us."

Laila paused. She wasn't exactly ready to talk about what happened, but she needed to think through it somehow. Suddenly she found herself telling Ali everything that had happened, even in the river Styx. The words just tumbled out of her mouth, while Ali nodded silently. When she'd finished Ali leaned her head back against the sofa.

"Wow, you died, like *actually* died." She shook her head.

"I don't know what to think," said Laila as she set her empty mug on a side table and stroked the Bogey-cat in her lap, he mewed at her before shutting his eyes again.

Ali nodded, "Now I get why you didn't tell everyone. But Talen and Jerrik know, right?"

"Not all of it, but yeah."

Ali thought for a moment. "Why did you say you were sorry to Jerrik?"

"I don't really know." Laila blinked. "Maybe because I felt like I had failed in dying, or because I was leaving the rest of you to face the Demons alone?"

"Hm…" Ali pursed her lips.

"What?"

"It didn't have anything to do with your lingering feelings for Jerrik?"

Laila frowned at her.

"You know I don't judge you, right?" The Fae gave her a caring look.

Laila nodded, but to be honest, she had no idea why she had said it. It just sort of came out.

"And how about Frej?" Ali asked. "Is he forgiven?"

Laila groaned. "I don't know. I'm sick of fighting. I forgive him for not telling me, and clobbering Jerrik, but…." He was still in love with Regina.

"Well, you don't have to decide now."

Laila shifted to face Ali, "How are you holding up? Have you heard from Mato?"

"They're keeping him for observation, but the doctor said he should be able to go home in another day or two."

Laila searched her friend's face. "But how are *you* doing?"

Ali sighed. Laila could practically see the swirl of emotions in her violet eyes as the Fae fought to put her feelings into words.

"I don't know if I can do this," she whispered finally. "This is exactly what we were talking about the other day. How can I let someone into my life knowing that it will make them a target?"

Ali looked away at a small potted plant on the windowsill above the kitchen table. Three purple lilies grew there sparkling with magic. The flower of mourning for the Fae.

Laila sighed. "He's no stranger to the cruelty of the Demons. Perhaps he finds it comforting to know that you're not either, that you understand."

Ali sank back against the couch looking conflicted.

Laila reached out to place a hand on Ali's arm, but the moment she made contact she was hit with the strangest sensation.

Carlos bleeding on the ground.

The image flashed through Laila's mind.

Erin's wrists, raw from the ropes that bound her.

These weren't Laila's thoughts.

Mato moaning in agony. Bullets tearing through Torsten.

Laila realized she was experiencing Ali's thoughts.

A couple, their bodies burning side by side on a pyre.

Somehow, she knew they were Ali's parents.

This is all my fault.

The words echoed through her mind.

"No, it's not," said Laila firmly.

"What did you—?"

"This is not your fault," Laila whispered.

Tears welled up in Ali's eyes as, "Did you just read my mind?"

Laila nodded bewildered, and Ali choked out a noise that was something between a sob and a laugh.

"Probably the divine magic," suggested Ali.

Laila frowned. "I'm serious though, Ali, you can't keep blaming yourself for all of this."

Ali was always the one to console others and use her magic to help lessen their pain and grief. Yet here she was, possibly in need of more comfort than any of them.

Ali hesitated. "I think it's time for us to get some sleep."

Just like that, Ali had covered her anguish. Laila didn't like the way she changed the topic, but she had to agree. She was absolutely exhausted.

Laila carefully removed Mr. Whiskers from her lap. He yawned and curled up on one of Ali's decorative pillows instead.

"Thank you for listening." Laila hugged her. "What would I do without you?"

"Overthink everything," Ali teased.

Laila grabbed her breastplate that Darien had returned to her and climbed the stairs. When she opened the door to her room, she found Frej asleep on her bed. It looked like he'd been waiting for her when he fell asleep.

She paused, unsure of what to do. There was a part of her that truly understood that Frej didn't intend to harm her. Still though, she wondered if Frej had just chosen her because he couldn't have Regina. Laila realized that she wasn't angry with him, not truly, but her trust had been violated, and that would be a slow wound to heal. Then again, she struggled with her own feelings for Jerrik, whatever those may be, and she realized that she couldn't be angry at Frej, not when she wasn't free of guilt herself.

She shook her head, there had been so much violence and hurt in the last twelve hours. It was overwhelming. It made her realize that she didn't want to be alone, not now.

She silently shut the door. By the time she'd removed her bloodstained clothes and taken a shower, she felt a little more relaxed, although she did notice that a pale blue scar in the shape of an intricate knot covered the place where she had been stabbed.

Laila pulled on a thin tank top to hide the scar and cotton shorts before leaving the bathroom. Knowing she might regret it later, she gave in and crawled under the covers beside him.

"Hey," murmured Frej, stirring as she inched closer. "I wanted to talk."

"There'll be time for that in the morning. For now, I just want this." She nestled closer in his arms.

"How are you doing?" he asked, "Are you okay?"

"I'm fine," she said with a sigh, "it's just been a long day."

Frej groaned. "That doesn't even begin to describe it."

"This was a close call," admitted Laila, "the Demons are getting stronger. We need to prepare ourselves in any way we can."

"I'm afraid you're right, but I'll be here for you, every step of the way."

Laila rested her head on his chest and drifted off to sleep.

CHAPTER 50

Laila paused just outside the doorway. It wasn't too late for her to leave, but she'd put this off for too long already. Instead, she followed the guard inside and took a seat.

It was only a few days after they'd crushed the Vampire rebellion, and she was more or less recovered physically. Mentally, she was just as unsure as she'd been when she crawled out of that tunnel. Laila had a feeling that wasn't likely to change anytime soon though.

She waited on her side of the visitor's room at the Supernatural Unit of the New Metropolitan Detention Center. This new detention center had been rebuilt south of the Airport near Manhattan Beach after The Event, with the additional unit built to accommodate a variety of SNP prisoners.

A prisoner was shown to the seat on the opposite side of the glass. With his hair unkempt and his beard in desperate need of a trim, Laila hardly recognized the man. Hesitantly she picked up the phone receiver that would allow her to communicate with him.

"Colin," she said stiffly.

Slowly he lifted his grey eyes to look at her.

"What are you doing here?" he asked miserably through the receiver.

"You know." She folded her arms and gave him a stony look. "Why did you do it?"

He shook his head. "I didn't."

"I've heard there's proof that says otherwise."

"I didn't! I wouldn't!" Colin shook his head and clutched the phone in his hand as if it was a lifeline. "I don't know what's going on, but I would never betray this team, it's my life."

His eyes pleaded with her, but she knew better than to fall for it. She reached out with her magic to examine the energy surrounding the Werewolf. Her eyes narrowed as she sensed the Demonic energy attached to him. Not just trace amounts, but enough for Laila to tell he'd been spending time with a Greater Demon.

"I can't believe it, I actually trusted you!" she spat, glaring through the glass.

She was shaking with anger. Laila didn't know how to even comprehend this information. How could she miss this? Why didn't she realize that sometime in the last few months, Colin had become a Lesser Demon.

"I don't know what you are talking about," said Colin, giving her a desperate look.

"Did you intentionally drag me into that bar knowing the Demons would kidnap me?" she asked evenly.

"If anyone was going to be taken by the Demons, I thought it would be me!"

"So, you wanted to be taken?" asked Laila suspiciously. Perhaps he'd just wanted to initiate contact?

"I thought I—"

Laila held her hand up.

"I've heard enough," she started to hang up.

"Laila, Please! It's these headaches! I can't think straight. I—"

"Goodbye Colin, I have a funeral to go to." She hung up the phone, her face a cool mask of indifference.

She wanted to believe him, deep in her heart she did, but it would be foolish. Maybe something was wrong with him mentally? Or maybe he truly was that cruel? After all, the Demonic energy was clear as day. In any case, it wasn't her problem anymore. Colin had chosen his side, and it cut her all the more deeply knowing that she'd be saying her final goodbye to Torsten thanks to Vampires and their Demon allies.

Laila left the detention center and began her drive north along the coast, past the airport, before turning inland to the house. As she pulled up along the curb, Ali left the house and got into the passenger's seat.

"Where in the worlds have you been?" she asked, turning to Laila. "Erin told me you just left suddenly."

Laila took a deep breath and drove off down the street. "I had an appointment at the detention center. I had to look him in the eye and ask him myself if he did it."

"And?" Ali waited for her to continue.

"He insisted he was innocent, even as I felt the Demonic energy clinging to his body." Laila shook her head. "I just don't get it."

Ali sighed and nodded. "Honestly, I don't either."

The rest of the drive to the funeral home was silent, neither of them in a mood to talk. It was a warm and sunny day which seemed far too pleasant given the circumstances.

When they reached the building, they were directed to a small room where a small number of people were gathered. Laila recognized Torsten's wife and daughters who she'd met once before, after freeing the others from the fight rings. There were other Dwarves dressed in clothing from Svartalfheim, who Laila guessed were either friends or family members. Donald was there as well, sitting in the back row of chairs with Jerrik.

A heavy stone casket rested on a platform. It was tradition for Dwarves to bury their dead in stone. The casket was surrounded by arrangements of colorful geodes, carved stones, and flowers crafted of metal. These sculptures were every bit as beautiful as the floral arrangements the humans used but had been handcrafted in the tunnels of the Dwarven Kingdom.

The service was short. His family and friends spoke, and a priestess said a prayer in Dwarfish. It felt like her chest was caving in as she watched Torsten's wife and daughters. It just seemed so wrong.

The priestess finished the prayer and continued in the common tongue. "Does anyone else have anything they wish to say?"

Silence fell in the room, but Laila felt there was something she had to do. A deep breath helped to steel her nerves, as she stood. Then she began her song.

It was an ancient, haunting tune in Elvish. In fact, it is the oldest song to be written by Elves from a time of great strife, when war ravaged Alfheim. It tells the story of a great warrior who leads an army into battle, knowing the odds are against him. His men are outnumbered nearly ten to one, but he refuses to back down. He falls, but eventually, the rest of the army goes on to win the war. It was the traditional Elven song to sing for the fallen warriors.

Her voice was high and clear, and the audience listened while tears escaped their eyes. Many of them turned to watch her. Laila tried to force her own tears back, but she could feel the grief crushing down around her. She took a breath but faltered, when a sob escaped her throat. Laila paused, unsure of whether she should continue, but in her silence, another voice stepped in. Jerrik rose a couple seats away from her, his voice deep and resonate as he continued the melody. A moment later Laila joined back in, their voices blending harmoniously until they reached the end of the song, the last note fading slowly, like a distant memory.

The priestess ended with another prayer before the mourners approached the casket for one last goodbye. When it was Laila's turn, she stepped forward with Ali. The Fae placed a single purple lily on the stone casket, the tradition of the Fae. The flower glittered and glowed with an unearthly magic.

"Thank you," said Torsten's wife when they passed her.

"He's in Valhalla now." Laila embraced the woman.

"We can only hope," she sighed.

"No, I saw him." Laila pulled away and looked into the woman's eyes.

"What?"

Laila glanced down at the blue flames on her arms that glowed slightly beneath the silk of her blouse.

"Trust me," she told the woman. "I was there when he crossed over. He wanted you and your daughters to know that he loved you so much."

The woman watched her curiously as she left the room.

Laila and Ali returned to the lobby where they found Jerrik standing by Donald, who was sitting on a bench in the corner, his face hidden in his hands.

Laila was about to take a step forward when Ali stopped her.

"Let me." The Fae crossed the room and took a seat beside the Tech Wiz.

The walls of the building felt like they were too close and suffocating her. Laila stepped outside for some fresh air, but a set of footsteps followed her out to the sidewalk.

"So, did you tell him?" Jerrik asked beside her. "Did you tell Frej what Ubel did to you?"

Laila shook her head.

"You should." He glanced at her, his expression serious. "I may not approve of the giant lizard, but he does care for you. I'd even go so far as to say he's a good man. He deserves to know."

In the last week, the two men had worked together amicably, much to her surprise. She had a feeling that they had worked things out somehow.

"Soon," she said, "but not now."

She turned and walked away to stand by Ali's car, this time Jerrik didn't follow.

EPILOGUE

Laila sprawled on her bed staring at the ceiling. She was not ready for this party, not tonight. It had only been a week since the night they disassembled the Vampire rebellion, and it felt as though a dark shadow was hanging over her. Torsten hadn't been the only one killed that night, she'd read a long list of humans and Vampires who had died trying to help them. If only she had been able to prevent this somehow.

Perhaps it would have been possible if she had known how to use her divine magic? She had easily destroyed them at the end, but only after she managed to connect with the divine magic. When she died and came back to life, it was as though something had awakened within her, but now that power once again felt dormant.

Still, the guilt haunted her, particularly in her dreams. It was as if every time she closed her eyes, she saw the faces of the dead looking back.

"What do you think?" Ali called from the doorway, pulling Laila from her thoughts.

She spun around in a tiny, skin-tight navy blue dress that

exposed far more of the Fae's body than it covered. A pair of plastic handcuffs dangled from the belt around her waist, and she wore a black hat with a badge on it.

"Really?" asked Laila shaking her head.

Ali laughed. "Why not? Did you figure out what you're going to wear yet?"

Laila propped herself up on her elbows. "No, but that's okay, I don't think I'm up to it anyway."

"Laila, if I can't blame myself, then neither can you." Ali gave her a meaningful look before lighting up. "Everyone's going to be there. It'll be fun. Plus, I already bought you a costume." She gave Laila a mischievous look.

Laila cringed. "Now I'm worried. What am I going to be? A slutty nurse?"

Ali gave her a wicked grin. She was oddly secretive as she helped Laila into the costume, not even allowing her to take a look in the mirror until the transformation was complete.

"Why don't you take this off?" Ali tapped the necklace the Goddess had given her.

"I can't there's no clasp." She showed Ali what she meant. "In any case, it's probably safer to leave it on."

"That's strange, but at least it looks nice."

Laila changed the subject.

"I still don't understand the tradition of dressing up like something you're not." Laila tried not to flinch as Ali added another layer of makeup to her face.

"Originally humans used to dress up like evil spirits as they gathered offerings. Over the years it turned into whatever costume they wanted. I'm almost done."

Ali finished drawing on Laila's nose with black eyeliner and stepped back.

"There." Ali capped the eyeliner and spun Laila around.

Laila stared at the furry orange dress that seemed way too short. There was a white patch on her chest and a pair of fuzzy triangular ears attached to a headband. Ali had drawn a black spot on Laila's nose. She wore a pair of black ankle boots that Ali dug out of her closet.

"What exactly am I?" Laila turned to look at the tail behind her.

"A fox!"

As the realization dawned on Laila, she face-palmed. "Wow."

"I think you look awesome!" Ali put her makeup back into her bag. "I bet the guys will agree too."

Laila rolled her eyes and followed Ali downstairs where Lyn and Erin were waiting. They were watching an interview on the news.

"Don't tell me it's Fredrik Stacy," groaned Ali.

"Yup," said Lyn, "and the ungrateful bastard has gone right back to blaming the Supernatural community for everything."

Laila threw her hands up in exasperation. The politician had managed to calm his human supporters after his abduction, but it appeared that his gratitude only extended so far.

There was a familiar figure standing behind the politician on the screen, Colin's girlfriend, Lorel. Laila found it odd that she'd made no attempt to see Colin since his arrest. She hadn't tried to bail him out either, but then again, the bail had been set extremely high on account of Colin's involvement with the Demons. Still, something about her seemed odd.

"Shall we go?" asked Erin, switching off the television. "Frej texted me asking where we are."

Lyn grabbed her purse. "Yeah! Let's get the party started."

The Witch was dressed in a corset and a colorful skirt. Her boots were old-fashioned, and she had several gold necklaces dangling around her neck. Laila guessed she was probably a pirate. Erin's costume was a dress, tights, and fingerless gloves that were all black. She also had a drawn nose and whiskers as well as pointed ears on a headband and a tail.

"Really?" laughed Laila. "A cat?"

Mr. Whiskers stood on the back of the sofa eyeing Erin. She tried to scratch his ears, but he swatted at her and took off, hiding under the coffee table.

Laila and the others laughed as they headed for the car to fight the evening traffic.

Forty minutes later, they strode through the doors of the Club La Fae. For months it had been closed for repairs after it was vandalized by the Di Inferi gang. Finally, the owner—Orin—was prepared to reopen it this weekend, but he'd allowed Ali to rent it out tonight for a private Halloween party.

A large group of their friends and coworkers had gathered around tables of food while Orin poured drinks at the bar. The Fae winked at the ladies as they passed.

"I hope you plan to use those!" Mato eyed Ali's handcuffs as he sauntered over.

"You've got to take it easy still," scolded Ali, although there was a lustful gleam in her eyes.

Mato was on the mend and had been allowed to remove the immobilizer a few days ago. Laila and Jerrik had taken turns healing the Werebear's fractured bones, it turned out that with all the fractured pieces, it took more time and energy to heal than she'd expected. Mato would still have to rest it for another week or so.

Henrik embraced Laila. "I'm glad you started coming to meetings again this week."

"I am too," said Laila with a smile.

She didn't allow him to see the pain beneath the surface. The decision to go to the meeting was the result of the conversations she'd had with Torsten, who had reminded her how important they were.

"I'll be back," Laila mumbled, heading towards the bar for a drink.

Jenn and a handful of members from the support staff were hanging out off to the side, but she saw Laila and intercepted her on the way to the bar.

"How are you holding up?" asked the woman quietly.

Laila gave her a half-smile but knew she wasn't fooling Jenn, so she changed the subject.

"How did everything go today?"

"We're almost finished mapping out the tunnels," explained Jenn, "Those Vampires Talen sent over have been a real help with that. We also discovered more weapons today. They had Di Inferi's mark on them. Once we finish documenting evidence, the tunnels can be dismantled or sealed."

Laila nodded.

Jenn pulled her aside. "Rumors have been circulating about you. People say you were glowing or something."

Laila winced, "Yeah, weird stuff's been going on. Hopefully, I'll have more to tell you soon."

"Okay," said Jenn confused, "take care of yourself."

"Thanks."

Laila flashed her a smile—a genuine one—before continuing to the bar. Talen was chatting with Orin, he waved as she approached.

"We were just talking business," explained Talen, "I'd like to get more Fae and Elven customers, so I've been picking Orin's brain."

"I see." Laila leaned against the railing. With how attracted the Vampires were to Elven blood, Laila was sure it would only help to draw in more Vampires as well.

"Here you go." Orin passed her a glass of Elven wine.

"You're the best," She gave him a grateful look. It was her favorite drink.

Orin gave her a dazzling smile before moving on to help the next person.

"Anything new?" Laila asked Talen quietly.

He nodded and took a sip from his goblet of blood. "Sire Ashford is starting to talk. I think he realized that no one's coming to save him, so he's singing like a bird. Dagan's on the run, but I'm going to send you his most recent address. My underlings are standing guard to make sure no one sneaks in to steal the evidence."

Great, hopefully, they would find something in there about the Demons. They still lacked a lead as far as they were concerned, and Laila hated to think of what they were plotting next.

"I have a feeling that Sire Ashford knows more about the Demons too," added Talen as he watched the crowd. "Have you spoken to Jerrik yet? In the moment when he saw you die, he was greatly affected, he hasn't been the same since."

"I know." She turned away, back towards the bar. "But our relationship, well, what could've been our relationship, is history. I've moved on. As for me dying, I'm not sure that I want to discuss that. It's too... complicated."

"More so than your relationship?"

"Surprisingly, it is." She had more questions than ever, but she was no closer to finding the solutions on her own. It was maddening, but she was far out of her element when it came to the divine magic.

"Speaking of relationships," started Talen, "your lover is looking for you."

Laila turned to find Frej walking towards her.

Talen placed a hand on her shoulder. "If you ever need to speak to anyone about this... *evolution* of your abilities, you know where to find me."

Laila realized that he truly did understand. As Talen aged, he'd gained new abilities as well. He probably was one of the few that truly understood what she was going through.

She nodded in thanks.

Talen moved off to mingle in the crowd as Frej reached her and wrapped her in a hug. As he pulled her close, he kissed her slowly, but after a moment, she pulled away.

They were working to patch things up in their relationship, and it seemed to be working. The fact that Jerrik and Frej had apparently put their differences aside helped, but there was still the issue of Frej's feelings for Regina that left her conflicted. She had her own feelings for Jerrik that she was still trying to process and lay to rest though. So while her relationship with Frej wasn't without its struggles, perhaps at this point in time they just needed someone in their lives to help them move forward.

Laila also hadn't told him about her death. She needed to know more about her powers, how they worked, and why she'd been allowed to return to the living before speaking to him. A part of her realized that he would want to know, but there was too much she didn't know about him. After all, he worked for a different government. While she felt that his intentions were pure, and she wanted to believe that Regina wouldn't abuse that information, she knew that she couldn't risk it. She'd trusted Colin too, and that ended in betrayal. Even though her powers were a source of newfound strength, it was still possible for this information to be exploited. She couldn't risk that, not now when the Demons were becoming bolder.

"Nice costume," she said stepping back to admire his plastic chainmail and white tunic.

He laughed. "Not exactly practical, but it's lightweight. Are you still planning to make your announcement tonight?"

Laila nodded as nervous butterflies appeared in her stomach. So far only Frej and Ali knew about her decision. The party seemed like the best opportunity to announce it though.

Frej squeezed her hand. "It'll be fine."

"I know," she kissed him again.

Looking out at the crowd she saw that Benning had once again been returned to his smaller size. He stood there chatting away with Lyn. Jerrik was deep in conversation with Henrik and Mato, while Donald stood awkwardly by a group of support staff members. Even Adam had made it to the party, although Laila heard he would be flying back to D.C. in the morning. There was also a table with a memorial for Torsten. It was primarily an office party, aside from the few friends Ali had insisted on inviting.

"Can I have your attention, please," shouted Ali as she stood on a chair.

Gradually the room fell silent.

"I'd like to thank you all for coming," said Ali to the crowd. "I know this month's been difficult, and I think we all deserve a moment to let down our hair and enjoy ourselves."

There were nods of agreement throughout the crowd.

"But while you are all here," continued Ali as she sobered, "I think it's time for a few announcements." She waved for Laila to join her.

Frej gave her hand another squeeze of encouragement as the crowd turned to look at her.

"Hi." Laila gave an awkward wave. Gods she hated speaking in front of people. "I um, just wanted to let you all know that I'm taking a leave of absence for a month or so. I've been presented with an opportunity to advance my training, and with this last incident, it's become clear to me that this is necessary."

It was more than necessary, it was essential. She would not allow herself to be unprepared for whatever threat came next. While she hadn't been there to save Torsten, Laila would be there for others in the struggles to come. She hadn't asked for this power, but whether it was a curse or a blessing, it gave her the strength to fight for everything she cared about.

She continued. "I hate to leave you when there is so much work to be done. I really wish I could be here to help. Ali will be able to contact me if something comes up, but I'll be leaving for Germany in the morning."

There were hushed whispers and a general response of surprise. Laila noticed Jerrik's frown as Ali continued with the next announcement.

"I know the news about Colin has come as a pretty big shock, but as it stands, we need to appoint a new supervisor to the office."

Ali motioned for Adam to come forward as she stepped off the chair. He cleared his throat.

"Eventually it is possible that a new supervisor will be appointed from D.C., but there is a need for an acting supervisor. I've discussed the matter in depth with Ali, and we've determined that Darien Pavoni is the most suitable choice for this role."

A round of applause and cheers erupted. The support staff exchanged uncertain glances, but the rest of the crowd seemed generally pleased. Darien watched in shock. It was apparent he hadn't seen it coming. Those surrounding him clapped him on the back and congratulated him as he tried to process the news.

"A toast!" crowed Ali, "to Laila and Darien, may both of them continue to grow through these changes."

"And to Torsten!" added Darien. "Who's here with us in spirit."

Glasses clinked over the murmur of the crowd. Laila took a sip of wine and waited for the crowd to dissipate before approaching Darien.

"Congratulations!" She clapped him on the shoulder.

"I have no idea what just happened." Darien shook his head. "I didn't ask for this."

"No, but you'll do just fine. Don't worry."

"You're leaving so soon." He frowned.

"I can't help it. If I don't go now, there may not be enough time to prepare for whatever lies ahead."

"How are you coping with your powers?" he asked. "Talen told me about what happened with the Lesser Demon."

Laila made a face. "It's too weird for me to process, honestly. But it's not as if anything's normal in our lives these days."

"That's true." Darien nodded. "Well, I see a couple of Ali's Fae friends are here. Maybe I can win a couple of them over with my new promotion." He gave her a wicked look.

"Reputation!" Laila called after him, but he was already lost in the crowd.

Everything was truly growing crazier by the day, but Laila felt blessed to have so many people supporting them. On the positive side, she'd put an end to the treachery of Caine Ubel, and stopped a Vampire rebellion that could have seriously marred the city. But there was still the matter of the Demons and the Di Inferi. Hopefully, they'd find some shred of evidence to point them in the right direction because they needed any advantage they could get.

She returned to Frej, who wrapped an arm around her. This time away would be good for her, she needed the space to think things through with their relationship. Talking with him had helped, but there were still decisions she needed to make on her own.

Glancing around the room, Laila knew she would miss all of them, but this was the path she needed to take. Hopefully, when she returned, she would be strong enough to keep them all safe. Until then, she prayed to Thor to watch over this city and the people within it.

DID YOU KNOW...

Did you know that leaving a review is one of the most helpful things a reader can do for any author? If you have a moment, please leave a review online.

ACKNOWLEDGMENTS

When I began this series, it was little more than a hobby that served the function of distracting me from the stressors of college life. Years later I am now the author of three books. At times it completely blows my mind how far I've come, but none of this would be possible without the support of the people around me.

I want to take a moment to thank my parents—who are still my biggest supporters. They have been there to support me the entire way, and I feel so blessed to have such a wonderful relationship with them. I would also like to thank my beta readers Rene, Eric, and Tammi, as well as my Patreon patrons—especially my top tier patron Kristine. Finally, I'd like to thank my readers! You guys rock!

CHARACTERS

Laila Eyvindr – An Elf hired by the Interrealm Security Agency (IRSA). She is young for an Elf and appears to be in her mid-twenties by human standards but she is really 83 years old. She is a trained warrior and has a good amount of magical training. Laila is determined, hardworking, caring, and passionate.

Colin Grayson – A Werewolf in his mid 30's with brown hair, short beard and grey eyes. He is a descendent of Shifters who have lived amongst humans in hiding for generations. He is the supervisor of the IRSA team, and has been a part of the organization since it's foundation.

Alastrina Fiachra (Ali) – A Fae woman with long curly golden hair and purple eyes. Like Laila, she is an IRSA agent, but she has been around for much longer and has adjusted to life in Midgard. Ali's parents died a few years ago, so she cares for her adopted little sister, Erin. She knows how to have a good time and loves the Los Angeles nightlife.

Darien Pavoni – A male Vampire with black spiky hair, pale skin, and red eyes. Another member of Laila's IRSA team, he is arrogant, and may not always make the most professional decisions, but he genuinely cares about the work he does. In 1724 he died in a duel and was turned into a Vampire.

Erin Fiachra – A young Dragon who is trapped in her human form. She is Ali's adopted sister, and appears to be about fourteen, but she is actually around sixty years old. She's had difficulty contacting other Dragons to discover why she's stopped ageing.

Arduinna – The Celtic Goddess of the Black Forest in Germany. She is down to earth and wise, and is a friend of Ali and Laila's.

Sir Frej Ilmarinen – An Air Dragon and a Knight from the Dragon Kingdom. He has chosen to stay in Los Angeles to train Erin and to help the IRSA agents. He's also Laila's lover.

Orin – The Fae man who owns the Club La Fae. He's cheeky, but a reliable informant.

Lyn – A human witch who lives in Los Angeles. She owns a shop in Venice Beach called Lyn's Charms and Remedies, and helps Laila with the occasional case.

Jerrik Torhild – Svartálfr (plural: Svartalfar) or Dark Elf that was imprisoned in the same cellblock as Laila. He and

Laila had a short-lived romance until he left without a word. He now works with the IRSA team.

Torsten – A fatherly Dwarf that was also imprisoned in the same cellblock as Laila. He now works for IRSA developing weapons and tools to make the agents' jobs safer.

Donald – A male Witch, or Tech Wiz, as he prefers. A local witch hired to assist Torsten in enchanting equipment for the IRSA team.

Unknown Goddess – Appears to be watching Laila and enhancing her powers.

Caine Ubel – A Snake Shifter and a Lesser Demon, who was capturing and sending Supernaturals to the Demon-run fight ring and organized the summoning rituals that nearly killed Erin.

Marius – A.K.A. the Master of the Games. He's Fae and was the Greater Demon in charge of the illegal fight ring. He escaped IRSA's raid on the place, and is still at large.

Izel – Unknown. Connected to Marius and the Demons.

Queen Regina Halvard-Hilgard – A Fire Dragon and Queen of the Dragons.

Lord Issac Mavrik – An Earth Dragon and a close friend of Frej's.

Benning – A Giant who was sent, by the Demons, to terrorize Los Angeles. In reality, he wouldn't hurt a fly. He now works as a security guard at IRSA's front desk.

Captain Anderson – A human and captain of the LAPD's Gangs and Narcotics division.

Captain Romero – A human and captain of the LAPD's Homicide division.

Lorel – A Human and Colin's girlfriend.

Fredrik Stacy – A human and avid protester. He believes that strict regulations should be placed on Supernaturals for the safety of humans.

Carlos – A Human who was one of Ali's informants in the Old City until he was assassinated while meeting with Ali and Darien.

Mato – A Bear Shifter who was imprisoned by the Demons in the same cellblock as Laila. He's now dating Ali.

Henrik – A Mörkö (ice creature) who was imprisoned in the same cellblock as Laila. He's Mato's best friend and roommate.

Talen Veryl – A Vampire and Darien's sire. A powerful and influential man who is also kind and compassionate.

Richard – A Vampire who gained his wealth through smuggling and other unsavory business practices.

Jennifer (Jenn) Holdt – A human and special investigator with IRSA. She is practical and level-headed.

Meuric Drisscoll – An Abhartach who works as a medical

examiner for IRSA.

Jim Cleary – A human who works as a medical examiner for IRSA.

Adam Johnson – A human and an agent who works for the Inspector General's office. He's been sent to investigate the IRSA team.

Sire Ashford – A rogue Vampire leading a rebellion.

Arnold Koch – A rogue Vampire who is a part of the rebellion.

Dagan – A Vampire on the council, a group of powerful and ancient Vampires that ensure the order and safety of the local Vampires. He is very opinionated and outspoken.

Cedric – A Vampire on the council. He is deliberate in his actions and decisions.

Aalis – A Vampire on the council. Her appearance is rather opulent and gaudy, and she tends to take charge.

Sarnai (**Сарнай**) – A Vampire on the Council and one of Darien's ex-lovers. A cool and ruthless woman.

WORLDS

Asgard – World of the Gods.

Vanaheim – World of the Ancient Gods.

Alfheim (pronounced "ALF-hame;") – World of the Elves, Fae, Dragons and nature related beings. Large cites of note include:

> Ingegard – Elven City
> Tír na nÓg – City of the Fae
> Schonengard – City of the Dragons

Earth (or Midgard) – The world of the humans. For Millennia it was off limits to the other worlds as humans and other creatures of this world were not gifted in magic or strength. Over time, the humans have become a force to reckon with as they created amazing technologies that rival the magic that others possess. The people of Alfheim were the ones who proposed the truce that would keep the human world safe from the other worlds. There are creatures like human Vampires, human Shifters, and a hand full of other creatures who have managed to stay under the radar during the era before The Event.

Svartalfheim (pronounced "SVART-alf-hame;") — The world of Dark Elves or Svartalfar, Dwarves, and creatures of the earth. They are known for their mines and craftsmanship.

Jotunheim – The world of brutish creatures like Trolls and Giants. They are constantly at war with the races of Alfheim or other worlds.

Muspelheim – The world of the Dammed. The inter-realm prison where the worst criminals are banished. There is a political organization that has risen to power within this world known as the Demons. They have begun to gain connections in the other worlds, particularly Earth, and have begun to plot their escape and rise to power.

CAN'T WAIT FOR MORE?

Want monthly access to advance announcements, exclusive content and more? Check out Kathryn Blanche's Patreon page for more information!

patreon.com/kathrynblanche

ABOUT THE AUTHOR

Kathryn Blanche writes novels in her favorite local cafes when not indulging her love for travel. Aside from exploring the world, this California native may be found designing for the theatre, reading, fencing, or teaching. *Infiltrated by Demons* is the third novel in her Laila of Midgard series.

FOLLOW KATHRYN BLANCHE FOR UPDATES ON NEW RELEASES, EVENTS, AND MORE!

Website: www.kathrynblanche.com
Email: contact@kathrynblanche.com
Facebook: @LailaofMidgardSeries
Instagram: @kathryn_blanche
Twitter: @_kathrynblanche

THE ADVENTURE CONTINUES IN...

HUNTED
⟫—⟩ BY ⟨—⟪
DEMONS

LAILA OF MIDGARD
❖ BOOK 4 ❖

BY

KATHRYN BLANCHE

CPSIA information can be obtained
at www.ICGtesting.com
Printed in the USA
BVHW031002270519
549328BV00002B/364/P

9 781732 665163